'Clodagh Murphy is the queen of romantic comedy and her latest is witty and warmhearted, with fantastic characters, laugh out loud dialogue and plenty of intrigue. This was my favorite kind of read – one where you fall in love with the characters to the point that they feel like your friends.'

— SARAH PAINTER

'The intriguing plot kept me page turning well into the night.'

— FRENCH VILLAGE DIARIES

'Romance, humour, secrets and lots of warmth make this book unputdownable … I dare you not to love it.'

— JUST 4 MY BOOKS

'I loved the premise, I loved Lesley's voice, I loved the whole thing … A really fun read!'

— LILAC MILLS

'My gosh, it was a TREAT! This is a book I'll be looking at in my end of year "best ofs" ... Beyond recommended.'

— BR Maycock's Book Blog

'A lovely romantic comedy packed with humour, drama, secrets, misunderstandings and love. It had me laughing out loud.'

— Splashes Into Books

'Just lovely! A clever, sophisticated, funny novel that is definitely one to read.'

— Books Are Cool

'Light, funny, well written, and heartwarming too. It was definitely addicting.'

— Nurse Bookie

'A wonderful story full of laughter, misunderstandings, and a few secrets ... but it is the warmth and connection that I felt with the characters that make this story truly special.'

— Books of All Kinds

'A rom-com filled with snarky humor and a memorable, if somewhat reluctant, sleuthing duo.'

— Cheryl M-M's Book Blog

FOR LOVE OR MONEY

CLODAGH MURPHY

Balally
Books

FOR LOVE OR MONEY
CLODAGH MURPHY
Clodagh Murphy © 2020

ISBN: 9781916265615

Published by Balally Books

Cover design by Stuart Bache

For my readers

1

Lesley knew the singles dinner party was a write-off when she found herself turning it into an anecdote halfway through her deconstructed prawn cocktail. She was already trying out character sketches of her fellow guests, mentally rehearsing how she'd describe them to her friend Romy to make her laugh. By the time the perfectly done beef Wellington was served, she had composed a couple of witty tweets and was mulling over a Facebook post – something pithy and poignant about her relationship status remaining unchanged. Maybe she'd try to find a GIF to go with it.

She was more relieved than anything. Dinner Dates was legendary for its high success rate, and Helen O'Neill's talent for matchmaking meant that there was a lengthy waiting list for a place at one of her weekly dinner parties. But the truth was, Lesley was in no hurry to get into another serious relationship after her break-up with Rob. In fact, she was excited about being single again, and was only here tonight because her sister Katrina had kept on at her about it, and she'd eventually relented to get her off her back. At the time, the first available slot had seemed impossibly far away, and, after signing up, she'd promptly forgotten about it.

But her turn had finally rolled around on this cold Friday night in April, so here she was. She could see how Dinner Dates had earned its reputation as the golden ticket among Dublin's singles. Everyone was very nice, the wine was flowing, the food was sublime, and Helen, presiding at the top of the table, was the perfect hostess. But Lesley had known there was no one here she wanted to shag as soon as the ten assembled singletons had introduced themselves to each other over pre-dinner drinks in the conservatory.

'So that was that,' the man beside her said, breaking into her thoughts. She turned to him: Matthew, thirtyish, graphic designer; quite cute if you could overlook the hipster goatee, which Lesley couldn't.

He was looking at her expectantly, and she realised she had no idea what he'd been saying. She nodded and gave a vague smile that she hoped would cover all bases, hovering somewhere between sympathy, regret and wry amusement. Luckily, she seemed to have got away with it as Matthew smiled back at her. She should pay attention: be present in the moment. The trouble was she was crap at being 'in the now'. She knew that because she had done a Buddhist meditation course, and she had totally flunked it. She had paid a hundred euro to sit cross-legged on the floor of a damp basement in Rathmines every night for six weeks while she thought about what to have for dinner and wondered if the very fit young monk who taught them would be really kind and non-judgmental in bed, or whether he was even allowed to have sex. She wondered where Jampa was now ...

'So, what about you?' Matthew asked her. 'Have *you* ever ...?' He left the sentence hanging.

Fuck! She'd zoned out again. Ever what? Ever been married? Done a bungee jump? Hosted an orgy? *What?*

'Um ... just the once,' she said falteringly.

'Oh.' Matthew reared back, eyebrows raised. Lesley hoped she hadn't admitted to hosting an orgy.

She was relieved when Helen gave the signal for the men to move places as a couple of teenage girls acting as waitresses for the evening started to clear the plates.

'Finally! I've been waiting to sit here all evening.' Al, a thirty-something architect, was giving her a twinkly smile as he took a seat beside her. He was tall and ramrod-straight; handsome in an old-fashioned matinee idol kind of way. She could picture him in an old black and white movie, all stiff upper lip and quiet dignity as he led his adoring troops off to their death, while he doled out encouragement in his clipped, officer-class English accent.

Al was good-looking and friendly, but she'd already ruled him out when they'd chatted briefly in the conservatory. She liked her men more rough and ready. Besides, everyone here was looking for a serious relationship, and she was in no hurry to get coupled up again.

'I've never met a real-life private detective before,' Al said. 'That must be interesting.'

'It is. Though there's a fair amount of grunt work involved too. It's not all eating doughnuts out of a paper bag and watching people bonking through binoculars.'

'It's not?' Al looked disappointed.

'Well ... it mostly is,' Lesley said, feeling bad for shattering his illusions. 'I just said that because I don't like to boast.'

The fact was *she'd* never met a real-life private detective either, but she'd decided it would be fun to pass herself off as one tonight. She'd always fancied herself as an amateur sleuth, and since she'd already decided she wouldn't be seeing any of these people again, she figured there was no harm in it. Besides, it would be a lot more interesting for everyone else than struggling to make small talk about her freelance IT business.

'What sort of work do you do?' Al asked.

'It's mostly cheaters,' she said.

'Hence the bonking through binoculars. And is there a lot of demand for your services?'

'Oh yeah, I'm kept pretty busy. There are a lot of love rats out there. You'd be surprised.'

'Sorry for interrupting—' Orla, sitting opposite her, leaned across the table '—but I know someone who could really use your services. Do you do honey traps, by any chance?'

'Yes!' Lesley said. 'That's my favourite kind of work.'

'Honey traps?' Ronan, beside her, asked, fingering his collar. 'Is that a real thing?'

'Oh, yes.'

'And um ... how does it work exactly?'

'Well, I get chatting to men on social media, play along if they get flirty with me, and see how far they go. Let them send me snaps of their tackle and whatnot. When they suggest meeting up in real life, bingo! I bring them down.'

'Gosh,' Ronan gulped. 'Isn't that—'

'Brilliant!' Orla said.

'I was going to say illegal.'

'Well, I think it's great,' Orla said. 'I wish I'd known I could hire someone like you when I suspected my ex of cheating.'

'Me too,' Janice beside her said. 'Do you have a card?' she asked Lesley.

'Er ... no, not on me.'

'Well, give me your number, then.'

'I'd like your number too, please,' Orla said, reaching

down to take her phone out of her bag. 'I'd love to tell my friend about you.'

'Oh, well ... I don't like to ... I mean I have to be very discreet in my line of work. You understand,' Lesley said, tapping her nose. Damn! Why did she have to get carried away and take it too far?

'But you're not at work now, are you?' Ronan asked wide-eyed, fidgeting with his tie.

She was sorry she'd started this now. So she was glad of the diversion when the door was suddenly flung open and a harassed-looking man burst into the room.

'Helen!' he panted.

Their hostess looked up, startled. 'Conor? What—'

'Ian McKellen was at the show tonight. He's coming for supper!'

Lesley recalled that Helen's husband was a bigwig in one of Dublin's main theatres. She couldn't remember which one – she hated the theatre.

'So you'll have to get rid of this lot.' Conor gestured at the guests, who were all gazing up at him in astonishment. 'Have they eaten all the food?'

'Well, we've just finished the mains.'

'You'll have to rustle up something else, then. I've got Cathy stalling him in the green room, but he'll be here soon.'

'I suppose I could do a quick risotto. But we haven't had dessert yet.'

'What is it?'

'Gateau Diane.'

'You can give them doggy bags.'

The singletons watched this exchange as if they were at a tennis match, their heads swivelling between Helen and her husband. They turned to Helen now, the ball back in her court, all their hopes resting on her return.

'Good idea,' she said, and you could almost hear the collective groan as she lost the point. 'I'll start parcelling up cake for everyone to take home,' she said as she stood. 'And you can all have a refund, or come along another night for free, whichever you prefer.'

'But we haven't had a chance to talk to everyone properly yet,' Matthew piped up from the end of the table as Helen left the room.

'You've had two courses and pre-drinks,' Conor said. 'You've already made your minds up about each other. Haven't you?' he demanded, looking sternly around the table.

'Absolutely!' Lesley said, reaching down to grab her bag, as the other guests looked at each other uncertainly. She didn't need to be told twice.

'Oh, I didn't see you there, Aloysius,' Conor was saying as she hurried to the door. 'You're welcome to stay for supper, if you'd like.'

She turned around and realised he was speaking to Al. *Aloysius*! Well, he'd kept that quiet.

In the hall, Helen handed her a little cake box. 'Where's Al?' she asked, looking over Lesley's shoulder.

'He's still in there. I think he's going to stay – your husband said he's allowed.'

'But he's already eaten. And I thought you two would really hit it off.'

'Don't worry about not getting us all paired up. This isn't my first time at the fair. I know not everyone goes home with a prize.'

'Well, I'm sorry you didn't have better luck. But feel free to come back another time – no charge.'

'Thanks.' She didn't like to say it to Helen, who clearly felt bad about the way the evening had ended, but Lesley didn't think she'd be taking up the offer of a return visit.

She was a one-strike-and-you're-out kind of person: decisive. She liked that about herself.

She buttoned her coat and burrowed her gloved hands into the pockets as she went out, her shoulders automatically tensing against the frosty night air. It was still early and she didn't have far to walk. She'd be home by ten-thirty. She'd make a cup of tea and have her cake on the sofa with Graham Norton. On the whole, it had been quite a satisfactory evening. And she had the Ian McKellen story. As anecdotes went, it was a pretty good one.

2

S he was just out the gate when she heard the door close behind her.

'Lesley! Wait!'

She turned to see Al hurrying down the road after her.

'Hi,' he said, sounding pleased with himself as he caught up with her. He had a red scarf wrapped around his neck, and his hands were buried in his pockets. The tip of his nose was already turning red. 'Are you getting a cab?'

'No, I'm walking home. I'm not far from here.'

'Oh, me too,' he said, falling into step beside her.

Lesley was surprised. She could have sworn he'd said he lived in Blackrock.

'Well, that was interesting,' he said, smiling at her.

'Yeah, it's not every day you don't get to meet Sir Ian McKellen. It's definitely one to tell the grandkids.'

'So, I was wondering if you'd like to invite me back to your place.'

Lesley stopped dead and looked up at him. 'Oh, you were, were you?'

'Yes. I thought we could have our cake, and um ...'

'Eat it?'

'Exactly. We were meant to be sharing dessert anyway. What do you say?'

'No, thanks.' She started walking again.

'I'd ask you back to mine, only I'm, er ... having some work done on my kitchen,' Al said, keeping pace with her. 'But we could go and get a drink somewhere, if you like.'

'Look, just because we're the only two left doesn't mean we have to get together. That's not how it works. Are you new to the dating scene?'

'Um ... not exactly. Sort of. I'm a bit out of practice, I suppose.'

'Well, I'm an old hand, so let me give you a tip. You're not going to hit it off with someone every time. Don't feel you have to flog a dead horse just to get your money's worth. Just chalk it up to experience. Cut your losses and call it a night. That's what I'm doing.'

Al raised his eyebrows. 'But it's only ten o'clock.'

'What's that got to do with anything?'

'You can't call it a night at ten o'clock. It's a late evening at best.'

'I'm not saying you have to go straight to bed. You could watch some TV or ... I don't know, whatever you like to do.'

'I can? Gosh, thanks. Anyway, I'm not asking you out because we're the only two left.'

'Oh, so now you're asking me out? That escalated quickly.' She stopped and eyed him suspiciously. 'Are you a chubby chaser, Al?'

'A chubby chaser!' He laughed.

Lesley started walking again and he ran a little to catch up.

'No, I'm not a chubby chaser.'

'And yet here you are chasing me.'

'I just wanted to get a chance to talk to you, get to know you better.'

'Why?'

'*Why?* Well, wasn't that the point of this evening? I thought you seemed nice ... interesting, you know, and bright. And I liked the look of you.' He shrugged. 'You know, the usual.'

'No woman wants to be with a chubby chaser, Al – not even chubby women. I mean, they don't want that to be the *reason* someone's with them, you know?'

'I promise you I'm not a chubby chaser. Besides, you're not even chubby. You're—'

'If you say curvy, I might have to hurt you.'

'I wasn't going to say curvy. I would never say curvy.'

'What were you going to say, then? And it better not be cuddly – that's even worse.'

He looked at her warily. 'How do you feel about statuesque?'

'That means built like a brick shithouse, doesn't it?'

'No!' He frowned. 'It means built like a Greek goddess – the sort of woman who inspires sculptors to carve them in marble.'

'Oh.' She didn't want to smile, but her lips were curling annoyingly. 'I suppose that's all right.'

'So, what do you say?' he asked, stopping as they came to the corner of the road. 'Fancy a drink?'

'Well, I'm a bit tired, Al. Maybe some other time.' She gave him a polite smile and turned to the left, thinking they were parting ways. But he quickly fell into step beside her again.

'Are you still here? I already told you I'm not going out with you.'

'Still, I thought I could walk you home at least.'

'Walk me home? Is it nineteen-fifty all of a sudden and nobody told me?'

'I'm a gentleman. There aren't many of us left. You should snap me up while stocks last. Avoid disappointment.'

'I'll take my chances.'

'Look, I'm going this way anyway. But I'll walk on the opposite side of the road, if you'd prefer.'

'No, it's fine.'

'Good. Because this isn't actually the shortest route home for me. I only came this way as an excuse to talk to you,' he admitted cheerfully.

When they got to Lesley's house, she stopped at the gate. 'Well, this is me. Thanks for walking me home.'

Al's gaze flicked to the house. 'Are you sure you don't want to invite me in?' he asked with a winning smile.

Lesley sighed. 'Look, you're a really nice guy, Al, and you're very good-looking and everything.'

'Thanks.'

'But there's just no spark.' She could have added that she knew his real name was Aloysius and she couldn't see herself dating someone with such a ludicrous name, but that would be mean.

'Oh, don't you think so? I mean, I feel a spark.'

'You can't feel a spark, because I don't. It takes two. It's like starting a fire by rubbing two sticks together. You can't do it with one stick.'

'Actually, I think you can. I was a boy scout, you know.'

'That doesn't surprise me. Well, if you know of a way of sparking off all by yourself, I don't want to hear about it.'

'Oh.' Al's shoulders slumped despite the cold. 'Okay, then. Well, goodnight, Lesley. It was a pleasure meeting you.'

'You too,' she said as she opened the gate. 'Enjoy your cake.'

Al stood watching as she walked down the path and opened the door. When she turned to close it, he gave her a little wave and a regretful smile.

That hadn't been a bad evening all in all, she thought, as she went to the kitchen and put the kettle on. She put her piece of cake on a plate and carried it through to the living room, and was about to flick on the light when she saw that Al was still standing outside, fiddling with his phone and looking furtive. Curious, she watched from behind the curtains, wondering what he was up to. A couple of minutes later, a cab pulled up and he hopped in.

Hah! So he did live in Blackrock after all, Lesley thought, chuckling to herself as she drew the curtains. He hadn't been kidding when he said walking by her house wasn't his most direct route home. No wonder he didn't want to ask her back to his place. Still, she couldn't help admiring his initiative. And she had to admit it was flattering that he'd resorted to subterfuge just so he could walk home with her. She could definitely chalk tonight up as a success, she thought, feeling quite pleased with herself as she switched on the TV and flopped onto the sofa. Being single again was going to be fun.

3

'So how was it before Gandalf turned up and you all got kicked out?'

The following Monday morning, Lesley was sitting in her friend Romy's living room, telling her about Dinner Dates, while Romy's two-year-old son, Luke, was busily emptying the contents of a CD rack, chattering happily to himself as he stacked them up on the floor. Romy was a property developer and worked from home, so Lesley often called round for a coffee break on weekdays.

Lesley cupped her hands around her mug and thought. 'It was ... convivial,' she said, landing on the word with satisfaction.

'Convivial?' Romy scrunched up her nose. 'You didn't meet anyone interesting, then?'

'No. One guy did chase me home, though.'

'Oh! Well, in that case, I think you can call it an unqualified success. What was he like?'

'Pretty fit, but in a nice, normal sort of way – not all man boobs and unputdownable arms. But there was no spark.'

Romy gave her a look, but said nothing.

'What?' Lesley shrugged. 'I'm decisive. It's one of my best qualities.'

'You're too quick to write people off. They might surprise you if you gave them a chance.'

'They might. And you know I hate surprises.'

Romy laughed. 'I just think you might miss out on someone great because you don't feel some instantaneous spark.'

'Katrina's always telling me the same thing – only she's more worried I'll miss out on the perfect pair of jeans.' Lesley was just as quick and decisive when it came to shopping as she was about potential dates. 'She made me go to the Dundrum Centre with her last week for a girlie shopping day.'

'Doesn't she know you at all?'

'I know! I think she imagined it'd be like one of those movie montages. You know – the pair of us on a moving walkway, laden down with posh shopping bags, laughing and pointing stuff out to each other.'

'Having salad and fizzy water for lunch, and getting your nails done to an upbeat soundtrack.'

'Yes! Anyway, she soon regretted it. She kept moaning at me that I hadn't even looked. But I'm like Sherlock. I take it all in in one fell swoop – wrong neckline, frilly sleeves, clingy material, not my colour … it's like my superpower.'

Lesley had spent most of the day hanging around in doorways, playing with her phone while Katrina had gone through every single rail of clothes, item by item. Then they'd move on to the next store, where she'd begin the painstaking process all over again.

'I don't know how she ever gets anything done. She was always the same with men. She once went on three dates with a guy called Skunk! Three! I mean, his name was *Skunk* – that's all you need to know right there.'

'Well, I'm sure that wasn't his real name.'

'No, but that was what his friends called him – and they're the people who *like* him. Thank goodness she has Tom now. She's not safe to be let out.'

'Still, there's a happy medium between serial-dating complete gobshites and not even going out once with a perfectly nice man. This guy who chased you home, for instance—'

'Al, his name was.'

'Maybe he'd grow on you if you gave him a chance.'

Lesley considered this for a moment. 'Nah,' she said. 'If there's a spark, you feel it straight away, and if there isn't, there's no point in wasting everyone's time trying to manufacture one. I'm like Ellen Barkin in *Sea of Love*. You know when she says she believes in instant attraction and love at first sight, and she's all snappy fingers. That's like me.' Lesley sighed. 'God, I love that movie.'

'Well, that just proves my point. Ellen Barkin ends up with Al Pacino, even though she thinks there's no spark at first. Maybe it'd be like that with *your* Al.'

'No. For starters, *my* Al is short for Aloysius. I ask you!'

'Oh, dear!' Romy giggled. 'Still,' she said reasonably, 'it's better than Skunk.'

'Marginally. I mean, who's called Aloysius?'

'Well, there was the gay teddy bear in *Brideshead Revisited*.'

'He was cute. Still, I'm not going out with anyone called Aloysius. I have my standards.'

Luke tottered over to Romy and presented her with a CD. 'Thank you,' she said, taking it from him absently. 'So, are you going to go back to Dinner Dates for a freebie?'

'No. It's a bit too intense for me. The people who go to

those sorts of things are looking to settle down. Maybe I'll stick to speed dating in future. It's more my ... speed.'

'Or you could go back to internet dating.'

'I think I've already dated everyone on the internet.'

'You've been away a while. There must be some new stock.'

'To be honest, I'm really not in the mood for any of it. I might take a break from the whole dating scene.'

'Well, it's not that long since you broke up with Rob. Maybe it's too soon?'

'It's not that. I mean, it's not like I thought he was "the one" or anything.' She rolled her eyes at the idea. 'Though I'm still pissed off that he dumped me. The cheek of it! If anyone was the catch out of the pair of us, it was me.'

'Totally.'

'But he lured me in under false pretences. I mean, why bother looking for someone to go out with, if you just want to stay in all the time?' Rob had been a big fan of Friday nights snuggled on the sofa with a takeaway and a box set on Netflix. 'He was turning into an old fart, and he wanted to take me down with him. Now that I've got my freedom back, I just want to enjoy it for a while.'

'Well, if you've nothing better to do next weekend, you can join us old farts for a *Star Wars* marathon. Ethan wants Luke to watch the whole series, so he's up to speed when the last one comes out.'

'Isn't Luke a bit young for *Star Wars*?'

Romy smiled. 'Ethan says it's his heritage, so we should introduce him to it as early as possible.' Romy had met Luke's father at a Halloween party when he was dressed as Darth Vader.

Lesley looked across at the toddler who was now engrossed in trying to open a recalcitrant jewel case, all fingers and thumbs. 'Use the force, Luke,' she said in a ghostly voice. 'Are you going to watch the prequels?' she asked Romy.

'No! God, I don't think so.' Romy frowned. It seemed like the thought had just occurred to her. 'No, I'm sure not. If Ethan suggested that, I might have to divorce him – and we're not even married.'

'Okay, sounds good. Oh, thanks, Luke,' she said as the child handed her a CD with a big grin.

'So, how's business?' Romy asked as she poured them more coffee from the cafetière.

'Good.' Lesley picked up her mug and sank back against the cushions of the couch. 'I've got a big SEO job from a new client. Boring as all get-out, but it pays well, and it'll be ongoing for months. Sometimes I wish I wasn't so good at my job, but what can you do?'

4

Two months later, Lesley was beginning to question whether she was cut out for working from home. Business was good, but the latest big SEO project she'd taken on was boring the pants off her, and it was a constant struggle to resist the twin lures of social media and the biscuit cupboard, and focus on her work.

When her doorbell rang at eleven one Monday morning, she promptly sprang out of her chair to answer it, grateful for the distraction. Expecting it was Romy calling for a coffee break, she hurried into the hall. But her welcoming smile died on her lips when she saw the unfamiliar head of a man through the bubbled glass of the door. Damn! It was probably someone selling something or collecting for charity. Still, it was too late to hide and pretend there was no one in as he'd already seen her through the glass – and besides, any diversion was better than nothing. Maybe she could persuade him to come in for a cup of tea and a chat, whoever he was. She'd invited a couple of very nice Mormons in last week and had managed to keep them talking for almost an hour.

When she opened the door, she vaguely recognised the tall, russet-haired man standing in her porch, but couldn't quite place him.

'Lesley, hello!' he said with a friendly smile.

As soon as he spoke, she remembered. He was the posh English guy she'd met at Dinner Dates – the one who'd followed her home and asked her out. She was surprised he'd turned up. He'd seemed to accept her brush-off the night they'd met, and she hadn't pegged him as a stalker. He'd waited long enough, but maybe that was part of his MO – biding his time and lulling her into a false sense of security.

'Hello, um ...' She couldn't remember his name, but she knew it was something preposterous. 'I want to say Algernon?'

'Aloysius,' he said cheerfully, holding out his hand.

Of course – how could she have forgotten?

'But you can call me Al.'

'Like the song.' She gave his hand a brief but firm shake.

'Yes. Quite,' he said in a jaded tone.

'Oh, I suppose people say that to you all the time.'

'No, you're the first.'

'Really?' She smiled, surprised.

'Well, the first today.'

'Oh.' She laughed.

'So, can I come in?' Al asked.

Lesley hesitated. He seemed so sure of his welcome, like a big, friendly dog that was used to people doting on him. But while she'd be glad of the distraction, even if it did come in the shape of a stalker, she didn't fancy him, and she didn't want to lead him on. Better to let him down

quickly so he could get on with his life and find some other
woman to pester.

'I don't think that's a good idea,' she said.

'Oh.' He seemed taken aback. 'But I haven't even told
you why I'm here yet.'

'Well, it's not hard to guess. I mean, we met at Dinner
Dates. You followed me home.'

'Walked you home,' he corrected her.

'You say potato. Whatever. The thing is I didn't feel we
... hit it off really.'

'I'm not here to ask you out again, if that's what you're
worried about.'

'You're not?' Lesley felt irrationally miffed that he
seemed to have given up so easily.

'No. So, can I come in?'

'Well, all right.' Puzzled, she stood back to let him in,
and he strode off down the hall before she'd even closed
the door behind him.

'In here?' he asked, pointing to the open kitchen door.

'Yes,' she said, trotting after him.

'So you work from home?' he asked when she caught
up with him in the kitchen.

'Yes.' Lesley was about to invite him to sit down, but he
was already pulling out a chair for himself at the kitchen table.

'Make yourself at home,' she mumbled.

'Thank you,' he said, oblivious to her sarcasm. He
whipped off his coat, draped it on the back of the chair
and sat down, stretching out his long legs in front of him.

There was something about his air of utter assurance
that reminded Lesley of a stockbroker she had dated
briefly when she lived in London. 'You went to one of
those schools, didn't you?' she asked knowingly.

'What schools?' Al frowned.

'You know – the schools where they train posh boys for taking over the world. You learn how to barge around other countries, subjugating the natives and making them do all the work, while you lounge about on verandas inventing cocktails.'

'If you're referring to public schools, then yes.'

'I knew it!'

'Harrow, though,' he said, as if in mitigation.

'How does that make it any better?'

'Well, it's the coolest one, obviously.'

'Cup of tea?' she asked, automatically flicking the switch on the kettle.

'I'd love a coffee, thanks.'

'I only have instant,' she said. It was a lie, but she wasn't about to start making fancy coffee for Al. She still didn't know why he was here, so best not to encourage him.

'It'll have to do.'

'I hope your parents didn't waste too much money on that charm school,' she said under her breath. She folded her arms, leaning against the worktop. 'So if you're not asking me out, why did you come here, Al?'

'I want to hire you.'

'Oh!' She was instantly mollified. That explained his brusque manner – he was just in business mode. She shouldn't have been so hard on him. 'You know,' she said, 'I think I might have some real coffee after all.'

'Excellent!'

She opened a couple of cupboards and pretended to do a bit of rummaging before 'finding' the coffee. 'Aha!' she said for dramatic effect, holding it up triumphantly. Today was looking up, and a new client definitely deserved real coffee.

'So have you been back to Dinner Dates since?' she asked him as she spooned coffee grounds into the filter.

'No. Actually, I was only there the night I met you as a favour to Helen. I help her out sometimes if she's a man short at the last minute.'

'So you were there under false pretences?' Lesley gave him a hard look. 'What if some poor woman fancied you?'

He shrugged. 'I *am* actually single at the moment. So if I did hit it off with someone, it would be perfectly above board.'

Huh! If Lesley had known that at the time, she mightn't have been so quick to give him the brush-off. Maybe he'd have been up for a casual hook-up.

'What about you?' he asked as she placed two mugs on the table and sat opposite him. 'Have you been back?'

'No. I've kind of stopped looking for now.'

'Oh. You've met someone.' For some reason, his face fell.

'No, I'm just taking a break from the whole dating scene. I'm going to concentrate on my career for now.'

'Ah. Good plan. And that's where I come in! As luck would have it, I need a private detective. So it was quite serendipitous that I happened to have met you.'

'Oh.' Lesley's heart sank. She had forgotten about passing herself off as a private investigator that night. She hadn't expected it to come back to bite her on the arse.

'Is there a problem?' Al asked, watching her closely.

'Well, it's just – look, I'm sorry, but I'm afraid you've had a wasted journey. I wasn't exactly honest about what I do for a living at that dinner party. I'm not really a private detective.'

'Oh, I know that,' Al said calmly and took a sip of coffee.

'You do? How?'

'I Googled you,' he said with a satisfied smile. 'You didn't give me your number, so I looked you up online to find your place of business. And I found you. You're a web designer, right?'

'Yes.' She frowned. 'So why would you want to hire me as a private investigator, when you know I'm not one?'

'Ah, well—' He looked shifty. 'An amateur is likely a better bet for my purposes.'

Lesley couldn't help bristling slightly. 'You mean you think I'll work for free? If you expect me to do it just for the fun of it ...' She left the sentence hanging, because the truth was she probably *would* do it just for the fun of it.

'No, I would pay you, of course. So, what do you say? Will you take the job?'

'I still don't know what it is.'

'Right. Of course.' He took a sip of coffee. 'It's my uncle. He had a massive heart attack a couple of months ago.'

'Oh, I'm sorry.'

'Thanks. He's fine now. You may have read about it,' Al said. 'My uncle is Peter Bradshaw.'

'*The* Peter Bradshaw? The actor?' This was intriguing.

'Yes.'

'Oh, he's brilliant! I love him.'

Al smiled. 'Me too.'

'I hadn't heard he'd had a heart attack.'

'It happened when he was in LA. They were filming the last part of that ghastly Inheritor franchise—'

'They're not that bad. It's not my kind of thing, but I've seen worse.'

Al threw her a scathing look. 'Anyway,' he continued, 'he collapsed on the set. Like I said, he's fine now. He's recovered enough to come home. He'll be moving back next week – and he'll be bringing his girlfriend with him. He's got engaged.'

'Good for him! He must be ancient.'

'He's seventy-two.'

'Never too late, eh? There's hope for us all.'

'His fiancée is twenty-six.' Al gave her a meaningful look.

'Gosh! Still, I suppose that's not so unusual for Hollywood types.'

'It's unusual in my family.'

'Well, I suppose he's old enough to know what he's doing,' Lesley said, still not sure why Al wanted a private detective. 'Hang on, he's not still married to your aunt, is he?' She knew Peter Bradshaw had been married to the actress Jane Howard for years. They'd had one of those tempestuous on-again/off-again relationships that the gossip columns did their best to keep up with. But she was pretty sure they weren't still together.

'No, they're divorced. Have been for years.'

'Okay, so ...'

'The thing is we know nothing about this woman – Stella. She moved in with Peter right after his heart attack, and looked after him while he was recuperating. And now suddenly they're engaged. She's twenty-six and he's an old man with a dodgy heart. He's okay now, but he hasn't exactly looked after himself. He's ... lived life to the full.'

That was putting it mildly. Peter Bradshaw was a notorious hell-raiser and womaniser, almost more renowned for his legendary drinking binges and wild partying than for his acting.

'So he's not in the best of health,' Al said. 'And my family is very wealthy.'

'That's nice. Not about your uncle's health,' Lesley added hastily. 'But it's nice to have money, isn't it? Not that

I can speak from experience.' Damn, she was babbling. Focus, Lesley! 'So you think the fiancée is a gold-digger,' she said, to make it clear she wasn't slow on the uptake.

'It seems obvious, doesn't it? They got engaged right after his heart attack. For a while there it didn't look like he was going to make it.'

'And you think this Stella has her sights set on being a merry widow.'

'That's certainly what my cousins think.'

'You don't think she could be in love with him? I mean, I know he's old and everything, but he's still quite attractive for a crumbly. And he seems like a real laugh. I'd say he'd be great fun to hang around with.'

'He is,' Al said with a fond smile. 'But we're not talking about just hanging around with him, are we? Would you sleep with him?'

'Ew, no!' Lesley wrinkled her nose. 'But that's just me,' she amended hastily. 'Everyone's different, aren't they? I mean, I don't even fancy Ryan Gosling.'

'I bet you wouldn't turn your nose up like that at the thought of sleeping with him, though.'

Lesley considered. Ryan Gosling *was* very fit. 'Yeah, okay. I take your point.'

'So you would?'

'I wouldn't kick him out of bed for eating biscuits, no.'

'Like you said, there's hope for us all,' Al murmured under his breath.

'Look, you don't really need an investigator at all, do you?' All it would take was someone with a Wi-Fi connection and a few hours to spare. An eight-year-old child armed with a laptop could easily handle it. Still, it beat SEO into a cocked hat, and if he wanted to pay her, she wasn't going to argue. 'But if you really want me to help out with this, I can do a bit of poking around on the internet. It shouldn't take more than a couple of days.'

'Well, there's a little more to it than that,' Al said, looking uncomfortable. 'I want something a bit more ... above and beyond. Stuff that doesn't really come within the remit of a regular investigator.'

'I'll tell you right now I won't do anything dodgy,' Lesley warned him.

'No, I wouldn't ask you to. But we need a more personal sort of investigation – not just background stuff that anyone could dig up on the internet. We want to know who this Stella is, how she genuinely feels about Peter, why she wants to marry him. Which makes you ideal for the job – that and the fact that you're single.'

This was starting to sound *very* dodgy, Lesley thought. She hoped she wouldn't have to turn it down. 'I don't see what my being single has to do with anything. And what's this "above and beyond" stuff you want me to do?'

'Well, those two things are related, actually.'

'I can't say I like the sound of that.'

'The thing is, as a woman, you could get close to Stella – maybe become her friend, someone she confides in. In order to do that, you'd need a reason to spend a lot of time around my family.'

'Okay ...' Lesley tried to play it cool, but the idea of hanging out with the Bradshaws was thrilling. She might get to meet Peter and Jane's two sons, who were both well-known actors in their own right. Rafe had caused a sensation the previous year when he'd played Mr Darcy in a very sexed-up TV adaptation of *Pride and Prejudice*.

'So you're related to Rafe and Scott Bradshaw?'

'Yes, they're my cousins,' Al said wearily.

'Wow! That must be really exciting.'

'I try to take it in my stride.'

She couldn't help thinking Al looked a bit pissed off. He was probably fed up of being overshadowed by his hot cousins.

'Anyway,' Al continued, breaking into her thoughts, 'I thought the best pretext for you spending time with my family would be if you were to, er ... be my girlfriend.'

5

'Oh.' Lesley was conflicted. On the one hand, the prospect of working undercover to expose a gold-digger was about as thrilling as it got. She'd be like a modern-day Miss Marple. On the other, being Al's girlfriend would put rather a damper on any chance of getting off with Rafe Bradshaw.

'Would I have to be your girlfriend?' she hedged. 'Couldn't I be ... I don't know ... your maid maybe?'

'My *maid*?' Al screwed up his face.

'Well, I don't know,' she said huffily. 'Don't you have a housekeeper or something?'

'I have a cleaner who comes once a week, but we don't socialise.'

'That's very elitist of you.'

'What can I say? She has her life and I have mine. The arrangement suits us both.'

'Well, I could be your assistant, then – your PA.'

'Nope.'

'Why not?'

'My family know Janine.'

'Who's Janine?'

'My PA. Besides, I have no reason to bring a PA on holiday with me.'

'You want me to go on holidays with you?' Lesley perked up at the thought of a holiday.

'My family have a place in Nice, and we all get together there every summer. As my girlfriend, you would naturally come with me.'

'All of you? The whole family? Would Rafe Bradshaw be there too? And Scott Bradshaw?'

'Yes, both my cousins would be there.'

'Rafe Bradshaw would definitely be coming?' Lesley felt it was important to clarify this point.

'Yes,' Al said wearily, 'TV's Mr Darcy will be there. So you see, we'd be living in the same house as Stella for two weeks. It'd be the perfect opportunity for you to get close to her.'

And to Rafe, Lesley thought. 'What else would I have to do as your girlfriend?'

'Nothing too arduous. Just accompany me to family dos, and try to look at me like you think I'm the greatest thing since ... Ryan Gosling.'

Lesley laughed.

'We should probably have the odd PDA, for authenticity.'

'What sort of PDA exactly?'

'Just some light hand-holding, perhaps the occasional snog.'

'No tongues,' Lesley said quickly.

'What do you take me for – a Kardashian?'

'Just so we're clear.'

'You would have to share a bedroom with me when we're on holiday, of course – for appearance's sake.'

'Ah, now we get to it.' Lesley gave him a knowing look.

'I can promise you I'll behave like a perfect gentleman. I'll take the floor.'

'How do I know this isn't all an elaborate ploy because you have designs on my wotsit?'

'I can assure you your wotsit will be perfectly safe. It won't even know I'm there.'

'I doubt that.' Lesley chewed her lip, considering. She was trying to keep a level head and look at this offer from all angles, but it was hard to contain her excitement. 'It sounds pretty full-on,' she said. 'It wouldn't leave me much time for my other clients.' That would be absolutely fine by her, but there was no need for Al to know that.

'It is. The problem is we don't have much time. It was a "whirlwind romance", conducted almost entirely from his sickbed on my uncle's part. They've just sprung this engagement on us, and now they're coming home to plan the wedding.'

'Blimey! That's fast work.'

'Suspiciously fast.'

'But look, no offence, but your uncle isn't exactly known for, well ...' She tried to think of a polite way to put it.

'For keeping it in his pants?'

'For his lasting relationships,' Lesley said primly. 'Don't you think that once he's on his feet again, he'll be back to his old ways, shagging around all over the place? This woman will probably go the way of all the others.'

Al shook his head. 'I don't think so. He's never got engaged to any of them before. If you ask me, this heart attack gave him a scare, and now he's afraid of ending up alone. He wants someone tied to him. I think that's why he's in such a hurry to get this woman nailed down.'

'Wow, you make it sound so romantic! But maybe you should just accept it. I mean, your uncle's old enough to make his own decisions, even if they're stupid ones. Surely he can give his money to whoever he wants.'

'It's not just his money, though. My father and Peter are heirs to the Bradshaw fortune. My great-grandfather founded the company. Dad took over the running of the business, but they still own it jointly. Bradshaw Biscuits? No doubt you've heard of them.'

'Your father makes Bradshaw Biscuits?' Lesley gasped, eyes wide.

'Well, he doesn't actually make them himself—'

'Oh, my God, I love his biscuits!' She jumped up and opened a cupboard. 'Look!' she said, producing a packet of Bradshaw's Chocolate Extravaganzas. 'I can't believe your dad makes these! They're my favourite. Would you like one?'

'Um ... no, thanks. Not just now.'

'Oh, you're probably sick of them, aren't you?' She put the biscuits back in the cupboard and sat down again. 'Did you get loads of free biscuits when you were a kid?'

He smiled. 'Yes, I did, actually. Mostly the wonky ones, but still ...'

'Still,' Lesley said dreamily. 'Hey, I bet you were popular at that posh school of yours. Tuck is currency in places like that, isn't it? *Tuck*,' she said, pronouncing it in an upper class English accent.

Al just rolled his eyes in response.

'So your cousins are afraid of being done out of their inheritance. That's understandable. If I stood to inherit my own biscuit empire, I wouldn't want anyone else getting their hands on it.'

'They don't want their father being taken for a ride,' Al said coldly.

'Literally,' Lesley said with a laugh.

'Sorry?'

'Well, basically you're worried his bride is planning to bonk him to death on their honeymoon and make off with the cash, right?'

'I know it sounds a bit far-fetched.'

'Not at all,' Lesley said reassuringly. 'I'm sure these things happen all the time.'

Al gave her a dubious look. 'Anyway, we'd like to get rid of this woman before it comes to that.'

'Hang on,' Lesley said, holding up a hand to stop him. 'Before we go any further, I might as well tell you I don't do wet work.'

'*Wet work?*' Al screwed up his face in dismay. 'What on earth is "wet work"?'

'You know, carrying out hits. Offing people.'

'You mean ... *murder?*'

'Well, you said you wanted to get rid of her.'

'I didn't mean in the *Goodfellas* sense.'

'What, then? Scare her off? Rough her up a bit? Because I won't do that either.'

'I'm very glad to hear it. Besides, you wouldn't be my first port of call if I was looking to hire muscle.'

'I'm stronger than I look, you know. I could do it if I wanted to – which I don't.'

'I'll bear that in mind. But I don't think we'll require anything quite so ... hands-on. We just want you to get close to her, find out if we have cause to be worried.'

'And if there's nothing?'

Al shrugged. 'Then I suppose we'll wish them joy and dance at their wedding.' He drained his coffee. 'So, what do you say? Will you be mine?'

Lesley glanced out the window at the grey sky through the steady drizzle that trickled down the glass. So far, the Irish summer was proving to be a washout. Did she want to go to the south of France with Al and his glitzy family? Tough decision ...

'I'll think about it,' she said. No harm in letting him stew a little. 'I'll get back to you tomorrow.'

WHEN AL LEFT, Lesley daydreamed about sleuthing escapades in Nice as she loaded the dishwasher. She pictured herself in a wide-brimmed straw hat and dark sunglasses, sipping a glass of cold white wine at an outdoor café while she observed Stella from a discreet distance; then chasing her down narrow streets and cobbled alleys, ducking into doorways to avoid being spotted; perhaps hitching a ride on the back of the motorbike of a handsome French man to continue the chase. This fantasy, she realised, owed more than a little to one of those sixties caper movies starring the likes of Audrey Hepburn.

She knew there was no way she was going to be able to concentrate on work for the rest of the day, so instead she decided to start on some research, and Googled Sir Peter Bradshaw. She found some news stories about his recent heart attack, and there was a touching picture of his youngest son, Scott, at LAX, flying to his father's bedside. He had his hood up, his gaze averted from the intrusive lenses pushed in his face as he made his way through the airport. He looked strained and anxious, and incredibly hot. Scott was most famous for his role as a dangerously attractive and morally ambivalent vampire in a cultish TV show. He wasn't very tall, but he was rakishly handsome, and what he lacked in height, he made up for in charisma and raw sex appeal.

There was a photo of Rafe speaking to press outside the hospital, and Lesley was surprised to see Jane Howard, ashen-faced, standing beside him. But then, Peter was still her children's father, and it had looked like he was going to die. She was probably there for her sons, rather than for her ex-husband's sake.

There were lots of images of Sir Peter – posing on the red carpet at movie premieres and award ceremonies, or snapped by paparazzi outside smart restaurants, always with his arm around some woman. The names and faces changed, but they were all young, glamorous and beautiful. Some were up-and-coming actresses or well-known models; others were not considered significant enough in their own right to even warrant being named.

Lesley read the captions on all the photos, searching for Stella, but if she was there, she fell into the latter category. The most recent picture she could find was from a premiere just a couple of weeks before Peter's heart attack. He was smiling for the cameras with his arm around the waist of a leggy strawberry blonde. She was the most likely candidate for Stella, Lesley thought, peering at the photo. Did she look like a gold-digger? There was nothing in the slanting green eyes, high cheekbones or perfectly made-up face that could tell her. Besides, this might not even be Stella, so there was no point in trying to read anything into her expression or body language. What did a gold-digger look like anyway? Probably exactly like this, she thought – a twenty-six-year-old stunner draped on the arm of a frail septuagenarian. Case closed.

There was no shortage of photos of Rafe and Scott, of course, or the gorgeous, glamorous people who seemed to constantly surround them. As she clicked through the images, Lesley started to panic. What had she been think-ing? How could she possibly accept Al's offer? It was all very well fantasising about holidaying with the Bradshaws. But the reality of hanging out with these people in a swimwear scenario was another thing. She didn't have the figure for it – or the wardrobe. She'd have nothing to wear. And she couldn't possibly sport a bikini in front of Rafe Bradshaw! Thank goodness she hadn't accepted the job on the spot. She could still say no. She'd call Al in the morning and tell him she couldn't do it.

She clicked out of the internet and rang Romy to talk it through with her. She was the sensible one. She'd tell Lesley she should turn it down, and that would be that.

'So, he knows you're not really an investigator, but he wants you to do the job anyway?' Romy asked when Lesley had filled her in. 'And you don't smell a rat? I'm starting to seriously doubt your powers of deduction right now.'

'What do you mean?'

'This Al clearly likes you.'

'No, it's not like that. I turned him down when he asked me out, so he knows I'm not into him.'

'Well, don't say I didn't warn you if this job is more about hunting the salami than unmasking the gold-digger.'

'So you don't think I should do it?' Lesley asked.

'I didn't say that—'

'Good. Because—' she took a deep breath '—I'm going to do it!'

6

Stella Daniels woke to sun streaming in through the gap she had left in the blackout curtains, heralding the beginning of another perfect LA day. She had never been able to sleep in total darkness, but she hadn't slept well last night anyway, despite the comforting chink of light, her mind racing, spinning around and around in circles, refusing to let go and slip into unconsciousness. That was happening a lot in the past couple of weeks. Everything had happened so fast, and her brain seemed to be struggling to keep up.

She swung out of bed and pressed the remote control to open the curtains, light flooding the room and bouncing off the white stucco walls. Pulling on a robe over her silk pyjamas, she crossed the room, pushed open the French doors and stepped onto the terrace, the terracotta tiles warm beneath her bare feet. Below her, light sparkled and danced on the water of the swimming pool, its shimmering surface reflecting the intensely blue sky. Leaning on the railing overlooking the grounds, she closed her eyes and stretched her face to the early morning sun, absorbing its warmth. She breathed in deeply, inhaling the fragrant morning air and let out a contented sigh. Then she opened her eyes and looked out over the luxuriously planted garden to the sprawling city spread out in the distance, and wondered, not for the first time in the past few weeks, how she had got here. She couldn't believe this was her life now, and she still had a pinch-me moment every morning she woke up to find herself living with Peter in this luxurious house in the Hollywood Hills.

Peter's proposal had taken her by surprise. They'd only been dating a few weeks before his heart attack, and Stella hadn't expected it to be anything more than a casual, short-term thing. Peter was a notorious ladies' man and was never with the same girlfriend for long. She had liked going out with him. The age difference wasn't important to her, and Peter was great fun to be around. He really knew how to show a girl a good time. She had to admit she'd also liked the kudos of being seen around town with such a huge star. She'd had fun and enjoyed it for what it was, but she'd never for a moment expected it to last, especially after she'd told him all about herself – her true life story, complete and unabridged.

She wasn't naive. It had occurred to her that perhaps it only *had* lasted because she just happened to be with Peter when this huge, game-changing event had hijacked his life. It was strange to think that such a momentous turning-point could be down to something so serendipitous – like winning a very high-stakes game of musical chairs. Had she simply happened to be in the right place when the music stopped? If his heart attack had been a couple of months earlier, would Peter now be engaged to Carla Gonzales, the young actress he'd dated just before her?

These were the thoughts that flickered through her mind constantly and kept her awake at night.

She had surprised herself by saying yes to Peter. But at the time, she'd thought he was dying, and she had nothing to lose. It had seemed like the right thing to do; the kind thing. She would be making an old man happy in his last days. So she'd said yes in a reckless spirit of adventure, not thinking beyond it to the reality of marriage. She had just never thought it would come to that.

She couldn't deny she had been taken aback by Peter's recovery. Even the doctors were impressed with how quickly he'd rallied. And now she found herself with a living, breathing fiancé and a wedding to plan. It wasn't that she was put out about it exactly. She was very fond of Peter and she wished him well. She was happy he'd survived. But it put her decision to marry him in a whole new light, and she wasn't sure how she felt about it.

She looked down at her engagement ring. She still couldn't quite get her head around the fact that she was getting married. She'd been rattling around on her own in the world since she was sixteen, and she'd always travelled light, torching the earth behind her and moving on. This was something different, she thought, twisting the ring around absently. Marriage was weighty and solid, like the heavy stone on her finger. Marriage left traces.

She went back inside, and her eyes strayed to the suit-cases she had hauled out of the closet last night. She still hadn't managed to bring herself to start packing. The prospect of going back to Ireland next week with Peter was tying nervous knots in her stomach.

She didn't expect his family to be very welcoming. She could imagine what they would think – a lowly young make-up artist engaged to a wealthy, ailing man more than twice her age. You didn't need to be Sherlock to put two and two together and come up with gold-digger. Even she couldn't rule out the possibility that Peter's wealth might have influenced her decision to say yes. It was hard to tell if your motives were pure when money was involved. It would be naive to think it wasn't an inducement. Money made everything easier. She didn't care about the cliché stuff – the jewellery, the designer clothes, the five-star hotels. It was the more nebulous things that money could buy that she found enticing – silence, security, freedom. They were the things she might be tempted to sell her soul for.

She was going to miss this place, she thought, as she sat down on the bed. More than the perfect weather and the beautiful house with its lavish furnishings, she would miss the privacy and seclusion here. The move to Ireland did have one big advantage, however: she'd be closer to Dan. The thought brought a kind of comfort that she felt seep through her body like an analgesic.

Suddenly feeling an overwhelming need to speak to him, she checked her watch. It would be early evening in Ireland. She grabbed her phone from the nightstand and hit Dan's number.

'Stella!' The warmth and affection in his soft, husky voice was instantly reassuring. 'What's up?'

'I've got news,' she said, keeping her voice low. They never bothered with chit-chat. They spoke too rarely to waste precious time on small talk. 'I'm engaged.'

She heard his intake of breath. 'Engaged?'

'Yes. To Peter.'

'Peter Bradshaw?' Dan knew she'd been dating Peter. 'Fuck me!'

He fell silent then. He would know she was feeling

wobbly and insecure – he'd hear it in her voice, no matter how breezy she tried to sound. He would know she was looking for reassurance, that she wanted him to tell her it would be okay like he always had.

'Congratulations, I guess.'

'Thanks.'

'That was quick work. How much does he know about you?'

She smiled. That was the million dollar question. Trust Dan to cut right to the chase. 'He knows everything.'

'Really? And ... he's okay with it?'

'Yes, he is.'

'You're sure?'

'Yes. He knows who I am, and he still wants to marry me. Is that so hard to believe?'

'Hey, of course not. I just don't want you to get hurt.'

She sighed. 'I know.' He was just worried for her, she understood that.

'And you're happy?'

'Yeah, I guess I am.'

'You don't sound too sure.'

'It's just all happened so fast, I can't get my head around it. Anyway, the good news is we'll be moving back to Ireland. I'll be living in Dublin. We can see each other.'

'Great! It's been a long time.'

'Yeah.' He was the person she loved most in the world. It had been far too long. Tears welled in her eyes at the thought of being able to put her arms around him again, of seeing him smiling at her ...

'Look, I've got to go now,' Dan said. 'But let me know when you're back and we'll arrange something.'

WHEN SHE HAD SHOWERED and dressed, she went downstairs. Maria, the maid, squeezed her some fresh orange juice and she took it out onto the patio and sat on a bench at the front of the house overlooking the sloping garden, her long legs tucked beneath her. She would miss this house. She'd been happy here – which seemed a little strange, in the circumstances. She'd enjoyed the time she'd spent here with Peter, just the two of them. She'd felt useful, looking after him and keeping him amused. It had been almost like a holiday, a time out from real life – they'd played Scrabble and watched television, and taken gentle walks in the garden, a little further each day while Peter built up his strength.

She heard him talking to Maria in the kitchen, and then he joined her on the terrace.

'Good morning.' She smiled. He looked well – rested and handsome.

'Good morning.' He sat beside her on the bench. 'Maria's making huevos rancheros,' he said, putting an arm around her.

She frowned. 'But you're not supposed to eat too many eggs.'

'They're for you,' he said. 'I know they're your favourite. I'll just have some muesli.'

She smiled as he pulled her to his side and she curled into him, laying her head on his shoulder. This was nice. Maybe this was all marriage meant and she was silly to panic about it. It was just about having someone who knew what you liked, and who wanted to please you; someone who was on your side and would always have your back.

'Thank you,' she said, taking his hand and playing with his fingers.

'I'm sorry it's not been much fun for you here. I'm not usually such a boring old fart.'

'Don't be silly. I haven't been bored.' She lifted her

head and looked out over the gardens to the horizon. 'I hate leaving this. It's so lovely.'

'It is. But it's always good to go home, isn't it?'

Stella shrugged. She didn't feel any special connection to Ireland or any fondness for the grim little seaside town in Galway where she'd grown up. She had led a rootless, peripatetic existence since she'd left home at the age of sixteen, never looking back – well, except for Dan. He was the one thing she could never leave behind. 'I guess it's different when you have family,' she said. 'Home for me is wherever I live.'

'Wherever you hang your hat,' he said, smiling. 'Well, I'm glad you've decided to hang it at my house. I can't wait to introduce you to everyone.'

'What if they don't like me?'

'They'll love you,' he said, smiling into her eyes.

'Easy for you to say. You don't have to worry about meeting *my* family.'

'Poor Stella,' Peter said, tucking a lock of hair behind her ear. 'You're so young to be all alone in the world.'

'You'll be my family now,' she said, giving him a bright smile. 'When we're married.' As she said it, she realised she meant it. She could do this. She could be Peter's wife, and they could have a good life together. She would be faithful, and she'd take care of him. They'd be loyal and kind to each other, and she would prove to his family that she wasn't on the make. She'd show them that she was good for him.

She was going into this with her eyes open and she would do all she could to make their life together work. It would be fun too. Peter was rich, and they could travel and do interesting and exciting things. It would be an adventure. Looked at from that angle, it wasn't scary at all. It was just another new beginning, and she was good at those.

'You're not having second thoughts, are you?' Peter asked her. She realised she'd gone quiet.

'No,' she said. 'I want to marry you, Peter.'

'You do?' He smiled, leaning forward to kiss her.

This time, when she said 'yes', she really meant it.

7

Lesley waited until the following morning to contact Al and tell him she'd accept the job.

He called around in the afternoon to discuss the details.

'So, I'll take the case,' she told him as soon as they were sitting down. She'd already agreed to do it, but she'd always wanted to say that, and she might never get another opportunity.

'Good. Excellent.'

They were once more seated at the kitchen table. This time Lesley had brought out the good coffee in advance, and she'd bought some pastries from the local bakery, having decided she couldn't serve Bradshaw Biscuits to Al.

'I've already opened a file,' she said, tapping the manila folder in front of her. 'I've decided to call it "The Adventure of the Adventuress".' She pointed to the title written on the front of the file in black sharpie.

'Oh, is that usual – to name your cases like that?'

'Well, I've never done this before, but I thought it would be nice. What do you think?'

'Of the title?'

'Yes. I considered something with "mystery" in it, but this case doesn't seem all that mysterious, does it? It has more of a caper vibe, what with the whole undercover girl-friend thing, so "adventure" seemed appropriate.'

'You've given this a lot of thought.'

'Well, it's my first case, and – I'll be honest with you, Al – I'm very excited about it. But you're the client. If you don't like it, we can change it. Or it can have no title at all, if you'd prefer.'

'No, I like it. It's catchy.'

'It has a nice ring to it, doesn't it?'

'The Adventure of the Adventuress it is.'

'Great! Now,' she said, pulling a notebook from the folder and opening it, 'tell me everything you know about this woman.' She picked up her pen to take notes.

'Well, there's really very little,' Al said. 'Her name's Stella Daniels. She's a make-up artist. Peter met her on the set of his latest film. She's Irish. Um ...' He drummed his fingers on the table. 'She's twenty-six ...' He trailed off.

Lesley looked at her meagre notes. 'There's not much to go on. I suppose we'll have to wait until Stella gets here and we can find out more about her.' She took a Danish pastry and started pulling it apart. 'In the meantime, why don't we get started on our back story. I mean, if I'm going to be your girlfriend, I should know more about you.'

'Okay. What do you want to know?'

Lesley narrowed her eyes at him. 'What happened to your last girlfriend?' she asked.

'Nothing! You make it sound like you think I did away with her or something.'

'Did you?'

'Of course not. Why would you think that?'

'You're the one who brought it up.'

'Well, I didn't "off her", as you'd put it.'

'But you did piss her off.'

'What makes you think it was my fault?'

'It usually is the man's fault, I find.'

'Well, it wasn't. We just split up.'

'But why? There must have been a reason.'

'That's none of your business.'

'It is if I'm going to be your next victim.'

Al sighed. 'She cheated on me, if you must know.'

'Oh. Sorry. How long had you been together?'

'Off and on for a couple of years.'

'And when did you break up?'

'About five months ago.'

'And no one since then?'

'Nothing serious. Until you,' he said with a disarming smile.

'You don't need to flirt with me when no one can see us,' Lesley said sternly. 'Save that for when we're with your family.'

'I thought it would be easier if I tried to stay in character the whole time – it'll be more natural then when we're in public.'

'Suit yourself. We should get a few photos of us together to put up on Instagram – you know, nights out, doing coupley things.'

'That would mean we'd have to go on some nights out.'

'Don't look so pleased about it,' Lesley said. 'It's just business.'

'Okay.'

'You should change your Facebook status to "in a relationship" for starters. That's the easiest way to get the word out, and establish us as a couple. I'll send you a friend request so you can add me.'

'And you'll be changing your status too?'

Lesley thought, taking a sip of her coffee. 'I don't really need to, do I? It's only your family who need to think I'm your girlfriend, and I doubt we have any friends in common.'

'But we will have, once we go public as a couple. My cousins at least are bound to add you.'

Lesley felt a little childish thrill at the thought of having famous Facebook friends like Rafe and Scott Bradshaw. Everyone would be so impressed and jealous. Rafe was a huge heartthrob since *Pride and Prejudice*, and Scott was widely acknowledged to be sex on legs. The fact that he was gay was no bar to hordes of women worldwide casting him in their fantasies.

'You definitely have to be in a relationship with me,' Al said.

Lesley raised her eyebrows meaningfully.

'You know what I mean,' Al said, reaching for a cinnamon roll. 'How will it look if I say we're in a relationship and you have it that you're still single?'

Lesley sighed. 'I just don't want to deal with the barrage of questions I'll get from everyone if I put that I'm in a relationship. They'll all want to know who you are. My family will probably even want to meet you.'

Al shrugged. 'You'll be meeting *my* family.'

'That's different. Your family are cool.' Lesley considered for a moment. 'I could be "it's complicated"?' she offered.

'No, you can't be "it's complicated". That'll look just as bad as if you're single. It's not complicated. You're my girlfriend.'

'Okay, okay, keep your shirt on. I'll put that I'm in a relationship, and I'll tag you in photos, so my friends can look you up.'

Actually, now that she thought about it, it would be

good to have photos of Al on her page. A pretend boyfriend would be useful for getting her family off her back. Her mother had really pinned her hopes on Rob, and was more upset about the break-up than Lesley was. And if Rob should happen to see her hobnobbing with the rich and famous, all to the good. Maybe he'd realise too late how lucky he'd been to have her.

'We should get some photos of us out and about, doing activities,' she said.

'What sort of activities do you suggest?'

'I don't know. Do you play rugby?' she asked with a sudden flash of inspiration. Al looked pretty fit, and it would drive Rob nuts if she had someone who was better than him at rugby. 'I could go and watch your matches and cheer you on.'

'You like watching rugby?'

'I don't mind it. My ex used to play a lot.'

'Well, I don't.'

'I thought all those posh schools made you play rugby.'

'They did. They also made us create a diorama of the Battle of Hastings from a shoebox and wear a straw boater in public – none of which I've done since leaving.'

'Is there any sport you're into?'

'I did a lot of hillwalking with my ex.'

'Is that a sport? I thought it was supposed to be gentle and sociable – everyone chatting to each other while they're ambling along.'

'Not for Cassie. She's very competitive. She doesn't amble. The guy she cheated on me with was always first to the top,' he said sourly.

'We should definitely go hillwalking then – find a way to beat them at it so you can get her back.'

'I don't want her back; I'm over her.'

'I don't mean get her back as your girlfriend. I mean

have your revenge – get her back for cheating on you. Make her rue the day. Wouldn't you like her to rue the day?'

'Well, when you put it like that,' Al said, a slow smile creeping over his face. 'I don't see how we're going to beat them, though. They're both really fit.'

'Well, leave it with me. I'll think of something. So, what else do you like doing?'

'The usual, I suppose. I like going to restaurants, the theatre—'

'Ugh,' Lesley grimaced. 'I hate the theatre.'

Al reared back in shock. 'How can you hate the theatre?'

'It's weird and embarrassing. It's all so artificial. You can see it's just people pretending, and I feel mortified for the actors making eejits of themselves.'

Al laughed. 'Well, you'd better not say that to any of my family. They're practically all actors.'

'Not you, though.'

'I'm the black sheep.'

'So I get the good one,' she said, smiling at him. 'Were they disappointed when you went into architecture?'

'Well, obviously they'd have preferred if I'd run away with the circus. But they were always very supportive.'

'And you're not the only one with a proper job. Your dad's a baker. That must have paved the way for you.'

'Well, he's not so much a baker as a captain of industry.'

'Still, no shame in that. Anyway, I've no problem with actors as long as they stick to movies or TV.'

'Okay, so no trips to the theatre, then.'

'Eating out is fine. I love going out to dinner. Oh, we could go on a mini-break!'

'You want to go on a mini-break with me? This is all so sudden.'

'We wouldn't really have to go anywhere. We could just drive around and check in somewhere fabulous.'

'That sounds like going somewhere to me.'

'I don't mean actually check in to a hotel – just check in at a location on Facebook, so my family would see what a great time we're having and how much better you are than my last boyfriend.'

'Were you together long?'

'Just over a year.' Lesley knew it didn't sound like much when she said it out loud, but it was the longest relationship she'd ever had.

'Why did you break up?'

'He moved.'

'Oh, that's tough. You didn't want to try the long-distance thing?'

'*I* would have. But he wasn't willing to make the effort. So that was that.'

'Where did he move to?'

'The north side.'

Al raised his eyebrows. 'The north side of ...?'

'Dublin. Portmarnock, to be precise. It's nearer his work.'

'But that's only about a half hour drive.'

'Twenty minutes if there's not much traffic. But he doesn't have a car, in fairness.'

'Still, there's public transport. Surely if he really cared about you—'

'Yeah, well,' Lesley mumbled, 'it turned out he didn't. He was only going out with me because I was on his bus route and it was handy for him.'

'Well, I'm sure you don't need me to tell you you dodged a bullet there.'

'He was nice in some ways, though,' Lesley said, smiling wistfully. Rob had been as enthusiastic and energetic in bed as he was on the rugby pitch, and had always applied himself to getting her off with the same bullish determination with which he approached scoring a try.

'If you're thinking about sex—' Al began.

'How did you know I was thinking about sex?' Lesley asked, caught off guard.

'You had this goofy look on your face. It doesn't suit you.'

'I still miss him in some ways, that's all.'

'Well, don't miss him for sex, for God's sake. Anyone can do that – dogs, Neanderthals. It's not rocket science.'

'No, but some people are better at it than others. I mean, I'd like to be with someone who had a little more finesse than a dog.'

'Well, you could train them up. Sex is the easy part. It's the other things you want to look out for, you know – kindness, good sense of humour, decent cook, that kind of thing. Someone who's prepared to go that extra mile on the bus for you.'

'Very funny.' Lesley took a long gulp of coffee to hide her annoyance. 'Okay, before we go any further, we have to lay out some terms and conditions for my role as your girlfriend. I will accompany you to family dos and make googly eyes at you. I'll laugh at your jokes, even when they're not funny, and generally hang on your every word and give all appearances of finding you adorable. You will do the same, of course, for me.'

'Agreed. My jokes will be funny, though.'

'As for PDAs, here are the rules,' she said firmly. 'Kissing is fine, but no tongues. No boob action, no touching under the clothes, no nudity. Anything below the waist is definitely out. No—'

'Lesley,' Al interrupted, 'you do know what the P stands for in PDA?'

'Public.'

'Exactly. Do you honestly think I'd stick my tongue down your throat or grope your breasts in public?'

'I don't know what you might do, given half a chance.'

He flattened his mouth into a thin line of disapproval. 'Well, I wouldn't – even if you were really my girlfriend. And public nudity is definitely not my bag. Okay?'

'Okay,' Lesley mumbled, feeling told off. 'Oh, and I was going to say absolutely no trying to get me to touch your willy either.'

Al just sighed exaggeratedly and rolled his eyes.

'So tell me more about this holiday we're going on,' she said into the awkward silence that followed. 'Did you bring your ex last year?'

'Yes, I did.'

'Right, I want to see some photographs.'

'Why?'

'If she's that competitive, I need to know what I'm up against.' Lesley felt intimidated again at the prospect of being in a bikini-wearing situation with Al's glamorous family.

'You're not "up against" anything. It's a family holiday, not a competition.'

'Still, I want to know.' She jumped up and left the room. She went into the study and grabbed her laptop from her desk, rubbing her finger over the mouse to wake it up as she marched back into the kitchen.

'Right,' she said, plonking it on the table in front of Al. 'Show me.'

'Show you what?'

'You must have some summer holiday photos on Facebook.'

'I don't use Facebook much.'

'Well, go onto your ex's page then and find some – or your cousin's. I don't believe there aren't any that you can access online. Go on – I won't look while you type your password,' she said, covering her eyes with her hand.

'Oh, all right,' Al huffed.

She waited a few seconds while Al typed. When she took her hand away, he was scrolling.

'Okay, here's one,' he said, turning the laptop around to face her.

The photo had been shared on his timeline by a Cassie Lyons and was dated last July. Cassie had captioned it '*En vacance chez* Bradshaw, Nice'. Lesley recognised most of the faces seated outdoors around a long wooden table under trees hung with lanterns. As well as Al, there were his cousins Scott and Rafe, Jane Howard and Peter Bradshaw. They were all burnished by the sun, and looked relaxed and happy. Rafe had his arm around the shoulders of a pretty dark-haired woman who was presumably his girl-friend, and there was an older couple she didn't recognise.

'Are they your parents?' she asked Al.

'My dad and my stepmother, Joy.'

'Oh, are your parents divorced?'

He shook his head. 'My mum's dead.'

'Oh, I'm sorry.'

'Thanks. It was a long time ago. She died when I was eleven.'

'God, that's awful.'

'Yes, it was.' He gave her a sad little smile.

'You're an only child?'

'Yes, but Rafe and Scott are like brothers to me. We spent a lot of time together, growing up. After Mum died, I used to come and stay with Jane and Peter in the summer holidays.'

Lesley turned her attention back to the screen. 'So, this is your girlfriend?' she asked, pointing at the avatar of the smiling blonde who had posted the picture. 'Cassie Lyons?'

'My ex-girlfriend, yes.'

Lesley clicked on her profile and brought up Cassie's page.

'Hang on, I didn't say you could do that.'

Lesley ignored him, her heart sinking as she scrolled through Cassie's photos. Tall, blonde and athletic, Cassie was gorgeous and she knew it. Her timeline was full of posed selfies of her dressed up for nights out, pouting at herself in bathroom mirrors. Every photo had hundreds of likes and was liberally peppered with comments on how stunning she was.

Lesley scrolled through to last July until she found a picture of Cassie and Al on the beach at Cannes, both beaming at the camera. Cassie wore a skimpy green bikini, Al's arm around her teeny-tiny waist. She was surprised how fit Al looked in his board shorts. He wasn't exactly ripped, but he was more muscular than Lesley would have given him credit for.

'Stop ogling me,' Al said, peering over her shoulder. 'I object to being objectified.'

'So this is your ex,' Lesley said accusingly, jabbing her finger at the image of Cassie. 'Well, sorry, but this isn't going to work.'

'What isn't going to work?'

'You and me,' she said, waving her hand between them.

'Why not?' he frowned, aghast. 'You haven't even given us a chance.'

'Well, look at her! She could be a model.'

'Well, she's not. She's a systems analyst, actually.

Though, now that you mention it, she did do the odd bit of modelling while she was at school.'

'I knew it!'

'But so what if she was? What have you got against models?'

'Nothing. But what are people going to think when they see you with me? They'll never believe I'm your girlfriend.'

'Why not?'

'Well, look at me!'

Al looked her up and down, frowning. 'What's the matter with you?' he asked impatiently. 'You look fine to me.'

'Oh, thanks very much!'

'More than fine.'

'Okay, tell me one thing about me that you find attractive.'

'Well, there's——'

'Come on.' She snapped her fingers and tapped her foot. 'Give me a compliment – the first thing that comes into your head. Don't think about it.'

'Um, well, er – there's so many things ...' Al stammered.

'Come on. And if you tell me I have a good personality, I might throw something at you.'

'Well, I'm not loving your personality right now, to be honest.'

'See, you can't do it,' Lesley said triumphantly. 'You can't think of one fecking thing——'

'I can, I just——'

'What is it, then?' Come on,' she said impatiently, snapping her fingers once more, 'out with it.'

'Big breasts!' Al shouted.

'What?' Lesley froze, ceasing all foot-tapping and finger-snapping instantly.

'Aargh, sorry,' Al said, clutching his head in his hands. 'I don't know what came over me. I'm not good under pressure. You kept snapping your fingers at me, and shouting, and it just came out.'

'That was the first thing that came into your head?'

'Sorry. Let me try again. You have beautiful eyes.'

'Thanks,' Lesley said, secretly pleased. Her eyes were her best feature – after her amazing rack.

8

At six-thirty Peter gave up on sleep. He was still suffering from jet lag since returning to Dublin two days earlier, and had been awake since four. He threw off the duvet with a weary sigh, got out of bed and started performing a half-hearted salute to the sun, but abandoned it halfway through. Maybe he'd try again later. He was too stiff this early in the morning. It took him longer to limber up these days. Everything took longer, he thought with annoyance.

It was such a bore growing old, your body no longer doing what you wanted it to without complaint, fighting you every step of the way. It was nature's way of seeing you off, he supposed – all part of Mother Nature's evil plan. Your body became slower to heal, as it grew more prone to insult and injury. 'Insult' was the term one of his doctors in LA had used for what had happened to his heart. It seemed pleasingly apt – he *felt* insulted. He wasn't done with life yet – not by a long shot. He may not be as agile as he'd once been, but he was still fit. Catching his reflection in the cheval mirror, he gave his flat stomach a self-satisfied pat. Only last month he'd featured in a list of the hottest men alive, albeit in the over-seventies category and polling behind Harrison Ford.

He pulled on a robe and drew the curtains. The cool morning breeze was welcome as he stepped through the French doors onto the balcony. LA had nothing on this, he thought, breathing in a deep lungful of salty sea air. From its cliff-top position, his house had a panoramic view of the broad sweep of Killiney Bay.

Across the water, the sun was hovering just above the horizon, a shimmering yellow ball throwing a sparkling path across the water. The sky was shades of grey, shot through with pale rays of light. Peter closed his eyes and listened to the soothing sounds of waves foaming over the rocks below, intensely aware of how lucky he was to be here – to have escaped death and have the world restored to him; to be still breathing the delicious morning air, surrounded by so much beauty. He had lived a reckless, profligate kind of life, squandering his health, his marriage, the love of his life. But miraculously he'd got away with it and been given another chance – and he wasn't going to push his luck this time. He'd start living a quieter, healthier, more peaceful life – and this house was the perfect place to do it.

He heard the front door close softly and opened his eyes to see Stella slipping quietly out of the house in her running clothes, her strawberry blonde hair tied back in a ponytail. Her trainer-clad feet crunched across the gravel as she walked to the gate. Peter felt a shock of unfamiliarity at the sight of her, almost wondering what this woman was doing in his home – this virtual stranger who was his fiancée. He watched as she headed for the steps that led to the beach and disappeared out of sight.

He'd been with a lot of women since his divorce – and

before it, he thought with a pang of guilt – but he'd never considered settling down with any of them. It wasn't really the point of going out with younger women. When he was with them, he felt young and carefree, and his relationships had been light-hearted, casual fun. They had never promised each other anything beyond a good time.

He knew what a cliché he was, serially dating a string of nubile beauties less than half his age. He was well aware that in the public imagination he'd become the archetypal lecherous old man – he'd read the sneery articles and blog posts. But despite what people might think, however stunning his girlfriends had been, it was never just about their looks.

They were all beautiful, of course – lovely in a way they wouldn't even realise until it was too late. He couldn't deny the allure of their tight, smooth skin and supple bodies; their bright eyes and soft, silky hair. But that wasn't the sum total of their appeal. He knew how ridiculous it would sound if he claimed it was their conversation that attracted him, but it happened to be true – at least partly.

He loved the things they talked about – their hopes and dreams, their plans for the future. But even more than that, he loved the things they *didn't* talk about – disappointments and failures; regrets about the past. He adored their ignorance and superficiality – all the things they didn't know about time and loss; the lessons they'd yet to learn about remorse and defeat. The sense that they had more of life ahead of them than behind gave them the confidence to be bold and adventurous, and he admired their recklessness, the audacious risks they took with lovers, with careers; even with life and limb. They didn't need to play it safe because there was plenty of time. That was the real secret of their magical attraction: time was what everyone wanted, and they had it in abundance. So he had clung to their youth

like a life raft, as if it could save him if he stayed close –
almost as if it might rub off.

Then he'd had his heart attack, and he'd realised what
an idiot he'd been. It was as if a veil had been lifted, and
he'd seen things as they really were. He felt like he'd been
on a terrifying roller coaster with all these silly young
women shrieking and laughing their heads off, completely
oblivious to the fact that they were all hurtling full pelt
towards their doom. Suddenly their youthful folly wasn't so
adorable and seemed just that – folly. They were all too
young and naive – too bloody stupid – to see that no
matter how much you enjoyed the ride, it would always
end the same way. He was the only one with the sense to
be petrified.

Lying in his hospital bed, shaking with relief that he
had woken up to another day, he'd found himself craving
some calm and stability in his life. He'd wanted to get off
the roller coaster and be down on the ground with the
people who were strolling along hand-in-hand eating ice-
cream, perhaps walking a dog or watching a grandchild
wobbling around on a bike. He'd realised he didn't want to
die alone, and that was where he was heading. So he'd
grabbed the person nearest to him and clung on for dear,
dear life – and that person happened to be Stella.

It had been the impulse of a moment, asking her to
marry him, prompted solely by fear and panic. But it had
been fortuitous, and he didn't regret it. He realised now
that Stella was just the sort of person he should be with at
this juncture in his life. She was so much more mature and
self-possessed than he'd been at her age – than he'd been a
year ago, for that matter.

He was looking forward to making a life here with her.
When the weather was warmer, he'd take her out in the
boat to the little private cove, where they could sunbathe

naked. He felt a little stirring of desire at the thought, and he smiled. Mother Nature could fuck right off. There was plenty of life in him yet, and he was going to suck the marrow out of every last drop.

AFTER HER RUN, Stella stood on the beach, looking out over the glittering water of the bay as she did her stretches. It was so beautiful in the early morning sunshine, and she felt a sudden burst of joy and gratitude that somehow, after everything she had been through, she had washed up safe on this shore. Filled with a sense of peace and wellbeing that she hadn't experienced in a long time, she closed her eyes and said a silent prayer of thanks to whatever twist of fate had led her here.

She turned and climbed the steps up the cliff to the back of the house, entering quietly by the side door so as not to disturb Peter if he was still sleeping. In the kitchen she grabbed her mobile from the worktop and hit Dan's number. She listened to it ring as she opened the fridge and took out the stuff to make her morning smoothie.

'Hi,' Dan croaked, sounding sleepy. She smiled, picturing him rubbing his eyes, and ruffling his wayward hair.

'Sorry to call so early,' she said. 'Can you talk?'

'Yeah. It's fine.' He was speaking quietly, and Stella wondered if he was still in bed, his wife sleeping beside him.

'Just hang on, I'm going to go downstairs,' he said.

As she waited, she peeled a banana and threw it into the blender along with some strawberries.

'Okay,' he said, his voice louder now.

'So, when can I see you?' she asked.

'You're in Ireland?'

'Yes, in Dublin. We got here the day before yesterday.' She spooned yoghurt into the blender. 'We're in Peter's house in Killiney. You should see it. It's amazing!'

'I'd love to see it,' he said, and there was just the hint of a challenge in his tone, 'but I take it you're not inviting me to meet the fiancé?'

'No,' she said, some of her pleasure in talking to him draining away, 'but I can't wait to see you.'

'I know, me too.' He sounded conciliatory. He knew what power he had to make her feel bad. He was too sweet-natured to wield it. 'How about Friday?'

'Sorry. We have this thing with Annie's parents. It's their anniversary.'

Annie, his beautiful wife. They'd never met, but Stella had seen photographs.

'I could do next weekend,' he said.

'Okay. I could meet you in Galway? I'll book a hotel and stay over – somewhere with five stars and posh afternoon tea.' She was excited already, picturing the two of them in an elegant hotel lounge, drinking champagne and eating dainty sandwiches with the crusts cut off.

When they'd said their goodbyes, she couldn't stop grinning as she poured apple juice into the blender, slapped on the lid and switched it on. Talking to Dan always calmed and reassured her. He had a way of making her insecurities melt away. He'd always been able to make her feel safe, like nothing bad could really touch her when he was there. He'd whispered it to her in the dark so many times – 'It'll be okay. Everything will be okay'. It had been hard to see at the time how it could ever be okay for her, and it was only because she trusted him so completely that she'd been able to believe him. But he'd been right. Everything had turned out fine, and look at her now! She had put all the ugliness of the past behind her, and she was a healthy, great-looking twenty-six-year-old woman, living in this beautiful house with a wonderful man who wanted to marry her.

She poured her smoothie into a tall glass and stood looking out the window as she drank. It was sweet, cool and refreshing. Outside, the sun was high in a cloudless blue sky. It was going to be a beautiful day.

∼

Peter found Stella in the kitchen with her back to him, looking out the window.

'You're up early!' she said, turning to him with a bright smile.

'Not as early as you,' he said, pulling out a chair and sitting at the table. 'Been out for a run?'

'Yes.' She slid into his lap, winding her arms around his neck. 'It's too beautiful here to stay in bed.'

As he wrapped his arms around her lithe body, he was suddenly struck by how young and vibrant she was, so full of potential, and he felt a stab of guilt. She still had so much of life ahead of her, so much possibility for adventure and ... love. Would he be curtailing all that by marrying her? Was he cutting off access to all those open roads and steering her into a dead end?

'Am I being very selfish, marrying you?' he asked.

'Probably,' she said with a shrug. 'And I'm being very selfish marrying you. No one gets married for altruistic reasons, do they?'

He smiled. 'No, I suppose not.'

'You're not getting cold feet, are you?' She punched him playfully on the arm.

'Never.' He couldn't say exactly what he meant,

because that would mean acknowledging the elephant in the room; the thing both of them knew and neither of them had ever spoken of since his surprise proposal and her even more surprising acceptance. He wasn't sure there would be any going back if either of them were to say it out loud. It might not change anything. But he was pretty sure Stella didn't want to test their shaky foundations any more than he did.

'There's so much I don't know about you,' he said wistfully.

'Well, what would you like to know?'

'Have you ever been in love?' he asked on impulse, and then immediately regretted it. 'I mean, before me, obviously,' he added, losing his nerve.

'Only once.' A shadow flickered across her face. 'I didn't like it.'

It was probably as close as they'd come to admitting how they felt about each other. But they both had their reasons for wanting this marriage, and they were going into it with their eyes open.

'Whereas you, as we all know, fall in love every five minutes.'

Peter laughed. 'Yes, I'm a hopeless romantic. Always have been.'

'That's one way of putting it,' Stella said, rolling her eyes.

It was true. He had fallen in love easily and often. At least, he had been convinced it was love at the time. Now he wasn't so sure. He had been besotted with countless women. Those three little words had tripped off his tongue so many times. But now he suspected that his honest answer to the question 'have you ever been in love' would be the same as Stella's – only once.

'I was a lousy husband in my first marriage,' he said.

'But I'm older and wiser now, and I'll do better this time. I promise.'

'I'll hold you to that.' She gave him a quick peck on the lips.

'So, what do you want to do today?'

'I thought we could go for a walk on the beach later. It's so nice out. But first I want to make a few calls, try and scare up some work.'

'You don't need to work. I've got oodles of money – more than enough for both of us.'

'I don't want to be a freeloader, Peter.'

'It's not freeloading if you're married.'

'We're not married yet.'

'That's only a matter of time. Besides, we've got a wedding to plan. I'm told that's a full-time job in itself.'

'It doesn't have to be,' Stella said with a mischievous grin. 'We could elope.' Her eyes danced merrily.

'Run away together like a pair of star-crossed lovers? I'm a bit old for that – and not in shape for running anywhere.'

'Well, you *are* marrying a penniless girl from the wrong side of the tracks,' Stella said playfully. 'I'm sure your family will heartily disapprove.'

'All the more reason to do this properly.' Peter already knew his sons weren't exactly overjoyed about the news of his engagement. 'I'm not having some hole-and-corner affair. A big fuck-off wedding will show them we mean business.'

'Aren't I the one who's supposed to be hankering after the big fairy-tale wedding?'

'And you're not?'

'I guess I'm just not that kind of girl.'

He frowned. 'You don't really want to run off; do you?'

Stella bit her lip, her expression serious. 'Are you offering?'

'Seriously?' He was shocked to realise that she meant it.

'I could do without the fuss.'

He caught the slight panic behind her eyes. 'Don't worry, we can keep it private and low-key. Just family and close friends. We could even do it here in the house.'

'Okay, that sounds good – as long as it doesn't get out of hand.' She climbed off his lap. 'But I do need to work, Peter. I don't want to be financially dependent on anyone.'

He saw that this was a battle he wasn't going to win. 'Fine. But there's no point in looking for anything until we get back from France, is there?'

'No, I guess you're right. It can wait. Besides, I do have some savings. I can afford to take a break.'

'Good. You've earned one.'

'There's some bircher muesli I made last night in the fridge,' she said, heading for the door. 'I'm going to jump in the shower. And then we can start making some lists.'

9

On Saturday afternoon, Al arranged for them to meet Stella and Peter for lunch, so he could introduce Lesley as his girlfriend. He picked her up from her house.

'You look lovely, darling,' he said, leaning in to give her a peck on the cheek when she opened the door.

Lesley reared back. 'Hey, what are you doing?' She frowned. 'Nobody's watching.'

'I thought I should get into my role – have a bit of practice at being boyfriendly with you.'

Lesley eyed him warily. 'Okay, maybe you're right,' she said. She turned and locked the door behind her. 'But don't call me darling,' she said as she followed him to the Land Rover parked at the gate.

'You don't like terms of endearment?' Al asked as he went around to the passenger side and held the door open for her.

'Not *darling*,' she grimaced as Al sat in beside her and fastened his seatbelt. 'It makes you sound about a hundred. Only old farts say "darling".'

'Oh! Really?' He frowned.

'Did you call your last girlfriend darling?'

'Well ... never you mind.'

'I'll take that as a yes,' Lesley muttered.

'Okay, what should I call you then?'

Lesley thought. 'What about "baby"?' She'd been surprised by the effect that had had on her when Rob had blurted it out once during sex.

'Really?' Al frowned, glancing at her as he pulled away from the kerb. 'You like that?'

'I do. It makes me go a bit funny, if I'm honest.'

'Huh!' Al made a face. 'Well, much as I'd like to make you "go a bit funny", I can't say *baby*. I'm not an American hoodlum.'

'Okay, then. What about "sweetheart"?' That was the only other term of endearment she could think of that didn't make her squirm.

Al nodded. 'Okay, sweetheart it is. You look lovely, sweetheart,' he said, smiling at her.

Lesley made a face.

'What's wrong? You said you were okay with sweetheart.'

'I am, but ... it sounds put on when you say it, like you're in a play.'

'I told you I needed practice.'

'You weren't kidding. Anyway, it's probably best if you just stick to calling me Lesley most of the time.'

'Do you have any nicknames? Does anyone call you Les? Lezzles?'

'No – not if they value their lives. No nicknames. What about you?'

'Well, Al is a nickname, I suppose, but it's what everyone calls me, apart from people I don't know all that well – like Conor. Scott sometimes calls me Aloysius, but only to wind me up.'

'It was very unfair of your parents giving you a ludicrous name like that. It's just asking for bullying. What were they thinking?'

Al raised his eyebrows. 'My grandfather on Mum's side was Aloysius. He was lovely. I like that I'm named after him.'

'Oh.' Lesley felt chastened. It was sweet, she thought, that Al was happy to have such a stupid name because it was in honour of his grandfather.

It was one of the first warm, sunny days of summer, and half of Dublin seemed to be headed, as they were, for the coast. Lesley had been glad of the chance to wear her favourite Zara dress, but now as she looked down at her milk-bottle legs, she was beginning to regret her decision. She wouldn't stand out among her fellow Dubliners – the pavements were full of people in summer clothes, whose translucent skin was obviously getting its first airing of the year – but Stella had been living in California. Lesley would probably look like a ghost beside her.

She was glad she and Al were the first to arrive at the restaurant in Dun Laoghaire, so she could get her legs under the table before Stella and Peter turned up. They were shown to a table on a large terrace overlooking the harbour.

They'd just been given water and menus when Peter and Stella arrived. They stood as the couple weaved across the terrace towards them. They both had a healthy, golden glow about them that instantly made Lesley feel pale and washed out by comparison.

Even though she'd been expecting him, it still gave Lesley a jolt to come face to face with the legendary Sir Peter Bradshaw. Lean and rangy as a greyhound, he looked older in real life, but no less handsome for it. His thick silver hair was streaked with chestnut, and years of hard work and hell-raising had etched deep lines on either side of his mouth and around his soft blue eyes. When Al introduced them, he shook her hand and gave Lesley a smile that softened his whole face, and though she had never particularly fancied him, she found herself quite bowled over as he kissed her on both cheeks.

Stella was the strawberry blonde that Lesley had found in online images, and she was just as stunning in real life – long-limbed, and as tall as Peter, she was what magazine writers would call 'striking' rather than pretty, with high cheekbones and slanting green eyes that had a feline quality to them.

Peter ordered sparkling water and a bottle of champagne, and there was a lull as they all turned their attention to the menu. Lesley was disappointed when Stella and Peter both decided to have crab salad after a long consultation. She'd never been one of those 'I'll just have a salad' women, and she really wanted the lobster linguine. But she also didn't want to be the only one at the table mindlessly scoffing carbs like some sort of throwback who didn't know any better. So she was relieved when Al ordered fish and chips.

'Well, congratulations, you two,' Al said when the waiter had poured the champagne.

'Gosh, is that the ring?' Lesley nodded to the whopping diamond on Stella's finger as they all clinked glasses. 'Can I see?'

'Of course.' Stella held out her hand with a shy smile. 'It's lovely, isn't it?'

'Wow, it's beautiful,' Lesley said, taking her hand and making the appropriate gushing noises. It must have been worth a fortune. She didn't know anything about diamonds, but you didn't have to be an expert to see that it was bloody enormous. If Stella *was* a gold-digger, she'd hit pay dirt. 'So when's the big day? Have you set a date?'

'Not yet,' Stella said, 'but we're thinking of some time in September.'

'After we get back from France,' Peter added. 'Are you coming to Nice, Lesley?'

'Yes, she is,' Al said, smiling lovingly at her in a way that felt unnervingly real. Blimey, he was good at this pretending lark. She'd have to up her game.

'Well, it'll be great to have you there,' Peter said. 'I haven't been to the place since last year,' he told Al. 'I'd have gone in April if it hadn't been for that awful little shit going off the rails in the middle of everything and delaying filming.'

'Who?' Lesley asked, perking up. She loved gossip.

'Ronan,' Peter replied, pursing his lips.

'Ronan O'Hara?' Lesley gasped. Ronan O'Hara was the eponymous magical child of the Inheritor film franchise, and Peter played his dead father, who still watched over him, imparting wisdom and guidance from beyond the grave.

'Who else? They should have fired him and re-cast, if you ask me. But unfortunately the whole Inheritor universe revolves around the little oik, so we had to twiddle our thumbs until he came out of rehab.'

'*Rehab*? But isn't he, like, eight?'

'He was,' Peter said sourly. 'Once upon a time. But he grew up – as they all do, in theory. God preserve us from child stars.'

'Oh, he's not so bad,' Stella said, bumping his shoulder. 'He's just going through an awkward phase. And he idolises you.'

'I can't believe you're sticking up for him after he cornered you in his trailer that time.'

'He's a hormonal teenager,' Stella said. 'He didn't mean any harm. Just trying his luck.'

Lesley couldn't help thinking Stella looked sort of pleased, as if having a horny teen trying to feel her up was something to be proud of. Maybe she was one of those women who found catcalling and wolf-whistling flattering. Lesley thought women like that had gone out with the flood.

'And he blatantly stares down your top whenever you're doing his make-up,' Peter said peevishly.

'So do you.'

Peter grinned. 'Well … I'm allowed. We're engaged.'

'I can't believe he's a teenager,' Lesley said. 'I still think of him as a little kid.'

'Hideous child,' Peter shuddered. 'Please don't tell me you're a fan.'

'God, no!' Lesley said. 'He's way too boyish. Anyway, I'm not into the Inheritor movies at all. I can't stand all that magical Chosen One bollocks.' She suddenly remembered who she was talking to. 'God, sorry!' she gasped, clapping a hand to her mouth. 'I mean, I'm sure they're brilliant. It's just not my sort of thing. I don't even like Harry Potter!'

'You should tell him how you feel about the theatre,' Al said to Lesley with a mischievous grin. 'Since you're on a roll.'

'Don't worry,' Peter said, looking delighted. 'It's all a dreadful load of old cobblers, if you ask me. But I'm just an old whore at heart, so there I am.'

Nevertheless, Lesley was grateful for the waiter creating a diversion when he returned with their food.

'So you're a make-up artist?' she said to Stella as they all began eating.

'Yes. That's how I met Peter.'

'And you've been living in LA? Where are you from originally?' Stella's accent was hard to place — a strange mishmash of English and Irish with a slight mid-Atlantic twang thrown in.

'Oh, all over. I'm a bit of a nomad.'

'But you're Irish?'

'Yes, but I haven't lived here in a very long time.'

'Whereabouts are you from?' Lesley persisted.

'The west,' Stella said. 'A real Nowheresville. Honestly, it's too dull to speak of.' She took a sip of champagne. 'You know that song "Everyday is Like Sunday"?'

Lesley nodded.

'Well, that dreary seaside town is exactly where I'm from. When I was a teenager I used to think Morrissey was singing about the place I grew up in.'

Lesley exchanged a knowing glance with Al. Stella was being deliberately evasive. 'Do you still have family there?' she asked.

'Stella doesn't have any family,' Peter answered for her. 'So, what do you do, Lesley?'

'I'm a ... meditation teacher!'

'Oh, that's great,' Stella said, looking at her with interest as Al shot her a 'what the fuck' look. She didn't really have an answer. It had just come out. Maybe because she'd been concentrating so hard on not saying she was a private detective. Or maybe because she'd been working all week on a website for a meditation teacher, so it was the first thing that came into her head. Oh well — what the hell? It was as good a thing to be as any.

'Well, it's not as interesting as being an actor,' she said, 'or a baker, like Al's dad.'

'Have you met my brother?' Peter asked her. 'King of the gypsy creams.'

'No, you're the first,' Al said to him.

'Very wise,' Peter said with a twinkle in his eye. 'Best to introduce her to us in small doses – you don't want to scare the poor girl off.'

'I don't scare easily,' Lesley said. 'Anyway, even if I did, Al's worth it.' She took Al's hand and gave it a squeeze.

'Yes, Al is the best of us,' Peter said warmly.

Lesley thought it was touching Peter thought so highly of Al, even if it was a bit disloyal to his own children.

Peter tilted his head to the side, regarding Lesley closely. 'You know, you remind me a little of a girl Al used to go out with … oh, years ago now. Do you know who I mean, Al?'

'No.'

'Anyway,' Peter said to Al, 'I'm glad you've ditched … what was that awful woman's name?'

Al sighed. 'Cassie. And she ditched me.'

'Ah well, her loss. And our gain,' he said gallantly as he poured the last of the champagne into Lesley's glass. She realised she'd drunk practically the entire bottle single-handed. Al had only had a thimbleful as he was driving, Peter was sticking to water, and Stella sipped hers so slowly that she still hadn't finished her first glass.

'I've been trying to get Peter to start meditation,' Stella said to Lesley. 'You must send me your details.'

'Yeah,' Lesley nodded as she wound linguine onto her fork. Then she had an idea. 'Why don't you add me on Snapchat and I'll message you?'

'I don't have Snapchat,' Stella said with an apologetic smile.

'Friend me on Facebook, then?'

'I'm not on Facebook either.'

'Really?'

'Sorry. I don't like social media.'

'Oh.' That was a bit weird. 'Okay, well, give me your phone number and I'll send you on my info.'

'THAT WENT WELL,' Lesley said as they drove back to her house.

'Apart from you deciding to be a meditation teacher. Are you pathologically incapable of telling the truth about what you do?'

Lesley shrugged. 'It was just a spur of the moment thing. Anyway, it went down well, don't you think? Stella was very interested. Maybe it could be a bonding thing for us.'

'What if she decides to pursue it?'

'It'll be fine. I can breathe in and out with the best of them.'

'And you said you'd send her your details.'

'No problem.' Lesley had already decided she could use the site she was building for Madeleine. She could just tweak some of the content, replace Madeleine's photo and contact details with her own, and send Stella a link to the back end.

'Anyway, what did you think?' Al asked.

'Of Stella? She's pretty reserved, isn't she? I wouldn't say it's easy to get to know her.'

'That's why I'm paying you the big bucks,' Al said with a smile.

'She really clammed up when I asked her about her background, didn't she?'

'Yeah, she definitely didn't want to talk about it.'

'She's very solicitous of Peter,' Lesley said, thinking of how Stella had fussed over him, and he had consulted her about what he should eat. 'But that could all be an act. I mean, it's not as if she's going to show her hand at this stage.'

'And it's in her interests to keep him fit and well for now. She'd want to make sure he survives long enough to endow her with all his worldly goods.'

'She was different to what I was expecting, though,' Lesley said thoughtfully. 'More ... low-key.'

Al nodded. 'Me too. I suppose I thought she'd be more of a show pony,' he mused. 'You know, all platinum blonde hair, and acres of silicon cleavage.'

'So you were expecting your cliché cartoon gold-digging bimbo?'

'Exactly,' he said with a grin. 'Weren't you?'

'I was reserving judgement,' she said primly. If she was honest, she had expected a pneumatic airhead in high heels and a low neckline. The fact was, Stella could hardly have been more different from the blowsy sex bomb of her imagination. But she wasn't going to tell Al that. 'She *is* blonde, though. So you got that right. And she does have fake boobs.'

'Really?' Al's eyebrows shot up. 'You could tell?'

'I'm pretty sure.'

'Anyway, we're out of the closet now,' Al said. 'We should start going out together in public and cross-pollinating our Facebook pages. How do you feel about coming on a mini-break with me?'

10

The following Saturday morning, Stella sat in the plush lounge of the Hotel Meyrick on Eyre Square, watching the door anxiously as she waited for Dan to join her. She'd been up early to catch the first train to Galway and had spent a long time getting ready, choosing her outfit with care, and fussing over her make-up and hair. She wanted to look good for Dan – grown-up and in control. It was important to show him she'd got her act together. She didn't want him to worry about her. She was wearing a red polka-dot tea dress with low-heeled nude pumps, and her hair was tied up in an elegant chignon. The overall effect was sophisticated, demure and a little retro, perfect for afternoon tea in an upmarket hotel.

She fidgeted nervously, smoothing the skirts of her dress and sipping her coffee too quickly, jittery and excited about seeing him again after so long. Then he was there, being waved over to her table by a waiter. He was a little stockier than when she'd last seen him, his face doughier than she remembered. His thick, straw-coloured hair was still long, pulled back into a stubby ponytail. She could hardly believe he was really here, and tears pricked her eyes as he approached, his lovely warm face breaking into a broad grin. Stella stood and he pulled her into a hug.

'It's so good to see you,' she said, squeezing him tight.

'You too. You look amazing!' he said, as they sat side by side on the banquette.

They ordered coffee, and the waiter brought a cafetière on a silver tray, with fine china cups. Stella poured, and smiled fondly as Dan spooned two cubes of sugar into his.

'Why don't you just have done with it and order cake?' she asked as he reached for another.

Dan grinned and stirred his coffee vigorously. 'I'm watching my figure.'

'And calories consumed as liquid don't count?'

'Exactly. You taught me that.'

She laughed. 'So I did.'

He took a sip of coffee and sank back against the sofa cushion, digging the heels of his hands into his eyes.

'Tired?'

'Yeah,' he yawned. 'It's been kind of a long week.'

'Sorry for making you get up early on a Saturday.'

'That's okay.' He looked around the plush lounge. 'I've had worse gigs.'

'Where are you supposed to be today anyway?'

'I told Annie I had a job in Galway.'

'Devious.'

'Yeah.' Dan's smile faded and he looked uncomfortable.

'Sorry.' She knew he hated lying to his wife. She felt bad that he was doing it for her.

'Don't worry about it. I'm building you a new set of wardrobes, just so you know.'

'Yes, best to get our stories straight.' She laughed. 'In case this ever goes to trial.'

'What about you?' he asked. 'Where are you supposed to be today?'

'Peter knows where I am. I told him about you.' She knew it wasn't fair, when he couldn't tell Annie about her. 'We're getting married. I had to tell him everything. But he's the only one who knows.'

'It's okay. I get it.'

'So, what's up with you?' she asked, eager to shift the focus from herself. 'Tell me everything.'

'Actually, I've got news,' he said, his mouth widening in a grin. 'Big news.'

'Oh?'

'I was waiting until today, so I could tell you in person. Annie's pregnant.'

'Oh, my God!' Stella gasped. 'That's fantastic.' Her eyes welled up and she reached for his hand, too overcome with emotion to speak for a moment. Dan looked so happy he might burst. 'Congratulations!'

'Thanks.'

'I'm so happy for you, Dan.' She was, but it was tinged with sadness, and she resented that even the most joyful event was shot through with some melancholy.

His fingers curled around hers. 'You're going to be an aunt,' he said, and her smile faltered. Because she wasn't going to be an aunt, was she? Not really. Not in any way that counted. She would never see Dan's baby, never get to hold her tiny niece or nephew. She wouldn't take them to the park, or sing at their birthday parties, or buy them extravagant, impractical presents. She'd be a stranger to them. If they passed her in the street, they wouldn't know who she was.

She blinked hard, shaking off the unwelcome surge of self-pity. 'How far along is she?' she asked.

'Only ten weeks.'

He picked up his jacket from the seat beside him and pulled his phone from the pocket. After thumbing through the screen for a few moments, he held it out to Stella.

It was a picture of Annie, his beautiful wife. She was tall and athletic, with olive skin and long, poker-straight dark hair. Her wide smile was dazzling, her whole face lit up. She was dressed in grey jogging bottoms and a white tank top, one hand holding the camera out at arm's length, while the other rested significantly on her stomach. Stella had to look hard to make out the barely discernible bump.

'She looks so happy.' It felt odd to talk about his wife in such a familiar way, as if she knew her. But Stella felt strangely close to her, even though they'd never met.

'She's over the moon,' Dan said, glancing lovingly at the screen as she handed him back the phone. 'We both are.'

He was practically glowing, and Stella felt a surge of love for the woman who had made her brother so happy, together with a pang of longing to share in their joy and excitement. She yearned to wish Annie well, to be part of their family. But Annie didn't even know she existed.

'I wish you'd meet her, Stella,' he said, closing the phone and putting it away. 'You'd like her.'

'I know I would. But would she like me?'

Dan frowned. 'Yes, she would,' he said, defensive. 'She's a good person.'

'Sorry.' She rubbed his shoulder. 'I know she is.' She sank back against the sofa. 'I can't believe you're going to be a dad.'

'Me neither.' He gave a nervous laugh. 'I just hope I'm better at it than our old man.'

'Of course you will be.' She rested her head on his shoulder.

'Wouldn't be hard, I suppose.'

'Have you seen Mam and Dad lately?' she asked, her voice hardening.

'I saw them at Christmas. We exchanged crappy jumpers and socks.'

'How are they?'

'Still gobshites.'

'Are they excited about being grandparents?'

'We haven't told anyone yet – just you. God, I just wish you could—'

'I know.' She lifted her head. 'Me too. I'd love for you to be at my wedding. I'd love to meet your baby and get to know Annie.'

He clasped her hand, intertwining his fingers with hers. 'If it's just about Mam and Dad … you know that if it's a choice between you and them, I'd pick you, right? Every time.'

She blinked away tears. 'I know.' She nodded. 'But it's not just them. It's what happened with Steve, and—'

'That fucker!' Dan snarled, his hand tightening almost painfully on hers.

'Anyway,' she said, 'your baby should know its grandparents, however crap they are. I wouldn't want to be responsible for depriving your child of its family.'

'What about you? You're family too. I fucking hate that you're not going to be part of my kid's life.'

'It's just better this way. For everyone.' It was how she had chosen to live, cutting herself off completely from her past and everyone in it. Twice now she had shed her old self like a snake shedding its skin. It was easy moving on and starting over; finding new friends and new jobs, inventing new identities. She had developed quite a talent for it. There was nothing she missed, nothing pulling her back – except Dan. He was the only link to her past that she couldn't bear to break. She loved him too much, and she knew no one could ever love her more or know her as completely as he did, even if she told them everything. Because she was more than the sum of her secrets. Dan knew her from the start and he loved her as he always had. That was the one constant in her life, and she couldn't let it go.

The cafetière was empty, and the lounge had started to fill up as they talked. Stella looked at her watch. It was just after one. She felt slightly panicked at how fast the time had gone.

'Let's get afternoon tea,' she said to Dan, picking up the laminated card from the table.

She called a waiter over and ordered the most lavish option on the menu. He returned with a tall, tiered cake stand laden with dainty crustless sandwiches, light, fluffy scones and sweet, sticky pastries, along with a glass of Prosecco each.

'Well, here's to you.' Dan clinked his glass against Stella's. 'Engaged!' He made big scary eyes at her. 'You've really done it this time.'

'I know,' she said, mirroring his expression. 'Never thought you'd see the day, did you?'

'I don't know,' he said softly. 'You were always full of surprises.'

'True.' She watched him carefully, but she couldn't tell what he was thinking, how he felt about this. They'd been apart for too long. She used to know him as well as she knew herself.

'Bloody hell, though – Sir Peter Bradshaw! You won't be bringing *him* home to Bally-go-Backwards.'

She laughed. 'I wouldn't be bringing him home even if he was Joe Bloggs.'

'No. But isn't he a bit ...'

'Rich for my blood?'

'Too old for you, I was going to say.'

'I don't care about that. It has its advantages.'

'Such as?'

'Well, Peter doesn't live his life online, for one thing. He doesn't do social media much. So that's good.'

'Still, you'll be a stepmum to Rafe and Scott Bradshaw,' Dan said with a crooked smile. 'How fucked up is that?'

'It's not fucked up,' she said, frowning. 'I'm not going to be breastfeeding them or anything.'

'Aaargh!' Dan grimaced. 'Thanks a million for that image.'

'I mean, it's true that whenever I thought about having kids, I imagined them being a bit younger ...'

'Younger than you at least.'

Stella laughed. 'Yeah. Even Scott's a couple of years older than me, and he's the baby.'

'What about the fame thing? It doesn't worry you?'

'I could do without it. But we're keeping the wedding small and low-key, and it's not as if Peter's going to sell it to a magazine or anything. Anyway, even if photos did get out, what are the chances of anyone from back then recognising me now?'

'You've changed a bit all right,' he said with a grin. 'You look fantastic.'

'Thanks.' She smiled. 'I do my best.'

'So, what's Peter Bradshaw like, then?'

'He's lovely. He's been very good to me.'

'Christ, Stella!' Dan huffed, running a hand through

his hair. 'You're not a fucking rescue puppy! You don't need someone to be "good to you".'

'I didn't mean it like that. It's just … we take care of each other. It's nice.'

'Nice!' Dan rolled his eyes. 'It sounds very exciting!'

'Maybe I've had enough excitement in my life,' Stella said quietly.

'Yeah.' Dan's expression softened. 'I guess you have. I just don't think you should sell yourself short.'

'I'm not "selling myself" at all.'

'Hey, that's not what I meant.' He gave an exasperated sigh. 'I just think you're settling for so much less than you deserve.'

'This is already way more than I ever thought I'd have, Dan.'

'I know,' he said, throwing her a look that was at once apologetic and frustrated. She knew he only wanted the best for her.

'Peter's just what I need,' she said, anxious to convince him. 'I never thought I'd find a man I could be with like that – a man I could marry. I'm tired of being alone all the time. With Peter I can have a real family, someone to come home to at the end of the day.'

'And you're in love?'

She picked up the pot and poured them both more tea, not looking at him as she spoke. 'I think we can be really happy together.'

'That's not what I asked.'

Stella turned to face him. 'No, I'm not in love. But I like him a lot, and we get on great. I think we're good together.'

Dan shot her a pitying look. 'That'd all be great if you were looking for someone to keep you company in your twilight years. But you're twenty-six. It's not as if this is your last shot.'

'But maybe it is. Who can say?' She shrugged. 'Why does everyone think that's such a great basis for marriage anyway? I mean, look at all the arranged marriages that work out really well – and all the people who start out madly in love and wind up hating each other's guts after a few years.'

Dan sighed. 'I guess you're right.'

'Peter and I are already ahead of the game. We don't have any unrealistic expectations to live up to. And we won't have the disappointment of falling out of love because we've never been in love in the first place.'

'So he's not in love with you either?'

Stella gave a wry smile. 'If he's in love with anyone, I think it's his ex-wife.'

Dan's eyes widened in shock. 'Bloody hell! And you still want to marry him knowing that?'

'It just proves my point. So what if he's in love with her? It didn't make any difference, did it? He still couldn't make his marriage work. They still ended up getting divorced.'

'When did you get so mature?' he said, his expression softening.

'School of hard knocks, baby. I wouldn't recommend it.'

'And you're happy?'

She considered before answering. It wasn't a casual question. He really wanted to know.

'Yes, I am. Peter's a good man. I think we're going to have a great life together.'

'Well, that's all that matters,' Dan said.

11

'What's this?' Al asked, nodding to the whiteboard in the corner of Lesley's study. At the top she'd taped a photo of Stella and Peter that she'd printed off the internet, and she'd written Stella's name in large capitals with a big question mark beside it. Underneath there was a list of the information she had gathered so far –

West of Ireland (seaside town?)

No social media??

It was a very short list.

'It's my incident … area,' Lesley said. 'There's not much to it so far.'

'Well, it's early days.'

'Yeah. I'm going to keep digging on the internet, but I haven't found anything so far. It's kind of weird someone her age not having any social media footprint at all.'

They were interrupted by Al's phone ringing. He took it from his pocket and frowned down at the screen.

'It's Peter,' he said as he tapped in a reply, 'asking if I'm at your house for some reason.'

Another message pinged and he read. Then he looked up at her, eyes wide with panic. 'They're on their way over, him and Stella.'

'They're coming *here*? Why? How do they even know where I live?'

'Apparently you're having one of your drop-in meditation workshops tonight,' Al said with a weary look. 'You sent Stella the details?'

'Ah feck!' Why hadn't she checked Madeleine's content more thoroughly before sending it to Stella? She'd switched her photo and contact details, but she hadn't thought to check the class details at all. She turned to the laptop on her desk and pulled up the website. Sure enough, there it was on the home page, big and bold – a drop-in meditation session every Thursday evening at seven, free to first-timers. Bloody Madeleine and her hippy-dippy, all-welcome ways!

'Tell him ... tell him it's full up—'

But even as she spoke, there was a ring at the door. 'Right,' she said, snapping her fingers. 'Sit on the floor.' She threw her eyes around the room. 'Oh Christ, the board!' she exclaimed, her eyes landing on her 'incident nook'.

'What?' Al looked up at her. He had already obediently settled himself cross-legged on the floor.

'The board, the board!' She waved at it frantically. 'Get rid of it.'

Al jumped up to grab the board as she left the room.

'Hello!' she said as she threw open the door to find Stella and Peter standing in her porch. 'Lovely to see you again. But I'm afraid I'm a bit busy at the moment.' She lowered her voice and threw her eyes towards the living room.

'Yes, that's why we're here,' Stella said. 'For the meditation.'

'Oh! But ... you're not enrolled,' Lesley said, thinking quickly.

Stella frowned. 'It says on your website that it's a drop-in class.'

'Oh, yes. Well ... come in and we'll discuss it,' Lesley said, waving them both inside. She needed time to think, but it felt rude to leave them standing on the doorstep any longer. She thought quickly as they stepped past her into the hall.

'The thing is,' she said, turning to them as she closed the door, 'I'm afraid this evening's workshop is full.' She was so pleased with herself for coming up with this excuse on the fly that she couldn't help smiling. She hoped she didn't look too happy about turning them away.

Stella glanced through the door into the living room, where Al was sitting cross-legged in the middle of the floor. He smiled and gave her a little wave.

'It's just Al,' Stella said to Lesley.

'Yes, that's right. I like to give all my students one-to-one attention, so I only take one at a time. So like I said, the class is full. Sorry.'

'Oh.' Stella's face fell. 'I see.' She looked so disappointed that Lesley felt like a prize heel.

'You really ought to put that on your website,' Peter said.

'You couldn't even squeeze in a couple more?' Stella looked at her hopefully. 'Just this once?'

'I'd love to. But it's, um ... it's a health and safety issue!'

'Oh?'

'Yes! I'm not insured. What if you had an accident?'

Peter frowned. 'What sort of accident? Meditation isn't exactly a high-risk activity.'

'No, but ... you could trip and fall, for instance.'

'Really? I don't see how.'

'Well ... you might need to go to the loo. It's down two steps. You could have a fall then.'

'What if Al slips on his way to the loo? If you have public liability insurance—'

'Okay, it's not really about health and safety,' Lesley said. 'The truth is, I prefer to stick to just one student at a time. Any more ... um, drains too much energy from the room,' she said, trying to sound mystical.

'Oh. Okay.' Stella nodded. 'I understand. Some other time, maybe? Only I was hoping it was something Peter and I could do together.'

Oh, screw it, Lesley thought. It would give her an in with Stella, and it wasn't as if she had no experience to draw on. She'd done that meditation course. It was mostly just telling people to breathe in and out. How hard could it be? She'd just wing it as best she could. Besides, thinking on your feet and toughing out tricky situations was all in a day's work for a PI. At least she hadn't pretended to be a yoga teacher. She didn't fancy her chances of leading everyone in a downward dog.

'All right, then. You can stay,' Lesley told them. Her eyes flicked to the living room, and Al shot her a panicked look.

'Oh, great!' Stella beamed. 'Thank you.'

'Okay,' she said, clapping her hands. 'Follow me, and we'll get started.'

Al gave Lesley a 'what the fuck' glare as she led Stella and Peter into the living room. She shrugged helplessly in reply. She was glad to see the incident board was nowhere in sight.

'Okay, find a space,' she said, spreading her arms in a Christ-like gesture to encompass the room.

She stood by the mantelpiece as Peter and Stella joined
Al on the floor and looked up at her expectantly.

'Right,' she said, stalling for time, 'since we have some
newcomers tonight, why don't we start by going around the
room and introducing ourselves?'

Al gave a hoot of laughter that he quickly turned into a
cough, while Stella and Peter looked at each other in bewil-
derment.

'We all know each other,' Stella said.

'Well, yes, but … I don't really know you, Stella. Tell us
a little bit about yourself and what brought you here today
– your meditation journey, if you like,' she said, hitting her
stride.

'Um, okay.' Stella gave Peter a bemused smile. 'Well,
I've been living in LA for the past few years. I'm engaged
to this lovely man here,' she said, nodding to Peter, 'and
we've just moved back to Ireland. I'm supporting him in
his journey back to health and working on building a
healthy, happy life together. I thought meditation would be
a good place to start.'

Peter looked touched, and reached across to squeeze
Stella's hand.

'And you have some previous meditation experience?'
Lesley prompted.

'Oh, yes. I do a daily practice, and I've done a lot of
training over the years in various disciplines. Last year I
went on a Vipassana course in Nepal. Have you ever done
one, Lesley?'

'No, I … haven't got around to it yet. It's on my bucket
list.' Just her luck Stella would turn out to be a meditation
buff.

'It's pretty intense – ten hours of meditation a day for
ten days, no communication, no contact with the outside
world.'

'Oh.' Lesley gulped. 'Not even ... a mobile phone?'

'No. My teacher used to joke that we could have email, but no attachments.'

That was a joke? 'Ha ha. Very funny. Well, you'll find my style a little more ... easy-going.'

'What tradition do you follow?'

'Oh, it's quite eclectic, really – a sort of rag-bag I've picked up over the years. I originally trained with the Buddhist Monks of Rathmines. Have you heard of them?'

'No.'

'Well, I guess they're big fish in a small pond. I'd say they'd be the top dogs on the Dublin enlightenment scene.'

Al's lips were twitching, and Stella looked bemused.

'Right.' Lesley clapped her hands. 'That's enough chit-chat.' Improv was fun up to a point, but she was starting to break into a sweat. 'Let's get on with the show. Everyone close your eyes.'

They all obediently did so, and Lesley looked around quickly for some suitable accoutrements. She had a feeling there should be candles and incense, possibly even a gong. She didn't have anything very spiritual-looking, but there was a fat Jo Malone candle on the mantelpiece; that would have to do. She lit it and placed it on the floor at her feet.

'Focus on your breathing,' she said, softening her voice. 'In through the mouth and out through the nose.' She took a few deep breaths to demonstrate while she tried to recall everything she'd ever heard in meditation or yoga classes. 'Think about the space between your eyebrows – your third eye – as you breathe in. Feel the warmth of your breath on your face – that bit under your nose and above your lip ... where your moustache would be, if you had one. If a thought comes into your head, just let it go and bring your focus back to your breath. Empty your mind of all thoughts.'

She checked her watch. Christ, there wasn't even five minutes gone yet and she was already running out of steam. How was she going to keep this up for an hour? 'Notice the sounds and smells in the room ...' Gah, why had she mentioned sounds and smells? She hoped no one farted and thought she was drawing attention to it. 'Listen to the breathing of the other people around you ... focus on the lovely smell of the scented candle ... lime, basil and mandarin by Jo Malone ... just be aware of it, and let it go.

'Imagine you're on a beach,' she ploughed on. 'Feel the softness of the sand under you, the warmth of the sun on your skin. Listen to the sound of the waves on the shore, going in and out ... in and out ... in with the good, out with the bad. Out with the old, in with the new,' she said, pleased with this sudden flash of inspiration. 'Just be in the now ... experience this moment ... observe all the sounds you can hear going on around you ... on the beach, I mean, not in real life ... the waves swooshing in and out ... seagulls squawking overhead. Maybe there's a yappy dog or a child howling in the distance ... just notice them and then let them go. Try to empty your mind—'

Peter opened one eye and squinted at her. 'If you'd stop wittering on for a couple of seconds, it might help,' he said.

'Oh, yes. Good point. Okay ... be alone with your thoughts ... lack of thoughts ... I'll shut up now. Just focus on your breath ... be with what is ... in the now ...'

She trailed off, relieved that she could stop talking. But she was still in a sweat at the thought of having to stand here watching them breathe for another forty minutes. Maybe she could get them to open their eyes and stare at the candle flame for a while, just to mix things up a bit. She decided she might as well sit down, and sank to the floor. She wished she could get a book, but she didn't want to be caught on the hop if Stella should happen to peek. It would look very unprofessional. Al opened his eyes briefly and grinned at her. She smiled back and they exchanged a friendly eye-roll over her predicament.

After half an hour, Peter was starting to shift and fidget. Stella was still and serene, and looked perfectly relaxed sitting in a full-on lotus, her back ramrod straight. When Peter opened his eyes and started making faces at Lesley – comical grimaces of pain, silent calls for help, miming hanging himself – she decided enough was enough. She couldn't hold out any longer, and if Peter kept up his antics, she was going to either burst out laughing or go over and give him a clip around the ear, neither of which would be in keeping with her dignity as a meditation guru.

She got to her feet and grabbed a poker from the set of fire irons in the grate. Using it as a makeshift gong, she clattered it against the brass stand. 'And you're back in the room,' she announced, snapping her fingers for good measure.

Al sputtered a laugh, and Peter and Stella looked like they were only just holding it in.

'Well, that was … interesting,' Stella said, slowly unknotting her legs and stretching her limbs. 'It was certainly different.'

'Yes, well … that's the Rathmines lot for you. They're very cutting edge.'

'The time flew.' Stella glanced at her watch. 'I can't believe it's been—Oh!'

'Yes, as it's the last class tonight before we break for the summer, I decided to just do the half hour. I thought we could have tea and cake for the rest of the time, to celebrate the end of term.'

. . .

Lesley was relieved to be back on familiar territory as they all sat around the kitchen table. She and Al had big mugs of coffee and were tucking into doughnuts Al had brought, while Peter and Stella sipped green tea.

'Are you sure you won't have one, Stella?' Lesley asked, holding out the plate of doughnuts. 'They're really good.'

'No, thanks. We don't eat cake. Poor Peter can't, so I don't either. It makes it easier for him if it's just not around.'

'That's very nice of you.' Lesley was impressed. She didn't know if she'd have it in her to be so self-sacrificing. 'You obviously take great care of him.'

'She does.' Peter put an arm around Stella and smiled at her fondly. 'I'm very lucky to have her.'

Stella smiled back at him, blushing.

'So you're finished classes for now?' she asked Lesley.

'Yes. Probably for good, actually.'

'Oh?'

'Yeah. I don't think teaching meditation is really my forte.'

Peter hooted. 'That's putting it mildly.'

'Peter!' Stella gave him an admonishing frown.

'It's fine,' Lesley said. 'He's absolutely right. It was just something I was trying out as a side hustle, really.'

'What's your main job?' Peter asked.

'IT,' she said. 'Web design, SEO, that sort of thing.'

'Oh.' Stella looked relieved. 'Well, I must admit I've never heard squawking seagulls or howling children mentioned before during a meditation.'

'Or an advert for the Jo Malone scented candle range,' Al said.

'I think my favourite bit was when you brought the fire irons into play and said "you're back in the room" like some hokey stage hypnotist,' Peter said.

'Okay, so I need to work on my patter.'

They all laughed.

'Best leave meditation teaching to the top Buddhists of Rathmines,' Peter said.

12

On Friday afternoon, Lesley was packing for a weekend away with Al.

'So where's he taking you?' Romy asked.

'I don't know. Somewhere down the country. It's a surprise.' Lesley held the phone to her ear as she tossed underwear into the little suitcase open on her bed.

'Oh, very romantic!'

'It's a nuisance is what it is. You know I don't like surprises.'

'Don't worry, I haven't forgotten.'

Romy was under strict instructions to give Lesley plenty of notice if anyone was ever planning a surprise party for her.

'I mean, how am I supposed to know what to pack?' She held up a floaty silk top, wondering if they would be going somewhere dressy enough for her to wear it.

'Just bring a bit of everything.'

'What about togs? Do you think I should bring them?'

'Might as well, just in case. There might be a pool.'

'Or a spa,' Lesley said despondently.

Romy laughed. 'There probably won't be.' She knew Lesley hated spas.

'Anyway,' Lesley continued as she went to the drawers, 'Al will be here soon. He's picking me up and we're going in his car. No one else knows about him yet, so if anything happens to me, it'll be up to you to finger him to the police.'

'Okay.'

'And you can tell them I was last seen wearing black jeans, black suede boots and that purple wrap top, you know the one? Hang on, I'll take a selfie and send it to you.'

'He's probably not planning to do away with you, you know.'

'I know, but at least if he does, they'll have something to go on. I'd hate to leave behind a messy case with no leads.'

'So your family don't know about your new fake boyfriend?'

'Not yet, but it's only a matter of time.' Lesley still hadn't changed her Facebook status, but she knew she couldn't put it off much longer. 'Then they'll all be wetting their knickers with excitement and wanting to have him round for Sunday dinner.' She sighed. 'You know what they're like.' Her mother would have her married off to Al already, and Katrina would be itching to get a look at him so she could start picking faults.

'Right.' She squashed one last pair of shoes into the case and zipped it closed. 'I'll text you later to let you know where I am. And I'll get a photo of his car reg and send it to you.'

'Wow, the evidence is mounting against him already and you haven't even left the house.' Romy laughed. 'Well, have a great time. I hope it's somewhere lovely and spa-free.'

'Sorry I'm a bit late,' Al said when he picked her up just after two. 'I had a site visit this morning that went on longer than expected.'

'No problem,' Lesley said as he took her case from her and led the way to his car. He put her case in the boot, then went around to the passenger side and held the door open for her.

'So, where are we off to?' she asked as she fastened her seatbelt.

'Doonbeg, in Clare. We're going to stay with my aunt Jane.'

'Oh.' Lesley tried not to look too put out, but she'd been secretly hoping for a five-star boutique hotel (sans spa) or an exclusive country house that specialised in amazing yet hearty food. Then it dawned on her that he was talking about Jane Howard, Peter's ex-wife. The Howard family were Irish theatrical royalty, and Lesley had fond memories of Jane playing the starring role in a TV series of Jane Austen's *Emma* when she was a teen. But she'd given up acting and was now a successful writer of historical novels.

'She wants to discuss Peter's engagement. She's quite worried about the whole thing, and since neither of my cousins are in the country at the moment, I said I'd go see her.'

'Well, you might have told me,' Lesley huffed. She would have made more of an effort if she'd known they were going to meet his famous aunt.

'Why? You'll like Jane,' Al said, with what Lesley supposed was meant to be a reassuring smile.

'But I would have dressed up a bit more if I'd known we were going to stay with Jane Howard.'

'Don't worry about that. Aunt Jane doesn't set the bar very high. In fact, she's pretty scruffy when she's knocking around at home.'

'Gee, thanks a lot!'

'I didn't mean it like that. You look great.'

'So is she your aunt by marriage?'

'No, she's my mum's sister. And Dad and Peter are brothers.'

'So the two sisters married two brothers?' No wonder Al's family seemed so close-knit. 'Does she live on her own?'

'Yes, since she split up with Peter. I thought she might move after the divorce, but she's very attached to the place. It's her old family home – quite grand, or at least it used to be. But it's fallen to rack and ruin a bit in the last few years. I've made plans for renovating it, but she can't bear the upheaval, and I've never managed to persuade her to move out for long enough to get it done. So it's a bit of a wreck, really.'

Oh well, Lesley thought, at least there wouldn't be a spa.

AL'S CAR was a point in his favour, Lesley decided, as they bowled along the motorway. She liked four-wheel drives, but unfortunately most people driving them around Dublin had to be written off as wankers, thus cancelling out all their cachet. But as an architect, she figured Al had a legitimate excuse for having the Land Rover, evidenced by the hard hat sitting on the back seat alongside a neatly folded wax jacket and a scatter of rolled-up plans. There was even a pair of mud-splattered wellies, she noted with satisfaction.

She appreciated the comfort of the plush leather seats and the smooth suspension on the long drive to Clare, especially once they hit the bumpy country roads, and she had to admit Al was an excellent road-trip companion. He had an impressive stash of chocolate bars in the glove box, and his playlist met with her approval, apart from a brief foray into the Bay City Rollers – 'They were mum's favourite,' he claimed in his defence, so she made allowances as he yodelled along happily to 'Summerlove Sensation' and 'Shang-A-Lang', and she even did some harmonies on 'Bye Bye Baby' as a show of support.

It was just after five when they turned through an open metal gate onto a bumpy track overhung by tall trees, the branches of dense, unkempt fuchsia bushes scraping the sides of the car as they passed. They stopped in front of a large double-fronted house with stone steps leading up to a columned porch. It looked very stately, if somewhat run down, and Lesley imagined rooms draped with tapestries, a huge entrance hall with stuffed birds in a glass case, four-poster beds and toasted crumpets in front of a massive roaring fire. Maybe she'd have the country house experience after all, she thought, as she hopped out of the car.

Al got their bags from the boot, along with a large cool box. He dumped them on the gravel, then leaned into the back seat and took out several large brown grocery bags.

'Can you take these?' he asked, handing them to Lesley.

Then he led her around the steps to a door at the side of the house. He pushed it open and waved Lesley in ahead of him. She stepped into a big, old-fashioned country kitchen with a red-tiled floor. A wooden dresser painted a soft green and crammed with mismatched china stood against one wall, a dark green range beside it, covered in pots and pans. Under the grimy window there was a long table of unvarnished wood, piled high with newspapers, magazines and books. A rocking chair sat in one corner, stuffed with colourful squashy cushions. It had been a pleasantly mild day, but there was a chill in the air that had Lesley automatically rubbing her arms as she looked around. It seemed colder in here than it had been outside – darker too, she thought. But maybe that was down to the film of dirt on the windows. Greasy plates and coffee-stained mugs littered every surface and the sink was piled high with dishes sitting in a basin of murky water.

'It's cold in here, isn't it?' Al said cheerfully, rubbing his hands together.

'Bloody freezing!'

'I wonder where Jane is.'

'Do you think something's happened to her?'

'What do you mean?' Al frowned.

'Well, the state of the place …'

'Oh, she's working on a book,' Al said, as if that explained everything. 'Deadline looming, I believe.'

The noise of a door banging outside drew them both to the window.

'Ah, there she is now,' Al said as Lesley peered through the grime to see a figure emerge from a little shed at the bottom of the garden. She was clad all in black, the evening sun glinting off her tangled mess of wavy blonde hair. As they watched, she shielded her eyes and squinted back at them. Spotting Al, her face lit up with a smile and she gave them a little wave as she picked up her pace, striding purposefully towards the house.

The door opened.

'Al,' Jane beamed, rushing up to him. 'It's lovely to see

you!' She threw her arms around him and stood on tiptoe to kiss his cheek.

Now that she was closer, Lesley recognised the pixyish face, more fleshy and lined than the picture in her head, but still girlishly pretty, her amazing eyes intensely blue and luminous as moonstone.

'This is Lesley,' Al introduced her. 'Lesley, my aunt Jane.'

'Hello,' Lesley held out her hand to shake, but Jane pulled her into a hug.

'It's lovely to meet you.' She turned to Al. 'If I'd known you were bringing someone ...'

'You'd have baked a cake?' Al said.

'Well, no. But I might have tidied up a bit.'

'Good job I didn't tell you, then. I didn't want you to go to any bother. I know you're busy.'

'Sorry the place is such a mess,' Jane said to Lesley, looking around vaguely.

'It's fine,' Lesley said. 'He should have told you.' She gave Al a dig with her elbow. 'It was very inconsiderate.'

'Oh, it's no problem. It's lovely to see you.'

'I know you're on a deadline,' Al said, 'so I thought it would be a good idea to bring reinforcements.'

'But I did want to talk to you about ... that family matter.' Jane gave Al a meaningful look.

'Oh, don't worry about that. Lesley knows the whole story.' Al put an arm around Lesley's shoulders.

'She does?'

'Yes, you can speak freely in front of her.'

'Al tells me everything,' Lesley said, briefly laying her head on Al's shoulder.

'Okay, good. Sorry, Lesley,' Jane said, turning to her. 'This isn't much of a welcome for you. Sit down.' She pulled out a chair at the table. 'How about a drink? I was just about to have one. There's some whiskey in the dresser, Al,' she said, waving at it as she sat down beside Lesley.

Al rinsed a couple of teacups and a tumbler under the tap, then lined them up on the table and splashed generous measures of whiskey into them. 'Bottoms up!' He clinked his cup against Lesley's, then knocked back the drink in one go and shuddered.

Lesley sipped hers gingerly, wincing slightly as it burned her throat.

'There's some shortbread I made yesterday,' Jane said, grabbing a biscuit tin that was sitting on top of the pile of papers on the table and opening it. 'Would you like some?' she held it out to Lesley.

'Thanks.' Lesley took a piece. The sweetness was a nice antidote to the whiskey.

'So, how's the book going?' Al asked his aunt as he sat beside her.

She made a face. 'Not great. I'm almost finished, but I'm having trouble with the ending.'

'It doesn't help, not taking care of yourself, you know. You should take a break now and then – get out, see people, eat food. You need fresh air and vegetables.'

'I don't have time for fresh air and vegetables.'

'Well, Lesley and I will take care of that while we're here. Won't we?' he said to Lesley.

'Er … yeah.'

Jane smiled fondly at Al. 'Hold onto this one, Lesley,' she said, dropping her head onto his shoulder affectionately. 'He's one in a million.'

'I certainly think so,' Lesley said, giving Al what she hoped was a suitably adoring look.

'You two are probably hungry,' Jane said. 'We should have some supper.'

Lesley was ravenous, but said nothing, not wanting to seem too forward.

'Don't worry, I'll take care of it,' Al said. 'We don't want to interrupt your writing.'

'I was just knocking off for the evening anyway when I heard you drive up,' Jane said.

'We've brought loads of food.' Al opened the cool box and started to unload it into the fridge. 'It looks like we've come just in time,' he said, as he filled the shelves. 'What were you planning to eat tonight?'

'I think there's an egg around somewhere,' Jane said. 'I thought I might do something with that.'

'What have you been living on?' Al asked, shutting the door and turning to his aunt, his eyes sweeping around the kitchen.

'My wits – what's left of them.'

'That's what I was afraid of.' He pursed his lips and began unpacking the grocery bags onto the table. There were jars of roasted peppers and plump chick peas, cartons of eggs, loaves of crusty sourdough and brown soda bread, slabs of cheese wrapped in waxy paper, punnets of berries, and bags of colourful vegetables, as well as several bottles of wine. 'And yet you've been baking biscuits. I think that's what's known as fur coat and no knickers.'

'I was starving and shortbread was the only thing I had the ingredients for.'

'Well, you're not eating like that on my watch.' He glanced at the clock on the wall. 'It'd take hours to get this place fit to even start cooking,' he said, indicating the jumble of the kitchen. 'Why don't we go to the pub tonight? We can tackle this lot tomorrow.'

Who's we, Paleface, Lesley thought.

'Gosh, it would be good to get out,' Jane said. 'I'm starting to go stir crazy. But I'm not fit to be seen. The people around here think I'm enough of a daft old bat as it is.'

'You're a writer,' Al said. 'You're allowed to be a bit eccentric. Anyway, I bet they love having a local celebrity. It'll give them something to talk about.'

'My goal in life,' Jane said dryly. 'Anyway, I've nothing to wear – I haven't done any washing in weeks. And my hair's a mess. I'm practically feral.'

'Tosh! You just need a bit of a hosing down and you'll be right as rain. Besides, Lesley likes her grub and she gets cranky if she's not fed. You don't want to be responsible for my girlfriend falling out with me.'

'Well, I suppose when you put it like that,' Jane said, pushing away from the table and standing up. 'I'll have a quick shower and see what I can find.'

'Come on and I'll show you our room,' Al said to Lesley when she had gone. He picked up the bags and led the way up to the ground floor, through a spacious, dusty entrance hall and up a wide staircase to the first floor. He opened a door off the landing and Lesley stepped into a large draughty bedroom, the wooden floorboards mostly covered by a faded threadbare rug.

Al dumped their bags on the floor, and Lesley's heart sank as her eyes drifted to the bed, feeling awkward suddenly about having to discuss the sleeping arrangements with Al. Damn, why hadn't she brought it up sooner?

'This was Scott's room,' Al told her, striding across to the bed. 'And the beauty of it is ...' He hunkered down and slid out a mattress on wheels from underneath. 'Scott used to like having his friends over for sleepovers.' He looked up at Lesley. 'Happy?'

Lesley grinned, relaxing. 'Happy.' She was also

impressed that he'd realised she might be feeling uncomfortable. 'But what about Jane? Won't she think it's odd?'

'Oh, don't worry, she won't come in here.' He stood up. 'I'll show you where the bathroom is, if you want to freshen up before the pub.'

13

It was a short walk to the pub along a narrow road that sloped downhill to the sea, flanked on either side by a patchwork of green fields bordered by low dry stone walls. There was no traffic, the sound of their footsteps reverberating in the surrounding hush as they walked three abreast in the centre of the road. The only other noise was the chirping of birds and the muffled bark of a dog in the distance. Lesley had to hide her surprise when Al took her hand as they strolled along. She had to keep reminding herself that she was supposed to be his girlfriend. She relaxed and smiled at him as his fingers curled around hers, trying to act as if it felt natural.

It was only six-thirty, but the pub was already busy, a wall of heat and noise greeting them as they stepped inside. Lesley wondered where all the people had come from – the area seemed deserted for miles around. Jane was the centre of attention as soon as they arrived, and Lesley felt everyone's eyes following them as they made their way through the crowded bar, several people raising a glass in greeting or nodding hello as she passed. She had scrubbed up well, and was more recognisable now as the star Lesley remembered from her youth, wearing a simple black jersey dress, which she had tarted up with a chunky silver necklace and long silver earrings. She had aged well and was still a beautiful woman, but she had an indefinable something about her that was more than the sum of her pretty features and slim figure – a sort of magnetism that commanded attention as soon as she walked into a room. She drew many openly admiring glances as she led the way to a table in a quiet corner.

'It's bog-standard pub fare,' Jane told them as they sat and picked up laminated menus, 'but the food is really good.'

A burly bald-headed man slid out from behind the bar and came over to take their order, greeting Jane like a long-lost friend. He shook hands with Al, calling him by name, and Jane introduced him to Lesley as Liam. After a few pleasantries were exchanged, they all ordered fillet steaks and chips, and a bottle of red wine.

'Long time no see,' Liam said to Jane when he came back with the wine. 'What have you been up to?'

'Oh, nothing much – just writing.'

'Keeping out of mischief,' he said as he poured the wine. 'I thought maybe you'd started drinking in Clancy's.'

'No.' Jane smiled up at him. 'Don't worry, I've been doing my drinking at home.'

'Glad to hear it,' Liam said. 'And you're just down for the weekend?' he asked Al.

'Yes.'

'Good, good.' Liam had put the bottle of wine on the table, but still hovered. 'No sign of Peter?' he asked Jane, looking around as if expecting him to appear.

'Nope. Still divorced,' Jane said with a wry smile.

'Ah, that's a shame. He's missed around here. You don't get many like him.'

'No.'

'He's a terrible man, Peter,' he said, shaking his head ruefully. 'A terrible man.' He smiled to himself as if enjoying some private joke. 'Well, I'll leave you to it. Enjoy.'

While they waited for the food to arrive, Lesley got out her phone and found the pub on Facebook. She checked in and tagged Al. Then she took a deep breath and changed her status to 'in a relationship', quickly burying the phone in her bag again as Liam reappeared. She would deal with the fallout later.

'Gosh, that's a real farmer's dinner,' Al said happily as three massive plates were plonked down in front of them.

'It smells amazing!' Lesley said, already salivating as the smell of char-grilled meat and fried onions wafted up.

'How long more will it take you to finish the book?' Al asked Jane as they all began eating.

'It's due at the end of next week.'

Al raised his eyebrows knowingly. 'Not what I asked.'

'Another couple of weeks should do it, hopefully,' she said.

'So you'll be finished in time to come to Nice anyway,' Al said. 'That's good.'

Jane grimaced. 'I'm not sure I'm going to go to Nice this year.'

'What?' Al frowned, astonished. 'Why not?'

'Well ... it'll be a bit awkward, won't it, with her there? My replacement – this Stella person.'

'She's hardly your replacement,' Al said.

Jane sighed. 'That's what it feels like.'

'It was your idea to get divorced,' Al pointed out.

'It was. But it doesn't mean I want anyone else to have him.'

'Dog in the manger.' Lesley nodded. 'I get that.'

'Do you?' Al frowned at her.

'Yes, of course. Don't you?'

'Not really.'

'Peter was indeed a terrible man,' Jane said. 'But he was *my* terrible man.'

'Well, you'll have to get over it,' Al said briskly. 'You've got to come to Nice. Dad and Joy would miss you – we all would. And how do you think Scott and Rafe would feel?'

'They're not children anymore. They'll be fine.'

'But it won't be the same.'

'No, it won't be the same. But maybe we'll all just have to get used to things being different now.'

When they had finished eating, Liam cleared their plates and poured the rest of the wine. He returned just as Lesley and Al were draining their glasses.

'Now, what'll ye have?' he asked, rubbing his hands. 'Another bottle? Or will you go on to something else?'

'Oh, nothing else for me, thanks,' Jane said, lifting her almost empty glass. 'I'll go as soon as I've finished this. I need an early night. But you two go ahead,' she added to Lesley and Al.

'Jack wants to buy you all a drink,' Liam leaned down and murmured in her ear, nodding to a stout man leaning against the bar, who raised his pint in salute.

'Oh.' Jane waved to him and mouthed her thanks. 'Well, I do need to keep a clear head for the morning,' she said to Liam. 'But I suppose one more won't hurt. I'll have a Bailey's, please.'

Lesley ordered the same and Al asked for brandy.

'So, what's she like, then?' Jane asked Al when Liam had brought their drinks.

'Who?'

'The Queen of Sheba, who do you think? Peter's child bride. This Stella.'

'She's not exactly a child.'

'Not far off, from what I've heard. Young enough to be *Peter's* child at any rate. Anyway, you haven't answered my question.'

Al threw Lesley a 'help me out here' look.

'You've met her too, then?' Jane asked Lesley. 'Don't tell me you've been double-dating with your uncle,' she said to Al.

'Well, we did all meet up for lunch the other day. I thought it would be good for Lesley to get the measure of her. She's got good instincts about people.'

'And what did you think, Lesley?'

'She's ... very tall.' She took a sip of her Bailey's. 'Good at meditation,' she added.

'That's it?'

'She's hard to get a handle on. But she was very evasive about her background, wasn't she, Al?'

'She wouldn't even tell us where she was from originally. She's definitely hiding something.'

'She's not on any social media,' Lesley added.

'And Peter doesn't seem to know any more about her than we do.'

'And I suppose Peter's madly in love?' Jane said bitterly. 'Too bloody besotted to see straight.'

Al shrugged. 'He's infatuated with her, I suppose. You know what he's like.'

'He's been infatuated with lots of people. He never married any of them before. What makes this woman different to all his other flings?'

'Timing?' Al said. 'He proposed to her in a panic right after his heart attack. Maybe he's painted himself into a corner and now he feels he has to do the right thing.'

'Huh!' Jane said. 'He's changed, then. He never used to worry about doing the right thing when he was with me.'

Just as they finished their drinks, Liam appeared with another round.

'From Sean over there,' he said, nodding across the bar. Soon he was beating a regular path to their table with round after round of drinks, compliments of Jane's many admirers.

Several rounds later, they were all slightly tipsy, and as the evening wore on, the pub's clientele loosened up and there was a parade of locals stopping by their table to have a few words with Jane. They seemed quite in awe of her, shyly shuffling up to her and enquiring about 'the book' in reverent tones. But the talk always came back to Peter. They'd all heard about his recent brush with death and were avid for news of him.

'Ah, sure you can't kill a bad thing,' a weather-beaten man named Matthew said cheerfully when Jane told him Peter was making a good recovery. 'He's an awful divil, Peter.' He shook his head with a fond smile.

'Oh, a holy terror!' Sean said admiringly as he joined them. 'D'you remember the time he had that fella from Hollywood staying and they broke into Buckley's field in the middle of the night and tried to get a rise out of his bull. Playing at matadors, they were – legless, the pair of them.' He gave a wheezing cackle.

'Lucky for them it was a cow, not a bull.'

'Aye. The poor cow was never the same after it, though,' Sean said, sobering up. 'Suffered terrible from her nerves, she did. I believe she never gave a drop of milk since.'

'What about the time they took your goat up to Dublin

for the rugby?' another said to Liam as he appeared with yet another round of drinks.

Liam laughed. 'That bloody goat's got a better social life than I have.'

'You're joking!' Lesley said.

'No, true as I stand here. And there's the picture to prove it.' He nodded to the wall behind the bar. Lesley peered, and sure enough there was a framed photograph of a younger Peter with a huge grin on his face brandishing a pint, his arm around a white goat wearing an Ireland rugby shirt.

'You'd miss him around the place, all the same,' Matthew said sadly.

'Well, tell him we were asking for him.'

'I will,' Jane told him.

Finally they all drifted off and went back to the bar for last orders.

'My husband was very popular around here,' Jane told Lesley when they were alone again.

'You're not doing so badly yourself,' Lesley said, nodding to the large collection of drinks that had accumulated on the table.

Jane gave a little shrug. 'Peter was so good at this sort of thing,' she said, looking around the pub. 'Being one of the fellows – salt of the earth. And of course he's – he *was* – a great drinker, which helped. They all adored him. "Like one of our own", they'd say, which is the highest compliment an Englishman can get in these parts. I don't think they've ever quite forgiven me for divorcing him and depriving them of his company.' She drained her glass. 'It's not bloody fair,' she said. 'I *am* one of their own. They should be on my side.'

'Maybe you just didn't make as much of an effort with them,' Al suggested gently.

'He did always have that desperate need to be liked,' she said with a bitter smile. 'That stood him in good stead.'

'And he is very likeable,' Al said tentatively.

'Yes. I'll give him that. He's very bloody likeable.'

'Well, I'm sure you could get him back,' Lesley said. 'And it'd solve all your problems,' she said to Al. 'Kill two birds with one stone.'

'But she doesn't want him back,' Al said, frowning at her. 'Do you?' He looked to Jane for confirmation.

But Jane was silent, toying thoughtfully with the rim of her glass. 'It doesn't seem fair, does it, that I put up with him all those years when he was taking goats to Dublin on benders, and someone else gets to have him now that he's apparently a reformed character, and finally ready to settle down? At seventy-two,' she added drolly.

Lesley reckoned that that was answer enough. 'That's decided, then. You have to come to France.'

'I don't know. But in the meantime, why don't you go and see Conor?' Jane said to Al. 'He might have some ideas about what we should do.'

'WHAT MADE you think Jane wanted Peter back?' Al asked later that night when they were alone in their room. Lesley was in the high double bed, and Al was on the pull-out mattress on the floor beside her.

She propped herself up on an elbow, looking down at him. 'It seemed obvious, the way she was talking about him.'

'Well, it looks like you were right.' He grinned. 'She was looking up flights to Nice when I left her in the kitchen just now.'

'What about Peter, though? Do you really think he'd just dump Stella if he could get Jane back?'

'In a heartbeat,' Al said.

'It would certainly be an elegant solution,' Lesley said, laying back against the pillows. 'The family fortune would be safe, and your aunt and uncle would be back together. Happy days!'

'Except for Stella.'

'Yeah, except for Stella.' Lesley felt an unwelcome pang of guilt, and tried to brush it aside. After all, despite her sweet, caring facade, Stella was probably just a scheming gold-digger preying on a vulnerable old man. They'd be doing a good thing, foiling her evil plan.

'Well, goodnight,' Al said, snuggling down. 'I'm sorry this probably wasn't the kind of mini break you were expecting.'

'That's okay. I had fun tonight.' And at least there was no one trying to wrap her in seaweed.

14

The next morning, Al was already up when Lesley woke. She pulled on a cardigan over her pyjamas and went downstairs. She found him at the kitchen sink, elbow-deep in suds.

'Morning,' she yawned.

'Good morning!' He turned and smiled at her, continuing to scrub.

'You're a right little domestic goddess, aren't you?' Lesley looked around admiringly, impressed at the transformation he had already made. She wouldn't actually fear for her life if she ate in here now.

'I do my best.' He dried his hands on a towel. 'What would you like for breakfast? Toast? Scrambled eggs? A fry-up?'

'Just toast, please,' she said casually, hiding her surprise that he was going to make it for her as Al flicked on the kettle and started cutting slices from a crusty loaf of sourdough.

'Where's Jane?' she asked.

'Oh, she's already at work.' He nodded to the window.

'I didn't hear you getting up this morning.'

'No, you were fast asleep – still snoring your head off.'

Lesley reared up indignantly. 'I do not snore.'

Al glanced at her, a little smile on his face. 'Is that what your last boyfriend told you?'

'No,' she frowned crossly. 'I just know. A person can know if they snore or not.'

'Ah, okay. My mistake. It must have been a cow in the next field or something.' He smirked as he handed her a mug of tea and put a plate of toast in front of her along with a dish of butter and a couple of pots of jam. 'I recommend the rhubarb and ginger,' he said.

'Thanks. Have you already had breakfast?' Lesley asked him.

'Yes, I ate earlier with Jane.'

He went back to the sink as Lesley started eating.

'You *do* snore, by the way,' she said to his back. He was right about the rhubarb and ginger jam – it was fantastic.

'Sorry,' he said without turning around. 'I hope it didn't keep you awake.'

'It's fine,' she said. 'It was very quiet snoring, in fairness.' She didn't want to make him feel bad when he'd made her this lovely breakfast. But it was kind of a relief to discover he had *some* flaws. She'd been starting to worry that he was perfect, and she didn't want to fall for him. She was just here as his employee, and she should keep it strictly professional. It was never a good idea to mix business with bonking.

She took out her phone and finally got up the nerve to sneak a look at Facebook. Of course the predicted bombardment had started almost immediately after she'd changed her status. Her check-in post from last night had caused a deluge of comments, her friends all agog about her changed relationship status and looking for details. She was tempted to boast about Al's famous family, but decided it would be better to be cool and mysterious about it, and wait until she actually had some Bradshaws in her friends list, so she didn't reply to any of them. Instead she shut off her phone and watched Al, who was quietly humming a medley of Bay City Rollers hits as he tidied the kitchen.

LESLEY KNEW she'd have her mother on her case now that she'd outed Al as her boyfriend, but she hadn't expected it to happen quite so quickly. Her phone was ringing as she got out of the shower. She was glad she didn't manage to grab it in time before it rang off when she saw that it was her mother and she already had three missed calls from her. Bloody hell! Why hadn't she held off a little longer before going public? She should at least have waited until she was back in Dublin. She sighed and tossed the phone on the bed. She wasn't going to bother answering. She'd just wait for her to call back. She knew she wouldn't have to wait long.

She was glad she had at least managed to finish dressing before her phone rang again.

'Finally!' was her mother's greeting when she answered. 'I was starting to wonder if we should get the guards involved.'

'What?'

'I've rung you three times this morning and no answer. I was starting to worry.'

'Sorry. I'm just away at the moment.'

'So, I hear you have a new boyfriend,' she said. Her tone was accusing.

'Where did you hear that?'

'Katrina told me she saw it on Facebook. It's a nice

thing when every randomer on the internet gets to hear what's going on in your life before your own mother.'

'It's very early days. I only posted it last night.'

'Well, I hope you're not going to let the grass grow under your feet this time. You're not getting any younger, Lesley. Act fast, if you want to hold onto him, that's my advice. You don't have time to be wasting at your time of life.'

'Mam! I'm thirty!' Lesley rolled her eyes. Her mother was probably already looking at mother-of-the-bride outfits.

'I know what age you are – that's my point. And don't you roll your eyes at me, young lady.'

'I wasn't!'

'Don't think I can't hear you.'

'Well, you shouldn't be talking to me like that if you think I'm so ancient. You should have more respect for the elderly.'

'Where are you anyway that you can't answer your phone – Timbuktu?'

'As good as,' she said in a put-upon tone. 'Sorry, Mam. We're staying with Al's aunt in Clare – a place called Doonbeg. The signal isn't great here.' She crossed her fingers, hoping her mother had never been to Doonbeg. The signal was just fine. But her mother was a militant Dubliner and didn't really hold with other parts of the country. In her view, anywhere beyond the M50 was a wasteland, devoid of phone signals and other accoutrements of civilisation, inhabited by oddballs and bandits, and to be avoided at all costs.

'Doonbeg!' Her mother tutted. 'I don't like the sound of that at all.' She sighed heavily. 'So when are you going to bring him around so we can all have a look at him?'

'There's a photo on Facebook. Get Katrina to show you if you're so keen to have a look at him.'

'I wouldn't have to ask Katrina to show me if you'd just accept my friend request. What kind of person refuses a friend request from her own mother?'

'No one wants to be friends with their parents on Facebook, Mam.'

'Sheila Ryan is friends with all her children on Facebook.' Another martyred sigh. 'Anyway, I'm not talking about a photo. Bring him around for tea, so we can meet him properly.'

'Okay, but you'll all have to be on your best behaviour. I don't want to scare him off.' She hoped the prospect of Lesley letting another man 'slip through her fingers' would get her mother to back off.

'It's just tea, for feck's sake – a few sandwiches and a bit of cake. What type of eejit would be scared off by that? I'll get a Black Forest gateau. We haven't had that in a while.'

Lesley knew when she was beaten; she couldn't resist Black Forest gateau. 'I suppose it would be kind of nice.'

'That's settled, then. Bring him to tea and we'll all give you our opinion on him.'

'Great. Thanks, Mam.'

'No bother, love. Sure, what's a mother for?'

If only you knew, Lesley thought.

'I might even make a few scones.'

'Okay. But I'd better warn you now, he'll probably call them "scons".'

There was a moment's silence.

'Is he English, then?' her mother asked warily.

'He is.'

'Well, we'll keep an open mind,' her mother said gamely. 'I mean, you *are* thirty.'

· · ·

'GREAT, YOU'RE HERE!' Al said, rubbing his hands when she returned to the kitchen. 'Ready to get started on this lot?' He gestured to the newly scrubbed table, now covered in a colourful array of fresh vegetables – shiny, dark-purple aubergines, bright red and yellow peppers, deep-green broccoli and spinach, and bundles of fragrant herbs.

'Um ... I've only just had breakfast – it's a bit early for lunch.'

'It's not for you. It's for Jane – to keep her going when we're gone.'

'All this? She'll never get through it all before it goes off.'

'Oh, she won't have to. Anyway, I wouldn't trust her not to let it all rot and go on living on beans straight out of the can. So we're going to cook meals and fill up her freezer before we go.'

'Wow!' Lesley looked around dazedly. 'I feel like I'm in a fairy tale.'

'Oh!' Al looked surprised but pleased. 'Really?'

'Yeah, you know one of those stories where some poor unfortunate girl is held captive by an ogre and forced to spin her weight in gold.'

'Oh.' Al's face fell.

'Or like Cinderella, having to stay home and peel mountains of vegetables while everyone else goes to the ball.'

'Sorry,' Al said. 'I just worry about Jane. She doesn't look after herself when she's close to a deadline. She forgets to eat sometimes. And she needs to get her book finished so she can come to Nice.'

'So this is my mini-break – cooking and cleaning for your aunt?' Lesley said indignantly, but more because she felt she should make some token protest. She couldn't really be angry with Al for being so kind to his aunt. It was touching that he wanted to take care of her.

He sighed, putting his head to the side and looking at her. 'Sorry. I'm not giving a very good account of myself as your boyfriend, am I?'

Lesley smiled at him. 'I've had worse,' she said.

'Really?' He grimaced. 'Blimey!'

'Yeah, the bar isn't set very high, to be honest. But I could get in a real strop about this, you know, if I wanted to. Just FYI.' She didn't want him to get complacent, just because she was being a good sport about it.

'I know. You'd be perfectly entitled.' He glanced at his watch. 'If you'd like to have one now, you could squeeze it in before we start.'

'Nah, it's okay. Luckily for you I'm not that sort of girlfriend.'

See, I knew you were the one for me!' he said with a happy grin.

He hasn't abducted you, then? Romy texted Lesley later that night. *I don't need to contact the police?*

No, the constabulary can rest easy in their beds.

She'd kept in touch with Romy throughout the day on WhatsApp, filling her in on where she was and what they were doing.

Though I could have him up for forced labour, I suppose, she typed.

But it was all part of the mission to get Jane to France and oust Stella, so she couldn't really complain. Besides, the truth was she'd enjoyed cooking with Al, chatting companionably as they'd worked.

It turned out he was a very good cook, and as her signature dish was a bog-standard spag bol, she was happy to act as his sous chef and let him boss her around a bit. He had proper knife skills, and he'd shown her a great trick for dicing onions. After they'd filled up Jane's freezer with healthy meals, he'd made a fiercely hot Thai green curry for dinner, after establishing that that was how all three of them liked it, and he'd even baked a cake for dessert. She was beginning to suspect Al was the nicest boyfriend she'd ever had. It was just a pity he wasn't real.

Still, as far as her family were concerned, he was. At least he'd get her mother off her back for a while.

15

'I hope they like me,' Al said as they drove to her parents' house the following Saturday. 'The new boyfriend.'

She glanced across at him. 'Lead with being an architect – Mam will be impressed by that. But she's not fussy really, not now I'm thirty. She's afraid I've been left on the shelf, so as long as I've got a man, she's happy.'

'What about your dad?'

'He's married to Mam, so he's taken. She wants me to have a man of my very own.'

Al laughed. 'You know what I mean.'

'Yeah, he won't like you.'

'What?'

'It's nothing personal,' she said. 'He just doesn't think anyone's good enough for me.'

Al smiled. 'I bet I can win him round.'

Lesley raised her eyebrows sceptically. 'Knock yourself out. But I'm telling you now you'll be wasting your time.'

· · ·

'Lesley!' Her mother threw open the door and ushered them inside. 'And you must be Al,' she smiled, extending a hand to him. 'I'm Miriam.'

'It's a pleasure to meet you,' Al said as they shook hands.

She beamed at him, and Lesley could tell by the way her eyes lit up that she was already impressed. 'Well, your father will be happy to see you,' she said to Lesley as she led the way down the hall. 'He could do with cheering up.'

'Oh? What's wrong?'

'Ah, he's just a bit down because no one liked his breakfast on Instagram.'

'Oh, right.'

'Lesley!' Her father was sitting at the kitchen table, fiddling with his phone. 'You're a sight for sore eyes.'

'Hi, Dad.' She introduced him to Al and they all sat.

'Katrina's just taking Skipper for a walk,' her mother said. 'She'll be back shortly.'

'So, Mam says you're having problems with Instagram,' Lesley said, nodding to her father's phone. 'No one liked your breakfast?'

'Ah, now! That's a bit of an exaggeration.' He scowled at his wife. 'It wasn't *no one*.'

'What did you have?'

'Scrambled egg,' he said, handing Lesley his phone, 'with granary toast.'

'Nice picture,' she said, looking down at the screen.

'I even put a bit of parsley on the plate for a splash of colour.'

'So I see. Good effort.'

'The presentation is excellent,' Al said, looking over her shoulder.

'But you're not using any hashtags, Dad. I've told you before, Instagram is all about the hashtags. Here, I'll put in a few to get you going.' She went in to edit the photo and added all the food-related hashtags she could think of. 'There.' She handed the phone back to her father. 'See how you get on with that.'

'There's Katrina back now,' Miriam said as they heard the front door open and close. 'We'll just give her a minute to get Skipper sorted out, and then we'll go through to the dining room.'

Lesley felt Al looking at them curiously as they all sat listening to shuffling sounds in the hall before her mother decided they'd given Katrina enough time to get the dog stashed away safely. But when she opened the kitchen door, Skipper was still there in the hall with Katrina. At least he was still on his leash, but Lesley couldn't help wondering if her sister had done it on purpose to sabotage Al.

'Katrina, we thought you'd have him locked in the other room by now,' her mother said, nodding at the dog. 'We've got company.'

'Oh, no need for that,' Al said cheerfully, striding forward in that over-confident way of his before Lesley could stop him. 'I love dogs. Hi, I'm Al,' he said, holding out a hand to Katrina. Then he turned to the dog. 'And this must be—'

'No!'

'Stop!'

'Don't!'

'He'll take your hand off!'

They all yelled at him in unison, but it was too late. He was already down on his haunches, reaching out to pet Skipper.

Everyone gasped, hands clutched to their chests in fear as they held their collective breath. Lesley couldn't bear to look, her eyes squeezed shut as she waited for the inevitable growling and snapping. She was already calculating which

hospital's emergency department would be the most effi-
cient to take Al to. But weirdly, the only sound breaking the
stunned silence was Al telling Skipper what a 'lovely boy'
and a 'good dog' he was.

'Well, would you credit that.'

She opened her eyes to see her father shaking his head
in wonder as Al patted and stroked Skipper as if he was a
perfectly normal dog and not the homicidal psycho they all
knew him to be.

'I've never seen anything like it,' her mother said.

'He's not normally like this,' Katrina said to Al, and
Lesley tried to figure out if she sounded disappointed. 'He
hates people. He only really likes Dad.'

'He barely puts up with the rest of us,' Lesley said. 'But
anyone outside the family ...'

'He took the arse off Lesley's last boyfriend the first
time he came round,' her father said, chuckling merrily at
the memory.

'What a good boy,' Al cooed, rubbing Skipper's ears.

'You've obviously got the magic touch, Al,' her mother
said. 'But let's not push our luck. Katrina, put him in the
kitchen, and then come in for tea.'

LESLEY HAD to give her mother credit where it was due –
she put on a great tea. The table in the dining room was
covered with a Cath Kidston cloth, and she'd brought out
the best chintzy china. There were plates of crustless finger
sandwiches and savoury pastries, and tiered cake stands
filled with small, fluffy scones, thick slices of lemon drizzle
cake and the promised Black Forest gateau.

'So tell us about yourself, Al,' her mother said, passing
him a plate of sandwiches. 'We've heard practically

nothing about you,' she added with a pointed look at Lesley.

'There's not really much to tell.'

'What do you do?'

'I'm an architect.'

'Oh, very nice,' Miriam said, clearly impressed as Lesley knew she would be. 'That's a lovely profession.'

'And his father makes Bradshaw Biscuits!' Lesley said, feeling Al wasn't talking himself up properly.

'Bradshaw Biscuits!' her mother exclaimed. 'Really?'

'Well, he doesn't exactly make them—' Al began.

'No, but he's the brains behind the whole operation,' Lesley said.

'Well, that's an amazing coincidence,' her father piped up. 'We love the Chocolate Extravaganzas, don't we?' he said to his wife. 'We had one just this morning with a cup of tea.'

'Gosh, that's amazing, Dad,' Lesley said.

'It's like you were meant to be or something,' Katrina said.

'So Al's family are loaded, obviously,' Lesley said, resuming her boasting. 'And half of them are famous too. Sir Peter Bradshaw is his uncle, Jane Howard is his aunt – that's who we stayed with in Doonbeg – and Scott and Rafe Bradshaw are his cousins.'

'Well, that's incredible!' her mother gasped. 'Only the other day I nearly bought one of Jane Howard's books.'

'Small world,' Katrina said drily.

'I love Peter Bradshaw,' Miriam said.

'We'll be staying with them all when we go to France,' Lesley said casually.

Her mother frowned. 'You're going on holiday together? First I've heard of it.'

Lesley nodded. 'Al's family have a house in Nice.'

'And Scott Bradshaw will be there?' Miriam looked at Katrina. 'He's a bit of a heartthrob around here, isn't he, Katrina?'

Katrina shrugged. 'I really like him in *Nightshade.*'

She was obviously trying to act cool and blasé, but Lesley was pleased to see she looked a little green around the gills.

'So where did you two meet?' Miriam asked.

'At a dinner party a couple of months ago,' Lesley said.

'Oh, whose was it?'

'No one you'd know,' Lesley said, shaking her head. 'No one I know either, as a matter of fact. It was at Dinner Dates.'

'Oh, one of those lonely hearts things you go to,' her mother said. She tilted her head to the side, looking at Al sympathetically. 'Are you a lonely heart too, Al?'

'Mam!' Lesley protested, blushing. 'We're not lonely. We're just young, single and ready to mingle.'

'You're not as young as you used to be,' her mother said. 'It's about time you stopped "mingling" and settled down before it's too late. You've gone out with hundreds of men, but what's the point of it all if it never leads anywhere?'

'Hundreds? Really?' Al turned to her, his eyebrows raised, a mischievous smile playing around his lips. 'I feel so special.'

'Lesley's dated a lot,' Miriam told him, her tone disapproving.

'Yes, she's a very popular girl,' her father said, beaming at her proudly.

'Thanks, Dad.' Lesley grinned back at him.

'Hmm. There was a word for popular girls in my day,' Miriam said, pursing her lips.

'What word was that, Mam? Popular? It's the same now.'

'You know very well what I mean, Lesley.'

'Mam's calling you a slut,' Katrina chipped in helpfully.

'Katrina!' her mother snapped. 'I wouldn't dream of using such language, especially about my own daughter.'

'Don't mind her,' Katrina said, turning to Lesley. 'She's just jealous because she's only ever shagged Dad. Classic FOMO.'

Lesley snorted. 'True. She's a slut manqué.'

Miriam threw them both a filthy look. 'I'm sure you wouldn't talk to your mother like that, would you, Al?'

'I bet she wouldn't have called him a slut either,' Lesley muttered under her breath, glancing warily at Al.

'Well, I was only eleven,' he said quietly to her. 'My mother's dead,' he told Miriam.

'Oh, I'm so sorry, pet,' Miriam said, a hand pressed to her chest, her head tilted sympathetically.

'Thank you.'

'I'm just choosy,' Lesley said as she reached for a slice of cake, keen to draw her mother's attention back to her and away from the subject of Al's bereavement.

'Too picky if you ask me,' her mother sniffed, taking the bait.

'I suppose she's told you that she doesn't fancy Ryan Gosling?' Katrina said to Al.

'She may have mentioned it,' Al said, grinning at Lesley.

'She thinks she's great. As if he'd have her anyway. It doesn't make you so special you know,' she said to Lesley.

'I don't think it makes me special. It's just a fact, that's all.'

'You'd be singing a different tune if Ryan Gosling

turned up at the door looking for you,' her mother said. 'I bet you wouldn't turn your nose up at him then.'

'I would too.'

'Ah, the poor fella,' her father said. 'After coming all the way from Hollywood, you'd just turn him away?'

Lesley sighed. 'Okay, if Ryan Gosling ever comes all the way from Hollywood to ask me out, I promise I'll give him a chance, okay?'

'You can't say fairer than that,' her father said, while Katrina's eyes threatened to roll right out of her head.

'Right, I'm out of here,' Katrina said, standing up. 'I'm going over to Tom's.'

'That's Katrina's boyfriend,' Miriam put in with a smug smile.

'It was nice to meet you, Al,' Katrina said. 'And we're all very grateful to you for taking on Lesley. We'd almost given up on her. Thanks for the tea, Ma.'

She left the room, and moments later the front door slammed. As soon as it did, Miriam leaned conspiratorially towards Al.

'Katrina doesn't know it yet,' she said, her voice low and confidential, as if she was afraid of being overheard, 'but she's engaged! Well, almost engaged. Tom is going to ask her to marry him soon. He has this big proposal planned and we're all going to be in it. He's even putting it on the internet. We're going to be on YouTube!' she said excitedly.

'Sounds great!' Al said heartily. Lesley threw him a sceptical look.

'I know. Imagine me, at my age, becoming a YouTuber!'

'That's not what being a YouTuber means, Mam.'

'I believe you can make great money at it these days if

you're a hit,' Miriam said, ignoring her. 'Who knows? Maybe this time next year we'll be millionaires.'

Lesley reminded herself to Google whether excessive eye-rolling could be damaging.

Miriam gasped suddenly, eyes wide, as if she'd just had a wonderful idea. 'We should get Tom to put you in the proposal!' she said to Al with a wide smile.

'Oh, that's really not necessary—'

'No, I'm sure he'll find a little part for you. Consider it done!'

'Er ... thanks.' Al smiled weakly.

'No bother,' she said, smiling kindly at him. 'I'm sure YouTube will be nothing to you, Al, with your theatrical background. You'll probably put us all to shame.'

Much as she was enjoying this, Lesley felt she had to step in and rescue Al. 'Mam, there's no reason for Al to be in the proposal.'

'Of course he should be in it! He's practically one of the family now.' She winked at Al, and Lesley cringed.

'Mam!'

'Maybe Tom will return the favour when it's your turn.'

Lesley blushed. 'We'll probably never see him again once Katrina dumps him after this *La La Land* fiasco,' she said sulkily.

'Lesley, don't start that again. You've already ruined one of your poor sister's romances. Is that not enough for you? She'd be married to Derek by now if it wasn't for you.'

'He was a cheater!'

'Well, she'd have had to change him, of course,' her mother said begrudgingly, 'but all relationships take a bit of work.'

'I did her a favour, and you know it,' Lesley said.

Miriam ignored her. 'We're starting rehearsals next Monday evening, Al. I hope you're free then?'

'Um … yes. I can arrange to be.'

'Great! And you,' she said, turning to Lesley, 'do something with that bird's nest of yours. You can't go on YouTube with that hair.'

'This is the only hair I've got!' Lesley said indignantly. 'If you're so worried I'll mess it up, maybe I shouldn't even be in this stupid proposal video.'

'That's enough of that,' her mother said, pointing a finger at her. 'You'll propose to your sister if it's the last thing you do. Now, more cake anyone? Al, would you like a "scon"?'

'Well, you were a big hit,' Lesley said when they were outside in Lesley's car. 'Even Dad liked you.' *That's a great fella you've got there, Lesley,* her father had whispered in her ear as they were leaving. Lesley was a bit stunned. He'd never taken to one of her boyfriends like that before.

'So what did you do to break up your sister's last relationship?' Al asked.

'I found out her boyfriend was cheating on her.'

'Oh.' He grimaced. 'That's tough. How did you find out?'

'I carried out surveillance on him – followed him around, staked out his house, that sort of thing. That's where I earned my stripes as a PI.'

'She had her suspicions about him, then?'

'No, I did it off my own bat. I wasn't particularly expecting anything. But then I caught him red-handed.' She drummed her fingers on the steering wheel. 'Well, not exactly red-*handed*.'

'She had a lucky escape, then, thanks to you.'

'She wasn't as grateful as you might expect.' Katrina had acted almost as if the cheating was Lesley's fault – as though not knowing about it meant it wasn't real. 'Sorry you were bamboozled into being in the proposal. But it's your own fault, really. You were the one who insisted I change my Facebook status.'

'What exactly is it going to involve?'

'We're doing this big musical number – about twenty of their friends and family horsing around lip-synching, basically carrying on like we're all in love with Katrina and want to marry her.'

'That sounds quite ...'

'Shite! I know. Imagine what's supposed to be one of the most romantic moments of your life starting off with dad-dancing! Not to mention the pressure for poor Tom, popping the question with everyone they know standing there expectantly.' She did jazz hands, accompanied by a manic showbiz grin.

'Maybe Katrina will like it.'

Lesley shook her head. 'She won't. She'll hate it – which is a shame, because Tom's lovely. But Mam won't let me tell him, so I have to stand by and watch him crash and burn. Worse, in fact – I have to dance around the fire doing harmonies and pouring on petrol.'

'Well, maybe it won't be so bad.'

'You're kidding! It'll be hideous.'

'I know. I was just trying to be nice.'

16

'Where are we off to, then?' Lesley asked on Monday afternoon when Al picked her up. He had rung the previous evening and said there was somewhere he wanted to take her.

'Going to see a man about a dog,' he said as he pulled away from her house.

'Just FYI, I don't like surprises. As my boyfriend, you should know that.'

He glanced at her. 'Okay, we're going to the Players Theatre.'

'Is that your idea of a date? Going to a matinee in the middle of the afternoon like a pair of fecking pensioners? I know you're paying me, but I won't be putting that on Facebook.'

'Hey, calm down,' Al laughed. 'It's not a date. Jane suggested I talk to Conor, remember? He's the director of the theatre.'

'Wait, is this the same Conor who barged into Dinner Dates that night? Helen O'Neill's husband?'

'Yes, that's him. He's an old family friend.'

'How does Jane think *he* could help?'

'I don't know exactly. But he has a rep in our family as a sort of all-round Mr Fix-It.'

'Well, he sounds like a very unsavoury character, if you ask me – "fixing" things for his friends while he hides behind a mild-mannered theatre director facade.'

Al laughed. 'He's not shady. He won't "off" Stella, if that's what you're worried about. Jane just thought he might have some ideas. He *is* a good problem-solver.'

CONOR'S OFFICE was on the top floor of an old Georgian building adjacent to the theatre itself. It was a large high-ceilinged room, with an ornate ceiling rose and decorative coving. Across a wide expanse of thick moss-coloured carpet, Conor sat behind an imposing mahogany desk. He was writing in a thick leather-bound diary as they entered, and looked up at them briefly.

'Al,' he said, nodding hello.

'This is Lesley,' Al said.

Conor put down his pen. 'Have a seat. I'll be with you in a moment.' He waved them to a couple of squashy armchairs in front of his desk.

Al and Lesley sat, and watched Conor in silence as he picked up his pen and resumed his writing, his movements unhurried and careful.

'Right,' he said finally, closing the book. He looked up and flashed them a business-like smile. 'What can I do for you two?' He clasped his hands on his desk and leaned towards them, giving them his full attention.

'Well,' Al began, 'it's about Peter. I suppose you've heard that he's engaged?'

'Yes,' Conor said. 'Bloody idiot! Rafe's in quite a tizzy about it, isn't he?'

'None of us are exactly thrilled.'

'No. Understandably. How does Jane feel about it?'

'She's not happy,' Al said. 'Naturally she's worried about Peter.'

'Naturally. I never understood what those two were thinking, getting divorced.'

'Anyway, she suggested I talk to you. She thought you might be able to help. I'm not sure what exactly she expected you to do, but I said I'd come and see you, so – here I am.' Al smiled awkwardly.

Conor peered at Al over the top of his glasses and said nothing. Then he opened the big diary and began flicking through pages. 'We have the theatre festival coming up in October ... Have they set a date for the wedding yet?'

'They're thinking of September.'

'So soon.' Conor sucked air in through his teeth like a plumber about to give an exorbitant estimate, and flipped back through the diary.

'Right. We're doing some of Beckett's shorter plays in September,' he said, tapping a page as he spoke. 'I could put Jane and Peter into *Endgame*. Lorcan's directing. Rehearsals would be in August.' He looked up. 'How does that sound?' he asked, his eyes flicking between them both questioningly.

Lesley thought it sounded like a nightmare, but she said nothing. She had no idea what it had to do with stopping Peter marrying Stella anyway. Even if Peter was busy with the play in September, they could easily shift the date of their wedding. It would only delay it by a month or two at best.

Conor was still looking at them with a satisfied expression, as if he had just presented them with the perfect solution. He clearly wasn't the mastermind Al's family took him for. Lesley turned to Al and was glad to see he looked as confused as she felt.

'Um ... that sounds very interesting,' he said hesitantly. 'The whole Beckett thing, I mean. I'm sure it'll be great. But you know Jane doesn't act anymore.'

'She will if I ask her,' Conor said calmly.

'And Peter's been ill. He's not really fit to go back to work yet.'

'It's a short show, just an hour and a quarter, and there'll only be six performances. It'll be a nice way for Peter to ease himself back into work.'

'But what about the dustbins? Wouldn't that be a bit of a strain for him?'

'Your grandfather was crippled with arthritis when he did it. Peter's a trooper. He'll be fine.'

'What's this about dustbins?' Lesley asked, frowning.

Al turned to her. 'In *Endgame*, this old couple, Nagg and Nell, are in dustbins for the whole play. You can only see the tops of their heads sticking out.'

'Oh!' She looked at Conor. 'That sounds like elderly abuse to me.'

'That's certainly one interpretation,' Conor said complacently. 'You've never seen it? You must come.'

Lesley didn't think that'd be happening. 'Thanks, but I hate the theatre.'

Conor guffawed, as if she'd just told the best joke.

'She's serious,' Al said. 'She really does.'

Conor's laughter stopped abruptly and he scowled deeply, looking at Lesley as if she was some kind of alien monster.

'Anyway,' Lesley said, 'I don't see what shoving Jane and Peter into dustbins on a stage has to do with Peter marrying Stella.'

'Explain it to her, Al,' Conor said.

'Um ...' Al looked blank. 'I'm afraid I don't get it either,' he admitted.

Conor sighed wearily and leaned on the desk. 'Peter and Jane are actors,' he began, as if explaining something very simple to a couple of particularly stupid children.

'Jane isn't anymore,' Lesley interrupted.

'They met in a rehearsal room,' he continued, as if she hadn't spoken. 'They've spent half their lives on stage together. The theatre is their world, their family. Get them back in a show together and they'll soon come to their senses and remember who they are. They'll forget all this nonsense about splitting up and marrying other people.'

'Oh! Do you think that will work?' Lesley asked.

'Of course it'll work.'

His confidence was compelling. 'You know, you could be right.'

'I am,' he said calmly. 'I'm always right. Ask Al.'

'He is,' Al said.

'Now, if there's nothing else—'

'No, thank you for your time,' Al said.

'Hang on!' Lesley said quickly, holding up a finger to Al. 'There is one more thing you could help me with,' she said to Conor.

'Oh?' Al turned to her, eyebrows raised.

'I'm going to ask him about Katrina,' she said to him in a loud whisper.

'Your sister?'

She nodded. 'I'm going to ask him what we should do about the whole proposal fiasco.' It was like being in the presence of some sort of oracle. She had to grab the opportunity while she had his attention.

'Who are you going to ask, the cat's mother?' Conor said.

'Oh, sorry,' Lesley said, turning to him. 'That was rude. I'd like to have another question, please.'

'Go ahead. What's this about your sister?'

'Well, she has this boyfriend, you see, and he's lovely, only he's also a bit of an eejit. He's going to propose to her, and he's making a real song and dance about it – literally.' She explained the whole proposal-by-flash-mob plan, resisting the urge to preface her speech with 'Oh, great and powerful Oz'.

'So, what do you think we should do?' she asked when she'd finished.

'Well, my advice would be to keep the choreography simple, stay away from jazz hands, and depending on your budget—'

'No, no, no.' Lesley waved a hand to stop him. 'I'm not looking for advice about the routine. That's all sorted.'

'Really? What song are you doing?'

Lesley hesitated. She really didn't want to say it out loud. '"All of Me",' she admitted, cringing.

'Oh dear.' Conor gave her a weary look.

'I know.'

'And her *father's* going to be involved?'

'Look, I *know*! Not to mention me, her sister. It's horrible, and it's going to be a disaster. Katrina will hate it, and she'll hate Tom for doing it to her. But Mam won't let me warn him because she's desperate to be on YouTube—'

'So you want to find a way to call it off?' Conor interrupted.

'Yes. Please!'

Conor regarded her in silence for a moment, twiddling his thumbs as he thought. The silence went on so long, Lesley thought he was stumped.

'Pre-emptive strike,' he said then, decisively.

'What?'

'Your sister does want to marry this person, yes?'

'Yes, she does. We all want her to marry him.'

'Then suggest to her that *she* propose to *him* – and get her to do it before this song-and-dance debacle is planned to go off.'

Lesley blinked. 'Pre-emptive strike!' she said wonderingly. It was genius. Why hadn't she thought of it? Probably because it was genius and she wasn't. 'It's brilliant! Thank you so much,' she said as she stood. She was tempted to go around the desk and throw her arms around Conor, but she got the feeling he wasn't the huggy type.

'If that doesn't work, at least get this Tom to change the song you're doing. I'd suggest "Marry You" by Bruno Mars. At least that's more upbeat, and less creepy for her father to sing to her. Still odd as fuck in the circumstances, but what wouldn't be?'

'Thanks. Really, I'm so grateful.'

'Happy to help. Well, goodbye,' he said, waving them off. 'And good luck!'

'Your family are right about him,' she murmured to Al as they went to the door. 'He's brilliant, isn't he?'

LESLEY WAS SO BUOYED up by her meeting with Conor, that she didn't even mind going to rehearsal that night. Confident that it would all come to nothing in the end, she felt quite cheerful as she horsed through several rounds of 'All of Me' with family and friends in the playing field of a local school where one of Katrina's friends was headmistress.

'Well, I'm glad to see you've changed your tune, Missy,' her mother said to her, eyeing Lesley's smiling face with narrow-eyed suspicion.

'I even brushed my hair, see?'

The routine was unbearably corny, couples waltzing around, gazing into each other's eyes as they mouthed to the lyrics of the song blaring from Tom's car stereo.

'You're a very good singer,' Lesley said to Al as he crooned along in her ear. He had a lovely deep, rich voice.

'Thank you. I was in the choir at school.'

'Why am I not surprised?'

'You're a lovely dancer, Al,' her mother said, as she and Lesley's dad glided past. It turned out Al could properly waltz, and he even made Lesley feel quite graceful as he whirled them around the playing field.

'Thank you, Miriam. I took ballroom classes for a while when I was younger.'

'Is there anything you're not good at?' Lesley asked grumpily.

Al just smiled at her, unperturbed. 'Have you thought about how you're going to persuade Katrina to propose?' he asked.

'No, but I'd better do it soon. We don't have much time.'

'Maybe you should try and get Tom to change the song anyway, just in case.'

'I suppose I should. Though it'll still be a disaster.'

'But at least the ick factor wouldn't be quite as high.'

Lesley gasped. 'The ick factor! That's it! You're a genius, Al.'

'What?'

'That's how I'll get Katrina to propose – Miranda Hobbs.'

'Who?'

'You know – *Sex and the City*. Miranda!'

He shook his head. 'I can't say I'm familiar.'

'Well, all you need to know is that she was the best one, and Katrina idolises her.'

'Bringing in the big guns, then?'

'Believe me, pal,' she said, patting his shoulder, 'once I set Miranda on her, this shitshow is toast.'

LESLEY DIDN'T WASTE any time in putting her plan into action. She wanted to plant the seed in Katrina's mind before she left for France – light the fuse and flee the country, as it were. So on Friday evening, she suggested they get a pizza and have a *Sex and the City* marathon, picking three episodes each to rewatch.

'Not counting "A Woman's Right to Shoes",' she added, because it was a given they'd both pick that. She let Katrina go first, just in case, but she was confident she didn't have to worry about her choosing 'The Ick Factor' – the episode where Miranda proposes to her boyfriend Steve. Sure enough, it was her first choice.

'God, this show was so good,' Lesley said when they were deep into 'A Woman's Right to Shoes'. 'I hate when people rubbish it and say it's all about the consumerism. Especially this episode. It so misses the point.'

'It's not about the Manolos!' Katrina chimed in, as if they were debating some invisible adversary.

'Exactly!' Lesley tore off a slice of pizza. 'Carrie might be a bit of an eejit, but she earns her own money and she can spend it however the fuck she wants. It's no one else's business.'

'That smug mummy is such a wagon,' Katrina said, sloshing more wine into her glass.

'Yep. Miranda's right. She's a fucking bitch!'

'Miranda's always right,' Katrina said.

Lesley smiled as she bit into a slice of pizza. This was going to be a piece of piss.

They both cheered at the end as Carrie skipped down

the street in her brand-new Manolos, bought and paid for by the shoe-shaming mom.

'Ah, that was lovely,' Lesley sighed. 'A morality tale for our times. Right,' she said, getting up from the sofa. 'I'll get another bottle, and you cue up the next one.'

When she had opened another bottle of red and poured them both big glasses, she curled up on the sofa and Katrina hit play on the remote control.

'Aw, I love seeing Miranda and Steve so happy together,' Lesley said as 'The Ick Factor' started.

'They're the best couple,' Katrina murmured before falling into a rapt silence as Miranda proposed to her boyfriend over three-dollar beers.

'Now *that's* what I call romantic,' Lesley said. 'It's much more authentic than some contrived mushy bullshit.'

'Miranda's so cool,' Katrina said.

'I bet Tom would love if you proposed to him like that.'

Katrina turned to her. 'Do you think so?'

'Totally.'

'You know, sometimes lately I get the feeling that he's building up to ask me.'

'Do you want him to?'

'Of course. I just wish he'd hurry up and come out with it. I think it's stressing him out.'

'Then why wait for him to do the asking? Be like Miranda. Don't you want to be a modern woman in charge of her own destiny?'

'Well ... yeah.' Katrina took a sip of her wine. 'But I'd kind of like a nice ring too. If I propose to Tom, I won't get a ring, will I?'

'I'm sure he'd buy you a ring anyway.'

'And what if he didn't say yes? It'd be mortifying.'

'Of course he'd say yes. He's nuts about you. But he's so shy. If you have to wait for him to get up the nerve to ask you, you might be walking down the aisle with a Zimmer frame.'

Katrina smiled. 'I don't know ...'

But there was a gleam in her eye, and Lesley could tell the idea was already taking hold.

17

S tella sang along to the music playing in her earphones as she kneaded her bread dough vigorously, trying to focus on the task at hand and ignore the fluttering in her stomach. She'd been fidgety and on edge all day, ever since Peter had announced that Rafe was in town and he'd invited him over for dinner.

'You don't have to cook,' he'd added quickly, perhaps picking up on her anxiety. 'We'll go out, or order something in.'

'No, let's stay in,' she'd said. It was easier to stick to Peter's diet if they ate at home, and, besides, she was happy to throw herself into menu planning and cooking to take her mind off fretting about meeting Rafe. While it would be nice to get to know at least one member of the family before she was thrown in at the deep end with them all in Nice, the cowardly part of her just wanted to put it off for as long as possible.

So she concentrated on kneading and chopping, stirring and tasting, and pumped up the music in her earphones to drown out the negative thoughts that were trying to nudge their way in. Peter's sons were bound to be suspicious about her motives for marrying their father. Would Rafe have already made up his mind about her, or would he give her the benefit of the doubt? It would be unbearable if they couldn't get along.

Damn it! As she found her mind straying again, she turned up the volume on her iPod and blasted Lady Gaga in her ears. She forgot her anxiety as she danced around the kitchen, singing along to 'Just Dance' as she took a perfectly risen tray of multigrain rolls out of the warming drawer and slid them into the oven. As the song came to an end, she raised her arms above her head, and gave one last full-body shimmy as she spun around – and froze.

Rafe was leaning in the doorway watching her, arms folded, the hint of an amused smile playing around his lips.

'Oh! Hi!' Crap! How long had he been standing there? She felt her face heat up as she pulled out the earphones, already feeling at a disadvantage. She'd wanted to be calm and poised when they met, and instead she felt flustered and guilty, as if he'd caught her doing something wrong.

'Sorry. I didn't mean to sneak up on you.'

'I didn't hear you come in.' She indicated the earphones dangling from the pocket of her jeans. 'Have you ... been here long?'

'Just since the second verse.' He smiled crookedly as he shifted away from the doorframe. 'Hi, I'm Rafe,' he said, extending a hand as he moved towards her.

Stella wiped her hands on her apron. 'Stella,' she said. 'Lovely to meet you.'

'Likewise.' His hand was warm and dry as it clasped hers firmly, and he had the sweetest smile that softened his features and creased up the corners of his sea-green eyes. She was familiar with his ruggedly handsome face from movies and magazines, but up close in real life, the full impact of his square-jawed masculine beauty hit her like a physical force that took her breath away. At six foot, Stella wasn't used to men towering over her, but Rafe was so big and broad, he almost made her feel petite.

'Well, dinner's nearly ready,' she said, waving at the stove behind her.

'Need any help?'

'No, thanks. Peter's in the living room. Why don't you go in and say hello, and I'll be with you shortly.'

She sighed with relief when he was gone, glad to have a moment alone to regroup. She didn't really need to spend any more time tossing the salad or watching the bread rolls bake, but she needed to catch her breath. Rafe taking her by surprise like that had left her feeling off balance. So she spent a few more minutes fiddling with things until she was ready to face him again.

'THIS LOOKS GREAT,' Rafe said as they sat down to eat. She had made a pear and walnut salad to start, served with the rolls still warm from the oven.

'Stella's a wonderful cook.' Peter smiled at her proudly. He poured Rafe a glass of wine and set the bottle back on the table.

'You're not having any?' Rafe asked, looking between Peter and Stella.

'No, we don't drink. We're teetotallers!' Peter told him with a delighted grin, like he was delivering the punchline to the most marvellous joke.

'Really?' Rafe raised his eyebrows.

'Don't worry, I haven't had some road to Damascus-style epiphany. It's doctor's orders.'

'So what's your excuse?' Rafe asked Stella. 'Recovering alcoholic? Mormon?'

'No,' Peter said, 'the darling girl's gone out in solidarity.'

'It's fine,' Stella said. 'I don't miss it, and I'm better off without it anyway.'

'Well, I suppose congratulations are in order,' Rafe said, raising his glass.

'Thanks,' Stella said shyly as she and Peter clinked their glasses of sparkling water against his.

'This is really good,' Rafe said as they ate.

'And it's healthy too!' Peter said. 'Stella's so clever.' He turned to her. 'You should have your own cooking show.'

'Hardly!' Stella laughed.

'You should,' Rafe said, smiling at her. 'Just you, cooking and dancing. I'd watch.'

Stella blushed and stood up to start clearing away the starter plates, glad of the excuse to escape to the kitchen for a while.

'SO, WHEN'S THE BIG DAY?' Rafe asked as Stella served the main course – a Mediterranean fish stew, fragrant with herbs and garlic, accompanied by new potatoes.

'We haven't set a date yet,' Peter said.

'Well, there's no rush, is there? You've got plenty of time.'

'I'm not sure that's true for me, dear boy,' Peter chuckled. 'Although the way this one looks after me,' he said, nodding at Stella, 'I'll probably outlive the lot of you.'

'We're thinking about September,' Stella said.

'Yes, if we can work out the logistics,' Peter said. 'Obviously, we want the whole family to be there, so we have to see when we can round everyone up.'

'Well, I'll be around. Shooting doesn't start until October.'

Stella knew that Rafe's next project was being filmed at Ardmore Studios and on location in Dublin.

Rafe glanced at his father. 'Actually, I've decided to move back to Dublin permanently. I'm going to get stuck into house-hunting as soon as I get back from Nice.'

'Oh, that's marvellous news!' Peter beamed. 'Well, you must stay here with us while you're looking. Mustn't he?' He looked to Stella for confirmation.

'Yes, of course.' She smiled to cover her consternation. She wasn't entirely comfortable with the idea of having Rafe at such close quarters in the long-term. She felt safe in her little bubble with Peter, and anything that threatened to pierce it seemed a bit scary.

'Well, if you're sure I wouldn't be intruding?' Rafe looked between his father and Stella.

'Of course not. There's loads of room here, and we'd love to have you. And Francesca too, of course,' Peter added a little uncertainly. 'It is still Francesca, isn't it?' he asked with a frown.

Rafe shook his head. 'Francesca and I split up.'

'Oh. Sorry to hear that,' Peter said, not appearing at all surprised. Rafe was notorious for hooking up with his co-stars on whatever project he was working on at the time, but the relationships didn't tend to last much beyond the shooting schedule.

Rafe shrugged. 'It's fine.'

'What happened?'

'She found out she was pregnant.'

'Oh!' Peter reared back in his seat in shock. 'Well, that's ...'

'It's not mine,' Rafe said quickly. 'Turns out she was sleeping with her agent for ages. But he's doing the decent thing now and leaving his wife for her.' He drained his glass, reached for the wine bottle and poured himself another.

'Oh. Is that the decent thing?' Peter asked.

'Francesca thinks so.' Rafe smiled crookedly. 'I doubt his wife would agree.'

'Well, you certainly don't seem too cut up about it.'

'Fair play to her,' he said. 'She always wanted kids.'

'And you didn't?' Stella asked, regretting the words as soon as they were out of her mouth. It was too personal. She'd only just met Rafe.

He looked at her in silence for a moment. 'Not with her,' he said finally.

'Wait,' Peter frowned, 'didn't you and Francesca have the same agent?'

'Not anymore. There's a limit to my forbearance.' Rafe grinned with relish.

'Good for you! Hit him where it hurts, eh?'

'Right in the heart of his fifteen percent.'

Peter laughed. 'Still, it's a pity she won't be coming to Nice. I thought she could be a friend for Stella.'

'Yes,' Rafe said, his eyes flicking to Stella, 'you could have arranged a play date for them.'

So he was going to be like that about it, Stella thought, her heart sinking. But Peter *had* made her sound like a child he needed to keep amused.

Peter gave his son an admonishing look. 'It'd be nice for Stella to have another girl her own age around.'

Girl. She cringed at Peter's use of the infantilising word. But *of course* that was how he thought of her. She was in the same age bracket as his sons, after all – his *boys*.

'Anyway, Lesley will be there now,' Peter said brightly.

'Lesley?' Rafe frowned.

'Al's girlfriend,' Peter told him.

'That's new.'

Peter nodded. 'We had lunch with them last week. She's lovely.'

'What about Mum?' Rafe asked. 'When's she coming out?'

Peter hesitated, throwing Stella a cautious glance. 'I'm not sure she's going to make it this year,' he said casually.

Rafe raised his eyebrows. 'That's a shame.' His eyes flicked to Stella.

'Yes, such a pity,' she said, lifting her chin. 'I was looking forward to meeting her.'

She excused herself to get dessert, hoping they'd have moved on from the subject of Jane when she returned. She was lying when she said she'd been looking forward to meeting her. She'd been shocked to discover there was any question of her joining them in France, and hugely relieved that she was probably choosing to stay away. She knew she'd have to meet Jane some time – as the mother of Peter's children, she would always be part of his family – but she was in no rush for it to happen.

She didn't know if Peter had said something to Rafe, but there was no more mention of Jane when she returned to the dining room. She relaxed as they ate grilled peaches with honey and yoghurt, and the conversation turned to the neutral topic of the Dublin property market.

STELLA WAS surprised when Rafe came into the kitchen as she was stacking the dishwasher and suggested going to the pub for a nightcap.

'Oh.' She straightened. 'What about Peter? Is he coming?'

'No, I'm not,' Peter said, coming into the kitchen carrying a handful of dishes, 'but you should go, darling.

It'd do you good to get out. And you can have a proper drink without worrying about making me jealous.'

She had to admit, it *would* be nice to go out for a change.

'Okay, then. I suppose we could just go for one,' she said.

'Just the one!' Peter laughed, shaking his head. 'God, I miss that.'

'You could come,' Stella said. 'One drink wouldn't do you any harm.'

He shook his head. 'I've never had just one drink in my life, and I'm not sure I'm up to learning new tricks at this stage. Best not chance it.'

'Okay, then,' Stella said. She was nervous about being alone with Rafe, but if he was making an effort to be friendly, she wasn't going to do anything to discourage him.

'Besides,' Peter said, 'it'll give you two a chance to get to know each other. As long as you don't take the opportunity to tell Stella what a terrible old reprobate I am and warn her off,' he added to Rafe.

'She hardly needs me to tell her that,' Rafe said. 'A quick Google search would give her enough reason to run for the hills, if she's so inclined.'

'Which I'm not.' Stella smiled at Peter. 'Just let me finish clearing up this lot and I'll go get changed.

'You go,' Peter said. 'I'll finish up in here.'

Stella ran upstairs and quickly changed out of her jeans and T-shirt. They were only going down the road to the local pub, so she didn't need to get dressed up, but she didn't want to wear the clothes she'd been cooking in all day. She threw on a short green shift dress that showed off her long, tanned legs, tied a matching scarf in her hair and touched up her make-up.

'You look gorgeous, darling,' Peter said when she came downstairs.

Rafe said nothing, but she saw the admiration in his eyes and felt a little gleam of triumph. Rafe wasn't going to be a problem, she decided. He was a man, after all. Even if he was unsure about her, she could get him on her side. Sometimes she forgot what potent weapons she had at her disposal. This face, this body – their power could still sometimes catch her by surprise.

18

It was a short walk downhill to the local pub. Some of Stella's confidence drained away as soon as Rafe pushed open the door and they were greeted with a wall of noise, the background hum of conversation punctuated by shrieks of laughter and the tinkle of glass. A group of five or six burly young men hugged the corner of the bar, pints of beer clutched in their fists. Stella felt their eyes flick towards her as she passed, and wished she hadn't changed out of her jeans after all. She instinctively shrank into herself a little and clung closer to Rafe as he led them through the crush.

'Are you okay?' He frowned down at her.

'Yes, fine.' She smiled reassuringly at him to disguise her discomfort. 'It's just a bit noisy in here. I guess I'm not used to it – I haven't been out in a while.'

Rafe glanced at the group of men and guided Stella to a table at the back.

'What'll you have?' he asked as she settled onto the squashy sofa.

Stella had planned to just have mineral water, but now

she decided it would be a good idea to have a proper drink to take the edge off. 'I'd love a Rusty Nail. Do you have that here?'

Rafe shrugged. 'I'm sure it can be arranged.'

When Rafe went to the bar, Stella glanced across at the group of lads. They were turned away now, talking loudly among themselves. They were perfectly harmless, she realised – just a bunch of friends in high spirits enjoying a night out together. They weren't paying the slightest attention to her.

Rafe returned with their drinks and sat beside her on the sofa instead of taking one of the chairs opposite.

'Well, cheers!' He lifted his glass.

Stella knocked her glass against his, then took a sip of her cocktail, feeling the warmth of it spread through her. It was delicious, the perfect ratio of Drambuie to whiskey. It had been a long time since she'd had a proper drink, so she should be careful. It'd probably go straight to her head when she was so out of practice.

'Good?' Rafe asked.

'Really good. Thank you.'

'You do drink, then.'

'Yes, but not around Peter. I was never a big drinker anyway, so it's not hard for me. It's not so easy for him.'

'Yeah, drinking was pretty much his favourite thing. He was good at it, too.'

'Well, it's hardly a talent,' Stella said.

'No, but … he was never morose or belligerent with it. He really enjoyed it. And no matter how messy it got, he never regretted any of it.' A shadow passed across his face. 'Well, almost never. It wasn't so much fun for Mum.'

'Maybe she should have joined in more, shared his life.'

'With two young kids? Someone had to be the grown-up. She was stuck with looking after me and Scott.'

'I'm sure she doesn't regret being a good mother.'

'No, but maybe she resents being pushed into that life – not having a real choice.'

'She must have known what he was like. He was the man she married.'

'He's the man *you're* marrying.'

'Not really. He's changed. I'm marrying a teetotaller, remember.'

'A retired drunk,' Rafe said. 'It's not quite the same thing. A man old enough to be your grandfather.'

'And I'm perfectly aware of that. I know what I'm getting into.' Stella took a sip of her drink, looking at him thoughtfully. Then she put her glass down and took a deep breath. 'I hope you don't mind,' she said, facing him squarely.

'Mind?'

'About me marrying your father.'

'I'm not thrilled about it, to be honest.'

'Oh.' Her face fell.

'You did ask,' he said without a hint of apology.

'Yes, I did.'

'Look, it's nothing personal.'

Stella gave a bitter little laugh. 'If that's not personal, I don't know what is.'

'It's not about you. I don't even know you. But look at it from our point of view. Dad's old, rich and has a dodgy heart. You're young and … gorgeous,' he said, his eyes lingering on her face. 'We've all seen this movie.'

Stella couldn't help the thrill of pleasure that spread through her at the compliment.

'You could have any man you want,' Rafe finished.

'What makes you think I don't? Is it so hard to believe I could want to be with your father for himself?'

'Don't get me wrong; I know what a charmer Dad can be when he wants to be. But for someone like you—'

'Someone like me?' She bristled. 'You just said yourself you don't know me at all.'

'Someone so young is all I meant. I don't see the appeal of tying yourself to an old man.'

'Apart from money, of course.'

'It's an old story.'

'Well, if that's what you all think, there's probably nothing I can say to convince you otherwise.'

'Oh, I don't know.' Rafe grinned. 'You could call off the wedding.'

She shook her head. 'Not going to happen. Sorry.'

'Ah well.' He shrugged. 'It was worth a shot.'

Stella smiled nervously. 'I'd like if we could be friends, Rafe.'

'If you marry Dad, we'll be a lot more than that. You'll be my stepmother.' He tossed back a slug of whiskey. 'I hope you're not going to be wicked.'

'It depends how much of a brat you are to me,' she said with a smirk.

'Seriously, though, all this might seem fine for a while – playing at Darby and Joan, having long walks on the beach and quiet nights in. But what about when the novelty wears off?'

'That's what you're worried about? That I'll get bored?'

He shrugged. 'It's not much of a life for a woman your age.'

'It suits me. I was never much of a party girl anyway. There's nothing I want that I can't have with Peter.'

'And what's that?' he asked softly. 'What do you want?'

'Same as anyone really,' she said. 'A good life.'

Rafe gave her a knowing look.

'A *happy* life,' she amended. 'I'm not talking about money.'

'You could have that with someone your own age.'

'Maybe. But Peter's the one I found. I didn't go looking for this, you know – it just happened. And yes,' she rushed on, 'I know that maybe he wouldn't be marrying me at all if he hadn't had that health scare. I get that. But he *did*, so ... here we are.'

Rafe was silent for a moment, staring into his drink. Then he looked up at her. 'What if you *were* talking about money?'

'What?' She frowned. 'I'm not!'

Rafe heaved a sigh and leaned forward, running a hand through his thick, dark hair. 'But say you were,' he said, turning to Stella. She opened her mouth to speak, but he held up a hand to silence her. 'Just humour me for a moment. If it *was* a question of money—'

Surely he wasn't calling her a gold-digger to her face? Stella couldn't believe he'd be so upfront about it. She must be mistaken. 'It's nothing to do with money!'

'Just hear me out. There's no need to act all outraged. You must know it's what everyone will think.'

She felt herself turning red. No wonder he'd wanted to get her alone. So much for being friends! 'They can think what they like. It's not true. Peter and I want to be together, and I don't care what anyone else thinks. It's none of their business.'

'What about his family? Don't you care what we think?'

'Well, you can sleep easy if that's what you're worried about.'

Rafe picked up his glass, looking down at it as he swirled the whiskey around thoughtfully. 'So if I were to offer you money and you could walk away right now a rich woman ... a rich *single* woman ...' He left the question hanging as he drained his drink with a rattle of ice cubes.

'You can't be serious! You're actually saying you'd pay me off? Give me money to ditch Peter and disappear?'

'I wouldn't think badly of you for taking it,' he said. 'We're all very grateful to you for everything you've done for Dad. Why shouldn't you get something out of it?'

She frowned. 'I didn't do it in the hope of some cash reward.'

'Nevertheless, there's no reason why you shouldn't be compensated. I'm talking about a substantial sum of money. Granted, not as much as you'd stand to get if you were married. But enough that you wouldn't need to work again. And you'd be free to do as you please. No ties, no obligations.'

Stella was stunned. He was actually completely serious – and just for a second she was tempted. But only for a second. Because it was the ties and obligations that she wanted. She wasn't marrying Peter for his money, no matter what anyone thought. Of course, there was no denying it would be nice to be rich. But that was just the icing on the cake. There were things she wanted from this marriage that couldn't be bought – family, roots, a sense of belonging; someone she could depend on to be there for her.

'So what would you say to me if I were to make you an offer like that? Not that I am, mind. Just hypothetically …'

'Hypothetically, I'd tell you to shove it,' Stella said with a little smile, suddenly feeling very calm. There was really nothing Rafe could say to shake her because she wasn't in the wrong here – he was, and he knew it.

'Don't you even want to know how much?' he asked.

Stella couldn't help being curious, but she couldn't

admit to Rafe that she had the slightest interest in his offer, not even academically.

'I'm not bluffing,' he said, 'in case you think this is some kind of perverse test of your integrity.'

Stella shrugged. 'Same answer,' she said, and took a sip of her drink, burying her face in the glass to hide her smile. She was enjoying thwarting Rafe. She got the feeling it didn't happen often.

'Oh well, can't blame a guy for trying,' he said, smiling ruefully. 'No hard feelings?'

19

A week later, Rafe's outlandish offer didn't seem so easy to dismiss. It was a balmy July evening as Stella sat after dinner with Peter, his brother Michael, his sister-in-law Joy, and his ex-wife Jane in the garden of the Villa Aurore. Cicadas chirped gently in the trees, and the scent of thyme and wild lavender perfumed the night air. The conversation flowed as they passed a bottle of wine around the table and idly nibbled on cheese and fruit from a large platter at its centre.

Peter's family were entertaining company, and Stella enjoyed listening to them as their stories fed into each other, weaving together seamlessly into the tapestry of their shared history. They were charming and witty, and their obvious affection and happiness at being together was endearing. But she couldn't help feeling left out, and if Rafe were to repeat his proposition to her right now, she might actually be tempted to take the money and run.

It wasn't their fault, and she knew they didn't mean to exclude her. Michael and Joy had been warm and welcoming, and even Jane, whose arrival this morning she had dreaded, had been surprisingly friendly and pleasant – albeit with a hint of effort. Joy had been especially kind, and had gone out of her way to put Stella at ease and make her feel like one of the family. But sometimes it was almost as if they'd forgotten she was there as they talked around her, swapping memories she didn't share, and drawing on a frame of reference she couldn't access. She did wonder at times if Jane was doing it on purpose, harping on their shared history to highlight her outsider status. But she told herself she was being paranoid. Jane and Peter were friends now, nothing more. It was only natural that they'd talk about old times when they got together.

Peter wasn't much help, seeming oblivious to her discomfort. Happy to have an audience, he went into performance mode at every opportunity, hogging the limelight and falling into what was clearly a well-worn double act with Jane as soon as she arrived, the two of them in perfect harmony, as if singing from a hymn sheet only they could see.

So she was looking forward to Al and Lesley arriving in the next couple of days. It would be nice not to be the only new girl in town.

'You should try this,' Peter said to her now, pointing to a wedge of pale crumbly cheese threaded with blue veins. 'It's fantastic.'

'No, thanks.' Stella shook her head.

'Don't deny yourself on my account,' he said. 'I promise I won't be jealous. I've had more than my fair share of this stuff in my time.'

But Stella steadfastly refused. 'Really, I'm fine,' she said. She knew it must be hard for Peter to deprive himself when he was surrounded by such indulgence, and she thought the least she could do was keep him company.

Meals at the villa were a minefield of rich patés and fatty rillettes, oozing cheeses and buttery patisserie, and baguettes spread thickly with pale, unsalted butter – all accompanied by seemingly bottomless jugs of pastis and bottles of rosé. She had gone into Nice as soon as they'd arrived and spent the afternoon stocking up on legumes and grains, and had taken over cooking for her and Peter. While the rest of them sat around after dinner picking at cheese as they constantly topped up their glasses, she and Peter grazed on grapes and nuts, and drank sparkling mineral water, limiting themselves to the occasional single glass of wine with the meal.

'You two are putting us all to shame,' Michael said as he cut himself a thick wodge of brie.

'Oh God, don't say that,' Peter said. 'I have no wish to be some sort of poster child for asceticism.'

'I don't think you need to worry about that, you old reprobate.' Jane laughed. 'You have way too much ground to make up before anyone would look to you as a paragon of healthy living.'

'I'm very glad to hear it.'

'It's paid off, though,' Joy said. 'You look really well, Peter.'

'You do.' Michael nodded. 'Better than you ever looked before you had the heart attack, if you ask me.'

'Well, that's entirely down to Stella,' Peter said, smiling at her. 'I'm sure I'd have been back to my old ways long before now if it weren't for her.' He put an arm around her and squeezed her shoulder affectionately. 'She has the patience of a saint and takes exceptional care of me. She can even make gerbil food taste good.'

'Well, I take my hat off to you,' Jane said to Stella, doffing an imaginary cap. 'Remember that time we all tried to go macrobiotic?' she said to the others.

'God, yes!' Peter hooted. 'We lasted all of about ten days.' He turned to Stella. 'It was the seventies. Everyone was doing it at the time. It was the clean eating of our day.'

'I made you that awful birthday cake,' Jane said. 'A wholegrain brick with a few strawberries on top as a concession to the occasion.'

Peter chuckled. 'I think we used it in the foundations of our extension in the end, didn't we?'

'Well, it certainly wasn't worth eating.'

'And then Monty came over for dinner, and when he saw what we were having, he stormed off in the most frightful huff and came back with a massive Chinese for everyone, and insisted we eat that instead.'

'We didn't take much persuading, as I remember,' Michael said.

'Nothing has ever tasted as good before or since as those pork ribs.' Peter licked his lips.

'And that was the end of our macrobiotic phase,' Jane said. 'We never looked back.'

'Good old Monty,' Michael said. 'I haven't seen him in years. I wonder what he's up to now?'

'I bumped into him not long ago outside Leicester Square tube,' Jane said. 'The last time I was in London. He and Jules have split up.'

'Oh no, when did that happen?'

And they were off again, howling over some anecdote about Jules and Monty's riotous wedding reception. Stella had no idea who Monty was, and she tried to appear content and relaxed as they batted stories back and forth about him. But she felt out of place again, and she was relieved when Joy touched her arm and asked if she'd help her with the coffee.

She nodded gratefully, glad of the chance to escape. The others hardly seemed to notice as they got up and excused themselves, and Stella followed Joy into the cool of the kitchen.

'I hope you're not feeling too out of it,' Joy said to her kindly, as she spooned coffee into the machine. 'Honestly, sometimes when that lot get together, they forget there's anyone else around, and that some of us haven't been Bradshaws for the last hundred years.'

'I'm fine,' Stella said with a grateful smile.

'I came late to the party, so I know what it's like,' Joy said. 'When they start talking about the good old days, they get carried away, and I think they sometimes forget that we weren't all part of it. I mean, I have no idea who this Monty character is that they're all talking about.'

'Oh good.' Stella laughed. 'I thought it was just me.'

Joy shook her head ruefully. 'And we weren't all macro-biotic in the seventies, were we? I wasn't for one. Goodness —' she put a hand to her chest '—you wouldn't have even been born then, would you?'

'No.' Stella shook her head, a little taken aback by this stark reminder of just how significant the age gap was between her and Peter.

'But they don't mean anything by it,' Joy said. 'They're just so happy to get together, they sometimes forget their manners.'

Stella smiled, relaxing. Joy was so nice. It must have been hard for her to join this family, taking the place of a much loved wife, sister and mother, perhaps wondering if they all resented her for it. 'It is a bit … intimidating,' she admitted.

'Well, don't let it get to you.' Joy smiled sympathetically, switching on the machine. She took cups and saucers from the cupboard. 'You'll be fine. It just takes a bit of time. Don't worry, you'll find your feet soon enough.'

'Thanks, Joy.'

'You've been really good for Peter. We can all see that, and we're very grateful to you for it.'

Stella felt her eyes welling up. 'Thank you,' she said.

She helped Joy load up a tray with cups, coffee and milk, and they took it outside. Peter was mid-anecdote, and didn't even break his flow as she took her place beside him, just flashing a wide smile at her. But she felt better after her chat with Joy in the kitchen, less of an outsider already. She had something to contribute and she'd earned her place in this family. They all loved Peter, and she saw that they valued and appreciated what she'd done for him. She may not be able to share in their reminiscences, but they would make new memories together that they'd share next year and all the years in the future. As she watched them chatting and laughing, she found herself looking forward to becoming a Bradshaw.

20

L esley loved hanging around the airport, and she was delighted that Al had no objection to setting off far earlier than necessary on Saturday morning for their eleven o'clock flight. She liked to have plenty of time to relax over a leisurely breakfast and have a wander around the shops.

'But I thought you didn't like shopping,' Al said.

'The airport is different. It's got the novelty factor, and I like the limited options. It focuses the mind.'

They went for breakfast after going through security, and Lesley kicked off the holiday with a full Irish. They split up for a trawl through duty-free, and met up again in the airport lounge, where they waited for Scott, who was on the same flight, to join them.

'Here he comes,' Al said, glancing behind her. He stood to wave his cousin over.

Lesley looked around and felt a strange shock of recognition as she saw Scott Bradshaw walking towards them. It was disorientating and slightly surreal. He was so familiar, she almost felt like she already knew him, and yet at the same time she experienced a little rush of fan-girl excitement that it was actually him. Lean and tanned, he was casually dressed in jeans and a figure-hugging T-shirt that showed off his toned upper body. He carried a large duffel bag slung over one shoulder as he weaved between the tables.

'Aloysius!' he said loudly, grinning as he pulled Al into an enthusiastic hug, with lots of mutual back-slapping. 'Great to see you,' he said, with a final clap of Al's shoulder.

He turned to Lesley then with a broad smile, and she felt a little off balance as he turned the full force of his charisma on her. He had a warm, expressive face, and kind, soulful eyes that made him look wise beyond his years – or maybe she was just confusing him with the ancient, world-weary vampire he played on TV.

'And who's this?' He slid onto the banquette beside Lesley, so close their legs were touching. 'Are you the lady who's going to be my new mummy?' he asked her in a childish voice.

Al cleared his throat as he sat back down opposite. 'No, your dad and Stella are already in Nice – they went out last week. This is Lesley.'

'Oh?' Scott didn't even glance at Al, but kept looking at her with blatant curiosity, a cheeky smile twisting the corners of his mouth.

'I'm with Al,' Lesley explained.

'Yes. Lesley, this is my cousin, Scott.'

'Pleased to meet you,' Scott said. Lesley gave him her hand to shake, and he held onto it far longer than was appropriate. 'So you two are ...'

'We're together, yes,' Al said in a tight voice.

'Ah!' Scott finally released Lesley's hand. 'I should have known.' He tilted his head to the side, looking Lesley over like she was a horse he was considering buying. 'You do have a slight look of Tits Maguire about you.'

Lesley had just taken a sip of her coffee, and almost spat it over the table.

'For God's sake, Scott!' Al protested, rolling his eyes.

'Sorry, should I not have mentioned Tits?' Scott said with an innocent air, belied by the mischievous glint in his eye. 'Have you not told Lesley about her?'

'Why on earth would I tell her about—'

'Well, it's not like it's something you have to hide. I mean, we all have a past, don't we?'

'Who the hell is she anyway?' Lesley asked.

'She was Al's first love,' Scott said with a wistful sigh. 'It was quite the romance. She was the first girl in our crowd to get a proper set of ti—' He broke off abruptly as Al shot him a furious look. 'She was the first young lady of our acquaintance to ... fill out,' he amended, miming cupping two huge imaginary breasts in his hands. 'Is that delicate enough for your genteel sensibilities, Miss Bennet?' he said to Al.

'No,' Al said flatly.

Scott ignored him, turning to Lesley. 'What I'm trying to say is the girl was stacked.'

'Yep, your little mime there was very subtle, but I managed to get the gist.'

'She had a rack like you wouldn't believe, Lesley.'

'Understood.'

'I hardly need tell you it didn't escape Al's notice. He was on that faster than you could say "tits ahoy". Well, I'm sure *you* know what he's like. He can't help himself. It's just the way God made him.'

Lesley couldn't help laughing.

'Please shut up, Scott,' Al said, surging to his feet. 'Can I get you something? Coffee? Gobstopper?'

'I'd love a coffee – a large Americano, and a blueberry muffin if they have one.'

'Right. I'll be back in a moment.' Al hovered, seeming reluctant to leave.

'We'll just talk amongst ourselves,' Scott said with a sly grin. 'Won't we, Lesley?'

'I'm sorry,' Al said to her. 'Please ignore him, and don't pay any attention to a word he says. He's just showing off. He's always like this with new people, but he'll calm down after a couple of months.' With that Al stormed off to the buffet counter.

'How long has this been going on with you and Al?' Scott asked her when he was gone.

'Not long. Only a couple of months.'

Al returned with coffee and a muffin for Scott, and sat down again at the table.

'So, how did you two meet?' Scott asked with a winning smile as he ripped open a sachet of sugar. 'Tell me everything. I'm a sucker for romance. Was it love at first sight?'

'Not exactly,' Lesley said.

'It was for me,' Al said, smiling at her.

Scott rolled his eyes exaggeratedly. 'Well, of course it was for you, Aloysius! I don't need to ask why Lesley here caught your eye. But what was it about young Aloysius here that got your juices flowing, Lesley?'

Lesley glanced at Al. 'Well, he's very handsome, obviously.'

'Obviously.'

'But I think what sealed the deal was that Al really likes women.'

'Don't we all, darling?' Scott gave her a lascivious grin.

'No, I mean he *likes* women. He's interested in talking to them and he pays attention. He didn't just ogle my chest all night and look at me like I was a piece of meat.'

She was glad to see that Al looked pleased by this.

'Well played, Al!' Scott drawled, holding his hand up for a high-five. He dropped it again when Al resolutely ignored it. 'Anyway, good for you. I didn't know you were bringing anyone.'

'It was kind of last minute. We haven't been going out long.'

Scott sighed. 'I've always wanted to have a whirlwind romance. Unless a quick knee-trembler by the bins round the back of The Ivy counts?'

'It doesn't,' Al said flatly.

'Even if it was Valentine's Day?'

'Was it with Louis?'

'No.'

'Then definitely not. Is he coming out to Nice later?'

Scott shook his head. 'No. I think we're finished.'

'Oh. Sorry. I liked Louis.'

'So did I.' Scott looked morose for a moment, but quickly brightened up again. 'Ah well, plenty more totty in the Mediterranean Sea. I'll just pick someone up on the beach.'

Lesley couldn't help thinking he didn't look very happy about it, despite his cheerful tone.

'Talking of romance, have you met my new stepmum-to-be?' Scott asked Al. 'Is she a total nightmare? Bitch on wheels? Come on, dish.'

'She seems nice enough, at least on the surface. Dad got an investigator to do a bit of checking into her background, but he hasn't turned up anything.'

'Nothing dodgy?'

'Nothing at all. Which is suspicious in itself.'

'Well, if all else fails, I could always step up.'

'And by "step up", you mean ...?'

Scott just grinned in response, and stuffed a chunk of muffin in his mouth.

Al raised his eyebrows. 'Your father's fiancée? You'd try and seduce her?'

'Jesus!' Scott rolled his eyes. 'We're not in a costume drama. But yeah, basically.' He shrugged. 'I'm single now. I could hook up with her – take one for the team.'

'That wouldn't exactly be great for family relations,' Al said.

'What makes you so sure you could do that anyway?' Lesley asked him.

'Lesley!' He reared back in mock horror, clutching his heart dramatically. 'You've been in my company now for —' he checked his watch '—almost half an hour. I'm wounded that you can still ask me that.'

Lesley rolled her eyes.

'I'm irresistible to women. Can't you tell?' Then suddenly his grin vanished and he shot her an intense intimate look that went straight to her groin.

'Don't you smoulder at me,' she said crossly, feeling herself flush. Damn him!

'Worked, though, didn't it?' He grinned happily.

'Feck off! Anyway, aren't you supposed to be gay?' she huffed, feeling flustered.

'I go wherever the wind takes me. I'm not averse to dipping my toe in female waters occasionally.'

Al gave him a sceptical look.

'Okay, not my toe,' he said.

'Right.'

'And not waters.'

'We get it, thanks,' Lesley said. 'We know what you dip where.'

Scott laughed, scrunching up the muffin wrapper and tossing it in the centre of the table.

Al glanced at his watch. 'We'd better go to the gate.'

21

It was a beautiful sunny afternoon when they arrived in Nice, and Lesley felt her whole body decompress as soon as they stepped outside and the heat wrapped itself around her. She quickly relaxed into holiday mode as they piled into a taxi and bowled towards the centre of Nice. Looking out the window at the spiky palm trees framed against the inky sky, she thought smugly of the heavy grey clouds she'd left behind in Dublin, and felt very pleased with herself for taking Al up on his unorthodox offer. She'd taken a bit of a chance, and it had paid off big-time.

'Have you seen TV's Mr Darcy recently?' Scott asked Al.

'No. He was in Dublin last week, but I didn't see him. He had dinner with your dad and Stella.'

'He has news, apparently,' Scott said broodingly. 'You don't know what it is?'

'No.' Al shook his head. 'No idea.'

'It had better not be that they're making him the next Batman, or I'll shoot myself.'

Al laughed. 'Or James Bond,' he said. 'That'd be worse.'

Scott groaned, clutching his hair. 'Oh God, I hadn't even thought of that. Bloody Darcy was bad enough.' He gazed out the window disconsolately. 'Do you really think he could be in the running for James Bond, though? Isn't he a bit old?' he asked, turning to Al. 'I mean, they'd want to get a few movies out of him.'

Al shrugged. 'He's only thirty-three. Roger Moore was way older when he started.'

'Too Irish, then?'

'Pierce Brosnan,' Al and Lesley said together, and laughed.

'And his English accent is brilliant,' Lesley pointed out. 'You'd never have known he was Irish in *Pride and Prejudice*.'

'Whose side are you on?' Scott scowled at her.

'Oh. I didn't know there were sides. Sorry.'

'I mean, how come *I* never get asked to play Darcy?' Scott said peevishly.

Lesley glanced across at him. 'Too short?' she said tentatively. She didn't want to offend him, but it seemed pretty obvious to her.

'Exactly,' Scott said. 'It's discrimination! Casting directors have no bloody imagination. I can totally play tall.'

In the centre of town, they turned away from the coast road and curved up a steep, tree-lined hill. They stopped on a quiet, leafy street in front of a set of wrought-iron gates set in a yellow ochre wall. A riot of deep-pink bougainvillea cascaded over the top, almost obscuring the keypad and a little plaque beside it that read 'Villa Aurore'.

Al paid the driver, and he and Scott took the bags between them as they were unloaded from the boot. Scott punched in a code and the gates opened to reveal a house that practically screamed summer, with sky-blue shutters at the windows and walls painted a sunny yellow.

A short middle-aged woman with cropped grey hair came around from the back of the house as they got to the door. She beamed warmly at them, throwing her arms open and hugging Al and Scott in turn.

'Lesley, this is my stepmum, Joy,' Al said, his eyes warm with pride and affection.

'Lovely to meet you, Lesley,' Joy said, as she led the way into the house. She had a kind, intelligent face and a sweet smile. 'Have you been to Nice before?'

'No, it's my first time.'

'Where is everyone?' Scott asked, dropping the bags in the hallway.

'Stella's gone into town. Michael and I are out by the pool with Jane, and TV's Mr Darcy is in the study with your father. He said he had some "business" to discuss,' she said, rolling her eyes. 'Another lecture about family responsibilities, I suspect.'

Scott threw back his head and laughed. 'He didn't waste any time!'

'Blimey!' Lesley said to Al. 'Isn't Rafe a bit old to be getting lectures from his dad?'

'Oh no, it's the other way around,' Al said. 'Rafe will be the one giving the lecture.'

'Oh!'

'Rafe's very alpha,' Scott whispered to her. 'We're all a bit scared of him.'

'Well, come and meet Dad,' Al said to Lesley, putting an arm around her shoulders.

It was a blazingly hot day, and as soon as they stepped outside, Lesley wished she'd had the chance to shower and change before meeting the rest of Al's family. She felt hot and clammy in the jeans and long-sleeved top she'd chosen

to travel in, hyperaware of her clothes clinging to her and
the trickle of sweat running down the back of her neck.
She could practically feel her hair turning to frizz already.

Jane was sitting on a swing seat beneath a large white
gazebo. Beside her, a heavy-set elderly man in a straw hat,
who Lesley presumed was Al's father, had nodded off over
a fat paperback that dangled limply in his hands.

Jane leapt up and hugged them all in turn. 'It's lovely
to see you again,' she said to Lesley. 'But I have a bone to
pick with you, young lady,' she whispered in her ear.

'Oh?'

'Later,' Jane said, side-eyeing Scott and Joy who were
nearby.

'Michael.' Joy gently nudged her husband awake. 'Al's
here.'

Al's father startled awake, blinking dazedly. He
collected himself as Al introduced Lesley, and smiled at her
warmly as they shook hands. He had a pleasant face – soft
and jowly, with a heavy smattering of freckles.

'It's a real thrill to meet you,' she told him.

'Me? Really?' Michael frowned in bemusement.

'Bradshaw Biscuits,' she explained. 'I'm a huge fan. I
consider the Chocolate Extravaganza one of the greatest
inventions of our time.'

'Well, that's very kind of you,' Michael said. 'I must
say, it's been very good to us.'

Just then, Peter came out onto the terrace, looking
rather harried, followed by Rafe – TV's Mr Darcy in the
flesh.

'Ah, you're here!' Peter's face lit up as he joined them.

Lesley couldn't help feeling a little star-struck as Al
introduced her to Rafe. She had to admit he was seriously
hot. With his square, stubbly jaw, thick black hair and
penetrating green eyes framed by long, sooty lashes, he

could have been a photofit of the quintessential romantic hero: the face that launched a thousand smutty fanfics. He didn't look quite so intimidating dressed in chino shorts and a pale-pink T-shirt, and without his trademark haughty scowl, but she still felt a sense of relief when he gave her a friendly smile as they shook hands.

The Bradshaws were so welcoming, and Lesley felt a little guilty for deceiving them as Peter pulled her into a hug. They were all touchingly pleased to be together, and soon everyone was babbling at once, talking over each other as they caught up on their news and remarked on how well Peter looked.

'Lesley!' Everyone turned to see Stella in the doorway to the garden, both hands full of shopping bags. She dropped them and raced across the terrace to throw her arms around Lesley. 'I'm so glad you're here!' Lesley was surprised but pleased that Stella seemed so excited to see her.

'Well, I expect you'd like to freshen up,' Al said to Lesley. 'Come on and I'll show you our room.'

AL SHOWED HER INTO A BRIGHT, airy room with pale wooden floorboards and walls painted a soft cornflower blue. Large shuttered windows opened onto a little railed balcony that ran along the back of the house, looking out over the pool and garden to the rooftops of the city beyond. He slung their bags onto a large wooden chest by the door, then joined her at the window, admiring the view. The family were still in the garden, gathered around the gazebo, and the sound of their voices drifted up.

'You can take the bed,' Al said in a low voice. 'I'll camp out on the floor.'

Lesley turned and looked at the bed properly for the

first time. It was vast. She didn't want to make Al sleep on the floor on his holidays, and they could easily share it without ever coming into contact with each other. 'No need for that,' she said.

'Are you sure?'

'Yeah, it's fine. You could fit the whole family in there. But we can make a pillow barrier down the middle, to be on the safe side.'

Lesley looked around the room. It was neat, and furnished with an eclectic mix of French shabby chic stuff and IKEA basics. A large bookcase stood in one corner, crammed with paperbacks. Her innate curiosity kicking in, she went over to study the rows of cracked and wrinkled spines, their colours faded in the sun. There were some generic thrillers, a small collection of classics and a few big bestsellers, alongside a couple of guides to the region and some well-thumbed French phrase books. But she was surprised to see a comprehensive set of Enid Blyton's Malory Towers novels, the complete *Twilight* series and all of Jilly Cooper's 'name' books.

'Oh, I loved these,' she said, pulling out *Harriet*, her favourite. 'I haven't read them in ages.' She flicked through the yellowed pages. It looked well read. 'So, this was your room?' she asked Al as she replaced it on the shelf.

'Mostly, yes. I shared with Scott sometimes if there were a lot of people staying.'

'Big fan of Enid Blyton, were you?' she asked, pulling out *First Term at Malory Towers* and waving it at him.

'Ah, an underrated modern classic,' he said, taking it from her. 'I longed to go to a boarding school like that – having midnight feasts, being on the lacrosse team and playing tricks on Mam'zelle.'

'But you did go to boarding school, didn't you?'

'Yes. But Harrow was quite a let-down after Malory Towers.'

'You've read all of these?' She ran a finger along the spines.

'At least once. That's Scott's influence. He said it would give us an insight into the female mind.'

'Huh! In other words, it would help you score with girls.'

'Exactly. He was all about the girls back then.'

'Did it work?' she asked.

'I bonded with my first girlfriend over our mutual admiration for Darrell Rivers,' he said with a smug smile.

'I was more of a *Harriet the Spy* girl myself.'

Al flicked through the pages of the book he was still holding, smiling down at it fondly. 'God, I'd forgotten how good this was. I might give it a re-read.' He snapped it closed. 'Well, you'd probably like to get freshened up. The bathroom's through here.' He opened the door to the en suite. 'I'll leave you to it,' he said when he'd given her towels, explained the shower controls and shown her the trick for adjusting the water temperature.

Lesley was dying to get out of her jeans and into something cooler. The weather in Dublin had been chilly for July, and she was wearing far too many clothes. As soon as he was gone, she locked the door and stripped off.

She felt much more human after a shower. She opened her suitcase and changed into a pair of cropped trousers and a loose sleeveless top, then slipped her feet into her cushiony thick-soled flip-flops.

She was usually pretty slobby about unpacking on holidays, only taking things out of her suitcase as and when she needed them. But as she'd be sharing with Al, she decided she should be on her best behaviour. So she unpacked completely, stowing her clothes in the wardrobe and drawers, and slid her empty suitcase under the bed. She was just finished when there was a knock on the door.

'You decent?' Al called.

She unlocked the door and let him in. 'I was just about to come down. I took half the wardrobe and the top three drawers,' she told him. 'The rest is all yours.'

'Great. I'll just have a quick shower and then we can go into town and I'll show you around a bit. Rafe wants us to go for a drink with him and Scott.'

'Oh! Just us?'

'Yes. I'm guessing he wants to talk about Stella.'

'Are you sure he wants me to come?' she asked. 'I don't mind if the three of you want to catch up. We don't have to be one of those couples who are joined at the hip.'

'No, you should come. If we're discussing Stella, I want you in on it.'

'But they don't know I'm an investigator, right?' She didn't fancy the idea of having to answer to Rafe.

'No. The fewer people who know that, the better. As far as they're concerned, you're just a mild-mannered web developer.'

'Well, it happens to be the truth,' she said.

22

It was a short walk through winding, leafy streets to the centre of town. They caught up with Scott and Rafe on the Promenade des Anglais. Al pointed out the famous Negresco Hotel to Lesley, but she knew they weren't there to see the sights as Rafe led the way down some steps to a bar right on the beach. Under large white canopies, little round tables were arranged on a wooden deck slightly raised off the shingle. On the beach, rows of sunbeds shaded by blue and white umbrellas were lined up in front of the sparkling blue sea. A waitress waved them to a table, and after some consultation, Rafe – in fluent, and very sexy, French – ordered a bottle of Perrier for himself, a Kir Royale for Lesley and Pernod for Scott and Al.

'So, I presume we're here to talk about Stella,' Scott said. He looked at Rafe, a grin on his face. 'What's your plan for ridding us of the troublesome wench?'

Rafe gave him a dry look. 'What makes you think I have a plan?'

'Because you always have a plan.' He turned to Lesley. 'We call him the Enforcer,' he told her.

'No, you don't,' Rafe said.

'Not to your face.'

'Who calls me that?'

'Everyone.' Scott grinned and took a sip of his drink.

'No, they don't,' Rafe said crossly.

'Not to his face,' Scott hissed to Lesley in a stage whisper. Rafe glowered at his brother and she suppressed a giggle.

'What have you got against her anyway?' Scott asked.

'What do you think?' Rafe said. 'It's nothing personal. I just want to protect Dad.'

'And our inheritance.'

'What's wrong with that?'

'Well, I think she's brilliant!' Scott said. 'So glam. I vote we keep her.'

Rafe gave him a quelling look. 'Just like that?'

'Why not? We could do with some sparkle.' He sipped his Pernod. 'I mean, granted we've got me. But we're down a bit of feminine pizzazz now that you've been dumped again.'

'I wasn't dumped,' Rafe said.

'That was his news, did you hear?' Scott said to Al. 'He's broken up with Francesca and he's moving back to Dublin.'

Al nodded. 'I heard.'

'Rafe's a tragic spinster, like Jennifer Aniston,' Scott said to Lesley. 'He just can't seem to hold onto a relationship.'

'You could say the same about yourself,' Lesley said.

'No, I'm more of a George Clooney. I'll settle down eventually, in my own time. Until then, I feel it's only right to play the field and give everyone a fair crack of the whip.'

Rafe rolled his eyes at his brother. 'What does your father think about it all?' he asked Al.

'He doesn't seem that worried. The background check didn't turn up anything. But I don't think he really expects the marriage to go ahead, to be honest. He thinks it's just Peter being Peter and it'll all fizzle out before anything comes of it.'

'Right.' Rafe sighed, leaning back in his chair. 'Well, where does that leave us? If there's nothing on her, and she won't be paid off—'

'*What?*' Scott shrieked, his eyes widening. 'What do you mean, "paid off"?' A slow smile spread across his face. 'Oh my God … you didn't?'

'What?' Al looked between Scott and Rafe. 'You offered her money?'

'Yes,' Rafe said defiantly. 'I certainly did.' He sipped his water grumpily. 'I'd say it's a sure-fire way to get rid of a gold-digger, wouldn't you?'

'I thought the whole idea was to stop her getting her hands on our money in the first place,' Scott said.

'It'd be a fraction of what she'd be worth once they're married. Worth it, if you ask me. If she'd go for it,' he added with a resigned twist of his mouth.

'But she didn't?'

'No.' He shook his head. 'So that's out.'

'Oh my God.' Scott grinned, hugely enjoying himself. 'How do you even say something like that? I mean, in this day and age? I bet she told you where to shove it.'

Rafe gave a little reluctant smile. 'She did, actually,' he said, his eyes softening.

'Well, I guess that's that, then,' Scott said.

'It doesn't mean she's on the level.' Rafe looked boot-faced. 'Anyway, it's not just the money.' He raked a hand though his hair. 'The whole thing is ridiculous, and they'll end up making each other miserable.'

'Dad seems happy,' Scott said.

'How long do you think that will last? You know what Dad's like,' Rafe appealed to his brother. 'He doesn't marry his girlfriends – and with good reason.'

'Maybe this one's different,' Scott said.

'Right. Like Mum was different.'

Scott's smile faltered, and he toyed with his glass, rattling the ice around.

'What happens when the next bright young thing comes along?' Rafe continued. 'Or when Stella gets tired of playing nursemaid to an old man? It'd be better for everyone if she'd just take the money and run.'

'There's not much we can do about it, though, is there?' Scott said. 'They're both grown-ups. I guess they know what they're doing.'

Rafe's jaw set stubbornly. 'Dad just isn't someone who should be married. It doesn't suit him. I thought he at least had the sense to realise that.'

'You don't think he's going to be playing around on Stella, though?' Scott said scathingly.

'Have you met Dad?'

'I know, but ... isn't he a bit old for all that stuff now?'

'Maybe,' Rafe said gloomily. 'But I doubt it.'

'I mean, he's not even sleeping with Stella. You know they have separate bedrooms?'

'That's just because of his heart attack, not because he's past it.' Rafe tossed back the last of his water. 'Anyway, I don't see what more we can do.'

'Well ... maybe you just didn't offer her the right incentive,' Scott said. 'If she's only into Dad for his money, she'd probably ditch him at the drop of a hat for the younger, hotter version – Mr Darcy himself, no less.'

'You think I should try it on with Dad's girlfriend?'
Rafe looked aghast.

'Just flirt with her, lead her on a bit. I'm not saying you
should follow through.' Scott shrugged. 'Just a suggestion,
since you're so determined to break them up.'

'And you're not?'

'I told you, I think she's fabulous. I love her already.'

'Anyway, it's not as if she'd fall for it, after I've tried to
buy her off, is it?'

'I don't see why not. That enemies-to-lovers thing is
sexy as hell. And you do that whole repressed Englishman
battling your feelings schtick so well – all smouldering
passion under your stiff upper lip. It totally plays into your
wheelhouse.'

Rafe looked thoughtful. Then he shook his head.
'Sorry, Lesley,' he said, as if he'd only just become aware
of her presence. 'You must think we're awful. We're not
usually this ... Machiavellian.'

'No worries,' she said. 'It's fine. I totally get it.' In fact,
she was having the time of her life. After all, she was sitting
in a bar in the South of France, drinking cocktails in the
afternoon and hugger-mugging with three gorgeous men.
It was like being part of some super-glamorous version of
the Famous Five.

'Right, well, I'm going to get back,' Rafe said, standing.
He took some euros from his pocket and tossed them on
the table. Scott got up with him. 'Are you coming?' he
asked Al.

'No, I think we'll stay here for a while, maybe have
another,' Al said, looking to Lesley.

She nodded in agreement.

'I want to take Lesley for a walk,' he said, 'show her
around a bit.'

'Okay, see you back at the house later.'

Lesley sank back against the cushioned seat as she watched Rafe skipping lithely up the steps to the promenade.

'Well, what do you make of all that?' Al asked, once his cousins were out of earshot.

'I can't believe Rafe actually tried to pay Stella off!'

'I know.' Al grinned, rolling his eyes. 'Sometimes I think he's really let Mr Darcy go to his head.' He called over a waiter and ordered another couple of drinks.

'This is the life.' Lesley sighed, tilting her face to the sun and closing her eyes. 'I'm really glad I came.'

'Me too. And Stella looked very happy to see you,' he said, smiling at her.

'Yeah.' She thought of the way Stella had pounced on her almost desperately as soon as she arrived. 'I'd say she was feeling a bit out of it with your lot, and is glad to have another outsider around.'

'Probably,' Al said.

'Well, it's all grist to the mill if it makes her glom onto me.'

23

Afterr another drink, Al took her on a short, leisurely walk along the seafront, admiring the miles of pebbly beach and glistening water.

She was starving by the time they got back to the house, and was glad to find Jane and Joy in the kitchen preparing dinner. Stella was hovering uncertainly in the door from the garden.

'Um ... should I make something separate for me and Peter?' she asked, watching anxiously as Jane poured olive oil into a large pan.

'No, don't worry,' Joy said, turning to her with a smile. 'We've got it covered.'

'We'll do our best not to kill Peter,' Jane said, looking at Stella over the top of her glasses. 'However tempting it might be,' she added.

Stella gave her a shaky smile. 'Maybe I should—'

'Don't mind her,' Joy said. 'We're having baked mullet, ratatouille and boulangère potatoes. There's nothing there he can't eat, is there?'

'No,' Stella said, her features relaxing. 'That's perfect.'

'You just relax and enjoy yourself. We don't want you to spend your whole holiday cooking.'

'Thanks, Joy.'

'Bubble, bubble, toil and trouble,' Jane whispered, stirring a pot as Stella disappeared back to the patio.

Joy chuckled, shaking her head admonishingly.

'Shit-stirring already?' Al said to Jane.

'I'm behaving impeccably, aren't I, Joy?'

'She's actually been very good,' Joy said. 'Practically saintly.'

'I wouldn't go that far,' Jane said.

'Go on out and have a drink,' Joy told them. 'We'll join you shortly.'

Out on the terrace, Scott was engrossed in a copy of *Fifty Shades of Grey*. Lesley hoped he wasn't looking there for insights into the female mind.

He looked up at them as they came outside.

'Enjoying that?' Lesley asked him.

'Bloody hell!' he said, shaking his head and grinning broadly. 'If I'd known straight sex could be like this, I might never have given it up.'

'Don't believe everything you read,' Lesley said with a sniff. 'Most women would still prefer a little spontaneity over a twenty-page contract. When it comes to sex, contracts aren't the things you want to be lengthy.'

'So you don't find this stuff a turn-on, then?'

'I always felt the humour would have gone off me by the time he'd got all his equipment set up.'

Scott laughed. 'Yeah, there's a lot to be said for a good old-fashioned shag.'

HOLIDAYING with the Bradshaws wasn't going to do her liver any favours, Lesley thought, as they drank pastis on the terrace before dinner. It was cool and refreshing, but she was starting to feel quite light-headed, and she was grateful when the meal appeared. They sat at a long wooden table laden with food and wine.

'Here's to the holiday!' Peter said when they were all seated, raising his glass of Perrier. 'It's great to be here with you all again this year,' he added with feeling.

'We're very glad you were able to make it,' Joy said softly, the glint of a tear in her eye as she bumped her glass against his. 'So what are everyone's plans?' she asked.

'Well, I'm going to spend some quality time with the manuscript of a rather marvellous book I'm reading,' Peter said, smiling at Jane.

'Oh, your new one?' Joy asked Jane, who nodded.

'Lesley hasn't been to Nice before,' Al said, 'so I want to show her around.'

'You'll love it,' Stella said to Lesley. 'It's my first time here too.'

'Then you should definitely visit Eze,' Rafe said, 'and Villefranche.'

'And Menton,' Scott put in.

'We have to spend some time at the beach, of course,' Jane said. 'We thought we might all go to Cannes for the day, maybe the day after tomorrow, when you're settled in a bit.'

'That all sounds great!' Lesley said.

'I was wondering if you'd come shopping with me one day,' Stella said quietly to Lesley.

'I'd love to,' Lesley said eagerly. It would be a perfect opportunity to spend some girly bonding time with Stella.

'Great!' Stella smiled happily.

'So have you two set a date for the wedding yet?' Scott asked, looking between Stella and Peter.

Suddenly everyone around the table seemed to be on high alert.

'Yes.' Peter took Stella's hand.

'As long as it's not a major stumbling block for anyone, we're thinking of September twenty-first,' Stella said.

'So if that's a problem for any of you,' Peter said, 'speak now or forever hold your peace. Otherwise, consider this your notice to save the date.'

There were subdued mumbles of acknowledgement, but everyone seemed a bit taken aback, as if the wedding hadn't been a reality until now. No one said it, but Lesley was sure they were all thinking it was happening very soon.

'That's not long for organising a wedding,' Joy said to Stella.

'I know. But we're keeping it small, so it shouldn't be too difficult to arrange.'

'It doesn't give me much time to scare up a date,' Scott said. 'I'd better hit the beach first thing tomorrow and find someone to bring.'

The tension around the table dissolved as everyone laughed.

They continued drinking long after dinner, and as the wine flowed, Lesley was alarmed to find the Bradshaws started to punctuate their conversation with snatches of songs and poetry. A hush fell over the table as Jane broke into an impromptu rendition of '*La Vie en Rose*' in a surprisingly sweet, high voice. It was lovely, and very evocative in the setting. But Lesley started to panic when Peter launched into a Shakespeare monologue.

'I'm warning you right now,' she said under her breath to Al, 'there'd better not be audience participation. If I have to do a party piece, I'm getting the next flight out of here.'

Al chuckled. 'Don't worry. You wouldn't get a chance

even if you wanted to. There are far too many show-offs here for you to get a look in.'

'A woman after my own heart!' Michael said, turning to her. 'Joy and I keep our heads down when they get like this.'

'The only poem *you* know,' Joy said, 'starts "There once was a nympho named Jill", and no one wants to hear that.'

Lesley laughed. 'I wouldn't mind; it sounds good.'

When Joy started clearing up, Lesley quickly sprang up and offered to help, seizing the excuse to scuttle off to the kitchen, just in case there was any chance she'd be called on to perform. Al followed and began stacking the dishwasher while she and Joy went back and forth carrying things in from the terrace.

'Peter's doing a dirty poem about Stella now,' she hissed at Al as she handed him a pile of plates.

He laughed. 'Is this true?' He looked to Jane, who was coming in with an armful of empty wine bottles.

'Swear to God,' Lesley said, 'all about having her long legs wrapped around him in bed. And he was looking right at her, in case anyone didn't get the message. Tell him,' she said to Jane.

'"My girl's tall with hard, long eyes" – you know the one,' Jane said to Al.

'It's E.E. Cummings,' Al told Lesley.

'Well, at least he didn't make it up himself. But I still think it's very inappropriate in front of the children,' Lesley sniffed.

'What children?'

'Scott and Rafe.'

Al looked at her askance.

'It doesn't matter how old they are, they're still *Peter's* children, and no one wants to have their parent's sex life rubbed in their face.'

'It does sound very unhygienic,' Al said.

Jane leaned on the worktop and sighed. 'It used to be all Yeats with him – all that yearning for Maud Gonne.'

Al shot her a sympathetic look; clearly Jane used to be Peter's muse for his after-dinner ramblings.

'Ah well, those days are "Gonne",' Jane said, smiling at the pun.

'But they'll be back,' Lesley said. 'Don't worry, you'll be treading on his dreams again in no time.'

When Jane had gone back to the garden, Stella came in and sidled up to Lesley.

'I thought maybe we could go shopping tomorrow,' she said. 'Unless you have other plans?'

Lesley looked to Al, who shook his head.

'No, tomorrow would be fine.'

'Great!'

Al removed himself, leaving Lesley alone with Stella.

'I didn't like to say it in front of Jane,' Stella said in a low voice, 'but Peter suggested I look for a wedding dress while I'm here. So I'd really be grateful for some help. I'm pretty clueless about wedding dresses.'

'I can't say I know much about them myself, but I'll do my best.'

'Thanks. It'd be great to have a second opinion. Or just some back-up for fighting off pushy sales assistants.'

'Now that I *am* good at.'

'SO WE HAVE A DEADLINE NOW,' Al said to Lesley later when they were alone in bed.

'Yeah.' She rolled onto her side and propped herself up on one elbow, so she was facing him across the barrier of bolsters and cushions he'd constructed between them. 'The end of September,' she mused. 'It doesn't give us much time.'

'But Stella seems very keen to be friends with you, so that's in our favour.'

'Yeah, that makes things a lot easier.' Lesley was delighted that Stella was looking on her as an ally already. 'And we're going wedding dress shopping tomorrow. That's the ultimate girly bonding experience.' She wished she didn't feel like such a fraud. But she mustn't let herself fall for Stella's charm. She was here to do a job, and she had to remain detached and professional.

'Hopefully she'll open up to you more when it's just the two of you,' Al said. 'You should go for a boozy lunch. Get her to loosen up a bit.'

'Good idea. If we got tipsy together, maybe I could even get her to be indiscreet. I could make a few drunken confessions of my own, to encourage her.'

'But be subtle. You want her to feel she can confide in you, and you can keep a secret.'

'Don't worry,' Lesley said, plumping up her pillows. 'Subtle is my middle name.'

Al turned away quickly and buried his face in his pillow, but Lesley still heard his muffled snigger. She resisted the urge to pick up one of the barrier cushions and whack him with it.

24

This is my kind of shopping, Lesley thought, as she sat sipping champagne on a chaise longue, while she waited for Stella to emerge from the dressing room of a fancy bridal boutique in the new town.

'What do you think?'

Lesley looked up as Stella pulled back the velvet curtains and stepped out. The sales assistant, a bird-like older woman with jet-black hair scraped back in a severe bun, rushed forward to fuss with the skirt of the dress as Stella stepped onto a raised platform in front of a huge mirror.

'Ooh!' Madame clapped her hands enthusiastically, then held them in prayer position at her mouth as she gazed delightedly at Stella's reflection. '*Très belle, non?*' She turned to Lesley for confirmation.

Lesley had to admit, Madame had a point. She felt like bursting into applause herself. 'You look amazing!' she said, standing up as Stella twirled in front of the mirror.

'It is lovely, isn't it?' Stella fingered the delicate lace at the neckline – hand-made by Parisian elves or some such, according to Madame; Lesley couldn't remember the exact details.

'I can't believe that's me,' Stella said as she gazed at her reflection. 'I look so …'

'Beautiful,' Lesley finished for her. There was no other word for it. 'It's gorgeous. That's got to be the one, right?'

Madame smiled at her almost tearfully, nodding her agreement.

It was a long narrow column, with a keyhole cut-out in the back revealing a tantalising glimpse of skin. The simple elegance of the design was perfect, the clean lines showing off Stella's modelesque figure. Anything fussier would have only detracted from the effect. In this dress, Stella was the main event, and she looked like a goddess.

Madame beckoned Lesley to come and have a closer look, then bustled off to give them a moment alone with the dress. Lesley stepped onto the platform behind Stella as she turned this way and that.

'I do love it,' she said in a low voice to Lesley, 'but it's ridiculously expensive.' She bit her lip. 'The first one was lovely too.'

This was the third dress Stella had tried on, and the most expensive. But it was also the clear winner, as far as Lesley was concerned. 'The first one was nice, but this is perfect. It could have been made for you.'

'Still, almost *three thousand euro* for a dress!' Stella frowned. 'How can I justify spending that kind of money on something I'm only going to wear once? It's ridiculous!'

That didn't sound much like the thinking of a gold-digger. 'But you don't have to worry about money, do you?' Lesley asked. 'You're going to be marrying Peter. He's loaded.'

'But *I'm* not, and I want to pay for this myself. Peter offered, of course, but I don't intend to be some kind of sponging trophy wife. Whatever his family may think,' she added under her breath. Then she laughed. 'Listen to me – trophy wife! As if I'm some kind of prize.' She shook her head. 'I can't believe I actually said that.'

'But anyone would think you were a prize,' Lesley said. 'Look at you!'

Stella smiled at herself in the mirror with real appreciation, as if she were seeing herself as Lesley saw her, and suddenly her eyes were welling with tears.

It struck Lesley as odd for a woman as stunning as Stella to seem so insecure about her looks. It was as if she had to be reminded how beautiful she was.

'You know, I wasn't even going to go in for this whole big wedding extravaganza,' Stella said. 'If I had my way, I'd be getting married in Vegas, in a nice dress from a high street store.'

'But now you've seen yourself in that,' Lesley said, nodding at Stella's reflection in the mirrors, 'the genie is out of the bottle.'

Stella smiled. 'I think you're right,' she said, her eyes running over her reflection again. 'I'm not going to be able to leave this behind, am I? I don't even want to take it off now.'

'Why don't we go and have lunch, and you can think about it?' Lesley suggested. She was hungry and the champagne was starting to go to her head.

'Good idea,' Stella nodded.

Madame helped Stella out of the dress, and they left with promises to return later in the afternoon when she'd made up her mind. Lesley led the way through the winding cobbled streets of the old town to a restaurant that Al had recommended on a side street off Place Rossetti, away from the touristy bustle of the square. They sat in the shade of a large red umbrella, while waiters bustled between the tables covered with yellow tablecloths, and pedestrians streamed past on the other side of the narrow street.

As so often happened to Lesley when faced with a menu, she wanted everything. The bowls of steaming pasta being delivered to the next table looked mouth-watering, but she also wanted to try the pizza, which Al had told her was amazing.

'What are you going to have?' she asked Stella.

'Salad niçoise and mineral water,' Stella said decisively after barely glancing at the menu.

Lesley's heart sank. She'd been counting on them at least sharing a bowl of frites. She wished Al were here; she figured he'd be happy to split half the menu with her.

'We're shopping for your wedding dress,' she said to Stella. 'We should celebrate. Let's get champagne. My treat.'

'Oh. I have to admit, it hadn't even occurred to me. But champagne would be lovely.'

'Great!'

'Shall we order?' Stella asked. 'Do you know what you're having?'

'I can't decide. Al says the pizza here is the best in Nice. But they're huge, and I really fancy some fries too.'

'That does look really good,' Stella said as a waiter passed, bearing two massive pizzas, the tantalising smell of herby tomato sauce and melting cheese drifting by in his wake. 'God, I can't remember when I last had pizza. Or fries,' she said, side-eyeing the bowls of crispy frites being delivered to another table.

'Fancy sharing? You've got a lot of mulling to do about that dress,' Lesley said. 'You need to keep your strength up. And we've got all afternoon.'

'You're right,' Stella said, picking up the menu again. 'Let's share.'

They ordered an aubergine pizza, a bowl of frites with aioli and a mixed salad as a nod to healthy eating, along with a bottle of house champagne.

'Thanks so much for coming with me today,' Stella said. 'You made it fun. And thank you for this.' She clinked her glass against Lesley's.

'It *was* fun,' Lesley said, surprised that she genuinely had enjoyed it. She took a sip of champagne. 'Now, what are you thinking about that dress?'

Stella smiled. 'Oh, I think we both know I'm going to go for it.'

'Really? I mean, it *was* stunning, but you'd look amazing in any of them.' It hadn't occurred to Lesley that Stella would be buying the dress herself, and she felt bad at the thought of her blowing so much money on a wedding that might never happen.

'No, hang the expense! You only get married once – at least I only intend to do it once.'

They were interrupted by the food arriving.

'Gosh, this all looks wonderful,' Stella said as the waiter bustled away. 'I'm so glad you suggested it. I've got so used to just zeroing in on what Peter can eat, I forget to consider what *I* want, even when he's not around.'

Lesley wondered was that really the reason. Stella seemed so into her looks. Maybe she was just worried about getting fat. 'So, how are you finding the Bradshaws?' she asked as she cut into the pizza, dividing it between their plates. The charred crust was just on the right side of burnt.

Stella hesitated, and Lesley could almost see the shutters coming down.

'It must be a bit daunting,' she prompted, 'being

thrown into the middle of them all like this — especially having Jane here. I mean, that must be weird for you.'

Stella took a bite of pizza and nodded, chewing thoughtfully. 'It was at first. I have to admit I dreaded her coming,' she said with a little laugh, 'but it's not as awkward as I was expecting, and she's been very friendly to me. She's nice, isn't she?'

'Yeah, I like her.'

'It must be quite hard for her too,' Stella mused, toying with her glass. 'She and Peter are still so friendly. Maybe I should be worried.' She darted an anxious look at Lesley.

'But they couldn't make a go of it,' Lesley said, sensing that she was looking for reassurance. 'It's one thing getting on well with someone; it's another being married to them. Jane couldn't put up with—' Lesley stopped herself.

'Don't worry,' Stella said, 'I know it was Peter's cheating that caused their marriage to break down. But he's changed. I wouldn't be marrying him if I thought he'd be unfaithful. Trust is very important to me.'

'What about the rest of them? Scott seems to have taken a shine to you anyway.'

'Scott's sweet,' she said, dipping a fry in aioli. 'Joy and Michael are lovely, especially Joy. She's been really kind. And Al, of course, is a sweetheart.'

'Well, I certainly think so,' Lesley said loyally.

'I mean, I'm not naive. I know they're probably not that happy about me. But they haven't been hostile at all. Well, except Rafe.' She took a slug of champagne. 'He straight out accused me of being a gold-digger to my face.'

'Pompous ass!'

Stella shrugged. 'It's what they're all thinking, I suppose. I can't blame him really. He's just looking out for his father.'

'And his inheritance,' Lesley pointed out.

'Yes, that too. You won't believe this, but he actually offered me money to call the whole thing off.'

'Bloody hell!' Lesley widened her eyes, acting surprised. 'How much?'

'I don't know. I told him I wasn't interested, so it didn't get that far.'

'Aren't you curious, though? I wonder would they pay me to break up with Al,' Lesley said dreamily.

'But you wouldn't consider it.'

'No, of course not. But I'd love to know what they'd offer.' She'd have to get Al to find out. 'Doesn't it worry you, though, that they think you might just be after Peter's money?'

'Not much I can do about it,' Stella said. 'I'll just have to tough it out. Eventually they'll see they were wrong.'

'Maybe it's not just about you, though. I mean, what if you and Peter were to have kids?'

Stella shook her head. 'We won't.'

'Really? You don't want children?'

'I ... can't have them.'

'Oh, sorry. But you could adopt. Or get a surrogate. There are lots of options nowadays, especially when you have money.'

'Peter would be a very old father. I don't think it would be fair to a child.'

'And you're okay with that?'

'I've known from a very young age that I couldn't have children. I'm used to the idea. So if that's what they're worried about, they can relax.'

'Well, they must see how good you are for Peter. He's a changed man, by all accounts.'

'Hmm. But maybe they resent me for that too,' Stella said thoughtfully. 'The old Peter may have been a drunk and a philanderer, but they loved him as he was. And now

I've come along and he's turned into this abstemious health freak. It's not entirely my doing, but no doubt the two things go together in their minds. I can tell they think I'm uptight and controlling.'

'Well, look how Peter ended up left to his own devices. He needs a firm hand. They're just glad to still have him around, and I'm sure they're grateful to you.'

'I guess. Anyway, I'm very glad *you're* here, Lesley.'

'Me too. This place is lovely, isn't it?' she said, looking around. She fished in her bag for her phone. 'I'd better get on Instagram and get busy making everyone jealous.' She took a photo of the restaurant and posted it. 'You're not on Instagram?' She thought it was worth asking, on the off-chance that Stella just kept her social media accounts private because she didn't want Peter's family to connect with her.

Stella shook her head. 'I'm not on any social media.'

'I'm kind of jealous. I'm a total addict.'

'I had a ... bad experience a while back.'

'Bullying?' That was common enough on social media.

'Sort of.' She looked down at her hands, fidgeting with the stem of her glass. 'An ex was ... stalking me, I suppose.' She lifted her head. 'It's a long time ago now. I deleted all my accounts.'

'And you've never been tempted to go back? Even to do a bit of covert cyber-stalking?'

'No.' Stella smiled sardonically. 'I'm afraid of what I might find. Anyway, I don't miss it. It's very freeing, actually, not being tethered to all that.' She nodded at Lesley's phone. 'The constant clamour for attention and applause, the comparisonitis.'

'The endless selfies,' Lesley chipped in.

'Oh God, the selfies!' Stella struck a pose, hand on hip,

chest thrust out, pouting at herself in an imaginary mirror while she held a phone out at arm's length.

Lesley laughed.

'I may be vain,' Stella continued, 'but at least I don't spend all my time broadcasting pictures of myself admiring my reflection.'

'You'd be perfectly justified if you did. I mean, there's no point in pretending you don't know how great you look.'

'Well, it's not as if I didn't earn it – literally,' Stella said, leaning forward confidentially. 'Bought and paid for it with my own money.'

'You mean ... plastic surgery? I must admit, I did wonder if you'd had a boob job.'

Stella nodded. 'And the rest.' She drew a finger over her face, along her jaw and chin. 'I've had a lot of work done.'

'Wow!' Maybe it was the effect of working in Hollywood, Lesley thought. But even there, she suspected it would be unusual for someone Stella's age to have had that much cosmetic surgery. 'That must have cost a packet.'

Stella nodded. 'It did. I spent pretty much all my money on it for years. But it was worth it.'

'Well, good for you!' Lesley raised her glass in salute. She was glad Stella was letting her hair down a bit with her. By the time they had drained the bottle of champagne and ordered another, she was really starting to loosen up.

'Lesley, can I ask you something?' She topped up their glasses. 'A favour?'

'Sure,' Lesley said readily, glad that she was gaining Stella's confidence.

'Would you be my bridesmaid?'

'*Me?*' she squeaked, taken aback.

'You don't have to, of course,' Stella said quickly. 'Feel free to say no if you'd rather not.'

'No, it's not that. I'm just surprised. I mean, you hardly even know me. You must have friends you'd rather ask.' Lesley knew she should be pleased, but instead she was horrified. If Stella's aim had been to make her feel like a prize snake, she couldn't have done a better job.

'That's just it, I don't. I haven't really got any close friends.' Stella gave a rueful smile. 'God, that makes me sound like such a loser. But it's just that I've moved around so much, and I'm not very good at keeping in touch. I'm a "live in the moment" kind of person, I guess.'

'Love the ones you're with,' Lesley said, nodding.

'Exactly. And now I'm with you.'

Being a bridesmaid could provide all sorts of excuses to nose around in Stella's life, and Lesley knew she should grab the opportunity with both hands. But she couldn't help feeling sorry for Stella. She was starting to really like her and to see her as a friend. It made her feel like such a fraud. Still, it was what she was being paid for. This was a good development, and she owed it to Al to ignore her reservations and make the most of it.

'Well, I'd be very happy to be your bridesmaid if you're sure that's what you want.'

'Thank you.' Stella beamed.

'And as your bridesmaid, my first job will be organising your hen do,' she said.

'Oh, don't worry about that.' Stella shook her head. 'I don't need a hen party. I hadn't even thought of brides-maids until just now when Madame asked me what they'd be wearing. Besides, who would you invite? I don't really know anyone in Ireland anymore.'

'What about before you moved?'

'Oh God, that was so long ago. Another lifetime.'

'Well, maybe I could organise a reunion. If you give me the info, I could dig up people you used to work with, maybe some old school friends ...'

Stella's eyes widened. 'I'm not a reunion sort of person. I don't like looking back.'

'Okay.' Lesley decided it was best to back off. Stella looked quite panicked, and it was a long shot anyway. Then she had another idea. 'It wouldn't have to be only women,' she said tentatively. 'I mean it's the twenty-first century. If you have any male friends you'd like me to invite ...'

Something flickered in Stella's face, but it was gone before Lesley could make out what it was. 'No,' she said. 'There's no one.'

She looked sad, and Lesley was struck by how lonely she must be. For whatever reason, she didn't seem to have anyone in her life – at least, no one she would admit to.

'Well, I don't intend to fall down on the most sacred of bridesmaid duties. I'm throwing you a hen party, even if it's just you and me.'

'Just you and me, then.' Stella raised her glass to Lesley.

'We'll have the fun of twenty women.' Lesley knocked back the last of her champagne. 'Now, let's go back and buy that dress. By the way, what *is* your bridesmaid wearing?'

'So, one day down and I'm Stella's bestie,' Lesley told Al later. They were lying side by side in bed, facing each other across the pillow barrier while she updated him on her progress.

'Well done! That was quick work.'

'Thanks.' She was pleased that she had something to report. 'I'm not getting a gold-digger vibe from her so far.

Do you know she didn't even ask Rafe how much he'd pay her to disappear?'

'Impressive. But it could be just an act, to show him she's not interested in the money. I mean, what if he was tricking her? She couldn't risk showing her hand. There'd be no going back if she took him up on it.'

'Or maybe she genuinely doesn't care how much he's offering because she's holding out for the jackpot.'

'Well, now that you're BFFs, maybe she'll show you her true colours,' Al said on a yawn as he lay back.

'Do you want the light out?' Lesley asked. 'I'm going to read for a while.' She picked up her paperback from the nightstand.

'No, that's fine. How are you enjoying that book?'

'It's great! Things are really hotting up in the first form.'

'Told you.'

'I'm almost starting to want to go to boarding school myself.'

'We could have a pillow fight if you like?' Al said, grinning at her. 'I wouldn't mind.'

'No thanks,' Lesley said. 'Though I wouldn't mind tying the sheets together and abseiling out the window. That sounds like a laugh.'

'Please don't. I don't want to spend tomorrow in A&E with you.'

25

The next day, Al took Lesley for a tour around Nice. First they walked up the hill to the Parc de la Colline du Château, a lush, shady park overlooking the city. It was a steep climb, but worth it for the spectacular views of the city and the Baie des Anges. Then they descended to the Old Town and spent the morning wandering through the narrow winding streets, overshadowed by tall sun-burnished apartment buildings painted in colourful shades of ochre, pink and burnt orange. Cascades of red and purple bougainvillea spilled from iron-railed balconies, and brightly painted shutters framed the windows. The tiny alleys opened out into wide squares drenched in sunlight and dotted with bustling pavement cafés, the tables shaded by colourful umbrellas.

Al was an enthusiastic guide, pointing out interesting architectural features, quirky little shops, the best gelaterie ('their lavender ice cream is to die for'), and favourite bistros and eateries ('We have to come back here, the pizza is amazing').

'What do you think so far?' he asked as they reached

the Cours Saleya, with its famous flower and produce market.

'Of Nice? I love it. It's pretty as a Pixar.'

The market was an explosion of colour and fragrance, delicious smells from the food stalls and cafés spilling out into the square and mingling with the heady scent of flowers. There were stalls selling everything from fresh fish and bottles of deep-green olive oil to jewel-coloured candied fruits and lavender-scented soaps.

'Hungry?' Al asked her. 'This place has the *best* crepes in Nice,' he said, leading her to a stall where a matronly woman was spreading batter on a wide rotating wheel. They ate a picnic lunch as they strolled around the market, grazing on savoury crepes and slices of pissaladière, and tasting samples of cheese and charcuterie. Al urged her to try socca, crisp chickpea pancakes cooked on huge circular pans, which tasted better than they sounded.

Al chatted easily to the stall-holders in rapid French, and many of them greeted him like an old friend, with warm smiles and hearty handshakes. Lesley felt proud to be with him, even if it wasn't real. Everyone seemed so glad to see him, and she liked how friendly and outgoing he was. As fake boyfriends went, she could do a lot worse.

Even though Lesley was already stuffed, Al insisted she had to try the 'best Nutella crepes in Nice' for dessert. They sat at a small table at one of the cafés in the centre of the market and ate the most delicious crepes Lesley had ever tasted, with cups of strong black coffee.

'Good?' Al grinned across the table at her, licking chocolate off his lips.

'Amazing,' she said. 'I just hope I can still fit into my bikini tomorrow.'

. . .

'It still fits, then,' Al said to her the next day as she pulled her sundress over her head and hung it on the hook under the parasol.

'Just about.' She tugged at the bra of her bikini self-consciously. Was it her imagination or was it already a little tighter than when she'd bought it? She was grateful that everyone else was too preoccupied with putting on sunscreen and settling themselves on sunbeds to pay attention to her.

'Well, it looks great.'

'Thanks.' It had been a while since she'd worn a bikini, but she felt good in it. She was relieved that she wasn't the only one wearing a bikini top. She'd been a bit nervous that toplessness would be the order of the day on the beach at Cannes. Not that she had any intention of stripping off, but she also didn't want to look like a fuddy-duddy. But she needn't have worried. Stella was even wearing a one-piece, albeit a skimpy one with cut-out panels in the sides and a high cut that elongated her already endless legs.

She pulled on her sunglasses and lay back on her sunlounger. This is the life, she thought. Going to the beach with the Bradshaws was an experience. They'd piled into two cars and driven to Cannes, then set up camp at an exclusive beach bar on the Croisette in front of a ritzy hotel. Luxurious sun beds with fat white mattresses were set in the white powdery sand, and smartly dressed waiters weaved between them, bearing trays of food and ice-cold drinks dripping with condensation. It was all a far cry from the picnic blankets, sandy sandwiches and lukewarm cans of lemonade of her childhood.

The sun sparkled and danced on the water like thousands of fireflies, and blue and white umbrellas stretched along the sand in either direction. White-sailed yachts floated across the horizon, while closer to shore, paddle-boarders skimmed effortlessly along the surface of the water.

The Bradshaws looked at home among the glamorous, moneyed crowd stretched out on the sand sunning themselves. Lesley wished she could put a photo on Instagram. She'd be the envy of social media if she could post about where she was right now. But as Al's girlfriend she had to act cool and take it all in her stride. So she had to satisfy herself with texting Romy.

She sent her a snap of the view from her sunlounger with the caption: *Loving the new job so far.*

Romy replied: *Well, I've just been to Lidl, so not jealous at all.*

Lesley laughed. *I'll be spending the day in a togs scenario with Rafe and Scott Bradshaw,* she texted back. *It's a tough job, but it beats SEO.*

And Al, Romy replied. *Don't forget your boyfriend.*

Lesley texted back a heart emoji, then pulled on her shades and lay back on her sunlounger to furtively ogle Rafe in his swim shorts. From where she was sitting, he had all the qualifications necessary to play James Bond. Though her 'boyfriend' was no slouch either, she thought, glancing at Al beside her.

'I think you've brought me here under false pretences, Lesley,' Jane said on her other side.

Lesley turned to her. She was looking straight ahead, her face almost completely obscured by dark sunglasses and a wide, floppy hat. Lesley followed her gaze to Stella and Peter walking hand in hand towards the sea.

Rafe and Scott had wandered off together in search of jet skis, and Michael was fast asleep under his umbrella, a fat paperback open on his chest rising and falling gently with his breath. Joy was paddling at the water's edge.

'His girl's tall with washboard abs,' Jane intoned softly as Stella walked along the sand, her hips swaying, her long, sun-streaked hair lifting slightly in the gentle breeze. 'I mean, how can I possibly compete with that?'

She had a point. Stella could be a Bond girl with her flat stomach, perky fake boobs and long, toned legs.

'I'll be brutally honest with you,' she said to Jane. 'You're not going to win the bikini round. I'll tell you that flat out.'

'Al, throw this one back.' Jane leaned across Lesley to speak to him. 'She's cruel.'

'Sorry, just telling it like it is. But you have to play to your strengths.'

'Which are? Evening wear? General knowledge?'

Lesley shook her head. 'It's only in stories that all the pretty girls are thick. Sorry.'

'True. It's a story the rest of us tell to comfort ourselves.' Jane said. 'Talent, then? I'm not a bad singer. And I can juggle a little. I had to learn it once for a part.'

'Well ... maybe if we get desperate. But no, where you're really going to come into your own is in the history section.'

'History?' Jane huffed a laugh. 'Thanks very much.'

'Think about it,' Lesley said, sitting up and swinging around to face Jane as she warmed to her theme. 'You and Peter had a whole life together. You've got children. Divorced or not, you'll always be family. Stella's known Peter for five minutes – a blip! You've had a quarter of a century together—'

'More,' Jane said quietly.

'Well, there you go. There's no way she can compete with that, no matter how good she looks in a swimsuit.'

'I don't know,' Jane said, her eyes drifting to Peter and Stella, paddling along the shoreline. 'It's true I used to know Peter inside out. Better than he knew himself − not that that was saying a lot. But the Peter I knew all those years was a drunk and a womaniser. He's changed. Maybe Stella knows him better than I do now.'

Perhaps she was right. Lesley was conflicted. Now that she'd befriended Stella, she didn't feel good about plotting against her like this. On the other hand, if she and Peter would be as miserable together as Rafe seemed to think, wouldn't she be doing her a favour in the long run?

'He might be a bit more domesticated, but he's still the same person,' she said to Jane. 'Back me up on this, Al.'

'She's right,' Al said, sitting up and turning to them both.

'And why should Stella swoop in and get the benefit after you put in all that work on him?' Lesley continued. 'If anyone's entitled to the new, improved Peter, it's you.'

'Am I, though? It was my decision to get divorced. Maybe I should leave them to it.'

'No.' Al shook his head. 'You said yourself Peter's changed. You wouldn't have kicked him out in the first place if he'd been even half as tame as he is now.'

'Plus you'd be rescuing him from the clutches of a gold-digger, don't forget,' Lesley added. 'Who knows what she has in store for him once she's got a ring on her finger?'

'I'm tempted to say it'd serve him right. He who lives by the sword ...'

'But you don't mean that,' Al said.

'No,' Jane said wearily. 'I don't.'

'So, history it is!' Lesley said.

Jane gave her a crooked smile, then lay back and picked up her book. But Lesley could tell she was still watching Stella and Peter over the top of it.

26

This was the easiest money she'd ever earned, Lesley thought, as she lazed in the sun, letting the heat seep into her bones. Suddenly she felt drops of cold water on her stomach, and she jerked upright to see Scott standing at the end of her lounger, shaking his head like a wet dog, sending a spray of water in every direction. Rafe was beside him, water glistening on his tanned, taut body.

'We've got jet skis,' Scott said, grabbing a towel and swiping randomly at his face and arms before tossing it onto a lounger. 'We got one for you too,' he said to Al. 'So who's in? Lesley?'

Al looked at her questioningly. She shielded her eyes and looked out at the powerful machines zipping around on the horizon, bouncing on the waves. It did look exciting. 'I've never been on a jet ski.'

'It's great fun,' Al said. 'You'll love it.'

'Okay, then. I'm game. Is it difficult to steer? Will I get thrown off?'

'No. Just hold on tight to me,' Al said. 'You'll be perfectly safe, I promise.'

'Hey, why do you assume you'll be driving?'

Al shrugged. 'You have to have a licence to do it here. Sorry, I just assumed you wouldn't have one.'

'Oh. Well, as it happens, you were right. I don't.'

'Anyone else?' Scott asked. 'There's room for one more.'

'Two more, surely?' Jane said.

Scott shook his head. 'My boyfriend's sharing mine.'

'Boyfriend?' Lesley frowned.

Jane looked around. 'Is Louis here?'

'No, he met someone,' Rafe said, rolling his eyes. 'Someone new.'

'What? When did this happen?'

'Just now,' Scott said to her. 'In the line at the jet ski place. His name's Leo. Or was it Larry?' He frowned. 'Anyway, I think I'm in love.'

'Not wasting any time,' Peter said, grinning. 'Good for you!'

'How about you, Joy?' Scott asked.

Joy shook her head. 'I think a pedalo is more my speed,' she said with a wry smile.

'Stella?' Rafe called across to her. 'Care to join me?'

She looked up from rubbing sunscreen onto her legs. 'Um ... I don't think so,' she said, glancing at Peter. 'Thanks.'

'Go,' Peter said to her. 'You'll enjoy it.'

'Yes, please come,' Lesley said. 'I don't want to be the only newbie.'

Stella smiled uncertainly at Rafe. 'Okay, then.'

～

PETER WATCHED Stella and Rafe as they walked away together, and felt a sudden sharp pang of longing – for quite what, he couldn't say. For their youth, perhaps: their lithe, supple bodies; their energy and vitality? Or for that feeling of possibility that they seemed to exude – of life opening up and the potential for new beginnings? Maybe he was nostalgic for a time when there were still new experiences to be had, first times and fresh adventures ahead of him.

As he watched, Rafe leaned in and said something in Stella's ear, and she threw her head back, giving an open-throated laugh. He was struck by how young she looked. It was good to see her so happy and relaxed, and he was glad that Rafe was being nice to her. He'd worried that he'd give her a hard time. Watching them together, he wondered, not for the first time, if he was doing Stella a disservice by marrying her. If he was out of the picture ...

If I was a jealous man, he thought ... and then he caught himself. He *was* a jealous man. He remembered the fierce burning pain he'd felt whenever Jane had flirted with another man. Just thinking about it conjured up a corrosive gnawing in his gut, like a visceral thing, as if it was happening right now.

Why was that? Why could he watch Stella with Rafe now and not mind? Was it simply because he didn't love her like he'd loved Jane? Or was it just one more thing age robbed you of? Everything else had slowed down and diminished. Perhaps feeling became muted too, and along with fading and failing senses, your heart lost the ability to burn and ache with want.

It should be a good thing to be calmer, more content. But he hated the way aging chipped away bit by bit at everything that made him who he was. Inside he was still the same person he'd always been. But only the people he'd known all his life saw that – saw *him*. To everyone else, he was just a gentle, subdued old man with everything he used to be consigned to the past.

'Can you believe that son of ours?' Jane said, flopping down on the lounger that Stella had vacated. 'Poor Louis not cold in his bed.'

'Scott?' Peter grinned. 'He was ever thus. He always made friends easily.'

'Yeah.' Jane smiled crookedly. 'He takes after you.'

'For better or worse.'

'I like to think our children have the best of both of us. That's why they're perfect.'

'At least that suggests I had *some* redeeming qualities.'

'You weren't the worst. The good always outshone the bad.'

'Almost always,' he murmured.

'Almost,' she said with a faraway look.

'Well, you're still speaking to me. That must say something.'

'It says a lot,' Jane said, smiling at him. 'I think we're doing okay for an old divorced couple.'

'We're bloody marvellous. I'm glad you were able to come,' he said to her. 'It's nice being back here, all of us together. It makes me feel like my old self again.'

'Your young self, you mean. That's what you really want.'

'Isn't that what we all want?'

Jane shrugged. 'I have no desire to be twenty again. I think it suits me being a wise old owl. I've grown out of my looks and into my personality.'

Peter raised his eyebrows. 'When did you get to be so mature?'

'Three-score years and ten will do that to you.'

'Or not,' Peter said with a cheeky grin.

Jane laughed. 'Or not.'

'Anyway, you haven't grown out of your looks. Age has not withered you.' It was true. She had a different kind of beauty now, but it was no less compelling.

'Says the man engaged to a twenty-six-year-old.'

'We didn't split up because I stopped fancying you,' he reminded her.

'No.' She smiled bitterly. 'We split up because you didn't stop fancying everyone else.'

Peter sighed. No good would come of picking at those old scabs. 'I finished your book,' he said, nodding to the iPad beside him.

'Well?' She raised an eyebrow, sitting up straighter, probably as glad to change the subject as he was.

'I thought it was marvellous.'

'Really?' Her face lit up with delight.

'Absolutely. Your best yet.'

'You always say that,' she said dismissively, but she still looked pleased.

'What can I say? It's always true. You get better and better. I don't have a single note.'

'Can you be my editor? Because I just got an email from Kate this morning, and she's got pages and pages.'

'Well, there was just one thing. It's very minor, but—'

He was interrupted by Jane's mobile ringing.

'Oh, hold that thought. Hello?' She stood as she answered the phone, making an apologetic face at him.

She went to the wooden walkway, and he watched her pacing back and forth as she talked on her phone. She returned after a few minutes, and plopped back down in the lounger next to him, tossing her phone on the table beside her.

'That was Jonathan,' she said. 'They're having a party on Saturday at their place and we're all invited.'

'That's nice,' Peter said. 'I haven't seen Jonathan and Sophie in ages.'

'Philippe will be there too,' Jane said. 'He's staying with them for the week.'

'Oh God, *really?*' Philippe — that idiot, Peter thought disgustedly. He'd always had the hots for Jane. And suddenly there it was — jealousy. He smiled, welcoming it back like an old friend even as it churned bitterly in his gut. It felt good. It felt like old times. He was almost grateful to Philippe.

'I don't know what you've got against Philippe,' Jane said, but her smug smile told him she knew damn well.

'Randy bugger! I don't know if I can stand an evening with him oiling his way around like he's God's gift. Maybe we should skip it. We can have Jonathan and Sophie over after he's gone.'

Jane fixed him with a weary look. 'Suit yourself,' she said, 'but I'm going.'

She picked up her book and opened it, reclining back in her chair.

'Yes, I suppose I'll go too,' Peter said. 'Be rude not to.'

27

'Y ou were right!' Lesley said to Al as they removed their life vests. 'That was brilliant!'

He grinned at her, revealing his even white teeth, water dripping from his face and hair, and she couldn't help thinking how handsome he was. If she fancied him at all, she'd be seriously lusting after him right now. Just as well she didn't, because she'd be seriously tempted to throw down right here, and sex on the beach really wasn't her thing.

'Glad you enjoyed it.'

Jet skiing had possibly been the best fun she'd ever had with her clothes on. She looked behind them at Stella and Rafe coming out of the water. They looked so perfect together. Stella was shaking out her long, blonde hair, laughing up into Rafe's face. She'd been so happy and exhilarated out on the water, laughing as they ripped through the waves, her long hair flying out behind her as she clung onto Rafe. She and Lesley had shouted and whooped over the roar of the engines as they zipped past each other. It was the first time Lesley had seen Stella cut loose like that. There was something so buttoned-up and contained about her usually. But out there, she'd looked carefree and excited, and ... young, Lesley thought with a little pang of pity. It was like she was acting her age for once, and the change in her was remarkable.

'Hungry?' Al asked, breaking into her thoughts as they walked up the beach.

'Starving!' All that sea air and salt water had given her an appetite.

When they had dried off and pulled on some clothes, they joined the others at the beach bar. Michael, Joy and Peter were already sitting at a long table set for ten, bottles of Perrier and rosé open in the centre. Jane was standing by the bar, talking on her phone as they passed.

Rafe and Stella followed them shortly after.

'Did you have fun, darling?' Peter asked Stella as she took a seat beside him.

'Yes, it was brilliant,' she said, darting a shy smile at Rafe.

Was Lesley imagining it, or was Rafe looking at Stella the way he used to look at Elizabeth Bennet when he was being Mr Darcy? His eyes had that soft, mushy look.

'Where's Scott?' Peter asked.

Rafe shrugged. 'Who knows?'

'Last we saw of him he was zipping off over the horizon with his new boyfriend,' Lesley said.

'Ah!' Peter nodded. 'He'll probably be married before us,' he said to Stella. 'I hope you won't mind being gazumped.'

'You won't believe who that was,' Jane said, returning to her seat and tossing her mobile onto the table.

'Don't tell me,' Peter said. '*Philippe?*' He pronounced the name with an exaggerated French accent, imbuing it with such venom, Lesley almost laughed out loud.

Jane rolled her eyes at him. 'No. It was Conor O'Neill. He offered me a part.'

'Good Lord!' Michael said.

Lesley and Al exchanged brief meaningful looks.

'How odd!' Peter reared back in surprise. 'He knows you gave up acting ages ago.'

'Yes, but ... he asked me if I'd consider doing this as a favour to him. He practically begged me, in fact.' Lesley could tell she was flattered. Good old Conor, she thought.

'Huh!' Peter exclaimed. 'What's the part?'

'Nell in *Endgame*. They're doing it in September. Lorcan's directing.'

'*Endgame*! Good Lord! We're not that old, are we?'

'Well, don't expect to be offered Hamlet anytime soon.'

'Did you tell him no?'

'Conor? You know what he's like. I said I'd think about it.'

'Really?'

She shrugged. '*You* try saying no to him.' She gave a smug little smile as she poured herself a glass of rosé. 'Because he's asking you to play Nagg.'

'WANT ME TO DO YOUR BACK?' Al asked, as Lesley creamed herself up for the afternoon.

'Oh.' Well, he was her boyfriend, after all. 'Yes, please.' She handed him the bottle of sunscreen and lay down on her stomach, flipping her hair to the side.

'So, Conor's come through, then,' she murmured, closing her eyes as Al began massaging the sun cream into her skin. His hands felt good – warm and firm – and Lesley sighed deeply as they moved over her back. 'Do you think Jane will go for it?'

'She seemed pleased to be asked. And Conor can be very persuasive.'

'I can see how he would be. Plus it'd give her an excuse to spend time with Peter.'

She felt a little tingle of pleasure as Al's hands moved over her waist and down to her lower back, and she had a sudden longing for them to go lower, to slip inside her bikini bottoms and—Gah! What was wrong with her? Al was just putting on her sun cream. It wasn't foreplay. She had to remember this was a job. They were just pretending. 'So who's this Philippe?' she asked, to distract herself.

Al chuckled. 'He's a cousin of old friends of theirs. He's always had the major hots for Jane.'

'Oh, interesting.' Lesley perked up. 'I wondered what Peter's problem was with him. He's obviously jealous. That's good.'

'He'll probably be at the Simpsons' shindig.' Jane had announced at lunch that they were all invited to a party on Saturday night.

'Even better,' she said. 'Jane should flirt with him.'

'I'm sure she will. There,' he said, 'all done.'

'Thanks,' Lesley said, turning over and resisting the urge to take off her bikini top and get him to do her boobs. She felt herself flush at the thought, and shoved her sunglasses back on.

'Now you do me?' Al asked, holding the bottle out to her.

'Sure,' she said, taking it from him. He lay down on his stomach, and she squeezed some cream into her hands and started rubbing it into his back, taking her time, allowing herself to luxuriate in the feel of his warm skin as her hands glided over the firm muscles of his back.

'Al?'

'Mmm?'

'Did you see the way Rafe was looking at Stella at lunch?'

'Yeah, he was laying it on pretty thick, wasn't he?'

'He said he wasn't going to make a move on her, though.'

'Did he?'

'Well ...' Lesley had the distinct impression that Rafe had said no, but now that she thought about it, she wasn't so sure. 'Are you sure he doesn't fancy her for real?' she asked as she worked down to the hollow of his lower back. 'He looked pretty ... smitten.'

'He's just a good actor. Do you think Stella might be tempted?'

'I don't know. But he's pretty irresistible, you have to admit. Especially when he goes full Darcy like that.'

'Hmm,' Al said. He didn't sound too happy about it.

'What? That's what you wanted, isn't it? If he can entice her away from Peter, all your troubles are over.'

Nevertheless, Lesley couldn't help feeling bad for Stella. She was starting to like her, and even if she was just marrying Peter for his money, it didn't necessarily mean she had evil intentions. They knew nothing about her background. Maybe she'd grown up in poverty, and just wanted a comfortable life. And who could blame her if she was tempted by all this, she thought, looking around at the rows of golden, pampered bodies stretched out in the sun, while liveried waiters catered to their every whim. It was pretty damn seductive.

As she worked down towards the top of Al's shorts, she felt suddenly aware of how almost naked he was, and once it occurred to her, all she could think about was the fact that it would only take pulling those swim shorts down and he'd be completely naked. If he turned around she'd see his dick. She could touch it. She wondered what he looked like; what he'd be like in bed. He was good at everything – he'd probably be brilliant. As she stroked her hands slowly over his broad shoulders, she wondered was this making him hard, even a little bit.

Gah! Get a grip, Lesley. What the hell was wrong with her? She had no interest in seeing Al's dick. It was too long since she'd had a shag, that was all, and all this sun and sea air was making her horny.

'There, done!' she said, giving his back a firm, businesslike slap. She replaced the stopper on the bottle and went back to her own lounger, lay down and picked up her book.

LATER, back at the villa, when she was sure Al was otherwise occupied, she went to their room and called Romy.

'I've been having … thoughts,' she told her, after they'd chatted for a bit.

'Thoughts?'

'About Al. And his penis.'

'Impure thoughts?'

'I don't think so. Just the fact that he has one, really.'

'But you always knew that, right?'

'Well, yes – in the back of my mind, I suppose. But it's sort of … come to my attention and now I can't stop thinking about it.'

'Come to your attention how? Did he flash you?'

'No! Nothing like that. But we were at the beach today, so I saw him in his togs, and I suddenly started thinking what it would be like to see him without his togs.'

'Are these thoughts troubling you, my child?'

'Well, it's a bit disturbing. I mean, I don't fancy Al, so it's not as if I want to get with him. But it's like – you know when you have a sexy dream about someone who you've never thought about like that before, and suddenly you start seeing them in a whole other way?'

'Yeah. It doesn't always work that way, though. I mean, I once had a sex dream about Mr Bean.'

'Ew!'

'I know. He still doesn't do it for me. So do you *want* to see Al without his togs? Because you probably only have to ask.'

'No, I don't. I'm just horny, I guess.'

'Well, why not take it out on Al? I'm sure he'd be happy to oblige. And you could do worse. You *have* done worse.'

'I don't know. I'm here to do a job. It's better to keep it professional. Besides, I don't think he's into me in that way.'

'He asked you out, didn't he, the first time you met?'

'Yeah, but ... he hasn't made any move on me since. I guess he wasn't that bothered.'

'Back to DIY, then?'

Lesley sighed. 'I don't even have my own room here because everyone *thinks* I'm shagging Al. So DIY is tricky.'

'Well ... I don't know what to suggest then. There's always the shower?'

'Yeah. I'll just have lots of cold showers, I guess.'

Romy laughed. 'I meant you could do DIY when you're alone in the bathroom.'

'Oh, yeah.' Lesley heaved a heartfelt sigh. 'Well, it's not my favourite, but I suppose I'll just have to make do.'

28

'Are you ready?' Stella asked Peter as she came out onto the terrace the following morning. 'We're leaving in a few minutes.'

Peter snapped his book shut and looked up at her. She was wearing a red and white polka-dot dress, a matching scarf tied in her hair. Her slanting green eyes sparkled, and her skin was dewy and radiant. Everything about her seemed to vibrate with youth and vitality. He felt weary just looking at her.

'I think I'm going to stay here,' he said. 'Laze by the pool and finish this.' He indicated the fat tome he was reading.

'Oh.' He saw the flash of disappointment in her face, but it was gone in a second, replaced by a placid smile. 'I'll stay too, then. Keep you company.'

Peter sighed, dropping his head back against the padded cushion of his chair. 'No, you should go – enjoy yourself. You'll love Villefranche.'

'But why don't you want to come? Are you feeling okay?' She frowned in concern.

He tried to swallow his annoyance. She was just being thoughtful. 'I'm fine,' he said. 'Just not in the mood. I've been to Villefranche. Bought the T-shirt, as they say. Don't worry about me, I'm just being an old fart.'

'Well, we could go together another time.' She sank onto the seat beside him. 'I'd rather see it with you anyway.'

Irritation bubbled up inside him. 'Oh, for God's sake, go, and stop fussing over me!'

Stella reared back, hurt etched on her face, and Peter felt a stab of remorse.

'Sorry,' he said gently, taking her hand. 'I didn't mean to snap. But I don't need a nursemaid. I'm not an invalid.'

She opened her mouth to say something, but shut it again.

'That's exactly what you are, Peter,' Joy said, coming out through the patio doors and surprising them both.

'Touché,' Peter said softly, smiling at her.

Joy looked from one to the other. 'You two had better get a wiggle on,' she said.

'I—I'm not sure if I'm going to go,' Stella said, twisting her hands and looking warily at Peter.

'I'm sorry, darling,' he said. 'I shouldn't have bitten your head off like that. But you go, have fun. I'm quite happy here on my own, honestly.'

'You won't be alone anyway,' Joy said. 'Michael and I are staying here too – he's not feeling well, poor love. And Jane wants to get some work done on her edits.'

'There,' Peter said to Stella. 'No need to worry about me. I'll have plenty of company.'

'Are you ready?' Rafe asked them, coming through the patio doors, and rattling car keys impatiently.

'I'm not coming,' Peter said to him. 'But this gorgeous

girl is.' He stood and pulled Stella up from her seat. 'You'll look after her for me, won't you?'

'Of course.'

As he watched Stella and Rafe walk away together, he thought once again what a beautiful couple they would make – and realised that the thought didn't bother him in the slightest.

'I DID OFFER to stay with Peter,' Stella said to Rafe as she slid into the passenger seat. He already disapproved of her enough. She didn't want to appear flighty and cruel, abandoning her aged fiancé so she could go off and have a good time. 'But he insisted I go with you.'

'He's right. It's your first time here. It'd be a shame to spend all your time sitting by the pool.' She couldn't see his eyes, just her reflection in his mirrored sunglasses, so she couldn't tell if he was sincere. 'Besides, it'll be nice for that lot to have some time alone together.'

That didn't put her mind at ease, and as they all piled into the car, she was half tempted to make a bolt for it and say she'd changed her mind and would stay at the villa after all. She already felt like she and Peter were starting to drift apart, and she didn't like the idea of him spending the day with Jane. It was different to when they were in LA. With his family around him, he didn't rely on her as much as he had then, and she felt they were losing the closeness they'd had when it was just the two of them. Maybe it had been a mistake not to start sharing a bed with him when they came here, but he had given her her own room on the first day, automatically continuing their arrangement at home. The longer they went without having sex, the more

of a big deal it felt, and she worried that it didn't seem to
bother Peter.

It was ironic really. Sex was supposed to be the whole
point of a man Peter's age taking up with someone as
young as her. They looked like a walking cliché, a tired old
joke to which everyone knew the punchline. The public
would be amazed to know the truth about their chaste relationship. But perhaps it had never been about sex for Peter,
and all he wanted was companionship, someone to look
after him in his old age. Or maybe he didn't want her in
that way because of what he knew about her ...

'Don't worry about Dad,' Rafe said, glancing across at
her. 'Believe me, he wouldn't hesitate to ask you to stay if
he was the least bit concerned he'd be bored or lonely. He's
not the self-sacrificing type.'

If he was trying to put her mind at ease, it wasn't working. She wasn't worried Peter would miss her. She was
afraid he wouldn't miss her at all.

LESLEY FOUND it an unusual experience walking around
Villefranche with Scott and Rafe. They attracted attention
wherever they went, little ripples of awareness following in
their wake. She felt eyes on them all the time, but the Bradshaws seemed not to notice the hushed whispers in the
harbour-side restaurant where they'd had lunch, or the
furtive nods and sidelong glances cast their way by passing
strangers as they explored the charming old town.

She was getting used to it herself, so she didn't pay
much attention when a man coming towards them in the
opposite direction seemed to be staring. She and Stella
were walking in front, Al and his cousins trailing a little
behind.

'Joanna!' She'd been so engrossed in their chat that she hadn't noticed the man had stopped right in front of them. It took her a moment to realise that he was looking at Stella. 'I don't believe it!' he continued. 'I haven't seen you in years.' He was speaking rapidly in an Essex accent, beaming at Stella like a long-lost friend. He had spiky black hair with dramatic white-blonde streaks and small beady eyes in his deeply tanned face. His short, compact body was squeezed into skin-tight jeans and a cropped T-shirt that showed off every muscle of his well-defined torso.

Stella seemed frozen, blinking at him dazedly. 'I'm sorry,' she said stiffly. 'I don't—'

'You don't remember me?' He looked surprised but a little pleased. 'You probably don't recognise me because I've lost a ton of weight. It's Adam,' he said, placing a hand on his chest. 'From Sassoon, remember? Used to be a giant tubster?'

'Sorry,' Stella cut in. 'You have me mistaken for someone else.'

Adam looked taken aback. 'No!' He frowned. 'You're having me on, right?'

'No, sorry.'

'But you did work at Vidal Sassoon?' Adam was looking a little uncertain now.

'No, not me.'

Lesley felt Stella's eyes slide to her momentarily.

'Oh! Right,' Adam said, glancing at Lesley. 'Sorry, my mistake. I thought you were someone I used to know.'

'I must have a doppelgänger,' Stella said.

'Well, sorry to have bothered you,' Adam said, his eyes widening as the others caught up with them.

'No problem,' Stella said.

Lesley turned to watch as Adam hurried away, her

heart racing with excitement. There was something fishy about the exchange between him and Stella just now. She wasn't convinced that it was a case of mistaken identity at all. Had Adam known Stella before, under a different name? There was something odd about the way they'd looked at each other before he'd clammed up and backed off. She couldn't let this possible lead slip away. She had to find a way to talk to him! She and Al exchanged significant looks.

'Who was that?' Rafe asked.

'Just someone who thought he knew me,' Stella said, but her voice sounded a little shaky, and she seemed rattled.

'Is there something you haven't told us?' Scott said playfully.

'What?' Stella frowned.

'Do you have an evil twin lurking somewhere in the background?'

'No.' She gave a stiff laugh. 'I guess I just have one of those faces.'

But she didn't, Lesley thought. Stella was striking and distinctive looking; she didn't have one of those faces at all.

She was pleased when Al took her hand and gave it a squeeze, glad there was someone who could acknowledge and share in her excitement. As they all walked on, she racked her brain, trying to think of an excuse for running after Adam before he got away. Then she had a flash of inspiration.

'Oh shit, my phone!' she gasped, opening her bag and rummaging through it. 'I must have left it at the restaurant.' She looked at Al in distress.

'We'll go back and get it. We'll meet you back at the car,' Al said to his cousins.

'We have to talk to that guy!' Lesley hissed once the others were out of earshot.

Adam was crossing the road now, turning up a side street. Lesley glanced behind her to make sure the others were out of sight before darting after him. Once they turned the corner, she started running, and she caught up with him at the top of the road.

'Excuse me!' Lesley called to his back. 'Adam!'

He turned at the sound of his name, and looked surprised to see her and Al.

'Oh. Hello?'

'Hi.' Lesley puffed. She was a little out of breath from the chase, and her heart was pounding with excitement. She hadn't thought about what she was going to say when they caught up with him, so she had to think quickly. 'Sorry to bother you but – you said you were a hairdresser …'

'Did I?' Adam looked confused.

'Well, you said you used to work at Vidal Sassoon.'

'Oh, yes.'

'Anyway, the thing is, I could really do with getting my hair cut while I'm here—'

'Yes.' Adam nodded, giving her hair the once-over. She decided she didn't like Adam.

'—and I'd love to find an English-speaking hairdresser,' she continued. 'I was wondering … do you know any around here by any chance?'

'You're in luck! I'm in a salon in St Tropez now,' he said, pulling a card from the tight pocket of his jeans with difficulty. 'Give that number a ring and ask for me. I'll sort that lot out for you.'

Yes! Lesley resisted punching the air in triumph. She was so happy, she didn't even care that Adam was being rude about her hair. 'Perfect. Thank you,' she said evenly, taking the card from him. 'I'll ring you tomorrow.'

Her heart was racing as she turned and walked away with Al, but she managed to contain her excitement until they'd turned the corner.

'Oh my God!' she burst out then, brandishing the card. 'That was so much fun!'

'You were brilliant!' Al grinned. 'Coming up with something on the spur of the moment like that—'

'I know!' Lesley beamed with pride. 'It's like bullshitting is my superpower.'

'This could be the breakthrough we've been looking for,' Al said as they walked back to join the others.

Lesley could kiss him when he talked like that. 'It could crack this case wide open.'

'So, what's our next move?'

Lesley decided not to reprimand him for the 'our'. It was fun having a sidekick, someone she could discuss everything with; she felt she might burst if she had to keep it all to herself. 'We're going to St Tropez!' she said. 'I'm getting a haircut.'

'Oh.' Al's face fell. 'Do we have to?'

Lesley was surprised how deflated she felt that he seemed reluctant to join in all of a sudden. 'You don't have to come if you don't want to,' she said. 'I just thought—'

'What? Of course I want to come! I wouldn't miss it for the world. Only ...'

'What?'

'You won't get too much off, will you?' he said, looking at the top of her head.

'Why do you say that?'

'I like your hair. The more of it, the merrier.'

Lesley rolled her eyes. 'You're not really my boyfriend,

remember. You're not allowed to say stuff like that to me – except in front of your family, of course.'

'I'm not allowed to say that you have nice hair?'

'No,' she said, feeling unreasonable. 'Well, only if someone is listening,' she conceded.

LESLEY COULDN'T WAIT to go to bed that night and discuss the whole thing properly with Al, but she had to try to tamp down her impatience.

'We're going hiking tomorrow,' Scott announced to everyone at dinner. 'Who's in?'

'Hiking?' Lesley thought she must have misheard. Hiking certainly didn't feature in her fantasies of a holiday on the French Riviera.

'It's something we do every year,' Al said to her. 'With a group of our friends here. It's sort of a tradition.'

'Oh, right. Well, you might have told me. I mean, I didn't bring my hiking boots, or my whatchamacallem ... crampons or anything. So I guess I'll have to sit this one out,' she said, attempting to sound regretful.

'Oh, don't worry. It's not difficult,' Al said. 'But didn't I tell you to pack walking boots?'

'I thought you were joking,' Lesley said, reasonably she thought. 'I mean what kind of holiday do you need to pack a bikini and walking boots for?'

'Well, obviously they're not meant to be worn together. Although ...'

'Get your mind out of the gutter. That would not be a good look on anybody.'

'I'm sure you could carry it off.'

'Anyway, don't worry,' Jane piped up. 'There are loads of spare boots here. I'm sure we can find you a pair in your size.'

'I'm a six,' Lesley said.

'Same as me!' Jane said. 'I have an old pair here you can borrow.'

'Great!' Clearly, she had no way out. 'In that case, count me in!'

'And me,' Stella said. 'We could do with the exercise.' She glanced at Peter. 'As long as it's not too strenuous.'

Peter shook his head. 'We leave that to the youngsters. But you should go, darling. You'll enjoy it.'

'Oh.' Stella bit her lip.

'We go into the hills behind Eze,' Rafe said to her. 'It's really beautiful. You should come.'

'Oh, well ... if you're sure you don't mind,' she said to Peter. 'I do miss hiking since leaving LA. I lived near some really good trails.'

'Not at all. I'll be perfectly happy here with the rest of the oldies.'

'Thanks very much!' Jane said with a roll of her eyes.

'It will be like old times.'

'But promise me you'll go for a good walk on the beach,' Stella said to him. 'Or at least have a swim.'

'Don't worry, Jane and Joy will look after me,' Peter said to her. 'Won't you?' He looked at Jane.

'We'll keep him on the straight and narrow,' Joy said to Stella with a kind smile.

'We'll return him in the same condition we got him in,' Jane added wryly.

'Well, that's me done,' Lesley said, yawning extravagantly as she pushed her dessert plate away. 'I'm off to bed. You coming, Al?'

'It's only nine o'clock!' Scott said, looking at her in astonishment.

'Yes, but ... we have an early start in the morning. I need to marshal my strength for the big hike.'

Scott grinned. 'You just can't wait to get Al into bed.'

'Okay, you got me,' she said with a laugh.

'I'll find those boots for you,' Jane said, getting up.

'I'll follow you up shortly,' Al called after her.

'Oh!' Al froze in the doorway of their bedroom, eyes widening. 'Um ... Lesley, you know I was joking about that look, right?' He nodded at her as she paraded up and down their room in her bikini and Jane's walking boots.

'You don't like it?' She struck a pose in front of the full-length cheval mirror.

Al gulped. 'Um ... I think it looks great. You should definitely wear that outfit tomorrow.'

Lesley laughed. 'Dream on! Jane just said I should walk around in the boots a bit to wear them in.' She'd been getting undressed and had already stripped down to her bikini when Jane had turned up with the boots, so she'd decided to walk around the bedroom a bit to break them in.

'Good idea,' Al nodded, not taking his eyes off her. 'You were wrong about it not looking good, by the way.'

'You think?' Lesley turned to him, her hands on her hips.

'Absolutely! You look fantastic. But then you'd look good in anything.'

Lesley blushed, but felt a little curl of pleasure at the compliment. Rob had never said things like that to her. But sometimes the way Al looked at her made her feel quite hot and bothered.

She started pacing again. 'So you know why I was so keen to get you up here?'

'Unfortunately, I am all too aware that it's not because

you couldn't wait to ravish me.' Al sat down on the bed. 'You walk, we'll talk.'

'What do you think that was all about today?' she asked. 'Do you think Stella really is Joanna?'

'It seems possible,' Al said. 'She *is* very cagey about her past.'

'And she seemed a bit shaken up by the whole thing.'

'I don't think that Adam guy was really convinced that it was a case of mistaken identity.'

'No,' Lesley said, 'but it was strange the way he backed off. It was like he was in on some secret that he realised Stella didn't want us to know.'

'But why would she have changed her name? I mean, that's pretty radical, isn't it?'

'Usually when people change their identity, they're either running away from a bad situation or—'

'Or they've done something they need to distance themselves from.'

'What if she's already married and she's planning to be a bigamist with Peter?' Lesley had a brief image of herself coming up with the crucial evidence just in time to stand up at Peter and Stella's wedding and declare the existence of an impediment, like in *Jane Eyre*. But exciting as that would be, she wouldn't like to do that to Stella on her wedding day, even if she *was* trying to marry Peter under false pretences – not without at least giving her a chance to explain herself.

'It could be even more sinister than that,' Al said.

'Like being a black widow,' Lesley said thoughtfully. 'Maybe she's done this before – married some rich old geezer and bonked him to death.'

'Or she could be on the run from an abusive ex.'

'She did tell me she'd deleted all of her social media accounts because an old boyfriend was stalking her.'

'Oh, that's good,' Al said. 'As a lead, I mean,' he added as Lesley threw him a disapproving look.

'Maybe it's even simpler than that. I mean, if she's spent a fortune on plastic surgery, she might just want a completely fresh start as the new improved Stella.'

She stood and picked up her laptop. 'Anyway, at least I have a bit more to go on. I'm going to look up Vidal Sassoon, see if I can find anything there. It's probably too much to hope for that there'll be any link to Joanna at this stage, but you never know.'

'Knock yourself out, Nancy Drew!' Al said as he got up and headed for the bathroom.

29

Stella sprang out of bed early the following morning after a restless night. She still felt unsettled after the encounter with Adam yesterday, but she tried to put it out of her mind as she pulled on her walking boots. She was glad to be going hiking today. Physical exertion was just what she needed to burn up some of the nervous energy that had left her feeling jittery. She swam every day here, of course, and went on long walks with Peter, but she was used to more vigorous exercise, and she was starting to feel lethargic from so much lazing around in the sun.

In the kitchen, she made herself a bowl of muesli, fruit and yoghurt, and went to join the others on the terrace. They were all seated around the table with coffee and a big plate of pastries and bread. They were leaving early to get the hardest part of the walk done before the real heat of the day set in, and Scott was bleary-eyed and half asleep, curled over a bowl of milky coffee and blinking in the early morning sunshine. Rafe, by contrast, looked fresh and wide-awake, in a lime-green T-shirt that brought out the colour of his eyes. He really was a breathtakingly beautiful man. No wonder all his co-stars fell for him.

She sat down beside Lesley.

'Coffee?' Lesley asked her.

'Yes, please,' Stella nodded, side-eyeing the plate of pastries as Lesley poured her a mug.

'Have one,' Scott said, pushing the plate towards her.

She shook her head. 'I'll just have this, thanks,' she said, nodding at her bowl.

'Go on,' Scott urged with a grin. 'Step away from the muesli. We won't tell Dad.'

Stella smiled, tempted. 'Well ...'

'I'll eat that for you, if it'd make you feel better,' Scott said, holding out a hand for her bowl.

'When in France,' Lesley said beside her, handing her a small plate.

'Okay, deal.' Stella handed Scott her bowl and took a pain au chocolat from the plate. 'Just this once.' She tore it in two, smiling guiltily as she smudged her fingers with buttery grease, and crumbs of pastry flaked onto her plate. She popped a piece into her mouth, savouring the luxury of it. Sighing, she closed her eyes as melting chocolate and soft pastry mingled on her tongue. It was heaven.

She opened her eyes to find Rafe watching her, his gaze dark and intense. Their eyes locked and held for a moment before Stella looked away, staring down at her coffee.

'You should eat chocolate more often,' Rafe murmured. 'It suits you.'

Her breath hitched as she looked up to find his eyes still on her. The air between them seemed to crackle with electricity, and she felt hot and flustered. Surely Rafe wasn't actually flirting with her – right in front of everyone? She was engaged to his father, for God's sake. She must be imagining it.

Nevertheless, maybe she shouldn't have agreed to go hiking with them today. She'd been disconcerted yesterday when Peter said it was something the young people did, not sure where she stood, which group she belonged to. Now she wondered had she done the wrong thing, aligning herself with the younger generation, thus putting more distance between herself and Peter. She should have opted to stay with him, and establish her place by his side as his partner. But it was too late to back out now.

'Put away your Mr Darcy look and leave Stella alone,' Scott said, rolling his eyes at his brother. 'You're putting me off my breakfast.'

Stella was grateful to him for making a joke of it and breaking the tension.

'Don't mind him,' Scott said to her. 'He can't help himself. Doesn't even know he's doing it half the time.'

'I don't know what you're talking about,' Rafe said stiffly. But he looked cross and uncomfortable, and Stella could swear he was blushing.

The intense panty-dropping look was gone in an instant, and Stella was relieved. It was just Rafe being Rafe, she told herself. Scott was right, flirting was simply a reflex with him. He was Peter's son, after all; it was in his genes. It didn't mean anything, but, try as she might, she couldn't shake off that look in his eyes, or the way it had made her feel.

'Is your new boyfriend coming with us?' Lesley asked Scott.

'No, unfortunately, he has to work. Those jet skis won't sell themselves.' He polished off the bowl of muesli and pushed it away.

Stella was relieved. At least it wouldn't be all couples. She didn't want to end up paired off with Rafe.

'Come on and we'll pack up the car,' Rafe said to Scott

as he stood. Al followed them, leaving Stella alone with Lesley.

'Maybe I should stay here with Peter after all,' she said, once they were alone.

'No! You have to come,' Lesley said. 'Please! You can't leave me alone with the guys.'

'I don't know ...' She bit her lip. She'd feel bad about ditching Lesley, and she had been looking forward to the hike.

'Don't worry about Rafe, if that's what it is. Like Scott said, it's just the way he is. He can't help himself.'

'You're right,' Stella nodded. 'I'm being silly.'

'Anyway, we're meeting up with friends of theirs, so there'll be plenty of other women around for him to practise his charm on.'

'True,' Stella said. But somehow she didn't feel as reassured as she should at the thought of Rafe flirting with other women. And that just made her feel more unnerved than ever.

LESLEY SAT beside Al in the front, as they wound around the twisty mountainous roads, climbing towards the hilltop village of Eze. The scenery was stunning as they drove along the coast, an endless vista of sun-dappled water and spiky green palm trees.

They found a space in the car park at the base of the village and stood in the sun, waiting for the others to arrive. Before long, a pale-yellow open-top car pulled up alongside them with a flurry of whooping and waving, and four people spilled out, engulfing Al and his cousins with enthusiastic hugs and back-slapping, while Stella and Lesley stood by and watched.

Al introduced them to everyone. Toby was floppy-

haired and pretty, with the same sort of posh English
accent as Al, and his sister Emma was a pale, long-limbed
beauty with a mane of blonde curls, dark glasses perched
on top of her head. Their friend Jill was petite, her short
dark hair worn in a chic pixie cut that showed off her elfin
features, and her boyfriend Luc was a wiry French-
Moroccan with a shaved head.

Lesley had been a little insulted when Al had offered
her a walking stick from the boot of the car, telling him
she wasn't a geriatric. But when she saw that the very cool
Emma was using one, she changed her mind and took it,
and she was very glad of it as they walked up a steep
incline towards the village. Rafe was in front with Alex
and Emma; Scott, Al and Stella a little behind them. She
was bringing up the rear with Luc and Jill, and they
chatted as they walked. Luc was in IT, and Jill was a
graphic designer, and they lived as digital nomads, travel-
ling the world in between bouts of living in France or
England.

Jill was originally from London, as were Toby and
Emma. Their families all owned properties in the area, and
they had been spending summers in Nice since they were
children. Jill had told her, 'We've all known each other
forever.'

It was a steep walk to the medieval village of Eze, but
nothing like as difficult as Lesley had expected. She really
didn't see the need for hiking boots. Eze was impossibly
pretty. Perched on a cliff overlooking the sea, it looked like
something straight out of a fairy tale.

They came to a little cobbled square, a few tables
dotted around on the terrace in front of a tiny café. Toby
and Emma were talking to a couple sitting at one of the
tables, and as they approached, the woman looked over
and waved. Al raised a hand in greeting, and joined them.

He bent to kiss the woman's cheek, then shook hands with the man seated opposite her.

'Oh,' Jill said, stopping beside Lesley. 'Shit! I didn't know she was going to be here.'

'Who?' Lesley asked, squinting at the woman, who looked strangely familiar. She tried to figure out where she might have seen her before. Maybe she just reminded her of someone.

'Cassie,' Jill said. 'Al's ex?'

'Fuck!' Scott breathed, coming to a halt behind her.

'Oh! I wondered why she looked familiar,' Lesley said, almost to herself, as they started walking again.

'Have you met her before?' Scott asked, surprised.

'No, but I've seen photos on Al's Facebook.'

'I wouldn't worry about it,' Jill said kindly.

'Oh, I'm not,' Lesley said quickly. 'I just ... wasn't expecting her to be here, that's all.' She wondered if Al had known she'd be here. If he'd been blindsided by it, he was doing a good job of hiding it, she thought, watching him chatting to the couple, his hand resting casually on the back of Cassie's chair.

'Yeah, her parents own a house in Cannes, and they come here around this time every year, same as the rest of us. She and Al first met over here. She was an old friend of Jean Claude's.' She nodded at the man sitting opposite Cassie.

'Oh, right.' Lesley tried to appear unfazed. But she felt very much out of the loop, and she didn't like it.

Scott grinned at her. 'Really, you don't have to worry about Cassie,' he whispered in her ear as they moved forward. 'You're much more Al's type. Come on, I'll introduce you.'

'Cassie!' Scott pulled Lesley forward as they surrounded her table. 'This is Al's girlfriend, Lesley. Lesley, this is Cassie, Al's ex, and Jean-Claude, the guy she dumped him for.'

'Hello, Lesley,' Cassie said. 'Lovely to meet you.' She shielded her eyes and looked at Scott in amusement. 'Scott, I see you're still as big a shit-stirrer as ever.'

'Just telling it like it is, darling.' Scott grinned.

Al put an arm around Lesley's shoulders and pulled her into his side, and she nestled closer, appreciating the gesture. She felt Cassie sizing her up us as they shook hands, and she did the same, pleased that Cassie wasn't as intimidatingly stunning as she was in her Facebook photos – clearly a fan of filters, Lesley thought.

'We didn't know you were going to be here today,' Scott said to Cassie. 'You didn't reply to the group WhatsApp.'

'It was a last-minute decision,' Cassie said. 'It's been so long since I've seen you all. I miss you.' Her eyes flicked to Al and she gave a playful pout. Al didn't respond, but Jean-Claude looked sulky anyway.

'Right!' Cassie slapped the table and stood. 'Are we ready for this hike, then?'

'Oh.' Lesley looked to Al uncertainly. 'Didn't we just do it?'

'The walk up from the car park?' He laughed. 'Hardly. This is just the starting point.'

'Oh. Right.' She tried not to look as dismayed as she felt as they all set off again up a winding path away from the village.

'Last one up's a rotten wanker!' Cassie turned to shout at the rest of the group, before she and Jean-Claude took the lead, racing ahead like a pair of mountain goats.

'First to the top gets to give me a blow job!' Jean-Claude yelled, charging after her.

'I think we already have a winner in the rotten wanker category,' Scott said, rolling his eyes.

'God, it's not a competition, is it?' Lesley huffed. Then she remembered what Al had told her about the man Cassie had cheated on him with – always first to the top. Poor Al – it must be hard on him seeing Jean-Claude and Cassie together like this.

'Are you okay?' she asked him, taking his hand and giving it a squeeze.

'Yes, fine!' He looked surprised by her show of solidarity.

She really didn't want to give Jean-Claude a blow job, but she felt the least she could do was make sure Al got to the top first.

'Come on, let's beat them to it,' she said, tugging on his hand.

'Don't pay any attention to them. It's not a race.'

'I'd still like to win. Come on – I've got a second wind. Quick before we lose them.'

HALF AN HOUR LATER, Lesley was red in the face, panting and dripping with sweat. She'd have killed for a sit down and a cold drink, but instead she staggered on after Al until her chest was bursting and her throat aching with the effort. The sun was beating down and her clothes were stuck to her. They'd raced ahead and passed out all the others, even leaving Cassie and Jean-Claude behind in their wake, but the initial sprint had taken too much out of her. She hated giving up, but she had to stop or pass out.

'I just ... have to ... stop ... for ... a minute,' she panted to Al's back, barely managing to get the words out. He'd strode ahead and hadn't noticed her slowing.

'Oh.' He turned and walked back to her. 'Are you okay?'

Lesley nodded as she didn't have any more breath to speak. She took a long slug from her bottle of water. 'Just need a little breather.'

'Are you sure?' Al frowned at her in concern. She dreaded to think how she must look. 'We don't have to do this, you know. It's not a race, despite what Jean-Claude might think.'

'No. I want to,' Lesley said, dragging air into her lungs. She didn't want to let Al down in front of his ex. He might not be real, but he was the nicest boyfriend she'd ever had, and she felt she owed it to him. She'd make it to the top before that pair of cheating sleazebags if it was the last thing she did – and it could well be. 'Come on,' she said determinedly, glancing down the hill. Cassie and Jean-Claude were catching up, Stella and Rafe close behind them.

Determined to stay ahead of them, she pressed on, but after another ten minutes, she had to admit defeat. She'd done her best, but it was no use. She couldn't go another step without collapsing – and that wouldn't impress anyone. She stopped, sinking down onto a large rock, her legs buckling beneath her.

'Are you okay?' Al looked down at her, frowning in concern.

'I can't go any further, Al. Sorry.'

'It's fine.' He sat down beside her and smiled.

'You go on ahead,' she said, waving at the path. 'I'm just slowing you down.'

'No way. If you're staying here, so am I. No one gets left behind.'

'You and your bloody boy scout code of honour.' She

rolled her eyes. 'Stop being noble, and save yourself! You can still be first to the top.'

He shook his head. 'No. I'm not leaving you here.'

'Sorry,' she said, feeling pathetic. 'But thanks for being so nice about it.'

'It's fine. I didn't really fancy giving Jean-Claude a blow job anyway.'

Lesley giggled. Then she had an idea. 'We wouldn't look like losers if we just stopped because we had better things to do.'

'What do you mean?'

'If we were overcome with lust, for instance, and we just had to throw down here because we couldn't keep our hands off each other.'

Al looked at her closely. 'It could happen.'

'They may be the first to the top, but they'd still wish they were us.'

Al's gaze dropped to her mouth. 'But we'd have to—'

Lesley shrugged. 'I'm game if you are. It wouldn't be so bad, would it? I'm a very good kisser, you know.'

'So am I.' Al grinned.

'Okay, quick,' Lesley said, grabbing Al as Cassie's booming voice could be heard getting closer. 'Kiss me!' She shifted off the rock onto the grass and pulled him down beside her as she pressed her lips to his. Al lay half on top of her, his mouth warm and soft on hers. Heat washed over her as she curled her hand into the short hair at the nape of his neck, the smell of warm grass mingling with the clean, soapy smell of Al's skin. She moaned loudly as she heard footsteps approaching, just in case Cassie wouldn't spot them. But in reality there was nothing moan-worthy about the way Al was kissing her. Maybe he was off his game because he was thrown by seeing Cassie. Or perhaps he was holding back

because he didn't want to take advantage of the situation, so
he didn't open his mouth, or try to slip her the tongue. He
was keeping it professional, which on the whole she appreciated – especially in light of her recent horniness. She lifted
her top as she heard the others approach. 'Stick your hand
up my shirt,' she hissed at Al, aware of Cassie and Jean-
Claude approaching in her peripheral vision.

He frowned and shook his head.

'Just do it!' When he hesitated, she grabbed his hand
and moved it under her T shirt herself. She was very aware
of her damp skin and the rivulet of sweat between her
breasts, but it was all for a good cause. His hand felt warm,
barely touching her skin as it hovered uncertainly over her
stomach and curled around her waist, carefully avoiding
going anywhere near her breasts. 'Oh Al,' she moaned for
effect.

She heard Cassie's disgusted tut when she saw them,
muttering something about acting like teenagers as she
passed, and she clamped Al's hand to her and continued
kissing him until the footsteps had faded into the distance.
She released her hand then, but he didn't move his, and
carried on kissing her.

'Um ... Al.' She pushed him away gently. 'They're
gone.'

'Oh.' He lifted himself off her, blinking dazedly, as if
waking up. 'So they have. Sorry.'

'Jeez, get a room, you two!' She heard Scott's laugh,
and looked up to see him and Stella looking down at them.
'Come on,' he said to Stella, grabbing her hand. 'We're
beating them to the top. I'm after that blow job from Van
Damme.'

Al sat up as Stella's giggle faded into the distance,
resting his elbows on his knees. Lesley was interested to see
that now he was the one out of breath.

He turned to her as she sat up beside him. 'Well, that was ... nice.' He smiled at her, his eyes crinkling, and she thought what a lovely warm smile he had.

'Yeah, it was.' She ran her hand idly over the grass. 'It was lovely.'

They sat in silence for a few minutes, both looking out over the view.

'So,' Lesley said finally, brushing blades of grass from her hands, 'should we go on to the top?'

Al shook his head. 'Let's just stay here for a while.' He looked at her questioningly. 'Enjoy the view.'

'Fine by me,' she said happily, relieved she wouldn't have to go any further. 'Plus that way we avoid being rotten wankers.'

30

'So, what are we doing today?' Adam asked, eyeballing Lesley in the mirror as he raked his fingers through her hair.

'Just a trim, I think.' It was the day of the Simpsons' party, and Lesley thought it would be a good excuse to get her hair done at the same time as quizzing Adam – kill two birds with one stone.

'Really?' Adam looked disappointed. 'You wouldn't like to go for something a bit different?'

'Well … maybe.' She didn't want to get too much off, but a quick trim wouldn't give her much time for grilling Adam. 'What would you suggest?'

'A different parting maybe? It's a bit old-fashioned.' Adam played around with Lesley's hair, parting it on one side, then the other, looking at it thoughtfully in the mirror each time, his head tilted to one side. 'I think it's best parted this way,' he said, sweeping Lesley's hair to the right. 'It suits the shape of your face better.' He looked at Lesley in the mirror, his eyebrows raised questioningly.

'Yes, that looks good.'

'And we could add some more layers,' he said, combing through her hair with his fingers. 'Give it a bit more movement.'

Lesley nodded. 'Whatever you think. But I don't want too much off. My boyfriend likes it long.'

'Well, he's not the boss of you, is he?' Adam said indignantly.

'No, but ... I like it long too.'

'Don't worry. We won't take much off the overall length, just add some layers and zizz you up a bit. Trust me, you'll love it. And so will he.'

'Okay, then,' Lesley said nervously, not sure what Adam's idea of 'zizzing up' might entail.

'Right, let's get you washed.'

'So are you here on holiday?' Adam asked, cranking up the pedal on her chair so Lesley's feet were lifted off the ground. She was back at his station, her newly washed and conditioned hair in snaky wet tendrils around her shoulders.

'Yes, I'm staying in Nice with my boyfriend and his family.'

'Very nice. And how do you know Rafe Bradshaw?' Adam asked.

'He's my boyfriend's cousin.'

'Really?' Adam drawled, widening his eyes enthusiastically. 'Lucky you! So is he staying with you too?'

'Yes.'

'So close and yet so far,' Adam shook his head. 'I don't think I'd be able to contain myself. He's gorgeous, isn't he?'

Lesley shrugged. 'I fancy my boyfriend more,' she said loyally.

'Good for you!'

'So how long have you been in St Tropez?' Lesley asked him.

'Almost two years now. Best thing I ever did.'

'And before that were you in London?'

'Mmm,' Adam murmured, concentrating as he snipped into the ends of Lesley's hair.

'You're not from London originally, though, are you?'

Adam shook his head, looking at her in the mirror. 'Barnsley. In Yorkshire.'

'I lived in London for a while,' she said in what she hoped was a casual conversational tone. 'Were you there long?'

'Fifteen years. I moved there as soon as I left school. I couldn't wait to get out of Barnsley. There, all done,' he said, whipping the towel away from around Lesley's neck with a flourish. He ran his fingers through it, fluffing it out. 'I'll finish off the fringe when I've dried it.'

'You're finished already?' Lesley asked in dismay.

'We've kept the length, like you wanted,' he said, pulling strands of her wet hair down on either side.

Lesley regarded herself in the mirror, turning her head this way and that, as if assessing the cut. 'I thought it'd look like more.'

'Would you like me to take a bit more off? Maybe add a few more layers?'

'Yes, please.'

'You're sure your boyfriend won't mind?' Adam asked with a playful wink at her in the mirror.

'Men aren't the best judge of hair anyway, are they? He probably won't even notice I've had it done.'

'You're right there.' Adam tucked the towel back into the neckline of Lesley's gown and she bent her head obediently as he started cutting again.

'Which branch of Vidal Sassoon were you in?' she asked.

'Chelsea.'

'With my friend's double, right ... Joanna?' Lesley screwed her face up as if not sure what he'd called Stella.

'Joanna, yes. Well, for a while. She left long before me.'

'It's weird how two totally unrelated people can look so alike, isn't it?' she mused.

'I wouldn't say it's that unusual. They say everyone has a doppelgänger.'

'Or maybe your friend and Stella are long-lost twins!' she said as if the idea had just occurred to her. 'I saw a video on YouTube about two women that that had happened to – identical twins who'd been raised apart. They didn't find each other until they were in their thirties, and then it was by pure chance.'

She thought the idea of being instrumental in reuniting two long-lost twins might make Adam more forthcoming and she could get him to tell her more about Joanna.

'Oh, I don't think that's likely. Like I said, it was a long time ago. I was just mistaken.' He stood back, whipping away the towel from around Lesley's shoulders again. 'What do you think? Enough?'

'Yes, that's perfect. Thank you.'

Adam busied himself pulling a hairdryer from a drawer, and lining up an array of combs, brushes and sprays. There was no point trying to talk over the roar of the hairdryer as he styled her hair. Anyway, she couldn't think of any more questions she could ask without sounding suspicious.

Adam finished fluffing Lesley's hair. 'Well, what do we think?'

Lesley grinned at him in the mirror. 'Brilliant! I love it.'

'Happy now that you let me have my way with you?'
He looked very pleased with himself.

'Very happy,' Lesley said. 'It was totally worth it.'

THE LONG-LOST twins angle was a good idea,' Al said later
when she joined him at a nearby café for coffee and a
debrief.

'If he'd taken the bait. Oh well, it was a long shot
anyway. And the way he dismissed it so easily convinced
me of one thing: this Joanna and Stella are one and the
same person, and he knows it.'

'Well, at least you've got more to go on now.'

'Yeah, I know where she used to work, and have an
idea of when. So it wasn't a total waste of time.'

'And your hair looks great. Am I allowed to say that?'

'Well, just this once.' Lesley smiled. She was really
pleased with it and felt rather fabulous.

'It's very swishy.'

'Thanks. But save the rest of your gushing for the party
tonight.'

31

'T hat's a great haircut,' Stella said as she brushed highlighter across Lesley's cheeks. 'It really suits the shape of your face.'

'Thanks.' Stella had offered to do her make-up for the party, and Lesley had jumped at the chance to have an intimate girly moment with her. 'Pity it's never going to look like this again after today,' Lesley said, admiring her hair in the dressing-table mirror. It was so glossy and shiny. 'I can never get it this smooth and silky. It'll be straight back to its normal frizz the first time I wash it.'

'I could do it for you,' Stella said with a shrug. 'I'm good at hair.'

'You are. Yours always looks amazing.'

'Well, I trained as a hairdresser originally.'

'When was that?'

'Oh, ages ago, right after I left school.' She picked up an eye-shadow palette from the dressing table and leaned in again. 'I didn't stick with it for long, but I can still turn my hand to a blow-dry.'

Lesley didn't think she was going to get very far with

this line of questioning, but she had to make the most of the opportunity to gain Stella's confidence and get her to open up. She decided to try another tack.

'So, how come you've got your own room?' she asked as Stella swept mascara over her lashes. 'Are you afraid Peter's family will be shocked if they find out you two are doing it before you're married?'

Stella laughed. 'No. The fact is, we're *not* doing it.'

'You're kidding. Come on, you can tell me. I won't judge you.'

'We're really not. We'd only been on a few dates before Peter's heart attack. And he's had to be careful since, so ...'

'You mean you've *never* slept with him? That sucks.'

'I think it's kind of romantic, saving it for after the wedding.'

She was forced to stay silent as Stella tilted her chin and applied lip liner. It may be a romantic idea to wait until they were married, but if Stella wanted to bonk Peter to death, it was also a clever strategic move. After all that build-up, it probably wouldn't take much to get him dangerously over-excited.

'There,' Stella said, with a final dab of lip gloss. She stood back and nodded to the mirror. 'What do you think?'

'Wow, you're a genius! You've actually made me look half human.'

'Shut up, you're gorgeous.'

Lesley looked wonderingly at her reflection in the mirror. Stella had done an amazing job – not surprisingly, since it was her actual profession – and she couldn't believe how glamorous and chic she looked. 'If I am, it's thanks to you. I can't believe you managed to do something with this mug.'

Stella pursed her lips. 'Stop that. You have fantastic

bone structure, and I know top models who'd kill for your skin. I only added a little polish.'

'Well ... I admit I haven't scrubbed up too badly,' Lesley said, which was as close as she could come to accepting a compliment graciously.

Stella shook her head, smiling. 'I suppose that'll have to do.'

THE SIMPSONS' house was a short walk from the Bradshaws' place, so when they were all ready, they strolled down the hill together in the early evening sunshine.

When they stepped out onto the Simpsons' large terrace, the party was already in full swing, the garden buzzing with conversation and the tinkle of glasses. Coloured lanterns were strung in the trees, and waiters moved among the guests bearing trays of champagne and canapés. Lesley was glad she'd made an effort as she took in the glitzy well-heeled crowd standing around in groups or sitting at long tables, drinking and talking, while music played softly in the background.

Al and his cousins were soon surrounded by friends, showering them with hugs and kisses.

'Lesley, you look stunning! Love the hair.'

Emma grabbed her and Stella as soon as they arrived and bore them off to join the 'girls' on a group of sofas, treating them like they were already old friends. Al raised his eyebrows and mouthed an 'okay?' at her questioningly as Emma dragged her away, and she gave him a thumbs-up. Jill was already sitting on the sofa, sharing a bottle of champagne with another girl who was introduced as Claire.

When they discovered Stella was a make-up artist and had worked in the movies, they were all agog, quizzing her about what actors she'd worked with and what they were like, avid for gossip about diva behaviour, on-set ructions and off-piste affairs. But Stella somehow managed to deflect all their queries in a friendly, good-natured way, while at the same time remaining tight-lipped and not betraying any insider secrets. It was quite impressive. Lesley knew she'd never have been able to withstand questioning like that and would be gagging to divulge any juicy gossip she had. She'd admire Stella's restraint if it wasn't making her job harder for her.

'So, tell us all about you and Al,' Emma said, and they all turned their attention to Lesley. 'Where did you two meet?'

'Oh, um ... it was at a singles thing, actually,' Lesley said.

'Good for you! And Al,' Jill said. 'It's good to have someone new around. Our friendship group is very incestuous. It's nice to have fresh blood.'

'Yeah, I was surprised to see Cassie and Jean-Claude at the hike yesterday,' Lesley said. 'You know, after what they did to Al.'

'Oh, we all go back years,' Jill said with a wave of her hand. 'It's all water under the bridge. Emma had a fling with Jean-Claude one year, didn't you?' she said to her friend.

'Well, so did you.' Emma laughed.

'Yeah. We've all had a go on Jean-Claude, haven't we?' Jill giggled.

'Oh.' Lesley wondered had they all had a 'go on' Al too.

'Not Al, though,' Emma said quickly, as if she knew what Lesley was thinking. 'None of us have ever been with him. Apart from Cassie, of course.'

'Can't say the same for Scott, though,' Jill said.

'Scott's had a go on Jean-Claude?' Lesley asked, wide-eyed.

'Oh!' Emma hooted. 'No, I mean we've all been with Scott at one time or another. He spreads his net even wider than JC.'

'He's just broken up with his boyfriend, apparently,' Claire said, looking across the garden at Scott. 'Maybe he'd go for a girl next time. I wouldn't mind a little summer fling.'

'He's already got someone new,' Lesley said. 'He met a guy at the beach the other day.'

'Ha, you're too late!' Emma said to Claire, laughing. 'You have to get in quick with Scott. He never stays on the market long.' She poured the remainder of a bottle of champagne into her glass and popped open another. She refilled Lesley's glass, but Stella refused a top-up, saying she was going to find Peter.

'Wow, she should get a job in MI6,' Claire said when she was out of earshot. 'Talk about tight-lipped. Name, rank and serial number only!'

'She's just a very private person,' Lesley said defensively as they all laughed.

'Well, she seems like a lovely girl,' Emma said. 'She's got to be after Peter's money, though, hasn't she?'

'I don't know,' Claire mused. 'I like older men. And Peter's still got something.'

'Well, I don't envy her,' Emma said. 'Mum says Peter's never got over Jane.'

'It must be weird for her with Jane still around.' Claire's eyes drifted to Jane and Peter chatting together on the terrace. 'Jane's so cool, isn't she? I really admire the way she and Peter are still friends, even though he dumped her for a younger model. It's so evolved. I'd like to be like that when I'm old.'

As Lesley looked around the garden, she saw Al standing under a tree with Cassie. He was leaning on the trunk as he talked to her, a drink in his other hand, and they seemed to be having an intense conversation.

'I'm going to go and find my boyfriend,' she said, getting up and taking her leave of the girls.

Curious, she crossed the garden circuitously, edging closer to Al and Cassie, but making sure they didn't see her. She moved behind them, staying out of their line of sight, until she was almost close enough to reach out and touch Al's sleeve, but hidden from view by the trunk of the large tree.

Cassie was touching Al's arm now '… made a mistake,' she was saying in a low voice. 'I mean, come on, it's Jean-Claude!' She gave a little huff of laughter. 'No one's supposed to end up with him.'

'Does he know?'

Lesley wished she could see Al's face.

Cassie shook her head. 'No. I'm going to talk to him tonight. I know he's going to be devastated.'

Huh! Ego much, Lesley thought.

'I knew it was wrong practically from the start.' Cassie sighed. 'What can I say? It was a moment of madness. Look, I know I don't deserve it, but do you think you can forgive me?' She touched Al's arm again, looking at him earnestly. 'I mean we were always friends, weren't we, apart from anything else?'

'Yeah, you're forgiven.'

'You're the best, Al.' She smiled happily at him. 'You do still love me, don't you? Even if I do act like the most enormous dick at times?'

'You know I'll always love you.'

Lesley's stomach lurched. What the hell did Al think he was playing at, lurking behind a tree with Cassie, telling her he still loved her? He was supposed to be *her* boyfriend. Well, she wasn't going to hang around to watch them mooning over each other any longer. Fuming, she wheeled around, and stormed off in the direction of the house, almost immediately crashing into a solid warm body.

'Oops! Sorry!'

'No harm done.' Scott grinned at her. 'What were you doing skulking around behind that tree? Come and dance.' He jerked his head towards the terrace by the pool. As darkness fell, the music had been pumped up, and fairy lights twinkled in the trees.

Then Scott's gaze drifted towards Al and Cassie. 'Don't worry about those two,' he said. 'There's no way Al would go back there after her cheating on him with JC.'

Lesley wasn't so sure. Cassie obviously regretted Jean-Claude, and it sounded like Al was all too eager to forgive her. She'd definitely been asking him for a second chance. She glanced back towards the tree to see Al pulling Cassie into a hug. Right! Two could play at that game, she thought, as she let Scott take her hand and lead her towards the crush of bodies on the terrace.

Lesley loved dancing, and she quickly shook off her annoyance with Al, giving it her all as she jumped up and down on the terrace, laughing and fist-pumping with Scott and her new friends.

Screw Al! If he wanted to let his cheating ex-girlfriend walk all over him and get away with it, that was his problem. There was no reason for her to get upset about it. It wasn't as if he was really her boyfriend. She was here to do a job, and she'd stick to the script even if he didn't.

When the music slowed, she collapsed on a sofa with Scott, breathless but invigorated, and reached for the bottle of champagne. She really should have eaten more. She felt quite light-headed as she poured them both a glass.

'That was fun.' Must pace myself, she thought, taking a big gulp. She collapsed back against the seat, fanning herself with her hand. 'Wow, it's hot.'

'*You're* hot,' Scott said, his eyes raking over her. 'Your hair is gorgeous.' He reached out to push a stray strand off her face.

'Thanks.' She swung her head from side to side, loving the silky feel of it, each strand seeming to move separately. She was beginning to sympathise with hair-flickers.

'So, where's your new boyfriend tonight?' Lesley asked him.

'He couldn't come. So I can focus my undivided attention on you.'

'Lucky me!' Scott was looking at her in a way that made her feel like she was the hottest woman alive. He was totally doing his smouldering thing, and she was enjoying every nerve-tingling second of it. Flirting was fun, even if it wasn't going anywhere. Because she knew there was no way Scott would hit on her for real – though it would serve Al right if he did.

'So, alone at last,' Scott said, edging closer until his thigh was nudging against hers. 'Wanna make out?' He fluttered his eyelashes.

'Probably best not, what with you being my boyfriend's cousin and all.' She took a sip of her champagne. Slow down, she reminded herself. Then she took another gulp.

'Suit yourself. You know, most women are gagging for a make-out session with one of my kind.'

'Your kind? Men? Bisexuals?'

'Creatures of the night.'

'Oh, that.'

'Honestly, you wouldn't believe the number of total strangers who ask me to bite them. You don't crave the vampire's kiss?'

'It's too bitey for my taste.'

'I could be gentle.' He gave her an intimate smile, his eyes dropping to her lips.

Lesley gulped. 'Well, I'll let you know if I change my mind.'

'Any time. Here, let me give you a top-up,' he said, nodding to her glass.

Lesley looked down as he took it from her hand, surprised to see that it was empty. 'Thanks.' As he poured her another glass, she vowed to pace herself this time. Slow sips all the way.

32

An hour and several more glasses of champagne later, Lesley was back on the terrace, dirty dancing with Scott, his hands sliding over her hips as they ground against each other suggestively. She was quite drunk, but in a lovely mellow way, and she felt wild and sexy and powerful, a veritable goddess of the dance floor as Scott spun her around and pulled her against him. She shimmied her ass against him as their hips swayed together. Then she took her hair in both hands and piled it on top of her head, baring her neck to him.

'Do it,' she said, tilting her head to the side. 'Give me a vampire kiss.'

Scott's hands tightened on her waist, and she closed her eyes as she felt the wet warmth of his lips on her neck. He really got into his part, his low growl vibrating against her skin as he opened his mouth wide, his teeth lightly grazing her neck. She gasped in shock as he nibbled her gently. Her eyes flew open and she froze as she saw Al glowering at her from across the garden.

Oh shit! What was she doing? Shame flooded through her like acid.

She felt suddenly sober, and looked around wildly, desperately hoping no one else had witnessed her behaviour, only to find Jane watching, quickly turning away just as their eyes met. Oh shit, shit, shit!

'Oh-oh,' Scott said with a grin. 'I think we might be in trouble.'

'Mmm. I should probably go,' she said, nodding to Al.

Oh, God, what had she been thinking, behaving like that with Scott in front of Al's family. They'd all hate her now. They'd think she was another cheating skank like Cassie. She may not really be his girlfriend, but he was paying her to keep up the illusion and she'd fallen down on the job big time. She'd never felt so shitty and miserable, and she just wanted to run away and hide and never have to face any of the Bradshaws ever again.

But she forced herself to walk over to Al, who was chatting to Toby, his back to her as she approached. He didn't turn around, but Lesley knew he was aware of her – and she could tell he was seething!

'Lesley,' he said coldly, turning to her at last. 'Are you ready to go?'

She nodded. 'Yes, if you are.'

The party was winding down, people starting to leave. Al took her hand, and Lesley was in an agony of anticipation as they made their way slowly through the garden, stopping every few minutes to say goodbye to someone. Part of her was dreading being alone with Al when he could let rip, but at the same time she wanted to get it over with.

'I'm really sorry, Al,' she said as soon as they were outside. 'I don't know what I was thinking. Well, I *wasn't* thinking. I drank too much, and then—'

She expected him to shout, but he didn't say a word, and that was worse – his set jaw, the blazing anger in his eyes, the jerky tension in his body. Then they were joined by Jane, and he couldn't say anything. The short walk home was passed in tense silence and felt like it took a life-time. Lesley was quite woozy and unsteady on her feet, and she had to cling onto Al's arm to steady herself. She knew he was probably dying to shake her off, but couldn't do it with his family watching.

'Nightcap, anyone?' Jane asked as soon as they were inside, throwing Lesley a sympathetic look.

'No, thanks,' Al said.

Even though the thought of any more alcohol turned her stomach, Lesley was tempted to take Jane up on the offer and delay the moment of confrontation with Al. She could sit out on the terrace, drink very slowly and think about what she'd done – and hopefully Al would be asleep by the time she went to bed. But she wasn't going to be a coward. Better to face up to it tonight and clear the air than have to deal with The Fear in the morning.

'No, thanks,' she said. 'I can't wait to get into bed … um, with Al,' she added, taking his hand and giving him what she hoped was a sexy smile. He just threw her a scathing look, and Lesley thought she might explode from the tension as they walked upstairs in stony silence.

As soon as they were out of sight, he dropped her hand and strode down the corridor ahead of her to their room. He stood back and held the door open for her, staring at the floor as she walked into the room. She flinched when she heard the door close behind her with a soft click. Only then did Al finally let rip.

'What the hell was that?' he asked, facing her, hands on his hips.

'I'm sorry. I didn't mean—'

'Jesus, Lesley!' he shouted.

Lesley gulped. 'I know. I was just—'

'You were just behaving like a complete tart! Flirting your arse off with Scott, of all people!'

'It's not how it looked. It wasn't even a real kiss – just a vampire one. We were just messing around, having a laugh.'

'You were dry humping him right in front of me. I was *right there*! Not to mention my whole family.'

'I know. I'm sorry.' She felt awful. Al was so nice. He didn't deserve to be humiliated like that in front of everyone. 'I just had a bit too much to drink – well, a lot too much, actually – and I lost the run of myself and forgot about you being my pretend boyfriend. I'm really sorry, Al,' she said miserably, tears springing to her eyes. 'It was a horrible thing to do.'

He looked a little taken aback, and she got the feeling she'd taken the wind out of his sails by not trying to justify herself. But she was in the wrong and she knew it. There was no excuse.

He took a deep breath and let out a heavy sigh. 'Look, I know you're not really my girlfriend,' he said stiffly, 'but as far as my family and everyone else is concerned, you are.'

'I know, I know!'

'So I'd appreciate it if you could try and act as such, at least while we're here.'

'Honestly, I feel terrible about the way I behaved. You're a lovely boyfriend even if you're not real, and you don't deserve that, especially when you're paying me. It was very unprofessional of me. But no one's going to think anything of it. I mean, it was *Scott*—'

'Right, of course. I suppose I should have anticipated this.'

'What do you mean?'

'Well, we all know how "insanely hot" my cousins are,' he said bitterly. 'Who'd blame you? He told you himself he's irresistible to women.'

'No, that's not what I meant. It's not about Scott. I was just drunk, and a bit lonely and—'

'Lonely?' He frowned.

She shrugged. 'Just a bit, you know.'

'But we've been spending practically the whole time together. My entire family was at the party tonight. And you were with Jill and Emma. Aren't they being friendly to you?'

'Yes, they are! They're being so lovely.' God, if he was trying to make her feel like a complete shit, he'd succeeded.

'And I keep you company, don't I? I didn't mean to abandon you tonight. But I thought you were fine, and you could have come and found me.'

'I did come and find you, but you were ... busy.' She knew she had no right to accuse him of carrying on with Cassie. He was perfectly entitled to after all, and he'd been very discreet about it. 'It's not you. You've been a model pretend boyfriend.'

'Well, then—'

'Maybe "lonely" isn't the right word ...' Lesley wavered, plucking at her top. God, why did she have to babble so much when she was nervous? She'd said she was sorry, now she should shut up.

Al looked at her, frowning. Then suddenly his face cleared. It was almost cartoon-like the way she could see a light bulb going on in his head. 'You have needs,' he said, looking her straight in the eyes.

'Um ... yeah. I suppose so.' Lesley hung her head and shuffled her feet. God, could this get any more mortifying? She really didn't think she should be discussing her needs with Al. Maybe if she concentrated hard enough, she could make the floor open up and swallow her. How hard could it be? All sorts of eejits did telekinesis on the telly.

'Is that it?' he asked her. 'You want sex? Or do you have a thing for Scott in particular?'

'Hey Al,' she said, looking up. 'I've got a great idea! Why don't we not have this conversation? Let's stop talking about it now and never speak of it again. What do you say?'

'It's nothing to be ashamed of, you know,' he said softly, walking towards her. 'It's perfectly normal.' He ducked his head so he could look up into her face. When she kept her eyes resolutely on the floor, he took her chin in his fingers, tilting it up so she was looking right at him.

'Why don't you let me take care of your ... needs?' he said.

'Ah, no. You're grand, really. Thanks, but I wouldn't want you to go to any trouble.'

'Lesley,' he said, his mouth quirking up in a smile, 'it would be my pleasure.'

Al was so damn polite, she wasn't sure how to take that. Did he mean it literally, or was it just an expression?

'I am supposed to be your boyfriend, after all,' he continued. 'And as such it is my duty to see to it that your needs are met.'

Lesley shook her chin out of his hand and turned away. 'No, it's okay, honestly. It's really nice of you to offer, but I'll be fine. I'll just ... have another shower. There's plenty of cold water.' It wasn't like her to turn down a shag from an attractive man, but it would be super humiliating if Al just had sex with her out of a sense of duty, while he was still hankering after Cassie. She didn't want to be 'serviced' like some brood mare.

'Fine,' Al said, all the warmth draining from his face.

'Look, we're both tired. Let's just go to bed and forget about it.'

With that he turned on his heel and stormed off to the bathroom, leaving Lesley standing dazed in the middle of the floor, not sure exactly what had just happened or how she felt about it. All she knew was that she needed to get into bed. She undressed quickly, and when Al came out of the bathroom, she went in. They moved around each other in silence. When she came back into the bedroom, he was already in bed, his stiff back turned to her. But she could feel the waves of hostility coming off him as she crawled miserably under the cover.

Despite how drunk she was, her mind was whirring and she couldn't get to sleep. Something had happened when she saw Al chatting with his ex, and it had unsettled her. She'd felt a stab of what felt horribly like jealousy. Had she gone and fallen for Al just when it was too late? Of all the rotten timing. Why hadn't she appreciated him before, and snapped him up when she had the chance? Clearly he was still in love with Cassie, but he'd asked her out. He'd been making an effort to move on. Maybe if she'd said yes ...

Oh sod it, she thought. It was probably just that she'd been faking having feelings for Al for so long, she'd started to buy into her own lie. It wasn't real. It was just that she was horny, and Al was looking very attractive tonight and he was so nice, and it had been lovely kissing him the other day ...

33

The next morning Lesley wished she was one of those people who had blackouts from drinking. But apart from being a bit fuzzy around the edges, she remembered the events of last night all too vividly. She was dreading facing his family – and the fact that she was suffering from a whopping hangover didn't help. At least she could hide behind dark glasses, and she was grateful for them as she joined everyone on the terrace, wincing in the clatteringly bright sunlight.

'Good morning,' she mumbled as she took a seat beside Jane at the table, trying to shrink into herself.

She was greeted with murmured acknowledgements. Stella was nauseatingly bright-eyed as ever, but Lesley was glad to see that both Rafe and Jane were looking rather the worse for wear, and Michael was pale and haggard, hunched miserably over a bowl of steaming coffee. At least she wasn't the only one.

The atmosphere was very muted, remorse hanging in the air between them. Lesley studiously avoided eye contact with any of Al's family, but, in fact, everyone seemed a little sheepish, mumbling to each other in hushed voices as they reached for croissants and poured coffee. Lesley had made a run to the bakery first thing as a peace offering, despite her pounding head and churning stomach. She was suffering from a lethal combination of hangover and a bad case of The Fear – made all the worse by the fact that she knew it was justly deserved.

Only Joy seemed really chipper, and didn't appear to be suffering any after-effects. She chattered away cheerfully, in an obvious effort to gloss over the awkwardness around the table. Despite the fact that she hadn't had much to drink, Stella was subdued, and Peter's mood was gloomy, though he hadn't been drinking at all.

'I think we're both in the doghouse,' Jane whispered to her.

Lesley turned to look at her, raising her eyebrows in surprise. She knew why *she* was in everyone's bad books, but Jane had done nothing wrong. Sure, she had got tipsy and flirted her arse off with Philippe, but she was single, and perfectly entitled. Nevertheless, she was right – Peter was glowering at her from the end of the table, throwing her thunderous looks. Lesley felt sorry for Stella. Peter was making it so obvious he was put out about Jane and Philippe. It was so unfair. She hadn't misbehaved at all, and look where it had got her.

'Bloody dog in the manger,' Jane muttered under her breath, but she sounded pleased.

'Good morning.' Al joined them, looking annoyingly fresh. But Lesley decided to forgive him for it when he made straight for her, put his arms around her from behind and kissed the top of her head. 'Morning, sweetheart,' he said, drawing curious looks from the rest of his family. She was grateful for his show of solidarity, but it made her feel more of a shit than ever.

'How are we all this morning?' Scott appeared, looking sleepy and dishevelled. He flopped into a seat beside Jane and started piling a plate with croissants and pain au chocolat.

'Ugh, I shouldn't drink,' Jane groaned. 'I'm too old. I can't handle hangovers anymore.'

'How about you, Lesley?'

Lesley blushed and threw him a filthy look from under her lashes, wishing she could make herself invisible. 'Not good,' she said weakly. 'But no better than I deserve.'

'Don't be so hard on yourself. We've all gone a bit "Girls Gone Wild" when we've had a few too many. And no one would blame you for wanting a bit of this,' he said, waving his hands over his body. 'Everyone knows I'm irresistible.'

She gritted her teeth, willing him to shut up. There might still be some people around this table who didn't know what she'd done last night.

'Good party, though,' Scott said as he smeared jam thickly onto a croissant. 'Philippe's a laugh, isn't he? He fancies the pants off you.' He grinned at his mother.

'I know,' she said, perking up.

'So, have you anything to tell us? Will Rafe and I be acquiring *two* new step-parents this year?'

'Oh, don't be silly.' Jane tossed her head dismissively, but her lips curled into a smile. 'We were just having a bit of fun.'

Scott had his iPad beside him and started scrolling idly through it, one eye on the screen as he chatted away, occasionally murmuring snippets of news and gossip that he came across, and showing kitten videos to Jane.

'Oh, you've made Celeb Watch in *Wow!* Magazine,' he said to Rafe, his finger pausing on the screen.

'Oh, *what?*' Rafe groaned, with a pained expression.

'Hang on.' Scott clicked a link and fell silent as he read, his eyes quickly scanning the screen. 'It seems you've been seen in Cannes, out and about with a – oh!' He broke off, grinning. 'With a mystery blonde,' he continued. 'That's you, Stella,' he said, turning to her.

'What?' She shot up and went around the table to look over Scott's shoulder. 'What does it say about me? Is there a picture?'

'Yep,' he said, grinning up at her, as he pointed to the screen. 'Not a great one, though. Rafe was spotted with you on the Croisette in Cannes and later you were frolicking on the beach together.'

'Frolicking?' Rafe rolled his eyes.

'You were looking very loved up, apparently,' he informed Rafe with a grin.

Rafe scowled in reply. 'For fuck's sake! Bloody gossip-mongers! Have they nothing better to do?'

'We were not looking loved up!' Stella shrieked in outrage. 'We were all there, for God's sake!'

'You do look a bit cosy together here, in fairness,' Scott said, pointing at the screen. 'And scantily clad.'

'Can I see that, please?' Stella's hand was shaking as she held it out for the iPad. She peered at the screen, frowning. 'This is ridiculous! Peter was there, on the other side, but they've cut him out to make it look like it was just the two of us.'

'I wouldn't worry about it too much,' Rafe said, giving her a sympathetic look. 'It's not a big deal.'

'Don't you mind?' she said fretfully. 'They've made it look like we're … together.'

'So they've got it wrong,' he said, shrugging. 'It wouldn't be the first time.'

'You're not worried Dad will think you're having it

away with Rafe, are you?' Scott asked, glancing cheekily at his father.

'Of course not,' Stella said stiffly. 'I just ... I don't like this kind of attention.'

'Sorry, darling,' Peter said to her, 'but it comes with the territory, I'm afraid. Don't upset yourself about it.'

Stella handed the iPad back to Scott and sat down again, but she still looked troubled, worrying at her bottom lip with her teeth.

'Don't let it get to you,' Rafe said to her. 'It'll blow over soon enough.'

'And think how stupid they'll look when it turns out you're actually with Dad and Rafe's still a tragic bachelor,' Scott said to her. 'You'll have the last laugh.'

Stella gave him a weak smile.

Scott left the iPad open on the table and Lesley picked it up. One picture showed Rafe and Stella walking along the Croisette. It was taken from behind. The other was on the beach and they were sitting side by side on sunloungers. It had obviously been taken from some distance and was a little blurred, but it was unmistakably taken the day they had all gone to Cannes, and it had been cleverly edited so that the rest of the group were nowhere in sight. Stella was in her orange one-piece, and Rafe was turned towards her attentively, tanned and handsome in his swim shorts. Lesley was amazed at how convincing it was. They looked just like a loved-up couple on a romantic holiday together. If she didn't know better and came across it in a magazine, she wouldn't have questioned it for a second.

The atmosphere became even more tense and fraught since Scott's discovery of those photos, so, when Al suggested they go out for lunch, just the two of them, Lesley practically bit his hand off. He'd been polite but cold with her this morning, and she really needed some time alone with him to clear the air.

So as the others set up for an afternoon of dozing by the pool, sleeping off their hangovers, Al took Lesley on a drive to Menton, where they walked along the seafront, checking out the restaurants that lined the harbour.

'What do you fancy?' Al asked her.

'I'm in serious need of a hangover feed,' she said, trying to get back on a more friendly footing. 'So it can't be anywhere where the food is too poncy. Nothing with shavings or foam, or *dust*. I can't be doing with shavings of anything in my condition.'

'Big portions, then, heavy on the carbs?' Al said. 'How about this?' He stopped outside a little Italian restaurant.

'Perfect.'

'This is my treat, by the way,' Lesley said when they were seated. 'It's the least I can do to make up for last night,' she added as Al began to protest.

'Really, there's no need for that.'

'Come on, I owe you one.'

'All right, if you insist.'

'I do. And have whatever you want.' Lesley looked down at her menu. 'But not the lobster,' she added. 'I'm not made of money.'

She was relieved to see Al give the hint of a smile. Maybe he was starting to thaw. 'I really am sorry about last night,' she said. 'But it honestly was nothing.'

Al shrugged. 'I probably over-reacted. I know it must be hard for you, pretending you're in a relationship, not being free to do whatever you want ... with whomever you want.'

'It's what you're paying me for,' she said. 'Anyway, I don't want Scott like that. I told you we were just messing around.'

'TV's Mr Darcy, then?'

Lesley thought it was touching that he didn't realise Rafe was way out of her league. 'It must be hard for you too.'

He lifted his head. 'How do you mean?'

'Well, everyone thinks you're taken, so you can't flirt with whoever you want without looking like a sleazebag. And Cassie obviously wants you back.'

'Really?' He frowned, looking at her closely. 'What makes you think that?'

'I saw you talking to her last night. You looked very cosy.' She tried not to sound snitty.

A slow smile spread across Al's face. He obviously liked the idea of getting back with Cassie. But she shouldn't be surprised. He'd only broken up with her because she cheated, not because he'd fallen out of love with her.

'Well, we could make it easier for both of us.'

'What do you mean?'

'What I said last night,' he began, and Lesley's heart sank. She was glad his mood seemed to have magically lifted, but she really wanted to draw a veil over the whole thing.

'Hm?' she squeaked, looking up at him from under her lashes.

'About taking care of your needs,' he continued cheerfully, without a trace of embarrassment or awkwardness. Lesley concentrated hard on her menu. 'I meant what I said.'

'Oh, right. Good to know, thanks.'

'Have you thought about it at all?'

'Um, yeah ... sort of.' Lesley was breaking into a sweat that had nothing to do with her hangover. She prayed for a waiter to come and rescue her.

'And?' Al looked at her expectantly.

'I think I'll have the steak frites. I need spuds.'

'Oh, right. But I meant—'

'What about starters? Do you fancy going halves on an antipasti platter?'

'Yes, sure – sounds good.'

'Have you decided what you're having? I was only joking about the lobster – have whatever you want.'

'Thanks. But I think I'll have the same as you.'

He put down his menu, and she was glad that subject seemed to be closed. He folded his hands on the table. 'Anyway, the offer still stands,' he said.

'Oh.' Shit, the subject wasn't closed after all.

'Any time you like,' he said, 'I'm at your disposal.'

'Great! Well, thanks. I'll … let you know if I change my mind.'

'If it helps, I've been told I'm very good. I can provide excellent testimonials.'

'Well … good for you!' She looked around frantically, trying to catch a waiter's eye. 'You should set up a website. Spread the word.'

'You'd have a good time. I'd make sure of that.'

'Okay, noted.' Lesley nodded seriously as if she intended to give it careful consideration.

'Excellent,' he said breezily. 'Well, now that that's out of the way, let's enjoy our lunch.'

Thankfully, Al dropped the subject after that, and Lesley was able to relax and enjoy the food, which was delicious.

'Stella was really shook up about that photo of her and Rafe online,' Al said.

'I know! It was kind of weird how she reacted, wasn't it?' Lesley perked up as the conversation turned to Stella and they were soon engrossed in discussing the latest developments.

'I'm starting to like Stella,' she admitted. 'I'm kind of hoping there's some innocent explanation for whatever it is she's hiding. Although the only innocent explanation I can think of wouldn't be something I'd wish on anyone.'

'Abusive ex?'

Lesley nodded. 'I'm sorry I haven't been able to find out much. I feel like a bit of a fraud taking your money when I haven't really achieved anything.'

'Don't feel like that. You're getting close to her. It takes time.'

'Time we haven't got.' Lesley sighed. 'But don't worry. I'm going to be her bridesmaid, so that will give me lots of opportunities to dig around and get more personal with her. I'll redouble my efforts when we're back in Dublin.'

'And there's always the chance Jane and Peter will get back together and solve the whole problem.'

'True. Jane did sterling work last night with that Philippe bloke.' Lesley ate her last chip and sighed, leaning back. 'I'm going to miss this,' she said, looking out at the blue water, sparkling with sunlight. 'I can't believe tomorrow is our last day.'

Al smiled sympathetically.

She was going to miss the heat of the sun and the intensely blue sky. But she felt a little pang at the thought of not being with Al all the time, chatting to him in bed at night about everything, bouncing ideas off him and going over the events of the day. She'd found it surprisingly easy being thrown together so intimately with him. She liked how friendly and confident he was, and she'd got used to him putting his arm casually around her shoulders or holding her hand. It felt nice, and she'd miss it. She wondered whether they could stay friends when the case was over.

'So am I forgiven?' she asked as they got up to leave.

'Yes, I've decided you were just acting out of jealous rage at seeing me with Cassie, so I've forgiven your momentary lapse.'

'Huh! Good story.' She knew he was joking, but it felt dangerously close to the bone.

'But I've assured you that you have nothing to worry about on that score, and now we're stronger than ever.'

'Sounds good,' she said. And even though there was no one around to see, she didn't protest when he took her hand in his as they left the restaurant.

34

'What the fuck?' Lesley was startled awake by a loud booming that seemed to permeate the walls of the house. It sounded like a long series of explosions, and she half expected to see the house crumbling around her as she tentatively peeled her eyes open. She quickly realised it was thunder when she saw the room lit up by sporadic flashes of lightning.

She squeezed her eyes closed again as the thunder rumbled on, hoping it would stop in a minute. She hated lightning. But when she peeked again, it was still flashing constantly at the window, lighting the room in jagged bursts like a strobe, and making her feel sick and dizzy. She'd never experienced such a dramatic electrical storm before.

'Al?' she whispered, groping for the switch on the bedside lamp. 'Are you awake?'

There was no answer. She was about to flick on the light, when she remembered you weren't supposed to touch anything electrical during a lightning storm.

'Al,' she hissed, louder this time. She leaned over and

peered down at him. His eyes were closed. 'Al!' she shouted.

'Huh?' He stirred.

'Are you awake?'

'Well, I am now,' he said, his voice thick with sleep as he looked up at her blearily. 'Something wrong?' He shifted up on one elbow.

She gave him an incredulous look. 'There's thunder and lightning.'

'So I see. It doesn't bother you, does it?'

'I can't say I'm a fan,' she said, cringing away from the window as there was another booming roll of thunder, and a spectacular flash. 'I've never seen lightning like this before.'

'It gets like that here sometimes. It's nothing to worry about.'

'That's easy for you to say all the way over there. I'm here next to the window. If anyone's going to be a lightning rod in this room, it's me.'

He blinked at her dazedly. 'Want to swap?'

She shook her head. 'What if the lightning got you, and I'd have to break it to your family that it was my fault?' She squealed as the lightning flashed brighter, squeezing her eyes shut. 'I don't want to have you getting burnt to a crisp on my conscience.'

'Well, you're welcome to join me over here, if you like.'

It was tempting. It definitely looked safer on his side. 'Maybe ...' Then there was a spectacularly loud boom of thunder and the light show seemed to crank up a notch. 'Okay,' she said, throwing off the duvet and diving across the pillow barrier as if trying to escape a bomb blast. Al pulled back his duvet and she scrambled onto the mattress beside him.

'Do you want me to go over to the other side?' he asked. 'I don't mind.'

'No, this is fine.' It was comforting to have the warmth of another body. It felt cosy and safe. Well, sort of ...

She yelped, clutching the sheet as there was another clatter of thunder. A flash at the window filled the room with piercing light, and she squeezed her eyes shut, turning away from it. When she opened them again, she found herself staring straight into Al's eyes, his face inches from hers. He was so close she could feel the warmth of his breath, and she suddenly felt very aware of the intimacy of the situation, their near-naked bodies crushed together. She only had knickers on under the short T-shirt she slept in, and Al was wearing nothing but boxers. Her heart started pounding very fast, and it had nothing to do with the storm.

She pressed herself closer to Al, huddling into his bare chest, and his arms came around her. His eyes dropped to her mouth as she leaned closer. When she touched her lips tentatively to his, he pulled back slightly, frowning at her questioningly.

'Lesley?'

'Just go with it,' she said, kissing him again, more forcefully this time, her lips lingering on his encouragingly. She sighed against his mouth as he started kissing her back, his arms tightening around her.

She parted her lips and felt his breath hot in her mouth, his lips warm and firm against hers ... and dry. She slid her tongue lightly along his lower lip, while she clutched him feverishly, aching for him to slide his tongue into her mouth and deepen the kiss. But to her increasing frustration, his kisses remained firmly PG-rated. Maybe he was just being polite, kissing her back because she'd kissed him first. But when she ran her hands over the bunched muscles of his chest, his heart was beating wildly, and when she ground her hips into his, seeking friction, she felt ... whoa! a rock-hard erection. He was definitely into this. So why was he holding back?

He pressed dry, closed-mouth kisses down her neck to the hollow at the base of her throat. Which was very nice as far as it went, but—

'Kiss me properly,' she murmured finally, unable to bear it any longer.

'I am kissing you properly,' he breathed against her skin.

Oh God, was he just a shit kisser, she thought, her heart sinking. Maybe she'd found the one thing Al wasn't good at. She wanted to howl with disappointment. She'd thought he was restraining himself out of respect that day on the hike, but maybe that was as good as it got.

'Seriously?' she said, grabbing his hair and pulling his head up. 'This is the best you can do?'

'Within the agreed parameters, yes.'

'Huh?'

'You said no tongues, remember?'

'Oh! Well, I've changed my mind.' She leaned in and ran her tongue along his bottom lip encouragingly.

'You want me to use my tongue?' His eyes glinted mischievously, and she suspected he was torturing her deliberately now, drawing out the agony.

'Yes. If it wouldn't be too much trouble,' she said, curling her hand around the back of his neck and pulling him to her.

'No trouble at all,' he said, his eyes crinkling as he smiled. Then he lunged in and kissed her again, his mouth opening over hers, and she gave a little whimper of relief and excitement as his tongue slid inside. The sensation went straight to her groin. He was an *amazing* kisser! She felt like whooping with delight as they devoured each other's mouths hungrily.

They kissed and kissed, and it all became more urgent and grabby, their breathing hot and ragged, their fingers clutching. Lesley hitched a leg across Al's, grinding against his erection, her breasts pressed against his chest. Her nipples were hard and taut, and she longed to feel his touch on her bare skin. But while she ran her hands feverishly all over his body, he kept his on her waist, so light he was barely touching her. When she couldn't stand it any longer, she took one of his hands and pressed it against her breast to give him a hint.

Finally he lifted his head a fraction, just far enough to mumble against her mouth.

'May I touch you under your clothes?'

'God, yes! Please. Knock yourself out.'

Then finally he pushed his hands up under her T-shirt and she felt them on her hot, flushed skin, sliding over her naked breasts. They both groaned as his fingers brushed against her hardened nipples and he kissed his way down to the neckline of her T-shirt as he pinched and rolled them, making Lesley squirm in pleasure, the delicious ache building between her legs.

'May I take this off?' he mumbled against her skin, tugging at the neckline.

'Yes,' she gasped. She knew what his game was now, and she could just tell him that the rules were off and he could do whatever he wanted. But the fact was his voice was incredibly sexy, and she was finding it a huge turn-on having him say what he wanted to do to her out loud. Besides, it was very hot making out like teenagers, teasing it out slowly.

She squirmed restlessly as his hand slid to the hem of her T-shirt. His fingers brushed lightly against her skin as he peeled it slowly upwards, and she shivered. She sat up a little and lifted her arms so he could pull it off over her head. He tossed it aside and looked down at her, his eyes darkening.

'Wow, you're gorgeous.'

Then his mouth was on her breasts, his breath hot on her skin as he licked and sucked, pulling one taut nipple into his mouth while his fingers teased the other, and Lesley felt the need gnawing at her insides.

'May I touch you below the waist?' Al breathed, his fingers drifting across her stomach.

'I might start screaming if you don't.'

She felt his smile against her skin as his fingers trailed lightly down her stomach, tracing a line across the edge of her knickers. Then he was kissing her again as his hand dived inside.

He groaned into her mouth as he slid a finger inside her, and Lesley gasped as his thumb started rubbing slow circles over her clit. The tension built inside her until she was on the verge of orgasm, when he pulled back, hooking his fingers into the sides of her knickers.

'May I kiss you below the waist?' he asked, his eyes dark and his jaw tense as he gazed down at her. 'With tongue?'

Lesley gulped and nodded furiously, too turned on to speak. He slid her knickers down her legs painfully slowly, and she was trembling with need as he nudged her legs apart and bent his head to her.

Her hands fisted the sheets as Al's tongue pushed her closer and closer to the edge. She was almost there ... any second now ... She let out a keening moan as the pleasure reached a crescendo. And then suddenly he stopped.

'Lesley?' Al had thrown the cover back and was looking up at her from between her legs. He looked sexy and dishevelled and very happy. Lesley felt like punching him, but she was afraid to move a muscle and lose all that lovely momentum.

'Mmm?' she whimpered, her mouth clamped shut.

'Is that you being scared of the lightning, or—?'

'What?' She'd completely forgotten about the storm.

'Only you were squealing like that earlier, so—'

Seriously? 'That was me enjoying myself, Al.'

'Okay. Good.' He grinned at her. 'Just checking.' Then his head disappeared under the duvet again, and he took up exactly where he'd left off. And thankfully, so did she.

Al certainly lived up to his notices, making her come twice with his fingers and tongue before collapsing beside her on the pillow. Little fluttering aftershocks were still rippling through her as she reached for his cock, stroking the hardness of his erection through his boxers. She couldn't wait to take him in her mouth. But as she reached for the waistband of his boxers, he slapped her hand away.

'Did I say you could touch me under my clothes?' he asked.

Lesley smirked, rolling her eyes. 'Is it okay to touch you under your clothes?' she asked.

He nodded and lifted his hips to help her as she slid off his boxers and tossed them aside to join her clothes on the floor. She stroked the length of his shaft, loving how hard it was beneath the silky soft skin. Then she crawled down the bed and bent her head to take him in her mouth.

'Did I say you could do that?'

'Sorry.' She looked up at him from under her lashes. 'Can I suck you off?'

'Well, I'm sure you *can*. I don't doubt your ability for a moment,'

'Seriously? You're going to quibble about my grammar at a time like this?'

'I'm a stickler for correct usage.'

Lesley sighed. 'Okay, then. May I please suck you off, Al?'

'Lesley,' he said, his breath shaky as he looked down at her, 'you may.'

Lesley enjoyed giving blow jobs and she knew she was good at them – the two things usually went together, in her experience. She loved the feel of Al's thick, warm cock in her mouth, and he made gratifyingly appreciative sounds of pleasure as she licked and sucked him. But she really wanted him inside her, and she was glad that he seemed to be on the same wavelength as he gently nudged her aside.

'Condom!' he said, and Lesley nodded eagerly. He darted to the bathroom and was back in seconds. Lesley even found the ripping of foil as he tore open the packet a turn-on – there was something incredibly hot about the statement of intent that it represented. She watched impatiently as he rolled on the condom. He got back into bed and instead of rolling on top of Lesley, he arranged her on top, straddling him.

'This is my favourite position,' he said, stroking her legs on either side, his features taut with barely suppressed need.

Lesley lifted herself a little, settling herself over his cock so the tip was just nudging at her entrance. 'Al,' she said, 'may I sit on your dick?'

'I thought you'd never ask.'

Lesley sometimes felt self-conscious when she was on top, too aware of how she looked, and unsure if she was getting the pace right. She worried about getting negative feedback. But with Al, she felt wild and sexy and abandoned. She didn't get the impression as she used to with Rob, that Al liked this position because he was lazy and wanted her to do all the work, but rather because he couldn't keep his eyes – or his hands – off her. He wanted to look at her tits as they bounced and jiggled, and he wanted to watch his hands stroking and fondling them. He made her feel beautiful, powerful and sexy in a way she'd never really felt before. He curled his hand around her bottom and squeezed her thighs tighter around him, pumping his hips up to meet her as she sank down on him, thrusting harder and deeper, as their bodies moved greedily against each other. He slid a hand between them to rub her clit, not taking his eyes off hers as he totally lost it and came with a deep groan. Seconds later, Lesley came too, in white-hot bursts of heat and light that matched the electrical storm still raging outside the window.

35

L esley had fallen asleep with Al's arms wrapped around her, their legs entwined. But at some point in the night they had shifted, and when she woke, he was turned away from her. She could tell from his slow, steady breathing that he was still asleep. Light was creeping in through a gap in the shutters, but it was a still, steady light, not the sickening strobing of last night. She yawned happily and stretched. She couldn't remember when she'd felt so content and sated. Even though she hadn't had much sleep last night, she felt refreshed and energised.

She also felt hot and sticky, and desperately in need of a shower. She eased herself carefully off the bed without waking Al and crept to the bathroom. The smell of sex rose up around her in clouds of steam as she stood under the shower and washed the sticky trails of saliva off her skin. She could still feel the imprint of his hands on her breasts, the rocking of his thrusts inside her. Her nipples were sore, licked and sucked raw, and there was a delicious feeling of fullness between her legs.

Well, that was a very pleasant surprise, she thought,

going over the events of last night in her mind. Al had been ... amazing, probably the best shag she'd ever had. Who'd have thought Al – lovely, polite Al with his perfect manners – would be such an animal in the sack? But it wasn't just that it had been hot – and it had been incredibly, toe-curlingly, breathtakingly hot. There was something else as well. It had been ... friendly, she thought, trying to put her finger on what had been different. It was like they were both in it together – which didn't make sense, because surely when you had sex with another person, you were in it together. There was give and take on both sides. But she was used to more push and pull, to having to take what she needed or risk not getting it. With Al it was like there was only one side. She didn't think she'd ever been so in sync with another person sexually. It was all very confusing.

Al still wasn't awake when she came out of the shower, and she got dressed quietly and went downstairs. The house was very quiet as she made her way through the kitchen and out onto the terrace. Some puddles of water and an overturned lounger were the only signs of last night's storm, a sheen of water across the terrace already drying in the morning sun. The sky was clear and calm.

She heard footsteps behind her and turned to see Scott coming into the kitchen carrying a body board.

'Some night last night!' he said, grinning at her.

'What?' Lesley blushed. How could he know?

'The storm.' He nodded towards the terrace. 'Didn't you hear it?'

'Oh. Yeah, it was something else. Where is everyone?'

'They've gone down to the beach for the day. You two seemed to be having a lie in, so we thought we'd leave you to it.'

'Right. Al's still asleep.'

'I came back for this.' He indicated the board. 'I was

just going to leave you a note, but now you're up. Join us when you're ready, if you feel like it.'

Lesley nodded. 'We will.'

'We'll be at Opéra Plage.'

When Scott left, Lesley was very aware that it was just her and Al in the house. Doubts started to creep in as she busied herself in the kitchen, feeling fidgety and on edge as she checked the contents of the cupboards and found supplies. Someone had been to the bakery, and they'd left croissants and ficelles. She was nervous about facing Al this morning. She hated the morning-after awkwardness and dreaded him acting all shifty and distant. And trapped in this house, with nowhere for him to run, it was even more awkward. Damn holiday shagging! What had they been thinking? No, what had *she* been thinking? She'd started it, so she had no one but herself to blame. She wished he'd just get up so they could get the whole thing over with. He probably hadn't really expected her to take him up on his offer to attend to her needs. She had to make it clear she knew that's all it was and that she wasn't reading more into it.

She decided to make scrambled eggs to occupy herself. She was just whipping the eggs in a bowl when she heard Al come into the kitchen behind her.

'Good morning.' He sounded very cheerful and breezy.

'Hi.' She turned to smile at him briefly. He looked crisp and fresh, his hair still damp at the ends from the shower, and she felt a wave of longing.

'Did you sleep well?' she asked, turning back to her eggs.

She heard him cross the kitchen and suddenly he was right behind her, his arms wrapping around her.

'Mmm, fantastic.' He pulled her back against him and

dropped a kiss onto her bare shoulder that made Lesley shiver.

Okay, this was weird. He was acting all ... normal. Like he was perfectly okay with what had happened between them – not even a little bit freaked out or remorseful.

'Ooh, are you making scrambled eggs?' he asked, spying the bowl on the worktop. He rested his chin on her shoulder.

'Yeah, would you like some?'

'Love some.' He turned her around in his arms and dropped a kiss on her mouth. 'You do that and I'll get the coffee on.' He released her and started busying himself with the coffee machine. 'Where is everyone?' he asked, as if he'd only just noticed they were alone.

'They've all gone to the beach. They said to join them later if we want to.'

'So we have the house to ourselves? Great!'

Lesley wasn't quite sure what to make of this chirpy morning-after Al. He was being so normal and friendly, acting as if they were really a couple. He seemed so cheerful and relaxed as they got breakfast ready together – as if he was really happy about last night. He casually rested a hand on her back as he reached behind her to get down plates, and she started to wonder if this was his way of dealing with it and pretending it hadn't happened. When the food was ready, they took it out to the terrace.

'Alone at last!' Al said when they were seated across from each other at the patio table.

Lesley couldn't take it any longer. If things were going to be weird between them she wanted them to get weird now, so they could get it over with and move on.

'You seem very cheerful this morning,' she said by way of an opener.

'I am.' Al grinned at her. 'Why wouldn't I be? I had a

great sleep, it's a beautiful morning.' He waved his knife at the sky. 'These eggs are great. I'm having breakfast with a beautiful woman. All's right with the world.'

'Thanks, but – look, I think we should talk about last night. Just clear the air, you know, about ... what happened.'

'Okay,' he said cheerfully, reaching for the butter. 'What would you like to say about it?'

'Well, are you okay with it?'

'Yes, why wouldn't I be?'

'Well, I mean, I just don't want there to be any awkwardness between us. If you want to pretend it never happened—'

'Why on earth would I want to do that?'

She shrugged. 'People do sometimes. I mean you might think it wasn't a good idea ... in the broad light of day.'

'I think it was a brilliant idea in any light.'

'Really? You don't regret it now?'

'Nope. *Je ne regrette rien.*' He frowned. 'Look, is there something you're not telling me? *Should* I have regrets? Did I fail you in some way? Commit some terrible faux pas? You did—'

'Yes!' she practically shouted. 'Yes, you were very ... thorough. You totally lived up to your reviews.'

'Good.' He grinned across at her. 'I'm very glad to hear it.' Then suddenly his face fell, his smile vanishing. 'Do *you* have regrets?' he asked her, and he looked so alarmed, Lesley wanted to go around the table and hug him.

'No,' she said quickly. 'Not at all. I thought it was absolutely brilliant.'

'Good.' His face sagged in relief. 'I told you you'd have a good time if you gave me a chance.'

'It's just that ... people like you don't usually act like this the morning after – all happy and cheerful and friendly.'

'Sorry to disappoint. How do you expect me to act?'

'Well, people like you tend to act all shifty the next day – avoid eye contact, disappear as fast as they can, that sort of thing. They certainly don't stay for breakfast.'

'You keep saying that. People like me how? Architects? Ex public school boys?'

'No, but, you know ... men.'

'Ah. Men. Well, I'll have to put my hands up to being one of them. But that is rather a large group that you're generalising about there. Surely there are regional variations?'

'I'm just saying, I don't want you to feel trapped just because we're stuck here together and you can't make a quick getaway. So if you want to run off, I'll turn my back and count to ten, and it can be like last night never happened.'

Al gave a hoot of laughter. 'You'll count to ten?' He drummed his fingers on the table thoughtfully and his eyes flicked to the door. 'That doesn't give me much of a head start.'

'Okay, twenty.' She grinned, relieved that he was teasing and obviously had no intention of scarpering.

'Well, that's very generous of you. If I want to take you up on it, I'll let you know.'

They ate in silence for a while. Lesley regretted having said anything. Al had been behaving normally and now she'd spoilt it by acting weird.

'Lesley,' Al's firm voice broke into her thoughts and she looked up. He put his knife and fork down and eyeballed her across the table. 'I loved it. Every second of it, okay? I wouldn't change a thing. Just so we're clear.' A smile nudged at the corners of his mouth.

'Okay,' she nodded, and she couldn't help the grin that

spread across her face. 'You don't have to look so smug about it, though.'

'I'm afraid that can't be helped. Sorry.'

'So you wouldn't change a thing?' She was aware that she was looking smug herself now.

'Nope. If you really want to know, it was the best sex of my life.'

'Oh,' she said in a small voice. 'That's a coincidence. Me too.'

Al grinned. 'A happy coincidence indeed.'

Damn it, why had she kept Al at arm's length for so long? If she'd found out sooner that they were dynamite together, they could have been shagging this whole holiday.

'Want to go back to bed and see if we can beat our personal best?' Al asked.

Lesley sighed. 'We should probably join the others at the beach,' she said reluctantly. 'It'd seem a bit rude to ditch them on our last day.' Maybe it would be better not to get hooked on Al when he was still hung up on Cassie.

'Really? You want to go to the beach?'

Oh, what the hell! Al was an amazing shag. She should just enjoy it while she could. 'No,' she said, sliding a leg across the table and running her bare foot up his leg. 'I really don't.'

36

'Y ou look well,' Katrina said grudgingly to Lesley a couple of days later as she let her in to their parents' house. 'Very tanned, and ... there's something else.' She tilted her head to the side and looked closely at her. 'Have you lost weight?'

'I've been having sex!' Lesley hissed excitedly.

'Well, yeah. I should hope so.'

Lesley forgot that everyone thought she was already having sex with Al, so there was no reason to be so excited about it. 'Well, you know ... holiday sex,' she amended. 'Lots of it. Day and night.'

'Thanks for the TMI.' Katrina narrowed her eyes at her. 'But there's something different about you.'

'Oh, I got my hair cut,' Lesley said, tossing her head.

'Yeah, that must be it. It's not bad.'

'Thanks,' Lesley said because she knew that practically constituted gushing for Katrina.

They walked into the kitchen, and Lesley stopped dead in the doorway because her mother was standing on top of the kitchen table doing a pile of ironing, while her father

sat at the table like a normal human being, fiddling with
his phone.

'Lesley!' Miriam looked up as they came in. 'You've
finally decided to grace us with a visit.'

'I only got back on Saturday night,' Lesley said sulkily.
'I needed to unpack and get my stuff sorted out. I have to
get straight back into work tomorrow.' In fact, she had
spent all of yesterday shagging Al, and he'd only gone
home this morning (quite reluctantly, she liked to think).
She hadn't been too sure where they'd stand once they got
back to Ireland, but she knew she didn't want the shagging
to stop. So she'd been very relieved when he'd asked her on
the plane if he could go home with her for the night.

'You look great,' her father said, hugging her hello.
'You have a sort of glow about you.'

'Must be the sun.'

'Where's Al?' her mother asked. 'Don't tell me you've
fallen out with him already.'

'He's going to the airport to pick up his aunt and drive
her home.' He was helping Jane move to Dublin for the
start of rehearsals, and he'd be spending the night in
Doonbeg. He'd invited Lesley to go with him, but she knew
she'd never hear the end of it if she let another day go by
without visiting her family. 'Anyway, never mind all that,'
she said as her mother unplugged the iron from the socket
board at her feet. 'What in the name of feck are *you* doing?'

'It's extreme ironing,' her father said proudly, standing
to hold her mother's hand as she stepped off the table onto
a chair and from there to the floor. 'She saw it on
YouTube.'

'Extreme ironing? Isn't that supposed to be on the side
of a mountain or something?'

'I'm working my way up to that,' her mother said. 'I'm
only starting.'

'Next stop, the Sugarloaf!' her father beamed.

'Well,' Miriam said tremulously, 'maybe the Hill of Howth first. I don't want to run before I can walk.'

'But why on earth do you even want to do extreme ironing?' Lesley said. 'Isn't that a young man's game?'

'Your mother has her heart set on being a YouTuber,' her father explained.

'There must be easier ways of getting on YouTube,' Lesley said as they all sat down.

'There are,' her mother said sourly, narrowing her eyes at Lesley. 'Did Katrina tell you her news?'

Lesley looked to her sister.

'I'm engaged!' Katrina held her left hand up, displaying the small sapphire on her ring finger.

'Oh wow! Congratulations!' Lesley grabbed her hand and pulled it towards her for a closer look. 'When did this happen?'

'Just last week,' Katrina said, smiling smugly. 'I asked Tom!'

'Good for you! And you got a ring and everything.'

'Of course she got a ring,' Miriam said crossly.

'You don't seem to be very happy about it,' Lesley said to her mother.

'I'm delighted. But I can't say I'm thrilled about the way it happened. Call me old-fashioned, but I think it's a sad day when a girl has to propose to herself.' She pursed her lips and shook her head sadly.

'She didn't propose to herself. She proposed to Tom. I think it's great!'

Miriam narrowed her eyes at Lesley again, but said nothing.

'So, when's the big day?' Lesley asked.

'We haven't set a date yet, but probably early next year.'

'Well, let me know if you want me to be bridesmaid, because I book up fast. I've already got one bridesmaid gig this year.'

'What? Who?' her mother asked.

'Stella, Peter Bradshaw's fiancée. She asked me while we were away.'

There was a low growling from the hall.

'I guess Skipper's ready for his walk,' Katrina said, getting up. 'I'll see you later.'

As soon as she left the room, Miriam let loose. 'Now see what you've done! Our big YouTube proposal is off. I hope you're happy.'

'I am, actually. But I don't know what you think it has to do with me,' Lesley said innocently. 'It's not my fault Katrina jumped the gun and proposed first.'

'Hmm. Don't try and tell me you didn't have some-thing to do with it. And now I have to resort to extreme ironing to get on YouTube. Well, on your head be it if I end up at the bottom of some ravine under a pile of your father's freshly ironed shirts.'

'Seriously, Mam. There are much easier ways to become a YouTube sensation. Besides, isn't extreme ironing a bit passé? Does anyone even do it anymore?'

'What would you suggest, love?' her father asked, while her mother continued to fume at her silently.

'Let's see what's trending right now,' she said, picking up her phone. 'I think soap cutting is pretty big.'

'Soap cutting?' her dad asked. 'What's that when it's at home?'

'Um ... it's exactly what it sounds like. It's basically whittling, only with soap.' She thumbed through her phone. 'Here, I'll show you.'

Her parents scooched together and looked over her shoulder as she opened a video.

'Hm! Looks like a waste of perfectly good soap to me,' her mother sniffed.

'I don't know,' her father said. 'There's something kind of ... mesmerising about it.'

'It's supposed to be very soothing, even just watching it,' Lesley said. 'And it's something you could do in the comfort of your own home.'

'I might give it a go myself,' her father said.

'It's not very environmentally friendly, is it?' her mother said, still not taking her eyes off the video, Lesley noticed. There *was* something strangely compelling about watching it.

'Since when have you worried about that?' Lesley asked.

'I'm every bit as environmentally aware as the next person,' Miriam said huffily.

'What if the next person is David Attenborough?'

'You always have a smart answer for everything!' her mother said, as if it was a bad thing.

The video came to an end. 'Will we watch another one?' her father asked.

'Sure. There are loads.' Lesley scrolled through the list of soap cutting videos to show them. 'And look how many hits they get.'

'They *are* very popular, aren't they?' Miriam said, and Lesley could tell she was weakening.

'And much more on trend than extreme ironing,' Lesley said.

'I do have that set of soaps the cleaner gave me last Christmas,' Miriam said thoughtfully. 'Fig and custard or some such ghastly concoction. I'm never going to use them.'

Her mother made tea, and they were all still watching YouTube when Katrina returned from her walk.

'What are you all looking at?' she asked.

'Soap cutting videos,' Lesley said.

'It's the latest YouTube sensation,' Miriam told her. 'I think I'm going to give it a go. The extreme ironing is very hard on my back anyway.'

'God, what's this sudden obsession with YouTube, Mam? How do you even *know* about YouTube at your age?'

'Oh, Liz from the bridge club showed me one of those proposal videos,' Miriam said airily, casting a sly look at Lesley, 'and I haven't been able to get it out of my head since. Such a lovely idea.' She sighed. 'So romantic!'

'Ugh! You think?' Katrina screwed up her face. 'If someone did that to me, I'd fucking castrate them on the spot and put *that* on YouTube.'

Miriam gasped, looking horrified. Lesley tried to catch her eye, but her mother was studiously avoiding eye contact with her. So she had to make do with smiling smugly to herself and trying to telepath 'Told you so' to her.

'How was Nice?' Romy asked later when Lesley called her.

'Fantastic! I had sex with Al!' Lesley squealed down the phone, glad to be talking to someone who realised this was big news.

Romy gasped. 'Really?'

'Still am, actually. Shagging him, that is. Well, not right this minute, but—'

'I should hope not. It was good then? The sex?'

'Yeah. It was ... kind of amazing, actually,' Lesley said, grinning to herself at the thought of it.

'So you fancy him now?'

'Yeah, I think so. I mean yes, I do.' She hadn't been too sure at first if it was just general free-floating horniness, and Al just happened to be the one getting the benefit. But she had decided over the last couple of days that it was definitely Al-specific.

'See, I told you it could happen if you gave it a chance.'

'You were right. Who knew?' Lesley said wonderingly. 'My first grower!'

But there was still a lot to process about her and Al too. She didn't really know what this thing between them was or where she stood. It had only started because she'd jumped him the night of the thunder storm. Were they just having sex? Was he attending to her needs as he'd offered to do, making it up to her because she couldn't be with anyone else while they were pretending to be together? She'd always felt he liked her more than she liked him. But now that she *did* like him in that way, she was starting to wonder if she'd not only caught up, but overtaken him.

Damn! Why did their timing have to be so out of whack? It'd be so much easier if she'd fancied him straight away when they met at Dinner Dates, and accepted when he asked her out. They'd be dating in a nice normal way, and she'd know what it was.

Still, she wasn't going to get all worked up and neurotic about it. She'd just enjoy it for what it was and see where it went.

37

F resh from her early-morning run, Stella sat at the table in Peter's kitchen drinking her breakfast smoothie as she went over her to-do lists for the day. In the week since they'd got home, she'd thrown herself into wedding preparations, and she was finding it surprisingly enjoyable. She liked the organisational aspect of it, and it felt good to be busy. She was still determined to keep it all as low-key as possible, but there was still lots to do, and in fact it turned out that foregoing a designated venue actually meant a lot of extra research and planning. She lived by her lists.

She'd booked the registry office, and was researching caterers for a small reception at the house. Hopefully this weather would keep up, she thought, looking out the window at the sun sparkling across the bay. The past week had been uncharacteristically hot and sunny for Ireland, and the terraced garden would be perfect for a party. She imagined how magical it would look with fairy lights and coloured lanterns in the trees and shrubs, and all the flowers in bloom.

Focusing so much on the details of the wedding in the last few days, she had found herself almost forgetting the marriage at the heart of it. But every so often, it would hit her where all this was leading, and she felt rather dazed that it was really happening. It was such an ordinary thing, really, despite the spectacle and romance. But she had never expected to have an ordinary life. Rings and white dresses and promises of ever-after belonged to other girls – girls whose smooth, straight paths through their well-ordered lives seemed to lead inevitably to the altar – and there was a little part of her that feared she'd be found out and exposed as an imposter, trying to lay claim to a life that wasn't rightfully hers.

'You're up early.'

She turned as Rafe came into the kitchen, dressed in a T-shirt and joggers.

'Mmm, lots to do today,' she said, indicating her lists.

'Coffee?' Rafe asked, as he switched on the machine.

'No thanks.'

He yawned and stretched while he waited for the coffee. 'Anything I can help you with?' He nodded at her notebooks.

She shook her head. 'It's wedding planning stuff,' she said, avoiding his gaze. Rafe had been friendly towards her since moving in with her and Peter after they'd returned to Dublin, but she still felt on shaky ground with him, and tried to avoid talking about the wedding when he was around. She didn't want to push her luck.

'Still going ahead with that, then?' His tone was flippant and teasing, but there was an undercurrent of antagonism to it.

'Yep.'

He poured a mug of coffee and sat across the table

from her with it. 'Well, you've been helping me with my house-hunting. The least I can do is return the favour.'

Stella had been delighted Rafe had accepted her offer to help with his property search. She was an avid watcher of all the TV property shows, and she loved looking around houses, so she enjoyed accompanying him on viewings. Plus she was good at it. She always knew the right questions to ask and had a good nose for when an estate agent was trying to hide something – unlike Rafe, who fell for the 'lifestyle' staging every time and never thought to look past it. But more than that, she was glad to have something they could do together to get on a more friendly footing with each other.

'Thanks for the offer. But Lesley's coming over later to help. Anyway, I don't think your heart would be in it.'

'What do you mean?'

'Well, wouldn't it be a bit like a bank manager helping a thief out with his plans for a heist? Since you think I'm intent on stealing the family jewels.' She blushed, realising what she'd said. 'Um ... so to speak.' Damn it, why had she said that? She didn't want a confrontation.

Rafe chuckled. 'Hardly.' He looked down at his coffee, then up at her, his expression serious. 'Come on,' he said softly, 'you can't blame me for being suspicious. I mean, much as we all love him, Dad's no prize. You can do better.'

His gaze was intense, and Stella had to look away.

'Your father is the best thing that's ever happened to me,' she said stiffly.

When she looked back at him, she was stunned by his expression. His eyes were narrowed as if trying to make her out, and he looked sad ... almost pitying.

'You're only twenty-six. Maybe the best is yet to come.'

'I'm counting on it,' she said softly. 'Look, Rafe, I know you don't like me, but——'

'I think we both know that's not true.'

She felt her face heat under the intensity of his gaze. 'Well, you don't approve of me, then,' she said, refusing to let him unnerve her.

'I don't think you're a bad person, Stella. But I do think you're making a big mistake.' He sighed, running a hand through his hair. 'But I guess there's not much I can do about it, is there?'

'Not a thing.'

'Unless I can persuade you to ditch Dad and run away with me?' he said jokingly. But again there was an undertone of something else, something that matched the intent in his eyes and caused her heart to flutter.

She forced a laugh. 'No, thanks. But I hope we can be friends.'

'I guess we can try.' He took a gulp of coffee. 'So, what's on the agenda for today?'

'Lesley and I are going to taste cakes this morning. I've found this company that do lovely bespoke ones with healthier ingredients.'

'Well, enjoy!'

'Thanks. Oh, by the way, I found you another couple of prospects,' she said, picking up her tablet. 'I thought we could make appointments to view them tomorrow. I'll send you the links——' She was interrupted by her phone buzzing, skimming across her notebook as it vibrated. She looked down at the display: Dan.

'Aren't you going to get that?' Rafe asked her, frowning.

'Um ... yeah.' She picked it up as she stood. 'Hi,' she said as she darted from the room.

'Hi.' His tone was subdued, and Stella immediately felt

something was wrong. 'I ... shit, it's hard to know how to tell you this. But anyway, I have ... bad news, I guess.'

Stella's heart started to pound. Oh God, was the baby all right?

'It's Dad,' Dan said. 'He died.'

'Oh.' Stella felt winded, blindsided by a dizzying mixture of emotions – relief, sadness, guilt and a bewildering sense of loss. But the overriding emotion was confusion. What the fuck was she supposed to feel?

'It was very sudden,' Dan was saying. 'He had a heart attack. Mam just found him dead in bed this morning.'

'God. Sorry ... I mean ... God.' It had been on the tip of her tongue to say 'sorry for your loss', to offer Dan her condolences in the traditional manner. But it was her loss too ... wasn't it? Was it? 'I think I need to sit down,' she said with a shaky laugh, sinking onto the bottom step of the stairs. 'How's ... how's Mam?' she asked, keeping her voice hushed in case Rafe could hear.

'She's in pretty bad shape. It was so sudden. It was a real shock.'

'And you? Are you okay?'

'Yeah.' He sniffed. 'I'm fine. It's ... weird, you know?'

'Yeah. I know.' God, she wanted so badly to be with him right now it ached. She wished they were in the same room and could put their arms around each other. They were the only ones who knew how this felt – how weird and wrong and bewildering.

'Anyway,' he said more briskly, 'the funeral's going to be on Wednesday, if you want to come.'

'Oh! Do you think I should?'

'No. I mean, that's not what I'm saying. I just thought I should tell you in case you wanted to. I know you probably don't, but ...'

'Do you think I should?' she asked again.

There was a brief silence. Then he said, 'Probably not.'

'Yeah, probably not a good idea. Has Mam ... has she mentioned me at all?'

'No. She doesn't even know we're still in touch.'

'Right.' She nodded dazedly. 'Best if I don't go, then. She's probably had enough shocks to deal with for now,' she added bitterly.

'Well, I'd better go – arrangements to make and so on. But I'll talk to you again soon.'

'Yeah. Bye. Take care.'

She hung up and sat for a moment, staring into space. Then she got up and walked back into the kitchen in a daze.

'Are you okay?' Rafe asked, frowning.

'Yeah, I'm fine, thanks,' she said, trying to shake herself out of her trance. She felt so hollow.

'You look like you've seen a ghost.' His eyes were wide with concern.

'Just some bad news,' she said, putting her phone on the table as she sat opposite him.

'Oh?'

'Yeah, that was ... an old friend of mine. His father just died.'

'Oh, I'm sorry. You were fond of him?'

'What?'

'Your friend's father?'

'Oh.' She smiled crookedly. 'Not really. He wasn't a very nice man.'

'Oh.' Rafe looked confused.

'He *really* didn't like me. Always had it in for me, in fact. But he was a big part of my childhood, I guess.'

'Right.' Rafe still looked baffled – understandably.

'And he wasn't *always* awful to me. I remember one day – I must have been about seven. It snowed, and he took me and my—my friend tobogganing. I fell on the ice and split my ear open, and he bought me a packet of Maltesers.' Her eyes welled up at the memory, and she blinked away tears.

'He bought you a packet of sweets? Big deal!'

She gave him a small smile. 'My childhood wasn't very happy,' she said, shrugging. 'I guess it makes the little things stand out.' Besides that *was* a big deal for her father. She knew it was pathetic that she was still touched by such a small act of kindness, but she couldn't help it.

That day was her best memory of her father. Dan's too. They talked about it sometimes – the fun, playful side of him that they'd fleetingly glimpsed as they hurtled down the snowy hillside together, squealing with delight. He'd made them the sled that morning from an old crate, and he'd laughed with them as they tumbled in the snow, cheering when they made it to the bottom of the hill without falling off. They always wondered where that affectionate, indulgent man had been up to that point; where he'd disappeared to again afterwards.

'So, are you going to the funeral?' Rafe asked.

'No. I'm not that close to the family anymore.'

There was a charged silence between them, and Rafe was looking at her strangely. She'd said too much, she thought – somehow without really saying anything, she'd said too much.

'Well, I'd better go and get ready,' she said, getting up. 'Lesley will be here soon. There are cakes to be eaten.'

'Are you sure you're okay?' Rafe narrowed his eyes at her.

'Yeah. I'm fine. I'll see you later.'

38

Lesley groaned with pleasure through a mouthful of vegan chocolate cake. 'Oh my God!' she said when she'd swallowed. 'Sorry you have to see my sex face at this hour of the day, but this is amazing!'

Stella laughed as she licked lavender icing off her fingers. 'It's really good, isn't it?'

'I think this is the one! And I mean that in the truest sense. Honestly, I'd marry this cake.'

'It's so beautiful too.' Stella sighed.

Lesley looked at the picture in the big book of cakes on the table in front of them. It was stunning – four tiers of dark chocolate sponge, decorated with delicate lavender piping, the whole topped with fresh roses. It was all vegan anyway, but Emma, the baker, had assured Stella she was happy to tweak any aspect of the recipe or decoration to her specifications.

'Well, that's another job done, then?' Lesley asked, picking up her tablet.

Stella nodded. 'It seems like an obscene amount to spend on a cake, though, doesn't it?'

The price was indeed eye-watering. 'But hey, it's your wedding,' she said to Stella. 'Anyway, you're going to be rich. You may as well get used to it.'

When they had ordered the cake, Emma told them to relax and take as long as they liked enjoying their tea and the rest of the samples.

'Might as well finish off the runners-up,' Lesley said, picking up a slice of carrot cake. 'So, how's Peter? Still not shagging him?'

Stella smiled. 'No. Actually I hardly see him since rehearsals started for his play.'

'Oh? They must be pretty full-on.'

'They seem to be going on longer each day too. And the last few nights, he's called to say they're all going out afterwards and he won't be home for dinner.'

'Does it bother you?' Lesley asked, though she could already tell from Stella's tone that it did.

'Well, I'm starting to feel more like his mum than his fiancée – always telling him to go easy and not to stay out too late. And I'm not sure I like the idea of him spending so much time with Jane. She's living in town now, you know. She borrowed some friend's apartment for the duration of the show.'

'Are you worried that he's actually just going back to hers when he doesn't come home?'

'No,' Stella said, shaking her head. But her dismissiveness was unconvincing, and Lesley could tell the thought had occurred to her. 'I mean, he's not even sleeping with *me*. I don't think I have to worry about him cheating.'

'Don't you miss sex, though?' Lesley asked, thinking dreamily of Al. They'd been shagging almost non-stop since they got back from France.

Stella shrugged. 'I don't mind waiting. To be honest,

I've always liked the closeness and cuddling more than the actual sex itself.'

'Yeah, I like that bit too.' Lesley smiled. 'But God, I love the main event.' Her mind flashed back to last night, Al pounding into her ... She shook her head. 'So you're living with Rafe now. Is that awkward?'

'What do you mean?'

'Well, I know he was a bit hostile to you at first.'

'No, it's fine. I think we've reached a truce.'

'That's good. Especially if Peter's been abandoning you.'

'He's not abandoning me,' Stella said, frowning. 'He's just ... busy.'

Lesley finished her cake and put down her plate. 'Right, what's next?' she said, picking up her tablet, and scrolling through her list of bridesmaid duties. She had coordinated to-do lists with Stella. 'Did you open an account on that budgeting app I sent you?'

Stella didn't answer. She seemed distracted, and had been zoning out now and again all afternoon.

'Are you okay?' Lesley asked.

'Sorry.' She shook her head. 'I was miles away. What did you say?'

'I just asked if you'd opened an account on that budgeting app.'

'Oh, yes. I did.'

'Great.' Lesley tapped on her tablet. 'Can you give me your login details? Then we can both access it and keep everything together.'

'Oh! I hadn't thought of that.' Stella hesitated.

'I just thought it would be handy,' Lesley said, trying to sound casual. 'No problem if you'd rather not.' She didn't want to be too persistent and arouse Stella's suspicions.

'No, it's fine,' Stella said. 'The username is my email. And the password ...' She hesitated, biting her lip.

'Look, if you don't want to give it to me, it's cool. I can keep track of whatever I spend and we can update it whenever we're together.'

'It's not that,' Stella said. 'It's just ... it's a bit embarrassing.'

'Ah, we've all been there. I won't judge you.'

'Okay, it's Babygirl star two hyphen zero.'

'Star as in asterisk?'

'Yes. All lower case, except for the B in Babygirl.'

'Ah, star for Stella? Very clever.' Lesley tapped it into her screen. 'Okay, I'm in! And we'll say no more about it. Anyway, at least it's not your birthday. That *would* be embarrassing. Plus I'd have to lecture you about it with my IT hat on. Now, do you want that last piece of coconut cake?'

Stella shook her head. 'It's all yours.'

LESLEY KNEW that people tended to be very lazy about two things online – passwords and usernames. Stella may not have used her birthday, but Lesley could have cheered when she heard the password. It sounded like something with personal meaning, the kind of password people clung on to over years. She'd bet her bottom dollar that she'd frequently used it or some variation of it as a login or handle.

When she got home that afternoon, she made herself a mug of coffee and sat down at her laptop, settling in for a long session hunting for Stella's internet trail. She typed Babygirl into the search engine, along with variations – using wildcards, or replacing the asterisk with the word 'star' or 'Stella'. Then she dug in and began trawling through the results. There were pages and pages of baby clothes, and most of the hits could be dismissed at a glance. She knew it was a long shot, and she wasn't really expecting to find anything, but there was the odd Twitter or Facebook profile, and she checked them all out. None seemed connected to Stella.

Then, deep into the tenth page of results, there were several links to a website devoted to make-up and beauty. Clicking on the first link brought her to a forum and someone using the name Babygirlstar commenting on the best green concealers for covering up redness. Another couple of links led to similar discussions on the same site, on topics as diverse as tips for keeping hair from going frizzy in humid climates (she made a note to come back to that one) and the best moisturisers for acne-prone skin. The threads were all from about five years ago. Babygirlstar seemed to be a regular contributor and someone other members looked up to as something of an expert – which Stella was.

The next link was to a thread on an area of the site devoted to general chat, where someone had posted a question about the etiquette of attending an ex's wedding, and various members were chipping in with their advice and opinions. There was nothing particularly revealing in Babygirlstar's comments, but it gave Lesley hope that there'd be more. She typed Babygirlstar into the site's search bar and brought up every discussion she'd contributed to – and there were a lot.

She started with the general discussions as they seemed more likely to reveal personal details, and began reading through them. She felt a spark of excitement when Babygirlstar (who she was already thinking of as Stella) mentioned in passing that she had started out working in hairdressing.

She felt like she was closing in on her target as she read Babygirl's comments on everything from difficult neighbours and weight loss to the best restaurants in LA and the perfect passive-aggressive wedding gift for your deadliest frienemy. Babygirl had a dry sense of humour, but didn't reveal much in the way of personal information. Still, Lesley started to piece together a sketchy profile from the few snippets she dropped. She'd never been married, didn't have much trouble controlling her weight, knew LA and London well, preferred coffee to tea and had no tattoos. Then she clicked on a thread headed 'My Crazy Ex-Boyfriend' started by someone going by the name of BirdofParadise. 'Birdy' as the other members called her, had just got engaged, but was being stalked by her abusive ex – a narcissistic asshole, if Lesley had ever heard of one, who had spent years manipulating and gaslighting her. She'd been to the police, but they hadn't been much use, and she didn't know what to do.

The make-up community were incredibly supportive, showering her with congratulations before weighing in with sympathy and suggestions. A lot of them shared stories about their own experiences with exes who couldn't let go, and Lesley got absorbed in the stories from regular contributors. She was starting to feel like she knew some of them at this stage. Then she scrolled to Babygirl's comment, and she started to hope it wasn't Stella after all as she told them about her own abusive ex – his violent rage when she'd broken up with him, his outrage that she'd had the audacity to leave him.

And then she saw two words that caused her stomach to lurch. Two words that could explain everything: Stella's reserve, her need for privacy, even her name change.

39

'As you can see, the garden is exceptionally large, and comprises an extra living space in itself,' the estate agent said, opening the French doors off the kitchen/diner and leading Rafe and Stella out onto a large deck. 'The current owners are keen gardeners, and it's been lovingly maintained. This space is perfect for outdoor entertaining,' she continued, sweeping an arm around the deck. A long table with six chairs was laid with a colourful runner, wine glasses and an ice bucket set on top. 'Or the perfect spot for enjoying a glass of wine in the evening.'

'Looks great,' Rafe said, glancing around appreciatively. Stella could tell he was already visualising family barbecues or quiet sundowners on the deck.

'Yes, but it's north-facing, isn't it?' Stella said.

'Oh?' Rafe frowned down at the brochure in his hands. 'I thought Hilary said it was south-facing?'

'I think it's the *front* garden that's south-facing, isn't it, Hilary?' Stella asked.

'Um ... yes, that's right,' Hilary said tightly.

'Oh, so it wouldn't get any sun at all?' Rafe frowned.

'No, not a spot,' Stella said briskly.

'Well, let me show you upstairs,' Hilary said, gamely keeping her smile pinned on as she led them back through the French doors into the house.

Stella glanced at her watch. 'I think we've seen enough.' She looked questioningly at Rafe, who nodded. 'There's no point in wasting your time,' she said to Hilary, smiling to soften the blunt statement.

'Oh, well ... if you're sure.'

'Do you have anything else to show us?' Stella asked.

'Well ...' Hilary rooted in her briefcase. 'I've a very nice property right in the village,' she said, pulling out a brochure. 'It needs a little work, but that's reflected in the price, of course,' she said as she handed it to Stella.

'Grade II listed,' Stella read.

'That's good, isn't it?' Rafe said, looking over her shoulder.

Stella shook her head. 'Not necessarily. There are a lot of restrictions on what you can do with a listed building, aren't there?' she said to Hilary.

'Well ... yes,' she admitted reluctantly.

'If it needs a lot of work, it might be more trouble than it's worth.'

Hilary sighed as Stella handed her back the brochure. 'Perhaps you should tell me precisely what you're looking for, so we don't waste anyone's time.'

'Well, nothing north-facing,' Stella said. 'South-west ideally – and take it as read that we're talking about the back aspect – but south or west is acceptable, and we might consider east at a pinch.' She looked to Rafe for confirmation and he shrugged. 'Somewhere in the Dalkey/Killiney area, and not listed if it needs a lot of renovation.'

Hilary was making notes on a pad as Stella spoke. 'Children?' she asked, looking up.

'Excuse me?' Stella stuttered.

'Sure, I wouldn't mind a couple of children thrown in,' Rafe said. 'Are they extra?'

Hilary smiled tightly, clearly not amused. 'I mean, do you have any children?'

'Oh, no, we're not – I mean, we aren't—' Stella stammered, blushing. She'd let it go if it weren't for the fact that Rafe was famous. But as it was, she felt it necessary to set the record straight.

'Any plans to start a family in the near future?' Hilary pressed on. 'Or will it just be the two of you?' she asked.

Was she just trying to get gossip about Rafe, Stella wondered.

'We're not ... together,' Rafe said.

'Oh?'

'No,' Stella told her. 'The house is for Rafe. I'm just helping him look.'

'Ah, very good.' Hilary straightened. 'Schools aren't a concern for you, then,' she said, ticking a box on her checklist. 'Well,' she said briskly, snapping her briefcase closed, 'I have a much clearer idea of what we're looking for now. Leave it with me.' She started leading the way to the door.

'I'll be in touch,' she said, showing them out. 'You know,' she said to Rafe as they were about to leave, 'since the property is just for you, perhaps it would be better if you did the viewings on your own. No point in being influenced by someone who won't be living there,' she said with a sour look at Stella. 'I mean, it's how it feels to you that counts, isn't it?' She flashed Rafe a flirtatious smile.

'Thanks for the suggestion,' Rafe said smoothly, 'but I trust Stella's judgement. She's much better at all this than I am. I'd probably have let you sell me this house just because I liked the idea of sitting at the garden table.'

'Oh.' Hilary pursed her lips. 'Well, whatever you think best, of course. But you know, there are many advantages to a north-facing garden.'

'Really?' Stella asked sceptically. 'Such as?'

Hilary looked stumped for a moment. Then she brightened. 'Skin cancer!'

'Oh? That's an advantage?'

'What I mean is, a shaded garden allows you to enjoy the fresh air without worrying about melanoma.'

'I'll buy a hat,' Rafe said. 'Then I can have the best of both worlds.'

'Right.' Hilary nodded. 'Great idea!'

'I DON'T THINK Hilary likes me very much,' Stella said as they walked back to Rafe's car.

'No, she's got you down as a troublemaker.'

'You, on the other hand ... '

'Oh, she definitely likes me.'

After several days of house-hunting, Stella was getting used to the reaction Rafe got from women whenever he turned up. There was a lot of fluttering, and even if they weren't openly flirting, there was always a sense of heightened awareness.

Her mobile rang as they got into Rafe's car. It was Peter.

'Hello, darling. How's the house-hunting going?'

'Great.' She glanced at Rafe. 'Are you at home?'

'No, that's what I was ringing to say. 'I'm going to eat with some of the company, so I won't be home for dinner.'

'Oh, okay.' She tried not to sound put out. She had wanted to tell him about her father later, when they were alone. It would be comforting to be able to talk about it with someone, and she knew he'd be sympathetic. But it would have to wait. 'Well ... enjoy yourself.'

'Thank you, darling. You too. It'll be a chance for you to have something really evil. You should order a pizza.'

'Yes, I might do that.'

'Dad?' Rafe asked her when she'd hung up.

'Yes, he was just ringing to say he won't be home for dinner.'

'Well, in that case, why don't I take you out for dinner as a thank-you for all this.'

'There's no need,' she said. 'I told you, I love it.'

'Still ... we have to eat anyway.' He shrugged. 'Besides, Dad's out enjoying himself, and you deserve a break.'

She considered. She liked Rafe. They got on well, and she felt they were friends now. And it *would* be lovely to go out for a change.

'Okay, then.' She smiled at him. 'I'd love to.'

'OH GOD, do you think they've seated us here on purpose?' Jane nodded to the wall behind Peter as he settled himself on the red plush banquette opposite her in Trocadero.

Peter turned to see he was sitting beneath a photograph of Jane. She was about twenty-five and breathtakingly beautiful. He could almost pinpoint exactly when it had been taken, shortly after they'd first met.

The restaurant had a long association with Dublin's theatre community, and the walls were lined with photographs of stars of stage and screen who had frequented it over the years. The faces of many old friends looked back at him as he scanned the room. He was up there too, a little further along the wall from Jane – young and preposterously handsome. They'd spent a lot of time here in those days, and he had fond memories of first-night suppers and long evenings of table-hopping with friends. The place was as warm and comforting as a much-loved cardigan, and it was a buzz to be back and feel part of it all again. Several of the waiters were old friends, and Peter enjoyed the attention they got, the little stir in the room as they walked in, the sideways looks from other diners who recognised them, the nods and waves from old acquaintances.

'God, look how handsome I was,' Peter said disgustedly. 'No wonder you fell madly in love with me.'

Jane laughed. 'I wasn't so bad myself.'

'You were stunning.' Peter turned back to her and smiled. 'Still are.' He took her hand across the table. 'Beatrice to my Benedick. I still remember that day like it was yesterday. The minute you walked into that rehearsal room on the first day, I was lost – completely bowled over. I knew my life would never be the same again. You slew me.'

'You recovered quickly enough,' Jane said, slipping her hand from his.

He shook his head. 'I'm not over it yet. And it was the same for you, don't pretend otherwise.'

'I'm not pretending anything. I was dazzled.'

'It was fate. We'd both met our match and we were helpless to do anything about it. Nothing could stand in our way.'

'Tough luck for that girl you were with at the time. Leah, was it?'

Peter felt a distant pang of guilt at the mention of the girlfriend he'd rapidly dispatched the moment Jane had come into his life. 'Leah, yes. The stage manager.'

Peter had always loved the first day of rehearsals, when it was all fresh and exciting – new people and ideas, the strange combination of competition and collaboration that electrified the room as they all tried to impress and outshine each other, buoyed up on a heady mixture of adrenaline, sexual tension and creative energy. And beneath it all was the ever-present promise of sex as they checked each other out, forming tentative friendships, making allies, finding lovers. That day he'd met Jane had been the most exciting of all, the energy crackling between them so fierce, he'd almost expected everyone else to be burned by the sparks.

'You were such a star,' Jane said.

'Me?' Peter reared back in surprise. 'Not then. I was just a chancer with more neck than talent. But then I met you.'

'I was no star myself.'

'No, nothing so crass. You were a queen.'

And she'd made him a king. Peter had been in awe of Jane's theatrical pedigree, coming from the legendary Howard acting dynasty. He'd always felt like something of an imposter in that world, but Jane had taken his hand and led him right to the heart of it, and for the first time, he'd felt like he belonged.

He'd been hugely impressed by her parents, and was gauchely thrilled to be marrying into theatrical royalty. He'd loved being part of her rather grand family, enjoying their expansive hospitality and unstinting generosity on long summer holidays at their *gîte* in France, or in the decaying majesty of their crumbling old house in Clare. Jane's parents were gregarious and colourful. They surrounded themselves with writers, actors and musicians, throwing lavish parties and casual kitchen dinners with the same tireless enthusiasm. It all seemed worlds away from his dreary industrial back-ground, and he'd been so grateful to Jane for sharing it all with him, like a wonderful dowry she gifted him when they married.

'God, we were gorgeous then,' he said wistfully, glancing at their photos again.

Jane shrugged. 'We were just young.'

'Is that all it is?'

'That's about ninety per cent of it.'

'God.'

Jane gazed over his head. 'I was twenty-six when that was taken,' she said, nodding at the photo of herself.

Neither of them said it, but Peter was sure they were both thinking the same thing: she'd been the same age Stella was now. What a strange thought.

The waiter came to take their order, and Peter could feel Jane's bemusement as he gave detailed instructions about how he wanted his food prepared, eschewing the rich sauces and oily dressings in favour of simply grilled fish and salad.

She was looking at him strangely as the waiter left with their order.

'I'm a changed man,' he said to her by way of explanation.

Jane frowned, looking slightly discomfited. 'Are you?' she asked. 'What are we doing here, Peter?'

'It's just dinner,' he said gently. 'We're just two old friends having dinner together.'

'You should be at home with your girlfriend. Where did you tell her you are tonight?'

'I said I was going to eat with some of the company.' Jane shot him a weary look. 'Well, it's true,' he said. 'You're one of the company.'

'Maybe you haven't changed at all,' Jane said, and even though he knew she didn't mean it in a positive way, Peter couldn't help feeling pleased at the thought. 'Maybe neither of us has. You'd think we'd know better at our age,' she said, glancing at the photograph above his head. 'We should have grown out of this by now.'

'Grown out of what?'

'Riding roughshod over other people's feelings. Philandering. Letting sex trump everything. But here we are, still sneaking around—'

'Not you. You were never a cheater.'

'I never used to be. But with you ...' She sighed. 'I was complicit. I knew you were with Leah when I met you, but I snuck off with you that first night anyway. I let you take me to bed when you should have been with her. I'm here with you now when you should be with Stella.' She gave an exasperated shake of her head, and Peter thought she was on the verge of walking out.

'We shouldn't be here, Peter. And yet ...'

'And yet?' He reached across the table, his hand open.

She put her hand in his. 'Here we are.'

40

S tella had been glad to have the wedding planning today to keep her busy. Having Lesley to talk to had really helped to distract her, and she'd managed to put everything else out of her mind while she was looking at houses with Rafe. She was grateful for the years of meditation practice that had given her the discipline to keep herself fully present in the moment and focused solely on what she was doing at any one time. But once she was alone again, her thoughts immediately drifted to home.

My father died today, she kept thinking as she showered and changed for dinner, trying to impress it on herself, struggling to feel it. But she just felt remote and detached from it. She wondered what Dan was doing now, what the funeral would be like. They'd be having the wake tonight. She thought of the house filled with her relatives; the old neighbours passing through; her father laid out in the living room. Would her mother think of her ... miss her?

Her mobile buzzed, vibrating on the nightstand, shaking her out of her thoughts. She picked it up and checked the caller ID – Dan. She swiped it quickly.

'Hi,' she said softly. She could hear noise in the background, and knew they must be in the middle of the wake. 'How's it going? Is it awful?'

'It's not so bad. Turns out everyone's really fond of Dad now he's dead. They're all going on about what a great guy he was.'

'Even Uncle Pat?'

'He's the worst of all. Inconsolable!'

Stella smiled. She couldn't remember a meeting between their father and Uncle Pat that didn't end in a punch-up. They couldn't stand each other. 'I don't suppose anyone's mentioned me?'

Dan hesitated a moment. 'No,' he said then.

'I saw the death notice.' She'd looked it up online. She wasn't surprised there was no mention of her, but it still hurt.

'I wanted to add you. He was your father too.'

'It's fine. It's how he would have wanted it,' she said bitterly.

'Yeah, I guess you're right.'

'I wish I could be there for you, though. I'm sorry you have to go through this alone.'

'I'm not alone. I have Annie. Though she might decide to leave me when she sees our fucked-up family in full swing.'

'Come on, it's a funeral. They'll have to behave themselves.'

Dan gave a humourless laugh. 'Don't be so sure.'

Stella wished she could reach through the phone and wrap her arms around her brother.

'Well, I'd better get back to the ham sandwiches. It must be at least two minutes since my last one.'

'Okay. Take care. I hope tomorrow isn't too awful.'

. . .

WHEN SHE HUNG UP, Stella paced the room restlessly. She sat at the dressing table to do her make-up, but jumped up again, unable to sit still. She felt agitated and unsettled, and desperately in need of someone to talk to who would understand. She picked up her phone to call Peter, but for some reason the thought of speaking to him only irritated her and she couldn't bring herself to dial his number.

He should be here, she thought, tossing the phone on the bed. She knew he'd care if she told him, and he'd come home if she wanted him to, but she resented having to prompt him. They were getting married. He was supposed to be there for her, and she shouldn't have to plea for his attention ...

She sighed, flopping down on the stool in front of her dressing table to finish doing her make-up. She was being unreasonable. Peter wasn't psychic. She couldn't expect him to know what was going on if she didn't tell him. She tried to put it out of her head as she finished getting ready and went downstairs to wait for Rafe in the living room.

But it was no use. Her mind was elsewhere, in her childhood home, with her mother and her brother, and her father in his coffin in the front room. She was consumed by a mounting sense that she needed to be there. Dan was right. He was her father too. She should be at the funeral tomorrow. She wanted to be with Dan; maybe even to see her mother ... She wouldn't cause a scene. She could hang back, stay on the edge of things. But she had to go.

She looked at her watch. It was almost seven. She would have to find something to wear. She stood up to go to her bedroom, but then sat down again. First she'd need to figure out a way to get to Gorebally for ten tomorrow. She picked up her phone to map out the journey. The first train in the morning was at seven-thirty, and didn't get into Galway until just after ten. It was about another hour by bus to Gorebally, so she would have to go tonight and stay over. She could arrange a taxi in the morning to drive her the rest of the way. Or maybe there was a bus ...

'Stella? What's wrong?' She looked up to find Rafe frowning at her in concern as he strode into the room. He slid onto the sofa beside her and took her hands. She realised they were shaking.

'I—' She stood up. 'I can't do dinner, sorry,' she said agitatedly. 'I need to go to Galway.'

'Tonight?'

She nodded. 'There's a funeral I have to go to in the morning.'

He glanced at her phone, tossed on the sofa. 'Your friend's father?'

She nodded; she'd forgotten she'd told him.

'I thought you weren't going to the funeral.'

'I changed my mind. My friend called and ... he needs me there. I have to find a train.' She picked up her phone.

'No, I'll drive you,' Rafe said, standing.

'Oh!' She couldn't think straight, her head spinning. If only she could take Rafe up on the offer, it'd be perfect. But she couldn't ... could she? 'Thanks, but that's not—I mean, it's really kind of you, but I couldn't ask you to drive all that way.'

'You didn't ask me, I offered. I'm not letting you go on the train. Apart from anything else, Dad would disown me.' He looked at his watch. 'It's only about two and a half hours to Galway. We could have dinner there, or somewhere along the way.'

'It's not Galway city, though. It's Gorebally.' She winced apologetically, rubbing her arms.

'Right, that's probably about another hour.' He pulled out his phone. 'Where were you planning to stay tonight?'

'I don't know,' she said. 'I hadn't got that far.'

'You're not staying with ... family?' he asked tentatively, as if trying not to pry.

'No. I was just going to find a B&B or something. Or stay in Galway for the night and find my way there in the morning.'

Rafe nodded and started thumbing through his phone. 'I'll sort something out, while you go and get your stuff together.'

'Thanks, Rafe.' She blinked back tears, overwhelmed with relief. She couldn't work out if it was a mistake involving Rafe, but right now she was just glad he was here.

'HAVE YOU SPOKEN TO DAD?' Rafe asked as he sat into the car beside her.

'Oh! No, I haven't. I suppose I should tell him where we've gone,' she said, pulling out her phone. But she hesitated to hit his number, reluctant to disturb him when he was ... what? Out shagging his ex-wife? The thought didn't sting as it should – it made her feel weary more than anything.

She'd thought she didn't care about the wedding, that she just wanted the marriage. But instead, she'd enjoyed organising the wedding, and now a cloud of inertia settled over her at the thought of what came after. She suddenly felt like being with Peter would be an enormous burdensome task that would crush her beneath its weight. Were they kidding themselves thinking it could work? She foresaw a life of endless effort, both of them trying too hard to jolly themselves and each other along and convince themselves they were happy. She wiped tears from the corners of her eyes and shook her head, trying to dispel her gloomy thoughts as she dialled Peter's number.

She couldn't tell him the truth with Rafe beside her listening, but Peter was kind and sympathetic when she told him Rafe was taking her to Galway for a family friend's funeral. She felt soothed as he spoke, the concern in his voice warming her. He apologised repeatedly for not being there.

'Do you want me to go? I could head off now and meet you there. Or join you tomorrow?'

'No, there's no need. I'll be home tomorrow.'

'Well, I'm glad Rafe was there to look after you,' he said. 'He's much more use than me in a crisis anyway.'

She felt a little better after talking to Peter, comforted and less wobbly about their future together. He was a sweet, kind man, and she did love him.

'Everything okay?' Rafe asked her.

'Yes, fine. Oh,' she gasped, suddenly remembering. 'You have that viewing tomorrow.'

'I'll cancel it,' Rafe said. 'I'd be useless without you there anyway.'

'Hilary would be over the moon to have you all to herself,' Stella said with a smile.

'Well, she's not getting me. I'll ring her in the morning and reschedule.'

'Did you find us somewhere to stay?'

'I booked us a couple of rooms at this place,' Rafe said, nodding at the satnav, where he'd put in the address of a small hotel on the outskirts of the town. 'It was the closest hotel I could find, and it's got decent reviews. But we can change it if you find something better.'

'It's pretty much the only show in town,' she said. She looked the hotel up on her phone. It had been spruced up recently, and looked much more welcoming than she remembered it. 'Apart from some B&Bs,' she said, thumbing through the accommodation website. 'And there's a pub with some rooms above it.'

'Well, if you'd rather stay at any of those ...'

She suppressed a shudder at the thought of staying at a local B&B. She'd probably know the landlady. As for the pub, that was where Dan had told her they were going after the funeral tomorrow. It was way too close for comfort. Her best shot at any semblance of anonymity and privacy was at the small hotel. 'No, this place looks good,' she said.

She felt increasingly anxious and queasy as they got closer to her home town, lurching nauseatingly between dread and wild optimism at the thought of seeing her mother tomorrow. She couldn't even imagine what it would be like to speak to her after more than ten years. She didn't dare acknowledge the tiny glimmer of hope that her mother would be glad to see her, and she tried to block out visions of tearful reunions, telling herself they were pure fantasy. But she couldn't help thinking what a frightening man her father could be, and how cowed her mother had been by him. She wondered if things might be different now that he was gone and she was out from under his thumb.

'So this is where you grew up?' Rafe said, looking around with interest as they drove through Gorebally's single street.

'Well, this is the downtown.' At the top of the same road she said, 'And now we're entering uptown Gorebally.'

'It's quite the metropolis.'

'Yes, but it's very well planned out, so it's easy to find your way around. No one ever gets lost in Gorebally.'

It was almost ten when they arrived at the hotel. Stella hung back a little at reception, keeping her head down while Rafe checked in.

'Are you hungry?' he asked her.

'Yes, starving actually,' she said, only realising now that she was.

'We never did have dinner.' Rafe turned back to the receptionist, who informed him that last orders in the restaurant were at ten, so they'd want to be quick.

Stella would much rather hide in her room and get room service, but it wouldn't be fair to Rafe after driving all this way to make him eat alone. So after quickly dumping their bags in their rooms, they went to the restaurant. She looked around surreptitiously while Rafe studied the menu, and relaxed a little when she didn't see anyone she recognised.

'Are you okay?'

She looked up to find Rafe looking at her with concern.

'Yes, fine. Sorry, I was miles away.' She shook her head and tried to concentrate on the menu.

'I'm sorry about your friend's dad,' he said gently. 'You were obviously close, despite everything.'

She shrugged. 'We used to be. He was ... almost like a father to me,' she said with a sad smile. 'But I hadn't seen him in a very long time.'

Stella ordered fish and Rafe had steak. The food was good, but, despite having been hungry, she found she could hardly eat.

'Is that not good?' Rafe asked her, nodding at her plate.

'It is. But suddenly I just don't seem to have an appetite.' She put down her knife and fork. 'Sorry, I'm just a bit weirded out about being back here.'

Rafe nodded understandingly.

'Thank you for driving me all this way, Rafe,' she said. 'I really appreciate it.'

'No problem,' he said. 'I was happy to.'

'Could I ask you one more favour? About tomorrow?'

'Of course. Anything.'

'The graveyard is a little way out of town and I'll need a lift—'

'Of course I'll take you. I presumed I would be.'

'But ... would you mind not actually coming to the funeral with me?' She felt awful asking him this when he'd been so kind to her. 'It's just ... I don't want to cause a fuss, and if I turn up with *you* ...'

'Sure,' he said, with a nod; 'I understand.'

'Sorry, it's just ...'

'Stella—' he leaned across the table, taking her hand '—it's fine, honestly. Please don't worry about it. I'll drive you to the church and wait outside to take you to the graveyard. It's not a problem.'

'Thank you.' She smiled, blinking back tears. He really was so kind.

He continued to hold her hand, and something shifted between them as their eyes locked.

'Well,' he said hoarsely, 'would you like to get a drink? Or do you want to go to bed?'

Rafe saying those words to her stirred something inside Stella that she hadn't felt in a long time, causing her stomach to flip and heat to spread through her. She thought how nice it would be to go to bed with Rafe, to feel his arms around her, to have him kissing her, touching her ...

'I'd like to go to bed,' she said, her voice coming out croaky. She cleared her throat. 'I mean, I'm really tired.' She had been exhausted from the strain of the day, her nerves stretched taut. But now she was suddenly invigorated, a different kind of nerves filling her with a weird energy.

'Yeah,' Rafe said, releasing her hand. 'Early start in the morning.'

41

Stella was glad her father had at least had the good grace to die in the summer, and during a spell of good weather, so she had an excuse to wear dark glasses at the funeral. She pulled them on as she sat in the car with Rafe, watching as mourners gathered outside the church. Her breath caught in her throat as the hearse arrived, and she saw her mother and Dan emerging from the funeral car. She should have been in that car with them. It felt so weird to be sitting here outside it all, watching from a distance, like she was a spectator to her own life.

'Well, here goes,' she said as Dan and her uncles shouldered the coffin, and the other mourners followed them inside.

Rafe gave her hand a quick squeeze. 'I'll be waiting here,' he said.

Her legs were shaky as she got out of the car. She was so nervous, she felt she might throw up. She pulled her wide-brimmed hat down, shading her eyes, hanging back as she joined the last of the stragglers making their way inside.

It was a big funeral – not so much, Stella suspected, because her father had been such a beloved local figure, but because it was the only show in a town where there was nothing to do. They spoke about a person she didn't recognise – a generous big-hearted man, a pillar of the community who was mourned by his wife Nora and son Dan. She had been obliterated from the ceremony as thoroughly as she had been from his life – unlike his drinking buddies, whose great loss was acknowledged repeatedly.

She stayed at the back of the church, hidden among the throng, and kept her head down as everyone exited the church. She'd texted Dan this morning to tell him she'd be here, and she could see him looking out for her, scanning the pews as he and her uncles carried the coffin down the aisle. He threw her a brief, furtive look of sympathy when he saw her. She shivered as the coffin passed, trying to feel something other than cold indifference. That was her father. But she couldn't summon any emotion.

She waited until everyone had filed past, following the coffin outside into the churchyard. She didn't even allow herself to look at their faces in case someone would recognise her. When the church was empty, she slipped out a side door and stood at the edge of the crowd gathered in the churchyard. Out of the corner of her eye she located her mother and Dan standing side by side, surrounded by friends and neighbours offering their condolences. No one seemed to notice her, apart from the odd curious glance.

Her heart pounded as she waited for her mother to spot her. Surely she would. She had dressed carefully for the funeral, and she realised now she had worn the chic black vintage Chanel suit with her mother in mind. She was a traditional woman, and she'd appreciate the mark of respect. But she also loved clothes, and Stella remembered her poring over fashion magazines when she was a child, gazing long-ingly at clothes she couldn't afford and would never have an occasion to wear. She'd always admired women who dressed stylishly, and Stella was sure she'd love her outfit.

She tried to get up the nerve to approach her. But the longer she stood there on the sidelines, watching her mother surrounded by friends and neighbours, the more she felt like an unwelcome intruder. Maybe she should just slip away quietly now, and her mother wouldn't even have to know she'd been here. Or should she stick around and wait until later, after the graveyard to talk to her, when the crowd would have thinned out, and they could meet without the whole town watching? As she pondered this, a light breeze lifted her hat, and she took it off, shaking out her hair.

'You!' Suddenly there was a shout from across the churchyard, and Stella turned to see her Uncle Pat looking right at her, pointing a finger accusingly. 'It's you, isn't it?'

Stella started as he began shouldering his way through the crowd towards her.

'You've got a feckin' nerve showing up here!' he roared. 'After what you put your poor father through.'

Faces turned towards her to see what the fuss was about, and Stella suddenly found herself the focus of attention. She turned to Dan, who stared back at her wide-eyed with alarm. He jerked his head in the direction of the gate, telling her to run, but she couldn't move. She felt rooted to the spot as Uncle Pat barrelled towards her.

Then her mother whipped around and saw her, and Stella felt the look in her eyes like a punch. Initial shock and disbelief was followed by horror and ... hatred.

'Could you not have had the decency to stay away?'

she said, her eyes narrowed as she advanced slowly towards Stella. 'Haven't you done enough? Isn't it your fault your father's in an early grave. You broke his heart—'

Stella didn't wait to hear any more. Suddenly galvanised into action, she turned on her heel and ran as her mother and uncles descended on her from all sides. Her heels caught in the gravel, and she slowed briefly to take them off, hopping on one foot at a time. Then she raced down the long driveway of the church, three of her uncles chasing after her, shouting.

'Come back here, ya bowsie!' Pat panted as he chased her.

'Wait till I get my hands on you!'

'Look at what you've done to your poor mother!'

Stella shot out the gate, tearful with gratitude at the sight of Rafe waiting patiently in his car. She tore open the door and flung herself inside.

'Drive, drive!' she hissed.

Rafe shot her a startled look, but quickly threw down the book he'd been reading and started the car. They sped away just as her uncles came barrelling through the church gates, looking around for her and shaking their fists.

'Jesus, who were those nutters?' Rafe asked.

Stella glanced behind her. The three of them were all bent double at the gates of the church, hands on knees as they tried to catch their breath.

'My uncles,' she said, adrenaline pooling in her body as she laid her head back against the headrest. 'Lucky for me they're not very fit.'

'So much for not creating a fuss.' Rafe threw her a worried look. 'So ... I guess you're not going to the grave-yard, then?'

Stella gave a hoot of laughter, but her eyes welled up

with tears. 'No,' she said. 'And I think I can skip the tea and sandwiches at the pub too.'

Rafe was obviously baffled, but Stella was grateful that he didn't ask any more questions. He drove back to the hotel and led her straight to the bar.

'I think you could do with a drink,' he said, eyeing her with concern.

She nodded. She felt dazed, and she was grateful that he was taking over. She sank onto a seat while Rafe went to the bar. What the hell had she been thinking? How could she have imagined for one second that her mother might have been happy to see her? She had been kidding herself. Her parents were a pair, united in everything, including their rejection of her. It was probably true what her mother had said, that she'd driven her father to an early grave. That kind of hatred was poisonous, corrosive – maybe it had eaten away at his heart until there was nothing left.

Rafe came back with whiskey and sandwiches. 'You hardly ate anything last night,' he said, pushing the plate towards her. 'You should have something.'

Stella ate and drank mindlessly, her mind in a whirl.

'I booked the rooms for another night,' Rafe told her, 'so you can take all the time you need.'

She nodded gratefully.

'So that funeral ...' Rafe prodded gently.

'It was my father's.' Stella took a gulp of whiskey.

'I'm sorry,' Rafe said.

Stella shrugged. 'There was no love lost. As you could probably tell.'

'But I thought—I mean Dad said—'

'That my parents were dead.' Stella nodded. 'I know. He knows it's not true, but that's what I tell people.' She sighed. 'They disowned me. Threw me out when I was sixteen, and I haven't seen them since. So I tell people they're dead. It's just ... easier.' She took another swig of her drink. 'At least, I thought it was.' Suddenly it felt very complicated, and she was overwhelmed with weariness from it all – the pretending and lying and hiding.

Rafe still looked confused. She could tell he had a million questions, and she was hugely grateful to him for not asking any of them. All he asked was 'Another?' as she drained her glass. She nodded and he went to the bar.

He'd just gone when Dan walked into the lounge. His eyes darted around, scanning the room, and she stood and waved him over.

'Dan, what are you doing here?'

Wordlessly, he pulled her into a hug, his arms wrapped tightly around her as he pulled her into the pillowy softness of his body, as if trying to absorb all the hurt of a lifetime. She laid her head on his chest and for a moment they just stood there, holding each other.

'Jesus, Stella!' He released her and they flopped down onto the couch beside each other. 'Never a dull moment with you around. What a fucking circus!'

'I know.' She bit her lip. 'I shouldn't have come. It was a stupid idea.'

He sighed and leaned back against the sofa. 'Well, you certainly livened things up,' he said, smirking. 'I've never seen anyone being chased away from a funeral before.'

Stella couldn't help smiling back at him, her brother's laid-back attitude dispelling her gloom.

'At least you gave them all something to talk about.'

'Is this guy bothering you?'

Stella looked up to see Rafe scowling down at Dan.

'*Seriously?*' Dan grinned, raising his eyebrows at Stella. 'Mr Fucking Darcy is threatening me?'

Stella giggled. 'I'm fine, Rafe. This is Dan. My brother.' Rafe put the drinks on the table. 'Dan, this is Rafe.'

'Your brother?' Rafe raised his eyebrows at Stella before extending a hand to Dan. 'Pleased to meet you.'

'Yes, I have a brother,' she said to Rafe as he sat opposite. She didn't know if it was the whiskey or finally publicly acknowledging Dan after all these years, but she felt quite giddy.

'Dan, will you have a drink?' Rafe asked him.

'No, thanks. I have to get back to Dad's send-off, unfortunately.' He turned to Stella. 'I brought you something,' he said, reaching into his pocket. 'I was looking through all the old photos for one to put on Dad's coffin, and I found this.' He handed her an old photograph, wrinkled at the edges. It was her and Dan, both in their teens, dressed up for some school disco.

'We look like a right pair of eejits,' Dan said, looking at it over her shoulder.

'Speak for yourself,' Stella said, with mock indignation. She was wearing what Dan used to call her 'mermaid wig', long snaky tresses streaked with pale blues and pinks. 'I looked fabulous.' She'd known that wig would get her into trouble, but she'd worn it anyway.

'May I see?' Rafe asked, and she handed it to him.

'You were so pretty,' he said softly, looking down at the image. Then he handed it back to her.

Stella looked at the photo. She didn't see pretty, but she tried to view it objectively, through Rafe's eyes, and she could see why he might think so. She'd forgotten what a good job she'd done even back then. 'I was always good at make-up,' she said. 'It's just smoke and mirrors.'

'Well, I'd better get back to the pub and rescue Annie.' Dan gave Stella an apologetic glance. He stood, and she walked with him to the door.

She grabbed his hand as he turned to go, holding him back. 'Did Mam—Did she say anything about me?'

He shook his head, giving her a pitying look. 'No. Dad's death hasn't magically transformed her into a human being with actual feelings. Sorry.'

Stella shrugged and gave him a rueful smile. It was exactly what she'd been hoping for after all.

'It's such bullshit all those people pretending they don't know you exist. I told her you should be mentioned in the service. But I'm sure you can imagine what she said to that.'

Stella nodded. 'That they don't have a daughter. That they never had a daughter.'

'Yeah.' Dan sighed. 'She's just as much of a gobshite as he ever was. There was a pair of them in it. Makes you wonder where they got us, doesn't it?'

'I know! I mean, we're great.'

'Sorry I can't stay longer, but I don't want to leave Annie alone with that lot too long.'

'No, of course not. Go. God, she must be wondering what that was all about at the church.'

'Can I tell her ... about you?'

'After all this time ... what would you say?'

'That I have a sister. That I've always had a sister.'

Stella's eyes stung with tears.

'And that my sister's a fucking legend.'

She took Dan's hand and nodded as she gave it a squeeze.

'She'll want to meet you.'

'I'd like that.'

'Okay, I'll be in touch.' He gave her a final hug and left.

42

'Wow, what a strange day,' Stella said when she rejoined Rafe, sinking back onto the sofa. She hardly knew how she felt, her emotions pulled in multiple different directions at once, veering dizzyingly between relief, melancholy and a devastating sense of loss that she couldn't even comprehend. Because what had she lost? Nothing she hadn't already left behind a long time ago. Her father had been dead to her for years. Her mother's rejection was nothing new. It shouldn't feel so sharp and shocking. If nothing else, this morning was confirmation that she'd been right to cut her ties to her parents. She'd wondered sometimes over the years if she should attempt a reconciliation, if things might be different, if they might regret how they'd treated her and just be waiting for her to make the first move ...

But nothing had changed. She hadn't been missing out needlessly simply for want of trying. At least she knew now she'd made the right choice, living the way she did. And what did it matter if her mother didn't love her and her family rejected her? It made no difference to the life she'd made for herself. She didn't need them. She had people in her life now who loved her for who she was. She had Peter ...

'Are you okay?' Rafe asked, sitting beside her and looking at her with concern.

'Yes.' She shook herself out of her stupor and gave him a reassuring smile. 'I'm fine.' In truth, she wasn't sure how she felt. Suddenly, her carefully coiled life was beginning to unravel, and even though it was scary and confusing, and her instinct was to wind it all up tight again, there was also relief in the thought of just letting go ...

'Well, I suppose we should be going,' she said, glancing at her watch. It was just after three.

'There's no rush. Whenever you're ready. Would you like anything else? Another drink?'

'No thanks,' she said. 'Let's go. I think I'm done here.'

THEY WENT to their rooms to change and pack their bags. Back in her room, Stella kicked off her heels, and threw her overnight case on the bed. She opened the wardrobe to grab the clothes she'd travelled in last night, and froze when she caught sight of herself in the mirror on the door. She felt a sudden stab of self-pity as she looked at her reflection. How ridiculous to have thought her mother would be impressed by any of this. The beautifully tailored suit was exquisite, her hair smooth and straight, with not a strand out of place, her nails perfectly manicured. She looked like she'd stepped out of the pages of *Vogue*. But it was all just surface polish, and her mother saw through it to the same grotesque, unlovable creature she'd always been. She flung off the jacket and threw it on the bed, blinking back tears as she unzipped the skirt and stepped out of it. She was pathetic, she thought, as she automatically folded her clothes neatly and put them in the case, her movements precise and robotic.

She tried to concentrate on the positive things that had happened today – like seeing Dan and introducing him to Rafe as her brother. But it was all tinged with such sadness and loss. Suddenly overwhelmed by all the turbulent emotions of the day, she sank onto the bed in her underwear, unable even to summon the energy to pull on her jeans, and gave into full-blown heaving sobs that racked her body and tore at her chest. Once she started, she couldn't seem to stop, and it was as if every unshed tear from the past twenty-six years was finally being unleashed.

She didn't know how long she'd been sitting there like that when her phone buzzed. She glanced down at it as it vibrated on the bed. It was Peter. But she couldn't seem to bring herself to pick it up. She just sat staring at it numbly until it rang off.

SHE HAD LET it ring out three times when there was a rapping at the door.

'Stella?' She jumped as Rafe called her name. She gulped hard, trying to stem the tears that kept on coming. 'Just a minute,' she called, swiping at her eyes. Her voice sounded thick and croaky. She grabbed a T-shirt and pulled it on, desperately trying to pull herself together. But it was no use.

'Are you okay?' Rafe called through the door. She opened it a crack and peered around it.

'Sorry, I was just—'

'Christ!' She saw the shock on his face, his eyes wide with alarm, and she stared at him helplessly as the tears continued to flow. She was powerless to resist as he pushed the door open fully and strode into the room, not caring that she was only half dressed as he gathered her into his arms. He manoeuvred them over to a chair by the window and sat, pulling her into his lap. Then he wrapped his arms around her and stroked her hair while she sobbed, clutching onto him fiercely, her head buried in his shoulder.

Finally she was all cried out, and her sobs subsided. She lifted her head, swiping at her eyes.

'Dad said he was ringing and you weren't answering,' Rafe said. 'He was worried.'

'I should call him,' she said, looking at her phone where it lay on the bed, but still not stirring.

'I think we should stay here tonight,' Rafe said. 'You can have a bath, get room service.'

Stella nodded. 'That sounds good.' She felt limp and washed out, completely drained after her emotional meltdown.

'I'll talk to Dad if you don't feel up to it.'

'Thanks. What did you tell him ... about today?'

'Not much, just that you'd had an upsetting day. I didn't tell him what happened at the church or about your family. And I won't, if you don't want me to.'

'It's okay. Peter knows about them. He knows they're not part of my life.'

'Well, why don't I call him, and you go have that bath?' Rafe said, pulling his phone from his pocket.

Stella nodded and stirred. A bath sounded good, but really she just wanted to stay right where she was, in Rafe's lap with his arms around her. Reluctantly she pushed herself up, a little shiver running through her as his hand brushed against her bare leg. Their eyes met and held, and Stella stood mesmerised as he held the phone to his ear, the air suddenly feeling charged with electricity.

'Dad,' Rafe said, his eyes flicking away, and the spell

was broken. She grabbed her pyjamas from the bed and made a dive for the bathroom, suddenly filled with adrenaline. She heard Rafe murmuring in the other room as she closed the door behind her and got undressed.

Shit! What the hell had happened out there? She couldn't think about Rafe like that. She was marrying his father, for God's sake!

A long hot soak in the bath soothed and calmed her, and she felt infinitely better as she got out and towelled herself dry.

'Better?' Rafe asked when she rejoined him, dressed in her pyjamas. She was glad she'd brought them because she really didn't fancy getting dressed again. They were light and comfortable, and respectable enough. Rafe was still sitting in the chair by the window, a glass of whiskey on the table beside him.

'Much, thanks. Sorry about earlier. I don't know what came over me.'

'Your father's funeral maybe, your uncles chasing you out of the church ... take your pick.'

She smiled, grateful for his understanding. 'Yeah, I guess it was a long time coming.' She hadn't cried at the funeral or when Dan told her their father was dead. She hadn't cried when her parents threw her out at sixteen. She'd known crying would only have made things worse when the other kids at school had bullied her. Even when she'd split her ear open on the ice, she'd managed to choke down her tears. Her father didn't like cry-babies. 'Did you talk to Peter?'

'Yes. He sends his love. Do you want something from the minibar?'

'Yes, please. I'll have one of those,' she said, nodding to his drink.

Rafe poured her a whiskey with ginger ale and handed her the room service menu.

'I'm too tired to be dealing with knives and forks,' Stella said, looking at it. 'Fancy sharing a pizza?'

They ordered pizza and a bottle of red wine, and, when it came, they ate on the floor, leaning against the bed, the pizza between them.

'So, what was that all about at the funeral today? Why are you estranged from your family?'

'So many questions.'

'Sorry.' He smiled ruefully. 'But I know so little about you. You're an enigma.'

'You know more about me now than most people.'

He raised his eyebrows. 'I find that hard to believe.'

'You know my mother's still alive. You know I have a brother.'

'Tell me something else that most people don't know.'

She arched an eyebrow. 'Aren't we a bit old for games of truth or dare?'

He shrugged. 'I don't remember offering you the choice. But if you like.'

'Dare, then.'

'Okay. I dare you to tell me something true.' He grinned, and she smiled back at him.

'Okay, but no questions. I'll choose.' She ran her fingers over her glass, toying with the idea of telling him something completely banal – like that she stole money once from a church collection when she was a kid. That was true, and not many people knew. But instead she took the dare in the spirit it was offered – as a challenge to share something more personal. 'I was bullied at school,' she heard herself saying. She took a gulp of her wine. 'Obviously lots of people knew at the time. But no one who knows me now. I never talk about it anymore.'

'What age were you?'

'Ten, eleven,' she said. 'Twelve. Thirteen. It went on for a while. It was worst when I was a teenager.'

'I guess girls that age can be pretty vicious. It was probably jealousy.'

She took a deep breath. 'It wasn't girls, though.' She grabbed another slice of pizza.

Rafe raised his eyebrows in disbelief. 'You were bullied by *boys*?'

She took a bite and nodded.

'As a former teenage boy, I find that hard to believe.'

'Well, it's true.'

'Did this bullying take the form of sexual harassment?'

'No. Just straight-up old-fashioned bullying. Teasing me. Being cruel. Generally making my life a misery. Believe me, it wasn't about wanting to get with me,' she said with a bitter laugh.

'Teasing you about what?'

'The clothes I wore. The way I looked. The things I liked to do.' She shrugged. 'Everything really. My hair. My face. My body.'

Rafe threw her a sceptical look.

'I didn't always look like this, you know. I've had some work done.'

It was fleeting, but she saw Rafe's eyes flicker over her breasts.

'My teeth were terrible,' she said and he laughed. That was true, but it was still an evasion. It seemed her confessional moment was over, the juiciest revelations still left unspoken.

'But I saw that picture of you. You were really pretty.'

'Still not pretty enough. And only after an awful lot of effort. My make-up was trowelled on in that photo.'

'I'm sorry,' Rafe said quietly. 'I'm sorry that happened to you.'

'It was a long time ago,' she said. But she had to blink back tears, touched by his concern.

'Tell me something else.'

She swallowed her last bite of pizza and lay her head back against the bed, thinking. 'How about I show you something?' She pulled her pyjama top and bottoms apart a little, revealing the small silver scar low on her stomach.

Rafe frowned, reaching out a finger as if he was going to touch it. But he didn't. 'What happened?' he asked, his hand hovering over the scar, tracing it in the air.

'My ex-boyfriend stabbed me,' she said, dropping her hands so it was covered again.

'Jesus!' Rafe reared back, eyes wide with shock.

'Well, he tried to.' She took a sip of wine. 'He didn't do a very good job of it. It's kind of a funny story, actually.'

'Sounds hilarious,' Rafe said dryly.

'He barely cut me really. Turned out he wasn't suited to a life of knife crime.'

'Thank God,' Rafe breathed.

'I'd just broken up with him, and he was very angry about it.' She frowned, remembering. 'Turned out he thought all along he was doing me a favour and I was really lucky he could be with a freak like me. He didn't think I'd ever leave him, because who else would have me. So he was furious when I broke up with him. He felt ... humiliated, I guess, that he'd ever been with me.'

She felt Rafe's eyes on her and wondered what sort of grotesque deformities he must be imagining.

'Anyway, lucky for me it turned out he was squeamish about blood. He barely nicked me, and he already looked kind of shocked at what he'd done, like he hadn't expected the knife to actually go in. The minute he saw the blood, he went white as a sheet, and then he just ... keeled over.'

'He *fainted*?'

'Yep. Went down like a tree. I made a run for it while he was still unconscious. That was the last I ever saw of him.'

'Did you report it? Have him arrested?'

She shook her head. 'No. I just wanted to get as far away from him as possible and never have to deal with him again.' She took a sip of wine. 'It didn't quite work out that way, though,' she said bitterly. 'He had worse up his sleeve.'

'Worse than *stabbing* you?'

'Well, much more effective at messing my life up anyway,' she said. 'But that's a story for another day. Maybe.' She drained her glass and put it down. 'Okay, your turn. Truth or dare?'

'Truth,' he said. 'It seems only fair.'

'Okay, then. Tell me something about yourself that no one else knows.'

He looked down at his glass, frowning broodily. 'I don't want you to marry Dad,' he said finally, looking up.

Despite herself, Stella flinched. She recovered quickly, anger pushing aside the hurt. She'd thought they'd got closer, that they were on their way to being friends. In the past few weeks, she'd felt that Rafe liked her and cared about her. And then he had to say something nasty like that. 'You haven't made any secret of that,' she said, unable to keep the bitterness out of her tone.

'No, I guess not. But the reason – that's something no one else knows. At least, I don't think they do.'

'Oh, I think we all know why. Because you think I'm a heartless mercenary, right?' she said, her tone brittle.

He shook his head. 'Wrong. Maybe I did think that at first. But that was before I knew you.'

He turned to face her, and suddenly everything seemed very still, the air in the room charged. Stella hardly dared to breathe.

Rafe sighed, looking down at his glass again. 'Okay, here's the truth. People think I'm like Dad, because I've dated a lot of women and I've never settled down.'

Stella gave a little derisive laugh. 'Like father, like son.'

'Yeah, that's what they say. But the truth is I'm not like him at all. I've never cheated on any of the women I've been with. But I don't think I was in love with any of them either. Dad falls in love every five minutes. Whereas I – I don't think I've ever really been in love.'

Stella could hardly breathe. She suddenly had an awful feeling she knew where this was going. Rafe was going to say something dreadful, something monstrous that would ruin everything and could never be unsaid. 'Until', 'before' – the words that would bring everything crashing down around them hung in the air. She had to stop him before he said them out loud.

'Not completely,' he was saying. 'Not—'

'Well,' she said, cutting him off and standing abruptly, 'I'm sure it'll happen for you eventually.' She brushed pizza crumbs off her pyjama top.

There was a brief flicker of anger in Rafe's eyes as he looked up at her. 'Yeah, maybe one day if I'm lucky I can have what you and Dad have,' he said sourly, frank challenge in his eyes.

Stella recoiled a little at his bitterness.

He sighed, his anger quickly extinguished, replaced by a look of resignation. 'Sorry.' He smiled ruefully, as if acknowledging that she was right and some things were better left unsaid.

'I don't fall in love easily either, Rafe,' Stella said gently. 'Does that mean I shouldn't want what other people have?

Does it mean I can't have a happy marriage, a family life? Do you think I should shut myself off from all that because I don't feel what I'm supposed to feel? It doesn't make me a bad person. It doesn't mean I don't care about anyone.'

He looked at her in silence for a long time. 'No,' he said eventually, his expression softening. 'I know it doesn't. You're a good person, Stella. I see how you look after Dad, and I know you ... care for him.'

She nodded stiffly in acknowledgement.

'You deserve to be happy. I hope you get everything you want.'

'Thank you,' she said, hardly able to see through the mist of tears. 'Well, it's getting late. I think we should get to bed.'

He nodded, standing up.

'Thank you for today, Rafe,' she said as he walked to the door. 'Goodnight.'

'Goodnight, Stella. See you in the morning.'

43

'Revenge porn?' Al repeated, frowning when Lesley told him what she'd found. She'd summoned him for a case conference, and they were seated at her kitchen table with mugs of coffee, the afternoon sun streaming in the window.

'It could explain why she changed her name,' Lesley said. She knew revenge porn could wreak havoc and have devastating consequences for the victims, completely wrecking lives and careers, and tearing families apart.

'It could,' he said thoughtfully. 'And you really think this Babygirl person is Stella?'

Lesley shrugged. 'I can't be sure, of course, but ... yeah, my gut feeling is that she is. It all adds up.'

'It'd certainly give her a good reason to avoid social media.'

'And to wipe out any trace of her online history.'

'Shit!' Al grimaced. 'Poor Stella.'

'I know. No wonder she's so private and reserved.'

'So, you think this is it? This is what she's been hiding?'

Lesley nodded. 'I'd say it's case closed.' She tapped the

file in front of her, 'The Adventure of the Adventuress' written on the cover in black sharpie. 'Are you going to tell your family?'

'There's no need for that, is there?'

'No.' Lesley was relieved Al saw it that way. 'She's been humiliated enough already. It'd be cruel to bring it all back up again.'

'Right. Well,' Al said, raising his mug in salute, 'congratulations on a job well done.'

'Thank you.' Lesley bumped her mug against his. 'I'm going to miss this,' she said, patting the file affectionately. 'I guess you never forget your first.'

Al glanced at his watch. 'Well, I have to get back to work. But we should celebrate this evening. Would you like to go out? Or shall we stay in and have champagne and sex?'

'Champagne and sex, please.' Lesley had discovered a newfound love of quiet nights in, and staying home with Al was her new favourite thing. Though they tended not to be very quiet, not with all the moaning and groaning that went on when the two of them got together. 'Why don't I call over to your house? Say around seven?'

'Oh! Um ... why don't I come here?'

Lesley frowned. That was the third time in the last few days that Al had put her off going to his house. 'We're always here. Why can't we go to yours for a change? I've never even been to your house. I'm beginning to suspect you're hiding something. I hope you don't have a sex dungeon or a creepy doll collection or something.'

'Oh no, nothing like that. It's just ... I'm, um ... I'm having work done on my kitchen.'

'*Still?*'

'What do you mean still?'

'You were having work done on your kitchen the first time I met you. That was ages ago.'

'Yes, well ... it's a big job. Big kitchen.'

'I'll have to take your word for it,' she said huffily. 'Okay, then. You come here.'

'Great!' he said, standing. 'See you later.' He bent to give her a quick kiss on the lips that turned into a long, lingering kiss that threatened to eat up the rest of the afternoon. God, how could she ever have thought he was a bad kisser?

'Mmm, mustn't start that,' Al said, breaking away reluctantly. 'Later.'

Lesley just sat there smiling dopily for a while after he'd gone. Then she picked up the folder and brought it into her office, filing it away. It had been fun getting to play amateur sleuth and she was very pleased with how the case had turned out, but now she needed to get back to real life and start tackling the backlog of work that had piled up in her absence.

But first there was one last investigation she needed to carry out on her own behalf. Al didn't know it, but she'd just given him a test, and he'd failed it. She couldn't suppress the niggling feeling that he was hiding something. Besides, lust had made her sloppy when it came to Al. She'd neglected to do the basic background checks she'd automatically undertake on a friend's behalf. She took out a new manila folder and wrote Al's name on the cover.

THREE DAYS LATER, she sat in her car across the road from Al's house. She'd parked a few yards down the street so that hopefully she wouldn't be spotted. But if she was, at least it would be easy enough to come up with a cover story. She'd watched Al setting off for work early in the morning, looking very handsome and capable with his hard hat in one hand and a bunch of rolled-up plans tucked under his arm. It had been over an hour since he'd driven off, and Lesley figured she could call it a day soon and return later for the evening shift. There was no point in watching an empty house.

Just as she was about to start the car, a delivery van arrived outside Al's house. As the driver got out carrying a parcel, she decided she might as well stay and watch. At least she'd have something to show for her morning's work. She watched as the courier rang the bell and waited – and then, the door opened. There was someone in the house!

Damn! She hadn't been prepared for that. She scrabbled for her binoculars, but the angle she was at made it impossible to see who was signing for the package before the delivery man handed it over. She wanted to growl in frustration as the door closed again and the courier went on his way.

Shit! She gave the steering wheel an angry thump. So she'd been right. Al was hiding something and he'd been lying to her. She'd never wanted so badly to be wrong. She picked up her bag and took out her book. She'd have to settle in for the long haul.

STELLA STOOD on the beach at Killiney, watching the sun rise over the bay. She was going to miss this. She'd come so close, she thought, twisting the diamond ring on her finger. Maybe they could still ...

But no. She shut off the thought. Peter had been so kind and sympathetic since she'd come back from Galway and told him what had happened at her father's funeral. He'd started talking about trips they would go on once his play was finished, and he'd invited Dan and Annie to come and stay whenever they liked. They'd been added to the wedding guest list and he was looking forward to meeting them. But she knew his heart wasn't in it, and he was always a bit distant at the same time, as if his head – and his heart – were somewhere else. She suspected they were on a stage with Jane.

The past few days she'd felt he was pulling back a little, and a couple of times she'd thought he was gearing up to say something. She could feel him steeling himself to break it off with her, throwing her wary looks as he seemed on the verge of speaking. But then the moment would pass and still nothing was said. The wedding was getting closer, and if one of them didn't put on the brakes soon ...

She didn't know if Rafe had told him about her meltdown in Galway, but Peter had been treating her like she was made of glass lately. And as the days wore on, it became clear that he wasn't going to do anything to stop this juggernaut hurtling to its natural conclusion. She sighed, turning towards the house. If one of them was going to say something, it was going to have to be her.

SHE FOUND Peter in the kitchen, nursing a cup of green tea.

'Good run?' he asked.

'Yes, great. It's going to be another beautiful day.' She sat down beside him at the kitchen table.

'So what's on the agenda today? No rehearsals, so I'm completely at your beck and call for wine choosing, flower arranging, menu planning. Whatever you want – I'm at your service! Well, maybe not flower arranging—'

Stella took a deep breath. 'You don't want to get married, do you, Peter?' she said, breaking into his flow. 'At least not to me.' She didn't want to sound accusatory, but somehow that was how it came out. Peter looked startled at first, then sagged in his chair – whether from relief that one of them had said it or defeat at being found out, she wasn't sure. He shifted around in his seat, looking uncomfortable. He raised his mug to his mouth and put it down again without drinking. He opened his mouth to say something, but closed it again. He seemed totally at a loss.

'You don't want to get married either, do you?' he said finally, a mixture of sadness and relief in his voice. It was sort of an answer.

'I wouldn't mind,' she said. She was immediately annoyed with herself. This was happening anyway. What was the point in making it harder for him?

Peter looked aghast. 'You'd still go through with it? But *why?*'

'Well, I've worked my arse off planning this wedding for one thing! It will be such a faff to call it all off.' She tried to make light of it, determined to let him off the hook. She might as well be dignified about it.

Peter smiled. 'Yes, I see what you mean. I suppose it'd be easier just to go through with it.'

'Much easier. It was going to be such a beautiful wedding too. Plus think of all the presents that were coming our way.'

'I did rather fancy that Ludmila Korol painting we had on our registry.'

'And I really wanted the pink Smeg kettle. Couldn't we at least wait until we get those?'

'Sorry.' He took her hand across the table. 'I can't.'

She wondered would he ever have said it. If she hadn't called a halt, would he have gone through with it? 'We could have had a good life together, Peter. I still believe that. I'm not saying this was a mistake.'

'There's just one little problem,' he said. 'We're not in love.'

'No. But then, we never were. It didn't stop us before. It wouldn't be a problem if you weren't in love with someone else.'

He withdrew his hand and sat back in his chair. 'I'm sorry, Stella. I never meant to hurt you.'

'I know,' she said. 'And hey, it's not so bad – at least you didn't break my heart.'

'I was never unfaithful to you, you know,' he said. 'If that's any consolation.'

It seemed strange to talk about infidelity when they'd never even slept together, but she was glad he hadn't slept with Jane. It would have been disrespectful and uncaring, and she liked to think that Peter thought more of her than that, even if he didn't love her. But it seemed odd that being in love didn't count when it meant so much more than a casual hook-up with some random woman.

Peter took a deep breath, his eyes wary. 'What about you and Rafe?' he asked.

'Me and Rafe?' She looked at him in confusion. 'What do you mean?'

'I thought perhaps ... I mean, you seem to have become close.'

Surely he didn't think that they'd been shagging in Galway?

'You know, I may not want to marry you, but—' His eyes darted away. 'I'm very fond of you, and I would love you to be part of our family.'

Stella's breath caught. Oh no, he did not just say that! She was glad he was looking down at his hands as he finished, so she had some time to disguise her shock. When he looked up again, she was smiling crookedly. 'You want to adopt me?'

Peter laughed, but there was a sadness behind his eyes. 'What will you do?' he asked.

'I don't know.' Start again, she supposed. But she had more now than when she'd first come here. 'I'll stay in Ireland, though,' she said. 'To be near Dan and Annie.'

'Yes, good decision. Family is the most important thing.'

She may not be marrying Peter, but she had gained a family anyway. How strange ... 'But first,' she said, standing up, 'we have to get busy dismantling this wedding. You said you'd be at my beck and call today.'

'Yours to command.'

'Well, get out the guest list and start making phone calls. I'll get on to the registry office and florist, and as for the cake and catering ... do you know anyone who could use a second-hand party?'

44

I t had been a couple of hours since the delivery man, and there had been no further movement in Al's house. Lesley sighed. Unless she took the bull by the horns, she'd have to spend the whole day parked here, hoping whoever was in there would eventually show their face. Well, she had better things to do than sit here all day, she thought, getting out of the car.

She marched up to Al's house and rang the bell. For a moment she thought whoever had been there earlier must have left somehow without her seeing them. Then she heard footsteps in the hall and the door was thrown open.

'Oh! Lesley, hi!'

Lesley felt her jaw drop as Cassie gave her a friendly smile. She was wearing a baggy T-shirt and leggings, her feet bare, and she looked very much at home. 'Hi!' She attempted to smile back, but she was sure it came out as more of a pained grimace.

'Were you looking for Al? He's gone to work.'

'Yes, I know. I'm well aware of Al's movements, thank

you.' The lying, cheating wanker! 'I just—I can't find my phone charger and I think I may have left it in the kitchen.'

'Well, come in, come in,' Cassie said, opening the door wider and stepping back. 'Let's have a look.'

She padded ahead of Lesley down the wood-floored hall and led her down a couple of steps into an open-plan kitchen/living room. Well, it was big – he hadn't lied about that. But there was feck all work being done on it.

'Would you like a coffee?' Cassie asked. 'I was just going to make one.'

'Oh, no thanks. I'm not staying.' Lesley moved around the kitchen, running a hand over the worktops as she pretended to look for her charger. It was a gorgeous kitchen, with purple high-gloss units and a big island in the middle. She could just imagine Cassie and Al tossing back glasses of crisp sauvignon blanc as they lovingly prepared meals here together, which they'd then eat at the table in the atrium at the far end of the room, being all English and long-legged together, talking about scons and not pronouncing 'sixth' properly. Why had *she* never been in Al's kitchen, she thought miserably. Well, no mystery there. You didn't need to be Poirot to figure that one out.

'No sign of it,' she said brightly to Cassie.

'Oh.' Cassie gave her a sympathetic pout. 'Well, I hope you find it. I'll ask Al if he's seen it when he gets home, shall I?'

When he gets home. Lesley wanted to howl at the casual domesticity of it. 'Are you ... here on holiday, then?' she asked.

'No, I moved back to Dublin this week,' she said, spooning coffee into the machine. She gave Lesley a curious look. 'Didn't Al tell you?'

So he'd taken her back. 'No, he must have forgotten to mention it.' Maybe he could never find the right moment since they spent most of their time shagging. It wouldn't be very polite to tell someone they were dumped when they were sliding up and down on your dick – and Al was nothing if not polite.

'Yah, I got offered a job here – a really good one. It was great timing because things weren't working out with Jean-Claude. Are you sure you wouldn't like a coffee? I'm gasping.'

'No, thank you. It'd choke me.'

'Okay,' Cassie said with a puzzled frown. She switched on the coffee machine and leaned against the worktop, folding her arms. 'So I decided to move back. And lucky for me, Al was kind enough to take me in.'

'Huh! So you got everything you wanted. Well, bully for you!'

Cassie gave Lesley a bemused smile. 'Um ... thanks.'

'Right, I'll go then,' Lesley said. Her voice came out shrill, and she didn't think she'd be able to hold it together much longer. She was furious and hurt, and furious for letting herself get hurt. Cassie wasn't helping, being all chummy and welcoming, like there was nothing wrong. She obviously thought Lesley already knew she'd been dumped and there were no hard feelings. It was Cassie's turn to 'have a go on' Al again, but they could still all be in a lovely incestuous friendship group together. Well, feck that!

'I'll tell Al you called,' Cassie said, accompanying her to the door. 'We must get together again properly soon, all three of us.'

'Yes, let's do that,' Lesley said stiffly as Cassie opened the door. 'Maybe when hell freezes over! How would that suit you?'

Cassie laughed. 'You're so funny, Lesley. Bye! See you again soon.'

. . .

THE FLOODGATES OPENED as she was walking down the path. She swiped impatiently at her eyes. She hated this and hated bloody Al for doing it to her. She was a complete mess as she drove home, barely able to see where she was going through the blur of tears. She wished she could go over to Romy's for wine and sympathy, but she was on holidays in Malta for the week. Instead she went home, curled up on the sofa and balled her eyes out while she waited for it to be a decent time to start drinking.

She couldn't remember ever being this upset about a man before. She certainly hadn't felt like this when Rob broke up with her. It wasn't fair, she thought as she howled. She'd really liked Al. He'd got under her skin with his Mr Nice Guy act, his open, affectionate manner and the brilliant sex. He'd made her think he was so into her too. And all the time he'd been having his cake and eating Cassie out too.

On the dot of six o'clock, she opened a bottle of wine and started drinking. Shortly afterwards, Al started ringing. She ignored the first three calls, but the fourth time, she decided to get it over with and picked up.

'Lesley, I—'

'I have nothing to say to you, Al.' Her tongue felt like it didn't quite fit her mouth, and her voice sounded a little slurry. 'Kindly stop calling me.'

'Are you okay? You sound awful.'

'I have a cold.' She did a big sniff to illustrate.

'Oh. Well, look, Cassie said you'd called round and you were acting very oddly.'

'Oh!' Lesley said haughtily. 'Well, I'm very sorry if your girlfriend didn't care for my manner.'

'Ex-girlfriend. Anyway, she said you were looking for some charger you thought you'd left in my house.'

'Correct.'

'But you've never been in my house.'

'And now we know why. I knew you were hiding something, Al.'

'It's not what you think. Just let me explain—'

'Nothing to explain. You lied to me.'

'No, I didn't. I never said—'

'You told me you were having your kitchen done up.'

'Oh! Yes, okay, I suppose I did lie about that, but—'

'Your kitchen is beautiful, Al.'

'Um, thank you.'

'Pristine. Not a hair out of place. Those purple cabinets ...' she gave a strangled sob.

'But listen, the only reason I lied to you was because—'

'Look, I get it. Obviously it's over with us and you're with Cassie now—'

'But I'm not! Would you just let me speak for a second!' Al was starting to shout.

'But you didn't have to lie to me about it. You were only pretending to be my boyfriend anyway. It wasn't real.'

'That's not true and you know—'

'We can break up now that the investigation's over. But you could have had the decency to tell me.'

'There's nothing to tell,' Al growled. 'Would you just listen to me for one—'

'I think I've listened long enough.'

'You haven't listened at all, you daft—'

'I think I should hang up now before you resort to name-calling,' she said with great dignity. 'No hard feelings. I was only having a go on you to pass the time while we were in France—'

Al gasped. 'That's a horrible thing to say!' He sounded

genuinely hurt, and Lesley felt a stab of guilt. Then she remembered Cassie standing in his beautiful kitchen making coffee in her bare feet ...

'Why did you never let me into your kitchen, Al?' she wailed.

'*What?* Sorry, is that a metaphor for something? Are you drunk?'

'Never you mind. And no, it's not a metaphor! You literally never let me into your kitchen. Or any other room in your house.'

Al sighed. 'Look, Lesley, can I just come round? If you'd let me explain—'

'No. It's over between us, Al. You're moving on and so am I. You have Cassie—'

'But I *don't*,' he yelled.

'And I'm going back to Dinner Dates next week to find myself a real boyfriend. For free!'

Al's only response was a growl of frustration before she hung up and went back to sobbing.

45

'Sorry I didn't get back to you yesterday,' Lesley said the next morning when she called over to Stella's for coffee. 'I wasn't really answering my phone.' She had woken this morning to a couple of missed calls and a voice message from Stella. 'So the wedding's off?'

'Yes.' Stella was giving nothing away, poised and self-possessed as ever. It was a stark contrast to what had faced *her* when she'd looked in the bathroom mirror last night – and again this morning. If only *she* could look that fresh and pristine when she was heartbroken. But then maybe Stella wasn't devastated like she was.

At least this meant her bridesmaid gig was off and she wouldn't have to see Al again – and Stella's secrets were none of the Bradshaws' business anymore. There was no need for them to ever know what she'd found out. She regretted even having told Al. She liked Stella, and she felt protective towards her now, knowing what she did.

'Who called it off?' she asked, deciding to try the direct approach.

Stella shrugged. 'I suppose I did technically. But it was

mutual really. We both knew it was the right thing. It's for the best.'

Lesley sighed. 'Must be something in the air with the Bradshaw men.'

'What do you mean?' Stella asked aghast. 'You're not telling me you've broken up with Al?'

Lesley chugged down half a glass of sparkling water in one before answering. She was alternating between strong black coffee and gallons of fizzy water to try and beat her hangover into submission. 'Yep,' she nodded, putting her glass down. 'He's back with Cassie.'

'*Really?* Are you sure?'

Lesley nodded. 'She's moved in with him.'

'I don't believe it! Al's crazy about you. It's so obvious.'

Huh! Maybe Al had the acting gene after all. 'I was at his house. I saw it with my own eyes. She's living there.'

Stella frowned. 'But that doesn't necessarily mean anything. I mean, Rafe and I both live in this house, but we're not together.'

Oh God. There was something about the way Stella said Rafe's name, something in her face when she talked about him that made Lesley's heart sink.

'That's not ... I mean Rafe's not the reason you broke it off with Peter, is he?' she asked cautiously. Bloody Rafe! She hated to think Stella had fallen for his act and been tricked into giving up the life she wanted.

'No,' she said with a derisive laugh. 'Definitely not.'

'Good. Because I know he can be very flirty and every-thing, but he's not someone you can take seriously.'

'I know.' She looked hurt, and Lesley had a horrible feeling she was lying. She really hoped Stella hadn't fallen too hard.

'So, what are you going to do now?'

'Well, first I have to cancel this wedding – which it

turns out is almost as much work as planning it in the first place.'

'Right, well, I'll help you with that.'

'Then I don't know. Find somewhere to live, get a job ...'

'But you're staying in Dublin?'

'Yes, I want to be near—Oh gosh, I haven't even told you about what's been happening the last couple of days. There's been so much going on.'

Lesley listened aghast as Stella told her about her father's funeral, her mother still being alive, Dan, the trip to Galway with Rafe ...

'Wow, you've had quite the week!' she said when she'd finished. 'So you went to Galway with Rafe? And you stayed overnight?'

'Yeah. He was really kind actually.'

Lesley studied her face closely. 'Did something happen between the two of you?'

'No, nothing like that.' Stella met her eyes frankly. 'But it could have. It almost did.'

'Oh God, you've fallen for him, haven't you?'

Stella shrugged. 'Maybe I have. But it doesn't matter. It wouldn't work out anyway.'

'I suppose it would be a bit awkward after you were with his dad. Even though you never shagged Peter.'

Stella smiled. 'It's not that.'

'What, then?' Lesley knew she shouldn't be pushing it, and she hated seeing Stella upset, but her natural curiosity got the better of her.

'I can't explain. There are things you don't know about me, Lesley.'

Lesley wondered if that was true. Did Stella have even more secrets yet to be unearthed? 'Well, I'm glad you're sticking around anyway.' She'd miss Stella if she was gone.

'Even though we won't have the Bradshaw connection, I hope we can still be friends.'

'Me too.'

'And I'm not cancelling your hen night. Just because you're not getting married doesn't mean we can't have a banging night out.'

∼

News of the cancelled wedding had travelled fast. Stella was glad for once that her share of the guest list was so sparse, so Peter bore the brunt of the fallout, and, since they'd started breaking the news yesterday, his phone rang constantly day and night with people offering their sympathy and eager for gossip.

He had decamped to Jane's apartment while Stella packed up and got ready to leave. He'd told her there was no rush and she could stay as long as she liked. It was a big house, he said, and besides, she was one of the family now 'like it or lump it'. But it didn't feel right, especially when it left her and Rafe here together. She'd started packing and would move out at the end of the week. She'd rented a short-term apartment in the city centre until she sorted out something more permanent.

She took her clothes from the drawers and folded them neatly before placing them carefully in the suitcase that lay open on the bed. Opening the wardrobe, she pulled out the black suit she'd worn to her father's funeral and held it against her, looking at her reflection in the mirror as she stroked the material. It was a beautiful piece, but she didn't think she could ever face wearing it again. She pulled it off the hanger and folded it before placing it in the pile that was earmarked for a charity shop.

'You're going, then?'

She looked up to see Rafe standing in the doorway.

'Yes.' She gave a little shrug. 'The wedding's off. What is there to stay for?'

'There's nothing else here you want?' His eyes were unblinking as he looked at her, his body so rigid he was almost trembling, his hands clenched tight by his sides.

'I don't want your money,' she said quietly. 'I never did.'

'I'm not talking about money.'

She knew he wasn't. She knew what he was asking, and she so wanted to say yes. Yes was the answer. 'No,' she said. 'There's nothing else here I want.'

He nodded, jerking his head away quickly, but not before she saw the hurt etched on his face. He dropped his head and sniffed heavily, a nasal sound that twisted her heart. 'I wish you'd stay,' he said so quietly she had to strain to hear him. He sounded crushed, heartbroken, and she longed to throw her arms around him and tell him the truth – that she wanted him just as much as he wanted her. But she'd have to tell him the whole truth – all of it – and she was too much of a coward, because what if he didn't want her anymore once he knew? She couldn't bear it if he were to look at her the way Steve had.

She'd told Peter, of course, but the stakes hadn't felt so high. She hadn't been in love with him. He said it didn't make any difference to him, but she could never be sure. Maybe it *had* put him off, even if only subconsciously. She couldn't help wondering if it was partly the reason they'd never had sex.

'I wish I could,' she said. 'But you don't really know me, Rafe. If you did, you probably wouldn't want me to stay anyway. I'm sorry.' It was better this way, she told herself, as tears tore at her throat.

'Well, I'm going to go down to Clare for a couple of

days,' Rafe said hoarsely. 'Will you still be here when I get back?'

Did he want her to be? 'Probably not. I'm moving on Friday.'

For a long moment they just stood gazing at each other. Then Rafe turned and walked quickly away without looking back. A few minutes later, she heard the front door slam, and he was gone.

46

The house felt eerily quiet once Rafe had gone. Despite having lived alone most of her life, Stella had got used to having people around all the time, and she'd miss the company. She was glad Lesley was coming over for the evening and should be here shortly. She'd decided she was going to tell her everything – if not tonight, then soon. She was putting down roots now. It was time to start being real with the people she cared about, even if – her mind strayed away from the thought, but she brought it back – even if it meant losing them.

That would be Lesley now, she thought, as she heard the front door open. Rafe must have bumped into her as he was leaving and let her in. She skipped down the stairs to meet her – and saw Rafe standing in the hall looking up at her.

'Did you forget something?' she frowned.

'No. Not exactly.'

'Oh.' She suddenly felt very aware that they were alone in the house together.

'Actually,' he said, 'I thought I'd take another crack at persuading you to stay ... with me.'

'Rafe—'

'Because I ran into Lesley just now, and she seemed to think—'

'Where is she?' Stella's eyes flicked to the door.

'She left. She said to call her later if you still want her to come over.'

'But what did she tell you?'

'Nothing.' He gave a rueful smile. 'Well, actually she told me I was an arsehole, and she seemed all set to tear me a new one.'

'What changed her mind?'

'I guess she's one of those women who can't stand to see a grown man cry. Bit of a softie, I suspect, when it's all boiled down.'

'You were crying?'

Rafe shrugged. 'Anyway, she seemed to think I'd been leading you on or something – coming on to you just so you'd break up with Dad.'

'Oh.' No wonder Lesley had seemed so keen to warn her off falling for Rafe.

'She got the wrong end of the stick, and I thought perhaps you had too. I realised I might not have made myself clear earlier. So I had to come back and tell you, just to make sure there are no misunderstandings. So, here it is: something true about me that not many people know.' He dropped his head and took a deep breath. Then he lifted his head and looked right into her eyes. 'I'm in love with you. Did you know that?'

She nodded. 'I guessed,' she whispered, tears welling in her eyes.

'I want to be with you. I want us to be together. And I was hoping you want the same thing.'

'Rafe, I don't know what to say.'

'You don't feel the same way.' He smiled sadly at her, and her heart twisted when she saw his eyes shone with tears. 'Okay. That's fine. Just so we're clear.' He turned to the door.

'Wait! Don't go.' She couldn't bear to see him looking so sad. 'Come and have a drink.' She skipped down the stairs and led him into the living room. She poured them both whiskey and sat beside him on the sofa. 'My turn,' she said.

He frowned questioningly.

'You told me something true about yourself. Now it's my turn.'

'Okay.'

'You want everything to be clear between us, no misconceptions. And there are things you don't know about me, Rafe. Things that might make you change your mind about wanting to be with me. Probably will, actually,' she said shakily. 'And that's okay.'

He took a gulp of his drink as if bracing himself for something. 'I doubt it, but go on.'

She took a deep breath, not knowing how to begin. 'Remember when I told you about being bullied in school?'

He nodded.

'And you were surprised that it was boys who bullied me. Why?'

'Well, look at you,' he said, his eyes glittering as they scanned her face.

'I told you, I didn't look like this then.'

'Even so, I'd have thought a girl – any girl – among a bunch of teenage boys ...'

She took a deep gulp of her drink, her hand shaking as she lifted the glass to her lips. 'I went to a boys' school,' she said. 'There weren't any girls.'

'That must have been tough, being the only one.'

'No, you don't understand. There were no girls – not one in the whole school.' She looked meaningfully at Rafe. She saw realisation dawning in his face, but there was still disbelief too.

'You mean...?'

'I mean not one. Not even—' She gulped, looking away. 'Not even me. I went to a boys' school because—'

'Because you were a boy,' he breathed.

She turned back to find him looking at her searchingly. It was obviously a shock, and he was struggling to get his head around it. But at least he didn't seem disgusted.

'That's why they bullied me. They hated me because I was ... different. It's why my parents kicked me out. It's why my boyfriend stabbed me.'

'He didn't know?'

'Oh no, he did. I was out then – not at work, but with friends. I hadn't even fully transitioned when I was with him. And he was fine with it ... as long as we were together. Or at least I thought he was. But when I broke up with him ... he was so angry. Like I said, he'd thought he was doing me a favour being with me. He couldn't handle the humiliation of someone like me leaving him. And he was ashamed, I guess, after the fact, of having been with me.' She rattled the ice in her glass, and knocked back the last of the whiskey. 'So he stabbed me, and when that didn't work, he plastered pictures of me all over the internet. Naked photos on revenge porn sites; videos of us doing stuff ...'

'But if he was ashamed of it, surely he'd have wanted to keep it quiet.'

'Oh no,' she said bitterly. 'Because every time someone liked or shared it, he took it as proof that he was a real man. Every vile, filthy comment reassured him that he hadn't fucked a boy. He was just one of the lads and any other red-blooded male would have happily "given me one" and been none the wiser.'

'Jesus!' Rafe dug the heels of his hands into his eyes, swiping away tears.

'It was after that that I decided to live in stealth. It seemed ... safer. After my final surgery, I changed my name – again – and moved to LA.'

'What was it before – your name?'

'Joanna when I first transitioned. My parents named me Joe.'

'Joanna!' he gasped. 'That guy in Villefranche ...'

'Yeah. So anyway,' she said, looking down at her hands, twisting in her lap, 'that's it – all the news that's fit to print. Or not.' She laughed nervously.

It felt like an age as she waited for him to say something. Then his hand covered hers, gently unknotting them. He lifted one to his lips, pressing a soft kiss to her knuckles, while his other hand cupped her face, his thumb gently stroking along her jaw.

'Stella,' he breathed. There was a world of tenderness in the way he said her name, and when she looked up at him, her breath hitched at the love she saw in his face. Achingly slowly, he leaned in and kissed her, his lips firm and warm on hers, and she felt like she was melting, all the knots of tension in her body dissolving under the warmth of his touch. He pressed butterfly kisses to her cheeks, her nose, the corners of her eyes, kissing away the stray tears that escaped because she was so overcome with relief and happiness. She curled her fingers into the short hair at the back of his neck and kissed him back, loving the sandpapery rasp of his stubble against her cheek.

Things quickly got heated, and they were making out like a couple of teenagers, hands grasping urgently, pushing underneath clothes to reach for warm bare flesh. Stella jumped a little when Rafe slid his hand under her top and stroked along her stomach. But then she remembered that he already knew about her scar and everything else, and she relaxed because there was nothing to hide anymore. She gasped as Rafe slid a hand inside her bra, stroking her nipple while he sucked and nibbled at a pulse point on her neck. She undid the button of his jeans so she could slip her hand inside, rubbing his rock-hard erection through his boxer shorts. She slid her hand inside, and wrapped her hand around his cock. It was hot and hard, throbbing for her beneath the silky soft skin. As she began to stroke him, Rafe pulled away with a groan.

'Bedroom?' he said breathlessly, his eyes glittering with intent.

She nodded, and they held hands as they stumbled upstairs. Rafe led her into his room, closing the door behind him with a soft click. It was still bright, and Stella watched, mesmerised as he stood in the light of the window and peeled off his shirt, revealing a tanned muscular chest with a light spattering of dark hair that trailed tantalisingly down his lean, taut stomach to the top of his jeans. He was so beautiful, and Stella suddenly felt inadequate and intimidated. Then she remembered that she was beautiful too, and she'd never been so glad, because she wanted to be beautiful for him. She held his gaze unflinchingly as she undid the buttons of her blouse and peeled it off, then unhooked her bra and tossed it aside. His eyes blazed as they raked over her naked body, and she didn't flinch under his heated gaze.

Their eyes held as he walked towards her and took her in his arms, and Stella shivered as her naked breasts brushed against his bare skin. He looked into her eyes as he lowered his head to hers infinitely slowly, his lashes fluttering closed just as his lips touched hers. He kissed her softly, slowly, his mouth moving to her neck as he started to undo the button of her trousers, his fingers clumsy and awkward as they fumbled with the zip.

He lifted his head. 'I'm shaking,' he said with a self-deprecating laugh.

'I make you nervous?'

'You terrify me, to be honest.'

Stella flinched, and looked away to hide the hurt she was feeling.

'Hey, that's not what I meant.' He grabbed her chin and turned her back to face him.

She took a deep breath. 'We don't have to do this,' she said, her hands covering his where they cupped her face. 'If it's too weird for you ... You can't help it if I freak you out.' She swallowed hard. 'It doesn't make you a terrible person just because you don't want me.'

'Jesus, of course I want you!' The burning desire in his eyes, the tension in his face and the bulge in his jeans made her inclined to believe him. He raked a hand through his hair. 'It's just ... you're kind of a new one on me.'

'I get that. You've never been with someone like me before.'

'No. I've never been with a woman who—'

'Who was raised as a boy.'

He shook his head. 'Who means as much to me as you do.' He stroked her cheek with a finger. 'I'm scared of screwing this up.'

She put her hand over his. 'You won't screw it up,' she whispered. 'I won't let you.'

'Promise?' His voice cracked.

'I promise,' she whispered as he bent his head to kiss her again.

. . .

IT HAD BEEN a long time since Stella had given a blow job, but it came back to her quickly. She loved the feeling of Rafe's hot, thick cock in her mouth, his hands tangled in her hair, the way he groaned her name as he came.

When it was her turn, Rafe kissed his way down her body with agonising slowness, awaking every nerve ending slowly and methodically until her whole body was on fire. At last he was kissing along her thighs, pushing them apart, and she felt the rasp of his stubble as he nuzzled his face between her legs. He pressed soft kisses to her inner thighs, and Stella shook with want. Then suddenly he stopped, and looked up at her.

'What do I—I mean I'm not sure how to—' He frowned, hesitating.

'How to make me come?'

'Yeah.'

'The usual way.'

'I just—I don't know how it all works,' he said, his eyes flicking to her pussy.

'How it works?'

'I mean, can you get wet? Will it hurt when I'm inside you?'

'You're just thinking of this now?' she squealed desperately.

'Sorry,' Rafe said. 'I'm killing the mood, aren't I?'

'Just a bit.'

Stella would have found his hesitation amusing if it wasn't so frustrating. 'You've been with a woman before, right? Or would you like me to draw you a quick map?'

Rafe looked up at her anxiously, but then saw that she was smiling and broke into a grin.

'Or I could give you Dr Sterling's number,' Stella continued, 'and you could get back to me when you've spoken to him. I'll read a magazine while I wait.'

'Dr Sterling?'

'He's the one who created my vagina.'

He gave a groan of frustration, then ruffled his hair and shook his head as if waking himself up. 'No need for that,' he said. 'I'll just suck it and see.'

'Suck it and see?' She giggled as he bent his head to her again, kissing the tender flesh of her inner thigh.

'Okay, why don't I shut up now and show you what I mean?'

'That sounds like a very good idea.'

It was dark outside when Stella woke hours later, Rafe's arms tight around her, his warm body entwined with hers. She felt the soft rise and fall of his chest, his breath warm on her skin as she studied his beautiful face. She could still hardly believe she was here with him like this, that last night had happened. It was all a bit overwhelming. Tears welled in her eyes as she thought of everything that had happened, the things Rafe had whispered to her last night, the promises he had made against her skin.

She felt him stir, and his eyes fluttered open. 'Hey.' He reached for her, pulling her into his arms. 'I'm sorry.' He stroked her hair, kissed her cheeks.

She sniffed, pulling a little away to look at him. 'What are you sorry for?'

'Whatever I did to make you cry. I presume it's my fault.'

She smiled. 'You're right. It is your fault I'm crying.'

She saw him struggle not to flinch. 'Sorry. Whatever it is, I'll make it better, I promise.'

'They're happy tears, you dope.' She cuffed him play-fully on the chin and swiped at her eyes.

'Really? So you're not crying because it was a bit shit?'

She laughed. 'No. It was amazing.'

'Because if it *was* a bit shit, you should tell me now. I'll do better next time.'

'I don't think you could.'

'I could try. I'd Google it.'

She giggled. 'What would you Google? How to make a trans woman happy in bed?'

'Yeah. Something like that.'

'You know what the first hit would be if you Googled that?'

'What?'

'A picture of you.'

He grinned. 'Seriously?'

'Don't look so smug.' She frowned, but she couldn't stop smiling. 'I mean, there's always room for improvement.'

'Now that,' he said, pulling her closer, 'is fighting talk.'

47

Lesley looked along the candlelit table as the Dinner Dates guests took their seats, and wondered what she was doing here. She'd only said she was coming back to spite Al. She didn't have to follow through — it wasn't as if he'd know (or care) either way. It had been a mistake to come. She just wasn't in the mood for making an effort tonight, and even if she did meet someone interesting, she wouldn't be good company. They'd be seeing her at her worst, her absolute dullest. She was too down — too sad and lonely and pining for ...

'Hello.'

She looked up and was shocked to see Al slide into the seat across from her, like he had leapt out of her thoughts — her deepest longings made flesh.

'Hi, I'm Al,' he said, extending his large hand across the table to her. Dazedly she shook it.

'Lesley,' she said. Great! She wasn't even getting a real date opposite her. Helen was obviously a man down, and Al had stepped into the breach, helpful as ever. Despite the fact that she'd already given up any hopes for the evening, she still felt pissed off that she was being short-changed – her and all the other single women here.

She waited for Al to withdraw his hand and introduce himself to the women on either side of him. But when she tried to pull her hand away, he just gripped it tighter. He was being very rude, actually, completely ignoring everyone else at the table while he held her hand and gazed at her across the table.

'Nice to meet you,' she said tightly, yanking her hand out of his with such force that she shot back in her seat. She then proceeded to ignore him, forcing an animated smile onto her face and introducing herself to the men on either side of her.

On her right she had David, who blatantly looked down her top while she introduced herself and then pointedly turned his back to her and started speaking to the skinny blonde on his other side. On her left was a good-looking guy called Darren, who was already up a point for speaking to her face rather than her chest.

'What do you do, Lesley?' he asked her.

'I'm a freelance web developer,' she said.

'Oh, good for you.'

'How's business?' Al asked her, blatantly eavesdropping and interrupting them.

'It's great. I'm very busy.'

'Ah, you two already know each other?' Darren said.

'Oh, only slightly. So, tell me about you, Darren. What do you do?'

'I'm an assistant bank manager.'

'Oh.' Lesley tried not to look too disheartened. It was a perfectly sensible job, after all.

'Assistant bank manager by day,' he elaborated. 'Purveyor of laughs by night.'

'Sorry?'

'I'm cutting my teeth on the stand-up comedy circuit.'

'Oh dear,' Al murmured.

'That's great!' Lesley said enthusiastically even as her heart sank.

'Oh, it's not as interesting as it sounds. Being a bank manager, I mean,' Darren said, clearly in the belief that he was delivering a punchline.

'Ha! Very funny.'

'Not really,' Al drawled.

'Stop earwigging on our conversation, and talk to your own people,' Lesley said to him crossly, indicating the women either side of him. 'So, Darren, you were saying ... before we were so rudely interrupted.'

'Um ... yes.' He gave Al a frosty glare. 'Well, as I was saying, comedy is where my heart really lies.'

'Well, I think it's great that you're doing something you love, following your dream. Seizing the day and all that. Well done!' Lesley clapped him on the back. She knew she was going over the top, but she wanted Al to see her having a good time, hitting it off with someone else. 'Where do you perform?'

'Just small clubs at the moment – open mic nights, that sort of thing. I'm trying to build a following. It's very competitive.'

'I bet. But fair play to you! What sort of stuff do you do?'

'It's mainly observational comedy. I'm a keen observer of human folly,' Darren said, tapping his nose confidentially. 'In fact, this whole dating scene has given me lots of material.'

Great, so he was just here to gather material for his act. She wondered was there anyone here tonight who was looking for a relationship.

'Internet dating, for instance. Have you ever tried it, Lesley?'

'Yes, I've done a bit.'

'Well, I've got a whole bit about the, shall we say, euphemisms that people use to describe themselves on dating sites. It's like learning a whole new language.' He put down his knife and fork to give her his full attention, looking her up and down. 'Now, you would probably describe yourself as *curvaceous*, am I right?'

'Well, it's not a word I'd use—'

'Christ!' Al murmured under his breath.

'But when you've been around the block a few times, you get wise to what it really means. Translation: fat. You might as well call a whale a curvaceous fish.' He looked at her expectantly, and somehow she realised she was expected to laugh. He was giving her a taster of his comedy stylings.

'Oh, ha ha,' she said. 'Very good.'

'Bloody rude, if you ask me,' Al muttered.

'She—' Darren nodded to a girl at the far end of the table '—probably calls herself *athletic*. Wouldn't knock herself out running for the bus, in other words.' He chuckled, cracking up at his own wit.

'Right.' Lesley nodded. 'Flat-chested – I get it.' Oh, God, she shouldn't have encouraged him. It was going to be a very long night. But she was aware of Al's eyes on her the whole time, so she tried to look like she was enjoying herself.

Al was being very rude to the women on either side of him, she thought, ignoring them to stare across the table at her and Darren, and barge into their conversation. Okay, so he was just here as filler and he wasn't really looking to meet someone. But *they* didn't know that. He didn't have to make it so obvious that he wasn't interested. He could at least be polite. The two women had clearly given up on him, and were now talking to each other across him. At least they seemed to have hit it off and they were chatting away nineteen to the dozen. In fact, they seemed the most successful pairing at the table so far.

'I wish all my audiences were as quick on the uptake as you, Lesley,' Darren said, on a roll now. 'Now, what do you think it really means if a woman says she appreciates the finer things in life?'

'Um ... I suppose that she likes good food and wine? Staying at nice hotels maybe ...'

'Er-Er.' Darren made a buzzer sound to indicate it was the wrong answer. 'It means she's looking for a sugar daddy.'

'Oh. I see.' Oh God, when would it be dessert so he could switch seats and annoy someone else.

'A man with a *curvaceous* wallet,' Darren continued, grinning at her delightedly.

'Offensive,' Al mumbled.

'You shut up!' Lesley hissed across the table at him. 'You're being very rude.'

'You *are* being quite rude, Al,' Helen said to him.

'Sorry,' he said to her.

Al began talking to the woman on his right, and Lesley did her best to ignore him for the rest of the meal. But she realised that was going to be impossible when everyone changed places for dessert. The relief of getting rid of Darren was short-lived when he was replaced by Al.

'Don't talk to me,' she hissed at him out of the side of her mouth as he sat down beside her.

'Well, that's not very friendly. How can I sit here and not talk to you?'

'You seemed to manage all right with those two.' She nodded across the table, where the two women were ignoring the rules and had scooched beside each other to continue their chat. They were deep in conversation, talking animatedly.

'Lesley—'

'Stop!' She held up a hand to silence him, still refusing to look at him. 'If you talk to me, I'll tell everyone that you're here under false pretences.'

'What do you mean?'

'I know you're just here as filler. If you say another word to me, I'll expose you as the imposter you are.'

'I'm not an imposter,' he hissed at her as pots of chocolate mousse were placed in front of them.

Lesley was momentarily distracted by the arrival of dessert. She picked up her spoon and tasted the mousse.

'How's your dessert?' Al asked.

'Mind your own business. I'm not talking to you.'

'And I'm not just filler, by the way. That's a horrible thing to say.'

'Oh, I suppose you're here looking for love, are you?'

'As a matter of fact, I am.'

Lesley turned to him. 'Well, you're not going about it the right way. You didn't make any effort with those women. And now you're pestering me when I've told you I'm not interested. Anyway, I don't know why you're here bothering me at all when you've got a perfectly good girlfriend at home.'

'I don't. Look, Cassie's just—'

'I don't want to hear it.' She picked up her spoon and gently tapped the side of her glass, not loud enough for anyone to pay particular attention. It was just a warning shot. 'I'm going to make an announcement if you don't shut up. I'll tell everyone why you're really here.'

'Okay, okay.' He reached out and stilled her hand.

'Maybe I am here under false pretences. But it's not what you think.'

She turned and raised her eyebrows at him.

'I'm not *filler*. But you're right, I'm not looking for love. I've already met the woman I want.'

'Tell me something I don't already know.'

'Helen actually had a full quota of men for tonight. I had to nobble one of her guests, in fact, so I could get an invitation.'

'What? You're ... *evil*!' Lesley spluttered. 'What if he'd been my soulmate?'

'He wasn't. I'm your soulmate.'

'What about Cassie?'

'What about her? We're not back together, if that's what you think.'

'You lied to me about your kitchen being a mess.'

'You broke into my house under false pretences.'

'I didn't break in! She let me in. Your precious girlfriend.'

'She's *not* my girlfriend.'

'That's not what it looked like to me.'

'What, when you were spying on me behind my back?'

'Well, I could hardly spy on you in front of your face, could I? That's not how you do spying.'

'Did you put me under surveillance? Were you watching my house?'

'What if I was?'

'Right, you two!' Helen roared, giving the table an almighty whack that made them both jump and startled everyone into silence. 'If you can't behave yourselves, I'm going to have to ask you to leave.'

Lesley blushed to the roots of her hair as she realised all eyes were on her and Al. 'Sorry,' she said to Helen.

'Sorry,' Al murmured.

There was a brief pause, then the hum of conversation started up again.

'I'm not back together with Cassie,' Al said to her in a low voice. 'She's moved back to Dublin and she's just staying at my house for a couple of weeks while her apartment's being renovated.'

'Huh! Like your kitchen was being renovated?'

'I'm sorry I lied about it. But I was afraid you'd get the wrong end of the stick if you knew she was living there. It was only for a couple of weeks, so there didn't seem to be any reason for you to find out. I wasn't counting on you staking me out.'

'I wouldn't have had to stake you out if you hadn't lied to me. Why should I believe you anyway? Why would you let your ex stay with you if you're not—'

'Because we're still friends. But that's all.'

'Oh yeah, I know what your lot are like, all taking turns to have a go on each other and then going back to being chums.'

'That's ridiculous! Besides, Cassie is with someone else now.'

'Oh, who? And don't say Jean-Claude, because I know no one ends up with Jean-Claude.'

'Okay, that's enough,' Helen snapped. 'Outside, the pair of you.'

Lesley hadn't even realised they'd raised their voices again. They both stood, mumbling shamefaced apologies to Helen and the rest of the guests.

'Go out and think about what you've done, and don't come back until you can be civil to each other,' Helen said as they shuffled out of the room. But Lesley glanced back in the doorway and saw that she was smiling slyly to herself. She gave Lesley an almost imperceptible wink.

. . .

'WELL, I guess we're in the doghouse,' Al said when they were cooling their heels in the hall.

'Did you really nobble one of the guests so that you could come here and see me?' Lesley asked.

'Yep. I really did. Can't say I regret it either, I'm afraid.'

Lesley smiled, hope blooming in her chest. Because when she cooled off and thought about it rationally, why would he be here chasing her if he was with Cassie? 'Sorry I snooped around your house,' she said.

'It's okay.' He shrugged.

'You don't mind?'

'You wouldn't be you if you didn't carry out due diligence on me. And it's you that I love.'

'Really? You do?'

'To distraction.'

'But what about Cassie?'

'What about her? I told you, we're not together anymore.'

'But you want to be. I know you still love her. I heard you telling her at that party in Nice.'

'As a *friend*.'

'But you were delighted when I said I thought she wanted you back. You should have seen your face. It was like I'd just told you you'd won the lottery. Your whole mood changed like that.' She snapped her fingers.

'Ah, I admit that's true.' Al smiled. 'I was happy because you noticed and seemed quite put out about it. It gave me hope that you might be jealous.'

'Oh.' Now Lesley was smiling.

'I want to be your boyfriend again but for real this time. I want to kiss you with tongue, and touch you under your clothes. Lots of nudity, and everything below the waist is in play. And I want boob action – all the boob action I can get. What do you say?'

'Deal,' Lesley said, moving closer.

'And I'll invite you into my kitchen, of course,' Al said. 'We can go there right now, if you like?'

'I appreciate the offer, and I definitely want to see your kitchen again. But my place is nearer,' she said, slipping her hand into his.

A NOTE FROM THE AUTHOR

Thank you so much for reading *For Love or Money*. I hope you enjoyed it!

If you'd like to be the first to hear about new book releases, giveaways and more, you can sign up for my mailing list at :

www.subscribepage.com/clodaghmurphy

Building a relationship with my readers is one of my favourite things about being an author, so I'd love to stay in touch. I will never spam you, and you can unsubscribe at any time.

If you enjoyed this book, I would be very grateful if you could take a few minutes to leave a review on your retailer of choice (and tell your book-loving friends). Reviews make a huge difference in spreading the word about my books, which helps me to keep on writing.

I always love to hear from readers, and you can find me on Facebook or Twitter if you'd like to chat. I'd love to meet you!

ACKNOWLEDGMENTS

Massive thanks to:

My brilliant author friend, Sarah Painter, for all the pep-talking, cheer-leading and hand-holding, and especially for championing this book so fiercely. Thanks for talking me down off the ledge and persuading me to pull this one out of the fire.

Sarah and my other author pals who have shared knowledge, advice and encouragement so generously – not to mention wine! Thanks especially to Denise Deegan, Hannah Ellis and Keris Stainton for writing retreats and beta reading, and for being such great company on this writing adventure and making it a whole lot of fun.

As always, my sisters Trish and Emer for being my first readers and biggest fans.

My agent Ger Nichol for being on my side and having my back.

All the fabulous professionals who have helped make this book the best it can be, especially editors Helen

Falconer and Donna Hillyer, and cover designer extraordinaire Stuart Bache.

All the loyal readers who are still with me and who waited so patiently (or impatiently) for this book. Thanks for sticking around, and I'm sorry it took so long. You truly deserve a medal. But all you're getting is this book, so I sincerely hope you enjoy it.

ABOUT THE AUTHOR

Clodagh Murphy lives in Dublin, Ireland and loves writing funny, sexy romantic comedies. She always dreamed of being a novelist, and after more jobs than she cares to (or can) remember, she now writes full-time.

To learn more about Clodagh and her books, visit her website or Facebook page, or follow her on Twitter.

ALSO BY CLODAGH MURPHY

The Disengagement Ring

Girl in a Spin

Frisky Business

Some Girls Do

Scenes of a Sexual Nature (novella)

Made in the USA
Middletown, DE
30 October 2020

23063636R00246